Praise for
New York Times and *USA TODAY* bestselling author Brenda Jackson

"Brenda Jackson writes romance that sizzles
and characters you fall in love with."
—*New York Times* and *USA TODAY*
bestselling author Lori Foster

"Jackson's trademark ability to weave
multiple characters and side stories together
makes shocking truths all the more exciting."
—*Publishers Weekly*

"Possibly [the] sexiest entry in the Westmoreland
series.... Jackson has the sexiest cowboy
to ever ride the range."
—*RT Book Reviews* on *A Wife for a Westmoreland*

"Jackson's characters are wonderful, strong,
colorful and hot enough to burn the pages."
—*RT Book Reviews* on *Westmoreland's Way*

"The kind of sizzling, heart-tugging story
Brenda Jackson is famous for."
—*RT Book Reviews* on *Spencer's Forbidden Passion*

"This is entertainment at its best."
—*RT Book Reviews* on *Star of His H*

D1044394

Selected books by Brenda Jackson

BRENDA JACKSON

is a die "heart" romantic who married her childhood sweetheart and still proudly wears the "going steady" ring he gave her when she was fifteen. Because she's always believed in the power of love, Brenda's stories always have happy endings. In her real-life love story, Brenda and her husband of thirty-eight years live in Jacksonville, Florida, and have two sons.

A *New York Times* bestselling author of more than seventy-five romance titles, Brenda is a recent retiree who now divides her time between family, writing and traveling with Gerald. You may write Brenda at P.O. Box 28267, Jacksonville, Florida 32226, by email at WriterBJackson@aol.com or visit her website at www.brendajackson.net.

BRENDA JACKSON

TEMPTATION
& SPONTANEOUS

Harlequin®

Desire

Special thanks and acknowledgment to Brenda Jackson
for her contribution to the
Texas Cattleman's Club: The Showdown miniseries.

ISBN-13: 978-0-373-83770-0

TEMPTATION & SPONTANEOUS

Copyright © 2011 by Harlequin Books S.A.

The publisher acknowledges the copyright holders
of the individual works as follows:

TEMPTATION
Copyright © 2011 by Harlequin Books S.A.

SPONTANEOUS
Copyright © 2010 by Brenda Streater Jackson

Recycling programs
for this product may
not exist in your area.

Printed in U.S.A.

CONTENTS

Dear Reader,

I am honored to once again participate in a Texas Cattleman's Club continuity.

No two people needed each other more than Zeke Travers and Sheila Hopkins, and getting the couple to realize that fact was both a challenge and a joy. Zeke and Sheila's story is a special one, and I hope you enjoy reading it as much as I enjoyed writing it. And I'm always excited when I can reunite my readers with characters from past books, such as Darius and Summer from my last Texas Cattleman's Club continuity book, *One Night with the Wealthy Rancher.*

I want to thank the other five authors who are a part of this continuity. I enjoyed working with each of you.

Happy reading!

Brenda Jackson

TEMPTATION

To the love of my life, Gerald Jackson, Sr.

To the cast and crew of *Truly Everlasting: The Movie*,
this one is especially for you!
Thanks for all your hard work!

Though your beginning was small,
yet your latter end would increase abundantly.
—*Job 8:7*

* * *

Don't miss a single book in this series!

Texas Cattleman's Club: The Showdown
*They are rich and powerful, hot and wild.
For these Texans, it's showdown time!*

CHAPTER ONE

SOME DAYS IT didn't pay to get out of bed.

Unless you had a tall, dark, handsome and naked man waiting in your kitchen to pour you a hot cup of coffee before sitting you in his lap to feed you breakfast. Sheila Hopkins smiled at such a delicious fantasy before squinting against the November sun that was almost blinding her through the windshield of her car.

And the sad thing was that she had awakened in a good mood. But all it had taken to spoil her day was a call from her sister that morning telling her she wasn't welcome to visit her and her family in Atlanta after all.

That message had hurt, but Sheila really should not have been surprised. What had she expected from her older sister from her father's first marriage? The same sister who'd always wished she hadn't existed? Definitely not any show of sisterly love at this late stage. If she hadn't shown any in Sheila's twenty-seven years, why had she assumed her sister would begin showing any now? Not her sister who had the perfect life with a husband who owned his own television station in Atlanta and who had two beautiful children and was pregnant with her third.

And if that very brief and disappointing conversation with Lois wasn't bad enough, she had immediately gotten a call from the hospital asking that she come in on her off day because they were shorthanded. And of course, being the dedicated nurse that she was, she had agreed to do so. Forget the fact she had planned to spend the day working in her garden. She didn't have a life, so did it really matter?

Sheila drew in a deep breath when she brought her car to a stop at a traffic light. She couldn't help glancing over at the man in the sports car next to her. She couldn't tell how the rest of him looked because she could only see his profile from the shoulders up, but even that looked good. And as if he'd known she was checking him out, he glanced her way. Her breath caught in her throat and her flesh felt tingly all over. He had such striking features.

They were so striking she had to blink to make sure they were real. Um…a maple-brown complexion, close-cut black hair, dark brown eyes and a chiseled jaw. And as she continued to stare at him, her mind mechanically put his face on the naked body of the tall, handsome man whom she would have loved to have found in her kitchen this morning. She inwardly chuckled. Neither she nor her kitchen would have been able to handle all the heat her imaginary lover would generate.

She saw his head move and realized he had nodded over at her. Instinctively, she nodded back. When his lips curved into a sensual smile, she quickly forced her gaze ahead. And when the traffic light changed, she pressed down on the gas, deciding to speed up a little. The last thing she wanted was to give the guy the impression she was flirting with him, no matter how good he looked. She had learned quickly that not all nicely wrapped gifts contained something that was good for you. Crawford had certainly proven that.

As she got off the exit that led to the hospital, she couldn't get rid of the thought that she didn't know there were men who looked like him living in Royal, Texas. Not that she knew all the men in town, mind you. But she figured someone like him would definitely stand out. After all, Royal was a rather small community. And what if she had run into him again, then what?

Nothing.

She didn't have the time or the inclination to get involved with a man. She'd done that in the past and the outcome hadn't been good, which was why she had moved to Royal from Dallas last year. Moving to Royal had meant a fresh start for her. Although, Sheila knew that where she lived was only part of the solution. She had reached the conclusion that a woman didn't need to be involved with a no-good man to have trouble. A woman could do bad all by herself. And she of all people was living proof of that.

EZEKIEL TRAVERS CHUCKLED as he watched the attractive woman take off as though she was going to a fire or something. Hell, she wasn't the only one, he thought as he watched her car turn off the interstate at the next exit. Whoever was trying to ruin his best friend, Bradford Price's, reputation had taken things a little too far. According to the phone call he'd received earlier from Brad, the blackmailer had made good on his threat. Someone had left a baby on the doorstep of the Texas Cattlemen's Club with a note that Brad was the baby's father.

Grabbing his cell phone the moment it began to ring, he knew who the caller was before answering it. "Yeah, Brad?"

"Zeke, where are you?"

"I'm only a few minutes away. And you can believe I'll be getting to the bottom of this."

"I don't know what kind of sick joke someone is trying to play on me, but I swear to you, that baby isn't mine."

Zeke nodded. "And a paternity test can prove that easily, Brad, so calm down."

He had no reason not to believe his best friend about the baby not being his. Brad wouldn't lie about something like that. He and Brad had gotten to be the best of friends while roommates at the University of Texas. After college Brad had returned to Royal to assist in his family's banking empire.

Actually, it had been Brad who suggested Zeke relocate to Royal. He'd made the suggestion during one of their annual all-guys trip to Vegas last year, after Zeke had mentioned his desire to leave Austin and to move to a small town.

Zeke had earned a small fortune and a great reputation as one of the best security consultants in all of Texas. Now he could live anywhere he wanted to, and take his pick of cases.

And it had been Brad who'd connected Zeke with Darius Franklin, another private investigator in Royal who owned a security service and who just happened to be looking for a partner. That had prompted Zeke to fly to Royal. He'd immediately fallen in love with the town and he saw becoming a business partner with Darius as a win-win situation. That had been six months ago. When he'd moved to town, he hadn't known that his first case would begin before he could get settled in good, and that his first client would be none other than his best friend.

"I bet Abigail is behind this."

Brad's accusations interrupted Zeke's thoughts. Abigail Langley and Brad were presently in a heated battle to win the presidency of the Texas Cattlemen's Club.

"You have no proof of that and so far I haven't been able to find a link between Ms. Langley and those blackmail letters you've received, Brad. But you can bet if she's connected, I'll expose her. Now, sit tight, I'm on my way."

He clicked off the phone knowing to tell Brad to sit tight was a waste of time. Zeke let out a deep sigh. Brad had begun receiving blackmail letters five months ago. The thought nagged Zeke's mind that maybe if he had been on top of his game and solved the case months ago, it would not have gotten this far and some kid would not have been abandoned at the club.

He of all people knew how that felt. At thirty-three he could still feel the sting of abandonment. Although his own mother hadn't left him on anyone's doorstep, she had left him with her sister and kept on trucking. She hadn't shown up again until sixteen years later. It had been his last year of college and she'd stuck around just long enough to see if he had a chance in the NFL.

He pushed that hurtful time of his life to the back of his mind to concentrate on the problem at hand. If leaving that baby at the TCC with a note claiming she was Brad's kid was supposed to be a joke, then it wasn't funny. And Zeke intended to make sure he and Brad had the last laugh when they exposed the person responsible for such a callous act.

ONCE SHEILA HAD reached her floor at the hospital, it became evident why they'd called her in. A couple of nurses were out sick and the E.R. was swarming with patients with symptoms ranging from the flu to a man who'd almost lost his finger while chopping down a tree in his front yard. There had also been several minor car accidents.

At least something good had resulted from one of the accidents. A man thinking his girlfriend's injuries were worse than they were, had rushed into the E.R. and proposed. Even Sheila had to admit it had been a very romantic moment. Some women had all the luck.

"So you came in on your off day, huh?"

Sheila glanced at her coworker and smiled. Jill Lanier was a nurse she'd met on her first day at Royal Memorial and they'd become good friends. When she'd moved to Royal she hadn't known a soul, but that had been fine. She was used to being alone. That was the story of her life.

She was about to answer Jill, when the sound of a huge wail stopped her. "What the heck?"

She turned around and saw two police officers walk in carrying a screaming baby. Both she and Jill hurried over to the officers. "What's going on, Officers?" she asked the two men.

One of the officers, the one holding the baby, shook his head. "We don't know why she's crying," he said in frustration. "Someone left her on the doorstep of the Texas Cattlemen's Club and we were told to bring her here."

Sheila had heard all about the Texas Cattlemen's Club, which consisted of a group of men who considered themselves the protectors of Texas, and whose members consisted of the wealthiest men in Texas. One good thing was that the TCC was known to help a number of worthwhile causes in the community. Thanks to them, there was a new cancer wing at the hospital.

Jill took the baby and it only screamed louder. "The TCC? Why would anyone do something like that?"

"Who knows why people abandon their kids," the other officer said. It was apparent he was more than happy to pass the screaming baby on to someone else. However, the infant, who looked to be no more than five months old, was screaming even louder now. Jill, who was a couple of years younger than Sheila and single and carefree, gave them a what-am-I-supposed-to-do-now look as she rocked the baby in her arms.

"And there's a note that's being handed over to Social Services claiming Bradford Price is the father."

Sheila lifted a brow. She didn't know Bradford Price personally, but she had certainly heard of him. His family were blue blood society types. She'd heard they'd made millions in banking.

"Is someone from Social Services on their way here?" Sheila asked, raising her voice to be heard over the crying baby.

"Yes. Price is claiming the baby isn't his. There has to be a paternity test done."

Sheila nodded, knowing that could take a couple of days, possibly even a week.

"And what are we supposed to do with her until then?" Jill asked as she continued to rock the baby in her arms, trying to get her quiet but failing to do so.

"Keep her here," one of the officers responded. He was backing up, as if he was getting ready to make a run for it. "A woman from Social Services is on her way with everything you'll need. The kid doesn't have a name…at least one wasn't given with the note left with her."

The other officer, the one who'd been carrying the baby, spoke up. "Look, ladies, we have to leave. She threw up on me, so I need to swing by my place and change clothes."

"What about your report?" Sheila called out to the two officers who were rushing off.

"It's completed already and like I said, a woman from Social Services is on her way," the first officer said, before both men quickly exited through the revolving glass doors.

"I can't believe they did that," Jill said with a disgruntled look on her face. "What are we going to do with her? One thing for certain, this kid has a nice set of lungs."

Sheila smiled. "Follow procedure and get her checked out. There might be a medical reason why she's crying. Let's page Dr. Phillips."

"Hey, let me page Dr. Phillips. It's your turn to hold her." Before Sheila could say anything, Jill suddenly plopped the baby in her arms.

"Hey, hey, things can't be that bad, sweetie," Sheila crooned down at the baby as she adjusted her arms to make sure she was holding her right.

Other than the times she worked in the hospital nursery, she'd never held a baby, and rarely came in contact with one. Lois had two kids and was pregnant with another, yet Sheila had only seen her five-year-old niece and three-year-old nephew twice. Her sister had never approved of their father's marriage to Sheila's mother, and Sheila felt she had been the one to pay for it. Lois, who was four years older than Sheila, had been determined never to accept her father's other child. Over the years, Sheila had hoped her attitude toward her would change, but so far it hadn't.

Pushing thoughts of Lois from her mind, Sheila continued to smile down at the baby. And as if on cue the little girl stared up at Sheila with the most gorgeous pair of hazel eyes, and suddenly stopped crying. In fact, she smiled, showing dimples in both cheeks.

Sheila couldn't help chuckling. "What are you laughing at, baby-doll? Do I look funny or something?" She was rewarded with another huge smile from the baby. "You're such a pretty little thing, all bright and full of sunshine. I think I'll call you Sunnie until we find out your real name."

"Dr. Phillips is on his way and I'm needed on the fourth floor," Jill said, making a dash toward the elevator. "How did you get her to stop crying, Sheila?" she asked before stepping on the elevator.

Sheila shrugged and glanced back at the baby, who was still smiling up at her. "I guess she likes me."

"Apparently she does," a deep, husky male voice said from behind them.

Sheila turned around and her gaze collided with the most gorgeous set of brown eyes she'd ever seen on a man. They were bedroom eyes. The kind that brought to mind silken sheets and passion. But this wasn't the first time she had looked into those same eyes.

She immediately knew where she'd seen them before as her gaze roamed over his features. Recognition appeared in his gaze the moment it hit hers, as well. Standing before her, looking sexier than any man had a right to look, was the guy who'd been in the car next to hers at the traffic light. He was the man who'd given her a flirtatious smile before she'd deliberately sped off to ditch him.

Evidently that hadn't done any good, since he was here, standing before her in vivid living color.

CHAPTER TWO

THIS WAS THE second time today he'd seen this woman, Zeke thought. Just as before, he thought she looked good…even wearing scrubs. Nothing could hide the wavy black hair that came to her shoulders, the light brown eyes and luscious café-au-lait skin.

He wondered if anyone ever told her she could be a very delicious double for actress Sanaa Lathan. The woman before him was just a tad shorter than the actress, but in his book she was just as curvy. And she was a nurse. Hell, she could take his temperature any time and any place. He could even suggest she take it now, because there was no doubt in his mind looking at her was making it rise.

"May I help you?"

He blinked and swallowed deeply. "Yes, that baby you're holding…"

She narrowed her eyes and clutched the baby closer to her breast in a protective stance. "Yes, what about her?"

"I want to find out everything there is about her," he said.

She lifted an arched brow. "And you are…?"

He gave what he hoped was a charming smile. "Zeke Travers, private investigator."

Sheila opened her mouth to speak, when a deep, male voice intruded behind her. "Zeke Travers! Son of a gun! With Brad Price as quarterback, you as split end and Chris Richards as wide receiver, that was UT's best football season. I recall them winning a national championship title that year. Those other teams didn't stand a chance with you three. Someone mentioned you had moved to Royal."

She then watched as Dr. Warren Phillips gave the man a huge bear hug. Evidently they knew each other, and as she listened further, she was finding out quite a lot about the handsome stranger.

"Yes, I moved to town six months ago," Zeke was saying. "Austin was getting too big for me. I've decided to try small-town life for a while. Brad convinced me Royal was the place," he said, grinning. "And I was able to convince Darius Franklin he needed a partner."

"So you joined forces with Darius over at Global Securities?"

"Yes, and things are working out great so far. Darius is a good man and I really like this town. In fact, I like it more and more each day." His gaze then shifted to her and her gaze locked with his as it had done that morning.

The clearing of Dr. Phillips's throat reminded them they weren't alone.

"So, what brings you to Royal Memorial, Zeke?" Dr. Phillips asked, and it was evident to Sheila that Dr. Phillips had picked up on the man's interest in her.

"That baby she's holding. It was left abandoned at the TCC today with a note claiming Brad's the father. And I intend to prove that he's not."

"In that case," Dr. Phillips said, "I think we need to go into that private examination room over there and check this baby out."

A SHORT WHILE later Dr. Phillips slid his stethoscope into the pocket of his lab coat as he leaned back against the table. "Well, this young lady is certainly in good health."

He chuckled and then added, "And she certainly refused to let anyone hold her other than you, Nurse Hopkins. If you hadn't been present and within her reach, it would have been almost impossible for me to examine her."

Sheila laughed as she held the baby to her while glancing down at the infant. "She's beautiful. I can't imagine anyone wanting to abandon her."

"Well, it happened," Zeke said.

A tingling sensation rode up her spine with the comment and she was reminded that Zeke Travers was in the examination room with them. It was as if he refused to let the baby out of his sight.

She turned slightly. "What makes you so sure she's not Bradford Price's child, Mr. Travers? I recall running into Mr. Price a time or two and he also has hazel eyes."

He narrowed his gaze. "So do a million other people in this country, Ms. Hopkins."

Evidently he didn't like being questioned about the possibility. So she turned to Dr. Phillips. "Did that social worker who came by while you were examining the baby say what will happen to Sunnie?" she asked.

Dr. Phillips lifted a brow. "Sunnie?"

"Yes," Sheila said, smiling. "I thought she was a vision of sunshine the moment I looked at her. And since no one knows her name I thought Sunnie would fit. Sounds better than Jane Doe," she added.

"I agree," Dr. Phillips said, chuckling. "And the

social worker, Ms. Talbert, is as baffled as everyone else, especially since Brad says the baby isn't his."

"She's not his," Zeke said, inserting himself into the conversation again. "Brad's been receiving blackmail letters for five months now, threatening to do something like this unless he paid up."

Zeke rubbed the back of his neck. "I told him to ignore the letters while I looked into it. I honestly didn't think the person would carry out their threats if Brad didn't pay up. Evidently, I was wrong."

And that's what continued to bother him the most, Zeke thought as he glanced over at the baby. He should have nipped this nasty business in the bud long ago. And what Ms. Hopkins said was true, because he'd noted it himself. The baby had hazel eyes, and not only were they hazel, they were the same shade of hazel as Brad's.

He'd asked Brad if there was any chance the baby could be his, considering the fact Brad was a known playboy. But after talking to Brad before coming over here, and now that he knew the age of the baby, Zeke was even more convinced Brad wasn't the father. Warren had confirmed the baby's age as five months and Brad had stated he hadn't slept with any women over the past eighteen months.

"To answer your question, Nurse Hopkins," Dr. Phillips said, breaking into Zeke's thoughts, "Ms. Talbert wants to wait to see what the paternity test reveals. I agreed that we can keep the baby here until then."

"Here?"

"Yes, that would be best until the test results comes back, that is unless Brad has a problem participating in the test," Dr. Phillips said, glancing over at Zeke.

"Brad knows that it's for the best, and he will cooperate any way he can," Zeke acknowledged.

"But it doesn't seem fair for Sunnie to have to stay here at the hospital. She's in perfect health," Sheila implored. "Ms. Talbert has indicated the test results might take two weeks to come back."

She then glared over at Zeke. "Whether the baby is officially his or not, I would think your client would want the best for Sunnie until her parentage is proven or disproven."

Zeke crossed his arms over his chest. "So what do you suggest, Ms. Hopkins? I agree staying here isn't ideal for the baby, but the only other option is for her to get turned over to Social Services. If that happens she'll go into foster care and will get lost in the system when it's proven my client is *not* her father."

Sheila nibbled on her bottom lip, not having a response to give him. She glanced down at the baby she held in her arms. For whatever reason, Sunnie's mother hadn't wanted her and it didn't seem fair for her to suffer because of it. She knew how it felt not to be wanted.

"I have an idea that might work, Nurse Hopkins, granted you agree to go along with it," Dr. Phillips said. "And I'll have to get Ms. Talbert to agree to it, as well."

"Yes?" she said, wondering what his idea was.

"A few years ago the wife of one of my colleagues, Dr. Webb, was hit with a similar incident when someone left a baby on her doorstep before they were married. Because Winona grew up in foster care herself, she hadn't wanted the baby to end up the same way. To make a long story short, Winona and Dr. Webb ended up marrying and keeping the baby to make sure it didn't get lost in the system."

Sheila nodded. "So what are you suggesting?"

Dr. Phillips smiled. "That you become Sunnie's emergency foster parent until everything is resolved. I believe I'll be able to convince Ms. Talbert to go along with it, and given the fact the Prices are huge benefactors to this hospital, as well as to a number of other nonprofit organizations, I think it would be in everyone's best interest that the baby's welfare remain a top priority."

Sheila looked shocked. "Me? A foster parent! I wouldn't know what to do with a baby."

"You couldn't convince me of that, Ms. Hopkins. The baby won't let anyone else touch her and you seem to be a natural with her," Zeke said, seeing the merits of what Dr. Phillips proposed. "Besides, you're a nurse, someone who is used to taking care of people."

Although Brad swore the baby wasn't his, he would still be concerned with the baby's health and safety until everything was resolved. And what Zeke just said was true. He thought the woman was a natural with the baby, and the baby had gotten totally attached to her. He had a feeling Ms. Hopkins was already sort of attached to the baby, as well.

"And if you're concerned as to how you'd be able to handle both your job and the baby, I propose that the hospital agrees to give you a leave of absence during the time that the child is in your care. My client will be more than happy to replace your salary," Zeke said.

"I think that would be an excellent idea," Warren said. "One I think I could push past the chief of staff.

The main thing everyone should be concerned about is Sunnie's well-being."

Sheila couldn't help agreeing. But her? A foster parent? "How long do you think I'll have to take care of her?" she asked, looking down at Sunnie, who was still smiling up at her.

"No more than a couple of weeks, if even that long," Zeke said. "The results of the paternity test should be back by then and we'll know how to proceed."

Sheila nibbled her bottom lip, then Sunnie reached and grabbed hold of a lock of her hair, seemingly forcing Sheila to look down at her—into her beautiful hazel eyes, while she made a lot of cheerful baby sounds. At that moment Sheila knew she would do it. Sunnie needed a temporary home and she would provide her with one. It was the least she could do, and deep down she knew it was something that she wanted to do. This was the first time she'd felt someone truly, really needed her.

She glanced up at both men to see they were patiently waiting for her answer. She drew in a deep breath. "Yes. I would be happy to be Sunnie's emergency foster parent."

AFTER REMOVING HIS jacket, Zeke slid into the seat of his car and leaned back as he gazed at the entrance to the hospital. He felt good about Sheila Hopkins agreeing to take on the role of foster parent. That way he would know the baby was being well cared for while he turned up the heat on the investigation to clear Brad's name.

He intended to pursue each and every lead. He would not leave a stone, no matter how small, unturned. He intended to get this potential scandal under total control before it could go any further.

Now if he could control his attraction to Sheila Hopkins. The woman was definitely temptation with a capital T. Being in close quarters with her, even with Warren in the room, had been pure torture. She was a looker, but it was clear she didn't see herself that way, and he couldn't help wondering, why not? He hadn't seen a ring on her finger and, when he'd hung back to speak with Warren in private, the only thing his friend could tell him was that she was a model employee, caring to a fault, dependable and intelligent.

Warren had also verified she was single and had moved from Dallas last year. But still, considering everything, Zeke felt it wouldn't hurt to do a background check on her, just to be on the safe side. The last thing he wanted was for her to be someone who'd be tempted to sell this story to the tabloids. That was the last thing Brad needed. His best friend was depending on him to bring an end to this nightmare, and he would.

Zeke was about to turn the ignition in his car, when he glanced through the windshield to see Sheila Hopkins. She was walking quickly across the parking lot to the car he had seen her in that morning. She looked as if she was dashing off to fight a fire. Curious as to where she could be going in such a hurry, he got out of the car, walked swiftly to cross the parking lot and intercepted her before she could reach her vehicle.

She nearly yelled in fright when he stepped in front of her. "What do you think you're doing?" she asked, covering her heart with the palm of her hand. "You just scared me out of my wits."

"Sorry, but I saw you tearing across the parking lot. What's the hurry?"

Sheila drew a deep breath to get her heart beating

back normal in her chest. She looked up at Zeke Travers and couldn't do anything about her stomach doing flips. It had been hard enough while in the examination room to stop her gaze from roaming all over him every chance it got.

"I'm leaving Sunnie in the hospital tonight while I go pick up the things I'll need for her. I'm going to need a baby bed, diapers, clothes and all kinds of other items. I plan on shopping today and coming back for her first thing in the morning once my house is ready."

She paused a moment. "I hated leaving her. She started crying. I feel like I'm abandoning her."

A part of Zeke was relieved to know she was a woman who would feel some sort of guilt in abandoning a child. His own mother had not. He drew in a deep breath as he remembered what Sheila Hopkins had said about needing to go shopping for all that baby stuff. He hadn't thought of the extra expenses taking on a baby would probably cost her.

"Let me go with you to pick up the stuff. That way I can pay for it."

She raised a brow. "Why would you want to do that?"

"Because whether or not Brad's the father—which he's not—he wants the baby taken care of and is willing to pay for anything she might need." He hadn't discussed it with Brad, but knew there wouldn't be a problem. Brad was concerned for the baby's welfare.

She seemed to be studying his features as if she was trying to decide if he was serious, Zeke thought. And then she asked, "You sure? I have to admit that I hadn't worked all the baby expenses into my weekly budget, but if I need to get money out of my savings then I—"

"No, that won't be necessary and Brad wouldn't want

it any other way, and like I said, I'll be glad to go with you and help."

Sheila felt a tingling sensation in the pit of her stomach. The last thing she needed was Zeke Travers in her presence too long. "No, I'll be able to manage things, but I appreciate the offer."

"No, really, I insist. Why wouldn't you want me to help? I'll provide you with two extra hands."

That wasn't all he would be providing her with, she thought, looking at him. Besides the drop-dead gorgeous looks, at some point he had taken off his jacket to reveal the width of his shoulders beneath his white dress shirt. She also noticed the way his muscular thighs fit into a pair of dress slacks.

"We could leave your car here. I have a feeling you'll want to come back and check on the baby later. We can go in my vehicle," he added before she could respond to what he'd said.

She lifted a brow. "You have a two-seater."

He chuckled. "Yes, but I also have a truck. And that's what you're going to need to haul something as big as a box containing a baby bed. And in order to haul the kid away from here you're going to need a car seat tomorrow."

Sheila tilted her head back and drew in a deep breath. Had she bit off more than she could chew? She hadn't thought of all that. She needed to make a list and not work off the top of her head. And he was right about her needing a truck and wanting to return tonight to check on Sunnie. The sound of her crying had followed Sheila all the way to the elevator. She hated leaving her, but she had to prepare her house for Sunnie's visit.

"Ms. Hopkins?"

She looked back at Zeke Travers. "Fine, Mr. Travers, I'll accept your generosity. If you're sure it's not going out of your way."

He smiled. "I'm not going out of my way, I assure you. Like I said, Brad would want what's best for the baby even if she isn't his."

She arched a brow. "You certainly seem so sure of that."

"I am. Now, it's going to be my job in addition to making sure the baby is safe and well cared for, to find out who's trying to nail him with this and to clear his name."

Zeke paused a moment and stared down at her. "And speaking of names, I suggest you call me Zeke, instead of Mr. Travers."

She smiled. "Why, is Mr. Travers what they call your father?"

"I wouldn't know."

Sheila's heart skipped a beat when she realized what he'd said and what he'd meant by saying it. "I'm sorry, I didn't mean anything. The last guy who told me not to call him by his last name said the reason was that's what people called his daddy."

"No harm done, and I hope you don't mind if I call you Sheila."

"No, I don't mind."

"Good. Come on, Sheila, my car is parked over here," he said.

Sheila felt her stomach twist in all kinds of knots when she heard her name flow from his lips. And as she walked beside Zeke across the parking lot, a number of misgivings flooded her mind. For one thing, she wasn't sure what role he intended to play with her becoming Sunnie's foster parent. She understood Bradford Price was his client and he intended to clear the man's name. But she had to think beyond that. If Bradford wasn't Sunnie's father then who was? Where was the mother and why had the baby been abandoned with a note claiming Bradford was the father when he said he wasn't?

There were a lot of questions and she had a feeling the man walking beside her intended to have answers for all of them soon enough. She also had a feeling he was the sort of person who got things accomplished when he set his mind to it. And she could tell he intended to investigate this case to the fullest.

His main concern might be on his friend, but hers was on Sunnie. What would happen to her if it was proven Bradford wasn't the child's father? Would the man cease caring about Sunnie's welfare? Would it matter to him that she would then become just a statistic in the system?

He might not care, but she would, and at that moment she vowed to protect Sunnie any way she could.

CHAPTER THREE

WHILE THEY WERE on their way to the store to pick up items for the baby, Sheila clicked off the phone and sighed deeply as she glanced over at Zeke. "I just talked to one of the nurses in Pediatrics. Sunnie cried herself to sleep," she said.

There was no need telling him that she knew just how that felt. She was reminded of how many nights as a child she had lain in bed and cried herself to sleep because her mother was too busy trying to catch the next rich husband to spend any time with her. And her father, once he'd discovered what a gold digger Cassie Hopkins was, he hadn't wasted time moving out and taking Lois with him and leaving her behind.

"That's good to hear, Sheila," Zeke responded.

There was another tingling sensation in the pit of her stomach. She couldn't help it. It did something to her each and every time he pronounced her name. He said it with a deep Texas drawl that could send shivers all through her.

"So how long have you been living in Royal?" he asked.

She glanced over at him. "A year." She knew from his conversation with Dr. Phillips that he had moved to town six months ago, so there was no need to ask him that. She also knew he'd come from Austin because he wanted to try living in a small city.

"You like it here?"

She nodded. "So far. The people are nice, but I spend a lot of my time at the hospital, so I still haven't met all my neighbors, only those next door."

She switched her gaze off him to look out the window at the homes and stores they passed. What she decided not to add was that other than working, and occasional trips to the market, she rarely left home. The people at the hospital had become her family.

Now that she'd agreed to a fourteen-day leave of absence, she would have her hands full caring for Sunnie, and a part of her actually looked forward to that.

"You're smiling."

She glanced back at him. Did the man notice every single thing? "Is it a crime?"

He chuckled. "No."

The deep, husky rumble of his chuckle sent shivers sweeping through her again. And because she couldn't help herself, when the car came to a stop at the traffic light she glanced back over at him and then wished she hadn't done so. The slow smile that suddenly curved his lips warmed her all over.

"Now you're the one smiling," she pointed out.

"And is that a crime?"

Grinning, she shook her head. He'd made her see just how ridiculous her response to him had been. "No, it's not."

"Good. Because if I get arrested, Sheila, so do you. And it would be my request that we get put in the same jail cell."

She told herself not to overreact to what he'd said. Of course he would try to flirt with her. He was a man. She'd gotten hit on by a number of doctors at the hospital as well as several police officers around town. Eventually, they found out what Zeke would soon discover. It was a waste of their time. She had written men off. When it came to the opposite sex, she preferred her space. The only reason she was with him now was because of Sunnie. She considered Zeke Travers as a means to an end.

When he exited off the expressway and moments later turned into a nice gated community, she was in awe of the large and spacious ranch-style homes that sat on at least thirty acres of land. She had heard about the Cascades, the section of Royal where the wealthy lived. He evidently was doing well in the P.I. business. "You live in this community?" she asked.

"Yes. I came from Austin on an apartment-hunting trip and ended up purchasing a house instead. I always wanted a lot of land and to own horses and figured buying in here was a good investment."

She could just imagine, especially with the size of the ranch house whose driveway they were pulling into. The house had to be sitting almost six hundred or more feet back off the road. She could see a family of twelve living here and thought the place was definitely too large for just one person.

"How many acres is this?" she asked.

"Forty. I needed that much with the horses."

"How many do you own?"

"Twelve now, but I plan to expand. I've hired several ranch hands to help me take care of things. And I ride every chance I get. What about you? Do you ride?"

She thought of her mother's second and third husbands. They had owned horses and required that she know how to ride. "Yes, I know how to ride."

He glanced at his watch. "It won't take me long to switch vehicles," he said, bringing the car to a stop. "You're invited in if you like and you're welcome to look around."

"No, I'll be fine waiting out here until you return," she said.

He got out of the car and turned to her and smiled. "I don't bite, you know."

"Trust me, Zeke, if for one minute I thought you did, I wouldn't be here."

"So you think I'm harmless?" he asked, grinning.

"Not harmless but manageable. I'm sure all your focus will be on trying to figure out who wants to frame your friend. You don't have time for anything else."

He flashed a sexy smile. "Don't be so sure of that, Sheila Hopkins." He closed the door and she watched as he strolled up the walkway to his front door, thinking his walk was just as sexy as his smile.

ZEKE UNLOCKED HIS door and pushed it open. He had barely made it inside his house when the phone rang. Closing the door behind him, he pulled his cell phone off the clip on his belt. He checked the caller ID. "Yes, Brad?"

"You didn't call. How was the baby?"

Zeke leaned up against the wall supporting the staircase. "She's fine, but she cries a lot."

"I noticed. And no one could get her to stop. Did they check her out to make sure nothing is wrong with her?"

Zeke smiled. "She was checked out. Just so happens that Warren Phillips was on duty and he's the one who gave her a clean bill of health, although she still wanted to prove to everyone what a good set of lungs she had."

"I'm glad she's okay. I was worried about her."

Zeke nodded. "Are you sure there's nothing you want to tell me? I did happen to notice the kid does have your eyes."

"Don't get cute, Zeke. The kid isn't mine. But she's just a baby and I can't help worrying about her."

"Hey, man, I was just kidding, and I understand. I can't help worrying about her, too. But we might have found a way where we don't have to worry about her while I delve into my investigation."

"And what way is that?"

"That way happens to be a nurse who works at Royal Memorial by the name of Sheila Hopkins. She's the only one who can keep the baby quiet. It's the weirdest thing. The kid screams at everyone else, but she's putty in Sheila Hopkins's hands. She actually smiles instead of crying."

"You're kidding."

"No, I saw her smile myself. Warren suggested that Sheila keep Sunnie for the time being," Zeke explained.

"Sunnie?"

"Yes, that's the name Sheila gave the kid for now. She said it sounded better than Jane Doe and I agree."

There was a slight pause and then Brad asked, "And this Sheila Hopkins agreed to do it?"

"Yes, until the results of the paternity test come back, so the sooner you can do your part the better."

"I've made an appointment to have it done tomorrow."

"Good. And I'm going shopping with Sheila for baby

stuff. She's single and doesn't have any kids of her own, so she'll need all new stuff, which I'm billing you for, by the way."

"Fine." There was a pause, and then Brad said, "I was thinking that perhaps it would be best if I hired a nanny and keep the baby instead of—"

"Hold up. Don't even consider it. We don't want anyone seeing your kindness as an admission of guilt, Brad. The next thing everyone will think is that the baby is really yours."

"Yes, but what do you know about this nurse? You said she's single. She might be pretty good at taking care of patients, but are you sure she knows how to take care of a baby?"

"I'm not sure about anything regarding Sheila Hopkins, other than what Warren told me. She's worked at the hospital about a year. But don't worry, I've already taken measures to have her checked out. Roy is doing a thorough background check on Sheila Hopkins as we speak."

Suddenly Zeke heard a noise behind him and turned around. Sheila was leaning against his door with her arms crossed over her chest. The look on her face let him know she had heard some, if not all, of his conversation with Brad and wasn't happy about it.

"Brad, I need to go. I'll call you back later." He then hung up the phone.

Before he could open his mouth, Sheila placed her hands on her hips and narrowed her eyes at him. "Please take me back to the hospital to get my car. There's no way I'm going anywhere with a man who doesn't trust me."

Then she turned and walked out the door and slammed it shut behind her.

SHEILA WAS HALFWAY down the walkway, when Zeke ran behind her and grabbed her arm. "Let me go," she said and angrily snatched it back.

"We need to talk and I prefer we don't do it out here," Zeke said.

She glared up at him. "And I prefer we don't do it anywhere. I have nothing to say to you. How dare you have me investigated like I'm some sort of criminal."

"I never said you were a criminal."

"Then why the background check, Zeke?"

He rubbed his hands down his face. "I'm a P.I., Sheila. I investigate people. Nothing personal, but think about it. Sunnie will be in your care for two weeks. I don't know you personally and I need to know she's not only in a safe environment but with someone both Brad and I can trust. Would you not want me to check out the person whose care she's been placed in?"

Sheila sighed deeply, knowing that she would. "But I'd never do anything to harm her."

"I believe that, but I have to make sure. All I'm doing is a basic background check to make certain you don't have any past criminal history." After a moment he said, "Come on in, let's talk inside."

She thought about his request then decided it might be best if they did talk inside after all. She had a tendency to raise her voice when she was angry about something.

"Fine." She stalked off ahead of him.

BY THE TIME ZEKE followed her inside the house, she was in the middle of the living room pacing, and he could tell she was still mad. He quietly closed the door behind him and leaned against it, folding his arms across his chest, with one booted heel over the other, as he watched her. Again he was struck by just how beautiful she was.

For some reason he was more aware of it now than before. There was fire in her eyes, annoyance in her steps and the way she was unconsciously swaying her hips was downright sensual. She had taken center stage, was holding it and he was a captive audience of one.

Then she stopped pacing and placed her hands on her hips to face him. She glared him down. The woman could not have been more than five-four at the most. Yet even with his height of six-four she was making him feel shorter. Damn. He hadn't meant for her to overhear his conversation with Brad. Hadn't she told him she hadn't wanted to come in?

"You were supposed to stay outside. You said you didn't want to come in," he blurted out for some reason.

He watched as she stiffened her spine even more. "And that gave you the right to talk about me?"

His heart thudded deeply in his chest. The last thing he had time or the inclination to do was deal with an emotional female. "Look, Sheila, like I said before, I am a private investigator. My job is to know people and I don't like surprises. Anyone who comes in contact with the baby for any long period of time will get checked out by me."

He rubbed his hand down his face and released a frustrated sigh. "Look. It's not that I was intentionally questioning your character. I was mainly assuring my client that a child that someone is claiming to be his has been placed in the best of care until the issue is resolved by way of a paternity test. There's no reason for you to take it personally. It's not about you. It's about Sunnie.

Had you been the president's mother-in-law I'd still do a background check. My client is a very wealthy man and my job is to protect him at all costs, which is why I intend to find out who is behind this."

He paused for a moment. "You do want what's best for Sunnie, don't you?"

"Of course."

"So do I, and so does Brad. That baby was abandoned, and the last thing I would want is for her not to have some stability in her life over the next couple of weeks. She deserves that at least. Neither of us know what will happen after that."

His words gave Sheila pause and deflated her anger somewhat. Although she didn't want to admit it, what he said was true. It wasn't about her but about Sunnie. She should be everyone's main concern. Background checks were routine and she would have expected that one be done if they'd hired a nanny for Sunnie. She didn't know Zeke like he didn't know her, and with that suspicious mind of his—which came with the work he did—he would want to check her out regardless of the fact that Dr. Phillips had spoken highly of her. But that didn't mean she had to like the fact Zeke had done it.

"Fine," she snapped. "You've done your job. Now, take me back to the hospital so I can get my car."

"We're going shopping for the baby stuff as planned, Sheila. You still need my truck, so please put your emotions aside and agree to do what's needed to be done."

"Emotions!" Before thinking about it, she quickly crossed the room to stand in front of him.

"Yes, emotions."

His voice had lowered and he reached out and tilted

her chin up. "Has anyone ever told you how sexy you look when you're angry?"

And before she could take another breath, he lowered his mouth to hers.

WHY DID HER lips have to be so soft?

Why did she have to taste so darn good?

And why wasn't she resisting him?

Those questions rammed through Zeke's mind as his heart banged brutally in his chest at the feel of his mouth on Sheila's. He pushed those questions and others to the back of his mind as he deepened the kiss, took it to another level—although his senses were telling him that was the last thing he needed to do.

He didn't heed their advice. Instead, he wrapped his arms around Sheila's waist to bring her closer to the fit of him as he feasted on her mouth. He knew he wasn't the only one affected by the kiss when he felt her hardened nipples pressing into his chest. He could tell she hadn't gotten kissed a lot, at least not to this degree, and she seemed unsure of herself, but he remedied that by taking control. She moaned and he liked the sound of it and definitely like the feel of her plastered against him.

He could go on kissing her for hours…days…months. The very thought gave him pause and he gradually pulled his mouth from hers. Hours, days and months meant an involvement with a woman and he didn't do involvements. He did casual affairs and nothing more. And the last thing he did was mix business with pleasure.

SHEILA'S FIRST COHERENT thought after Zeke released her

lips was that she had never, not even in her wildest dreams, been kissed like that. She still felt tingling in her toes and her entire body; her every limb and muscle felt like pure jelly, which was probably the reason she was quivering like the dickens inside.

She slowly drew air into her lungs, held it a moment before slowly letting it out. She could still taste him on her tongue. How had he gotten so entrenched there? She quickly answered her own question when she remembered how his tongue had taken hold of hers, mated with it and sucked on it.

She muttered a couple colorful expletives under her breath when she gazed up at him. She should not have allowed him to kiss her like that. She'd be the first to admit she had enjoyed it, but still. The eyes staring back at her were dark and heated as if he wanted a repeat performance. She cleared her throat. "Why did you kiss me?"

Why had he kissed her? Zeke asked himself that same question as he took a step back. He needed to put distance between them or else he would be tempted to kiss her again.

"You were talking," he said, grabbing the first excuse he could think of.

"No, I wasn't."

He lifted a brow. Hadn't she been? He tried to backtrack and recall just what was taking place between them before she'd stormed across the room to get in his face. When he remembered, he shrugged. "Doesn't matter. You would have said something you regretted and I decided to wipe the words off your lips."

Sheila frowned. "I suggest that you don't ever do it again."

That slow, sexy smile that she'd seen earlier returned, and instead of saying he wouldn't kiss her again, he crossed his arms over his chest and asked, "So, what brought you inside? You said you were going to wait outside."

He had changed subjects and she decided to follow his lead. "Your car began beeping loudly as if it was going to blow up or something."

His smile widened to emphasize the dimples in his cheek. "That's my fax machine. It's built into my console in a way that's not detectable."

She shook her head. "What are you, a regular James Bond?"

"No. Bond is a secret agent. I'm a private investigator. There's a big difference." He glanced at his watch. "If you're ready, we can leave. My truck is this way."

"What about the fax that was coming through?"

"I have a fax in the truck, as well. It will come in on both."

"Oh."

She followed him through a spacious dining room and kitchen that was stylishly decorated. The living room was also fashionably furnished. Definitely more so than hers. "You have a nice home."

"Thanks, and if you're talking about the furniture and decorating, I can't take credit. It was a model home and I bought it as is. I saw it. I liked it. I got it."

He saw it, he liked it and he got it. She wondered if that was how he operated with everything in his life. "WHERE DO YOU want me to put these boxes?" Zeke asked, carrying two under his arms. One contained a baby car seat and the other a baby bath. He hadn't wanted to tell her, but he thought instead of purchasing just the basics that she'd gotten carried away. The kid would only be with her for two weeks at the most, not two years.

"You can set them down anywhere. I'm going to stay up late tonight putting stuff up."

After placing the boxes in a corner of the room, he glanced around. The place was small, but it suited her. Her furniture was nice and her two-story home was neat as a pin. He could imagine how it was going to look with baby stuff cluttering it up.

"I'm going to call the hospital again to check on Sunnie."

He bit down on his lips, forcing back a reminder that she had called the hospital less than an hour ago. And before that, while they had been shopping in Target for all the items on her list, she had called several times then, as well. It was a good thing she knew the nurses taking care of the baby, otherwise they would probably consider her a nuisance.

While she was on the phone, he went back outside to get more boxes out of the truck. Although she didn't live in a gated community, it was in a nice section of town, and he felt good about that. And he noticed she had an alarm system, but he would check the locks on her doors anyway. Until he discovered the identity of the person who'd tried to extort money from Brad, he wasn't taking any chances. What if the blackmailer tried to kidnap the baby back?

He had made several trips back and forth into the house before Sheila had finally gotten off the phone. He glanced over at her. "Is anything wrong?"

She shook her head. "No. Sunnie awakened for a short while, but she's gone back to sleep now."

Hell, he should hope so. He glanced at his watch. It was after nine o'clock. He should know since they'd closed the store. He figured that kid should be asleep by now. Didn't she have a bedtime?

"Okay, all the boxes are in, what do you need me to do now?"

Sheila glanced over at him, tempted to tell him what he could do was leave. He was unnerving her. He'd done so while they'd been shopping for the baby items. There was something about a good-looking man that could get to a woman each and every time, and she'd gotten her share with him today. Several times while walking down the aisles of the store, they had brushed against each other, and although both had tried downplaying the connection, she'd felt it and knew he'd felt it, as well. And he smelled good. Most of the men at the hospital smelled sanitized. She was reminded of a real man's scent while around him. And then there was that kiss she was trying hard to forget. However, she was finding it difficult to do so each and every time she looked at his lips. His mouth had certainly done a number on her.

She thought every woman should spend the day shopping with a man for baby items at least once in her lifetime. Sheila couldn't help remembering the number of times they'd needed assistance from a store clerk. Finally, they'd been assigned their own personal clerk, probably to get them out the store sooner. She was sure the employees wanted to go home at some point that night. And she couldn't forget how the clerk assumed they were married, although neither of them was wearing a wedding ring. Go figure.

"You can take me to get my car now," she said, tucking a loose lock of hair behind her ear and trying not to stare at him. She shouldn't be surprised that he practically dominated her living room by standing in the middle of it. Everything else seemed to fade to black. He was definitely the main attraction with his height, muscular build and overall good looks.

"What about the baby bed?"

She quirked a brow. "What about it?"

"When are you going to put it together?"

She nibbled on her bottom lip, thinking that was a good question. It was one of the largest items she'd purchased and the clerk had turned down her offer to buy the one on display. That certainly would have made things easier for her. Instead, he'd sold her one in a box that included instructions that would probably look like Greek to her.

"Later tonight."

A smile curved his lips. "I should hope so if you plan on bringing the baby home tomorrow."

She wrapped her arms around herself. She hadn't told him yet, but she planned on bringing Sunnie home tonight. It was getting so bad with her crying that the nurses hated it when she woke up. Her crying would wake all the other babies. She had talked to the head nurse, who would be contacting Dr. Phillips to make sure Sunnie could be released into her care and custody tonight. She was just waiting for a callback.

Zeke studied Sheila. Maybe his brain was over-reacting, but he had a feeling she was keeping something from him. Maybe it was because she was giving a lot away. Like the way she had wrapped her arms around herself. Or the nervous look in her eyes. Or it could be the way she was nibbling on the lips he'd kissed earlier that day. A kiss he wished he could forget but couldn't. For some reason his mouth had felt right locked to hers.

He crossed his arms over his chest. "Is there something you want to tell me?"

She dropped her arms to her sides. "Sunnie is keeping the other babies up."

That didn't surprise him. He'd heard the kid cry. She had a good set of lungs. "She's sleeping now, right?"

"Yes, but as you know, she probably won't sleep through the night."

No, he didn't know that. "Why not?"

"Most babies don't. That's normal. The older they get the longer they will sleep through the night. In Sunnie's case, she probably sleeps a lot during the day and is probably up for at least part of the night."

"And you're prepared for that?"

"I have to be."

It occurred to him the sacrifices she would be making. His concentration had been so focused on the baby, he hadn't thought about the changes keeping Sunnie would make in her life. When she'd been on the phone and he'd been hauling in the boxes, he had taken a minute to pull his fax. It had been the background check on her. The firm he used was thorough and he'd held her life history in his hand while holding that one sheet of paper.

She was twenty-seven and every hospital she'd worked in since college had given her a glowing recommendation. She was a law-abiding citizen. Had never even received a speeding ticket. One year she had even received a medal for heroism from the Dallas Fire Department because she'd rushed inside a burning house to help save an elderly man, and then provided him with medical services until paramedics got there. That unselfish act had made national news.

On a more personal side, he knew she had a sister whom she didn't visit often. She had a mother whom she visited once or twice a year. Her mother was divorced from husband number five, a CEO of a resort in Florida. Her father had died five years ago. Her only sister, who was four years older, was from her father's first marriage. Sheila had been the product of the old man's second marriage.

"Tell me what else I can do to help," he said.

She released a deep sigh. "I want to bring Sunnie here tonight. The nurses are contacting Dr. Phillips for his approval. I hope to get a call from him any minute. Either way, whether I get Sunnie tonight or tomorrow, I'll need the bed, so if you really don't mind, I'd appreciate it if you would put it together. I'm not good at doing stuff like that."

He nodded. "No problem." He began rolling up his sleeves. "You wouldn't happen to have a beer handy, would you?"

She smiled. "Yes, I'll go grab one for you."

And then she took off and he was left standing while wondering why he couldn't stop thinking about the time he had kissed her.

"WE'RE GLAD YOU'RE here," one of the nurses in Pediatrics said anxiously. "We have her packed up and ready to go," she added, smiling brightly.

"She's been expressing herself again, eh?" Zeke asked, chuckling.

Sheila glanced over at Zeke, wondering why he was

there. It hadn't taken him any time to put up the baby bed, and he'd taken the time to help with the other things, as well. Except for the fact Sunnie was a girl and the room was painted blue, everything else was perfect. By the time they'd left, it had looked like a genuine nursery and she couldn't wait for Sunnie to see it.

That brought her back to the question she'd wondered about earlier. Why was he here? She figured he would drop her off and keep moving. She had a baby car seat, so as far as she was concerned, she was ready to go. But she couldn't dismiss the nervous tension in her stomach.

Sunnie had clung to her earlier today when the police officers had first brought her in. What if she no longer had that attachment to her and treated her like the others and continue to cry all over the place? She drew in a deep breath, wanting to believe that that special connection between them was still there.

"Where is she?" she asked the nurse.

"Down that hall. Trust me, you'll hear her as soon as you clear the waiting area. You won't be able to miss it. All of us are wearing homemade earplugs."

Sheila knew the nurse had said it as a joke, but she didn't see anything funny. She was ready to get Sunnie and go home. Home. Already she was thinking of her place as the baby's home. Before tonight, to her it was just a place to eat and sleep. Now, taking Sunnie there had her thinking differently.

True to what the nurse had said, Sunnie could be heard the moment Sheila and Zeke passed the waiting room. He put his hand on her arm for them to stop walking. He studied her features. "What's wrong? Why are you so tense?"

How had he known? She released a nervous sigh.

"I've been gone over eight hours. What if Sunnie isn't attached to me anymore? What if she sees me and continues to cry?"

Zeke stared at her. The answer seemed quite obvious to him. It didn't matter. The kid was going home with her regardless. But he could see it was important for this encounter with the baby not to constitute a rejection. He wondered why he cared. He reached out and took her hand in his and began rubbing it when it felt cold.

"Hey, she's going to remember you. She liked you too much not to. If you recall, I was here when she was clinging to you like you were her lifeline, her protector and the one person she thinks is there for her."

He saw the hopeful gleam in her eyes. "You think so?"

Hell, he wasn't sure, but he'd never tell her that. "Yes, I think so."

She smiled. "Thanks, and I hope you're right."

He hoped he was right, too. They began walking again and when they reached the door to the room where Sunnie was being kept, he watched her square her shoulders and walk in. He followed behind her.

The baby was lying in a crib on her side, screaming up a storm, but miraculously, the moment she saw Sheila, her crying turned to tiny whimpers before she stopped completely. And Zeke wasn't sure how it was possible, but he wouldn't believe it if he hadn't seen it for himself.

The abandoned baby she'd named Sunnie smiled and reached her chubby arms out for her.

CHAPTER FOUR

THE ALARM WENT off and Zeke immediately came awake. Flipping over in bed, he stared up at the ceiling as his mind recalled everything that had happened the night before. Sunnie was now with Sheila.

He had hung around long enough to help gather up the baby and get her strapped in the car seat. And the kid hadn't uttered a single whimper. Instead, she had clung to Sheila like she was her very last friend on earth. He had followed them, just to make sure they arrived back at Sheila's house safely. While sitting in his truck, he had watched her get the baby inside before he'd finally pulled off.

At one point he'd almost killed the ignition and walked up to her door to see if she needed any more help, but figured he'd worn out his welcome already that day. Hell, at least he'd gotten a kiss out of the deal. And what a kiss he'd had. Thinking about that kiss had made it very difficult to fall asleep and kept him tossing and turning all night long.

His day would be full. Although Brad was his best friend, he was also a client; a client who'd come to him for help. Zeke wanted to solve this case quickly. Doing so would definitely be a feather in his cap. It would also further improve his reputation and boost the prospects of his new partner, Darius.

He eased out of bed and was about to slide his feet into his slippers, when the phone rang.

"Hello."

"Hi, Zeke. I just want to make sure the baby is okay."

He smiled at the sound of Darius's wife, Summer's, voice. Darius was presently in D.C. doing antiterrorism consulting work. "She's fine, Summer. The nurse who's going to be taking care of her for the next two weeks took her home from the hospital last night."

"What's the nurse's name?"

"Sheila Hopkins."

"I know Sheila."

He lifted a brow. "You do?"

"Yes… She and I worked together on a domestic-abuse case six months ago. The woman made it to the hospital while Sheila was working E.R. I was called in because the woman needed a place to stay."

Summer was the director of Helping Hands Women's Shelter in Somerset, their twin city. "I hope things turned out well for the woman," he said.

"It did, thanks to Sheila. She's a real professional."

He agreed. And he thought she was also a real woman. Before they'd gone to pick up the baby and while he was putting up the crib, she had showered and changed into a pair of jeans and a top. He wasn't aware that many curves could be on a woman's body. And he practically caught his breath each and every time he looked at her.

Moments later, after ending his call with Summer, Zeke drew in a deep breath and shook his head. He needed to focus on the case at hand and not the curvaceous Sheila Hopkins, or her sleep-stealing kisses.

The first thing he needed to do was to check the

video cameras around the TCC. According to Brad, there were several, and Zeke was hoping that at least one of them had picked something up.

Then he intended to question the gardeners who were in charge of TCC's immaculate lawns to see if they'd seen or heard anything yesterday around the time the baby had been left on the doorstep.

And he had to meet up with Brad to make sure he'd taken the paternity test. The sooner they could prove that Brad wasn't Sunnie's father, the better.

As he made his way into the bathroom, he wondered how the baby was doing. Mainly he wondered how Sheila had fared. Last night, it had been evident after taking several naps that Sunnie was all bright-eyed and ready to play. At midnight. He wondered if Sheila got any sleep.

He rubbed his hands down his face. The thought of her in jammies beneath the covers had his gut stirring. Perhaps she didn't sleep under the covers. She might sleep on top of them the way he did sometimes. Then there was the possibility that she didn't wear jammies, but slept in the nude as he preferred doing at times, as well.

He could imagine her in the nude. For a moment he'd envisioned her that way last night when he'd heard the shower going and knew she was across the hall from where he was putting the crib together, and taking a shower and changing clothes. Strong desire had kicked him so hard he'd almost dropped his screwdriver.

And there was the scent he'd inhaled all through her house. It was a scent he now associated with her. Jasmine. He hadn't known what the aroma was until he'd asked. It was in her candles, various baskets of potpourri that she had scattered about. But he'd especially picked it up when she'd come out of her bedroom after taking her shower. She had evidently used the fragrance while showering because its scent shrouded her when she'd entered the room she would use as the temporary nursery.

Last night it had been hard to get to sleep. To take the chill out of the air he'd lit the fireplace in his bedroom and then couldn't settle down when visions of him and Sheila, naked in front of that same fireplace, tortured his mind.

As he brushed his teeth and washed his face, he couldn't help wondering what the hell was wrong with him. He knew the score where women were concerned. The feeling of being abandoned was something he would always deal with. As a result, he would never set himself up for that sort of pain again. No woman was worth it.

A short while later he had stepped out the shower and was drying off when his cell phone rang. He reached to pick it up off the bathroom counter and saw it was Brad. "What's going on?"

"Abigail Langley is what's going on. I know she has a meeting at TCC this morning and I'm going to have it out with her once and for all."

Zeke rolled his eyes. "Lay off her, Brad. You don't have any proof she's involved in any way."

"Sure she's involved. Abigail happens to be the only person who'll benefit if my reputation is ruined."

"But you just can't go accusing her of anything without concrete proof," Zeke said in a stern tone.

"I can't? Ha! Just watch me." Brad then clicked off the phone.

"Damn!" Zeke placed the phone back on the counter as he quickly began dressing. He needed to get over to TCC before Brad had a chance to confront Abigail Langley. He had a feeling his best friend was about to make a huge mistake.

SHEILA FOUGHT BACK sleep as she fed Sunnie breakfast. She doubted if she and the baby had gotten a good four hours' sleep. The pediatric nurse had been right. Sunnie had slept most of yesterday, and in the middle of the night while most of Royal was sleeping, she had been wide awake and wanting to play.

Of course, Sheila had given in after numerous attempts at rocking her to sleep failed. Now Sunnie looked well-rested. Sheila refused to think about how *she* looked half-asleep and yawning every ten minutes. But even lack of sleep could not erase how it felt holding the baby in her arms. And when Sunnie looked up at her and smiled, she knew she would willingly spend an entire week of sleepless nights to see that smile.

And she could make the cutest sounds when she was happy. It must be nice not having any troubles. Then she quickly remembered Sunnie might have troubles after all, if Bradford Price turned out not to be her daddy. Sheila didn't want to think about could happen to her once Social Services took her away and put her into the system.

"We're not going to think about any of that right now, cupcake," she said, wiping Sunnie's mouth after she'd finished her bottle. "Now it's time for you to burp," she said, gently hoisting the baby onto her shoulder.

Dr. Phillips had referred Dr. Greene, the head pediatrician at Royal Memorial, to the case, and he had called inquiring how Sunnie was doing. He'd also given her helpful hints as to how to help Sunnie formulate a sleeping pattern where she would stay awake during most of the day and sleep longer at night.

A short while later, she placed the baby back in the crib after Sunnie seemed to have found interest in the mobile Zeke had purchased at the last minute while in the store last night. She had almost talked him out of getting it, but now she was glad she hadn't.

Sheila had pulled up a chair to sit there and watch Sunnie for a while, when her phone rang. She immediately picked it up. "Yes?"

"I was waiting to see if you remembered that you had a mother."

Sheila rolled her eyes, fighting the urge to say that she'd also been waiting to see if her mother remembered she had a daughter, but knew it would be a waste of time. The only reason her mother was calling her now was because she was in between husbands and she had a little idle time on her hands.

"Hi, Mom," she said, deciding not to bother addressing her mother's comment. "And how are you?"

"I could be better. Did you ever get that guy's phone number?"

That *guy* her mother was referring to was Dr. Morgan. The last time her mother had come to visit they had gone out to lunch, only to run into one of the surgeons from the hospital. Dr. Morgan was ten years her mother's junior. Did that mean her mother was considering the possibility of becoming a cougar?

"No. Like I told you then, Dr. Morgan is already in a serious relationship."

Cassie Hopkins chuckled. "Isn't everybody...except you?"

Sheila cringed. Her mother couldn't resist the opportunity to dig. Cassie felt that if she could get five husbands, her only daughter should be able to get at least one. "I don't want a serious relationship, Mom."

"And if you did want one, then what?"

"Then I'd have one." Knowing her mother was about to jump in about Crawford Newman, the last man she wanted to talk about, she quickly changed the subject. "I talked to Lois the other day."

Her mother chuckled again. "And I bet you called her and not the other way around."

"No, in fact, she called me." She didn't have to tell her mother that Lois had called to tell her not to visit her and her family in Atlanta after all. And that was after issuing her an invitation earlier in the year. There was also no need to tell her that Lois had only issued the invitation after hearing about that heroic deed Sheila had performed, which had gotten broadcast nationwide on CNN. She guessed it wasn't important any longer for Lois to let anyone know that she was her sister after all.

Her mother snorted. "Hmmph. I'm surprised. So how is the princess doing and has she said when she plans to share any of the inheritance your father left her with you?"

Sheila knew the fact that her own father had intentionally left her out of his will still bothered her mother, although it no longer bothered her. It had at first because doing such a thing had pretty much proven what she'd always known. Her father hadn't wanted her. Regardless of the fact that he ended up despising her mother, that should not have had any bearing on his relationship with his daughter. But Baron Hopkins hadn't seen things that way. He saw her as an extension of her mother, and if you hated the mother then you automatically hated the child.

Lois, on the other hand, had indeed been her father's princess. The only child from the first wife whom he had adored, he hadn't been quite ready for the likes of Cassie. Things probably wouldn't have been so bad if Baron hadn't discovered her mother was having an affair with one of his business partners—a man who later became husband number two for Cassie. Then there was the question of whether Sheila was even his child, although she looked more like him than Lois did.

She was able to get her mother off the phone when Cassie had a call come through from some man. It was the story of her mother's life and the failed fairy tale for hers. She got out of the chair and moved over to the crib. Sunnie was trying to go to sleep. Sheila would have just loved to let her, but she knew if she were to sleep now that would mean another sleepless night.

"Oh, no, you don't, sweetie pie," she said, getting the baby out of bed. "You and I are going to play for a while. I plan on keeping you up as much as possible today."

Sunnie gurgled and smiled sleepy hazel eyes up at her. "I know how you feel, trust me. I want to sleep, too. Hopefully, if this works, we'll both get to sleep tonight," Sheila said softy, rubbing the baby's fingers, reveling in just how soft her skin was.

Holding the baby gently in her arms, she headed downstairs.

ZEKE WALKED DOWN the hall of the TCC's clubhouse to one of the meeting rooms. The Texas Cattlemen's motto, which was clearly on display on a plaque in the main room here, said, Leadership, Justice and Peace. He heard loud angry voices and recognized Brad's and knew the female one belonged to Abigail. He wondered if they'd forgotten about the peace wording of the slogan.

"And just what are you accusing me of, Brad?"

"You're too intelligent to play dumb, Abigail. I know you're the one who arranged to have that baby left with a note claiming it's mine, when you know good and well it's not."

"What! How can you accuse me of such a thing?"

"Easily. You want to be the TCC's next president."

"And you think I'll go so far as to use a baby? A precious little baby to show you up?"

Zeke cringed. He could actually hear Abigail's voice breaking. Hell, it sounded as if the woman was crying. He paused outside the door.

"Dang, Abigail, I didn't mean to make you cry, for Pete's sake."

"Well, how could you accuse me of something like that? I love babies. And that little girl was abandoned. I had nothing to do with it, Brad. You've got to believe me."

Zeke inhaled deeply. The woman was downright bawling now. Brad had really gone and done it now.

"I'm sorry, Abby. I see that I was wrong. I didn't mean to get you so upset. I'm sorry."

"You should be. And to prove I'm not behind it," she said, still crying, *"I suggest we suspend campaigning for the election until the case is solved."*

"And you'll go along with doing that?"

"Of course. We're talking about a baby, Brad, and her welfare comes first."

"I agree," Brad said. "Thanks, Abby. And again, I'm sorry for accusing you earlier."

Zeke thought it was time for him to make his entrance before Brad made a bigger mess of things. At least he'd had the sense to apologize to the woman. He opened the door and stopped. Brad was standing in the middle of the room holding a still-weeping Abigail in his arms.

For a moment Zeke thought he should tiptoe back out and was about to do just that, when they both glanced over at him. And as if embarrassed at being caught in such an embrace, the two quickly jumped apart.

Zeke placed his hands in the pockets of his jeans and smiled at the pair. "Brad. Abigail. Does this mean the two of you are no longer at war?"

A SHORT WHILE later Zeke was getting back in his car thinking that he hadn't needed to put out the fire after all. Brad and Abigail were a long way from being best friends, but at least it seemed as if they'd initiated a truce. If he hadn't been a victim of abandonment himself, he would think something good had at least resulted from Sunnie's appearance.

Sunnie.

He shook his head. Sheila had deemed the baby be called Sunnie for the time being, and everyone had pretty much fallen in line with her request. He had refrained from calling her earlier just in case she and the baby were sleeping in late. But now it was close to two in the afternoon. Surely they were up by now. While she had been upstairs taking a shower last night, he had opened her refrigerator to grab another beer and noticed hers was barer than his. That meant, also like him, she must eat out a lot. Chances were she wouldn't want to take the baby out, so the least he could do would be to be a good guy and stop somewhere, buy something for her to eat and take it to her.

While at the TCC he had checked and nothing had gotten caught on the video camera other than a woman's hand placing the baby on the doorstep. Whoever had done it seemed to have known just where the cameras were located, which meant the culprit was someone familiar with the grounds of the club. Could it have been an inside job? At least they knew they could erase Abigail off the list. She had been in a meeting when the baby had been dropped off.

Besides, to say Abigail Langley had gotten emotional as a result of Brad's accusation was an understatement. He couldn't help wondering why. He knew she was a widow. Had she lost a baby at some point while she'd been married? He'd been tempted to ask Brad but figured knowing his and Abigail's history, he would probably be the last to know. He'd heard from more than one source that the two of them had been butting heads since they were kids.

After buckling his seat belt he turned his car's ignition and eased out the parking lot, wondering what type of meal Sheila might have a taste for. Still not wanting to disturb her and the baby, he smiled, thinking, when in doubt, get pizza.

SHEILA COCKED ONE eye open as she gazed over at Sunnie, who was back in the crib toying with her mobile again. She sighed, not sure how long she would be able to stay awake. It had been almost eighteen hours now. She'd done doubles at the hospital before, but at least she'd gotten a power nap in between. She didn't know babies had so much energy. She thought of closing her eyes for a second, but figured there was no way for her to do something like that. Mothers didn't sleep while their babies were awake, did they?

She had tried everything and refused to drink another cup of coffee. The only good thing was that if she continued to keep Sunnie awake, that meant when they both went to sleep, hopefully, it would be through the night. She glanced around the room, liking how it looked and hoped Sunnie liked it, as well.

Zeke had been such a sweetheart to help her put the baby equipment together and hang pictures on the wall. Although he hadn't asked, he had to have been wondering why she was going overboard for a baby that would be in her care for only two weeks. She was glad he hadn't asked because she would not have known what to tell him.

She tried to ignore the growling of her stomach and the fact that other than toast, coffee and an apple, she hadn't eaten anything else that day. She didn't want to take her eyes off the baby for even a minute.

She nearly jumped when she heard the sound of the doorbell. She glanced at the Big Bird clock she'd hung on the wall. It was close to four in the afternoon. She moved over to the window and glanced down and saw the two-seater sports car in her driveway and knew who it belonged to. What was Zeke doing back? They had exchanged numbers last night, merely as a courtesy. She really hadn't expected to see him again any time soon.

She immediately thought about the kiss they'd

shared…not that she hadn't thought about it several times that day already. That was the kind of kiss a girl would want to tell somebody about. Like a girlfriend. She'd thought about calling Jill then had changed her mind. On second thought, maybe it was the kind of kiss a girl should keep to herself.

The doorbell sounded again. Knowing she probably looked a mess and, at the moment, not caring since she hadn't anticipated any visitors, she walked over to the bed and picked up the baby. "Come on, Sunnie. Looks like we have company."

ZEKE WAS JUST about to turn to leave, when the door opened. All it took was one look at Sheila to know she'd had a rough night and an even rougher day. Sunnie, on the other hand, looked happy and well-rested.

"Hey, you okay?" he asked Sheila when she stepped aside to let him in. And he figured the only reason she'd done that was because of the pizza boxes he was carrying.

"I'm fine." She eyed the pizza box. "And I hope you brought that to share. I've barely eaten all day."

"Yes, I brought it to share," he said, heading for the kitchen. "The kid wore you out today?"

"And last night," she said, following on his heels. "I talked to the pediatrician about her not sleeping through the night and he suggested I try to keep her awake today. That means staying awake myself."

He stopped and she almost walked into the back of him. He turned inquisitive dark eyes on her. "Sunnie hasn't taken a nap at all today?"

"No. Like I said, I'm keeping her awake so we can both sleep tonight."

He found that interesting for some reason. "When do babies usually develop a better sleep pattern?"

"It depends. Usually they would have by now. But we don't know Sunnie's history. Her life might have been so unstable she hadn't gotten adjusted to anything." She glanced at the baby. "I hate talking about her like she isn't here."

Zeke laughed. "It's not as if she can understand anything you've said."

He shook his head. Sheila had to be pretty tired to even concern herself with anything like that. He glanced around the kitchen. It was still neat as a pin, but baby bottles lined the counter as well as a number of other baby items. It was obvious that a baby was in residence.

"Why did you stop by?" she asked.

He glanced back at her. Her eyes looked tired, almost dead on her feet. Her hair was tied back in a ponytail and she wasn't wearing any makeup. But he thought she looked good. "To check on the two of you. And I figured you probably hadn't had a chance to cook anything," he said, deciding not to mention he'd noticed last night she hadn't had anything to cook.

"So I decided I would be nice and stop and grab something for you," he said, placing the pizza boxes on the table. He opened one of them.

"Oh, that smells so good. Thank you."

He chuckled. "I've gotten pizza from this place before and it is good. And you're welcome. Do you want to lay her down while you dig in?"

She looked down at Sunnie and then back at him. "Lay her down?"

"Yes, like in that crib I put together for her last night."

"But…she'll be all alone."

He frowned. "Yes, but I hooked up that baby monitor last night so you could hear her. Haven't you tried it out?"

"Yes, but I like watching her."

He nodded slowly. "Why? I can imagine you being fascinated by her since you admitted yesterday that you've never kept a baby before, but why the obsession? You're a nurse. Haven't you worked in the nursery before?"

"Of course, but this is different. This is my home and Sunnie is in my care. I don't want anything to happen to her."

He could tell by her tone that she was getting a little defensive, so he decided to back off a bit, table it for later. And there would definitely be a later, because she wouldn't be much use to Sunnie or anybody if she wore herself out. "Fine, sit down and I'll go get that extra car seat. You can place her in it while you eat."

A short while later they were sitting at her kitchen table with Sunnie sitting in the car seat on the floor between them. She was moving her hands to and fro while making sounds. She seemed like such a happy baby. Totally different from the baby that had been screaming up a storm yesterday. Every once in a while she would raise her hazel eyes to stare at them. Mainly at him. It was as if she was trying to figure him out. Determine if he was safe.

Zeke glanced over at Sheila. She had eaten a couple slices of pizza along with the bag salad he'd bought. Every so often she would yawn, apologize and then yawn again. She needed to get some sleep; otherwise, she would fall on her face at any minute.

"Thanks for the pizza, Zeke. Not only are you nice, but you're thoughtful."

He leaned back in his chair. "You're welcome." He paused for a moment. "I got a folder with stuff out there in my car that I need to go over. I can do it here just as well as anywhere else."

Her forehead furrowed as if confused. "But why would you want to?"

He smiled. "That way I can watch Sunnie."

She still looked confused.

"Look, Sheila. It's obvious that you're tired. Probably ready to pass out. You can go upstairs and take a nap while I keep an eye on the baby."

"But why would you want to do something like that?"

He chuckled. She asked a lot of questions. Unfortunately for him they were questions he truly couldn't answer. Why had he made such an offer? He really wasn't sure. All he knew was that he liked being around her and wasn't ready to leave yet.

When he didn't give her an answer quick enough, she narrowed her gaze. "You think I can't handle things, don't you? You think I've taken on more than I can chew by agreeing to be Sunnie's temporary foster parent. You think—"

Before she could finish her next words, he was out of the chair, had eased around the baby and had pulled Sheila into his arms. "Right now I think you're talking too damn much." And then he kissed her.

For some reason he needed to do this, he thought as his mouth took possession of hers. And the instant their mouths touched, he felt energized in a way he'd never felt before. Sexually energized. His tongue slid between her parted lips and immediately began tangling with hers. What was there about kissing her that was so mind-blowing, so arousing, so threatening to his senses?

This kind of mouth interaction with her was stirring things inside him he'd tried to keep at bay with other women. How could she rouse them so effortlessly? So deeply and so thoroughly? And why did she feel so damn good in his arms? Even better today than yesterday. Yesterday there had been that element of surprise on both their parts. It was still there today, but surprise was being smothered by heat of the most erotic kind.

And it was heat he could barely handle. Not sure that he could manage. But it was heat that he was definitely enjoying. And then there was something else trying to creep into the mix. Emotions. Emotions he wasn't accustomed to. He had thought of her all day. Why? Usually for him it had always been out of sight and out of mind. But not with Sheila. The woman was unforgettable. She was temptation he couldn't resist.

He felt a touch on his leg and reluctantly released Sheila's mouth to glance down. Hazel eyes were staring up at him. Sunnie had grabbed hold of his pant leg. He couldn't help chuckling. At five months old the kid was seeing too much. If she hadn't gotten his attention, he'd probably still be kissing Sheila.

He shifted his gaze from the baby back to the woman he was still holding in his arms. She was about to step back, so he tightened his hold around her waist. "I'm going out to my car and getting my briefcase. When I come back inside you're going to go up those stairs and get some rest. I'll handle Sunnie."

"But—"

"No buts. No questions. I'll take good care of her. I promise."

"She might cry the entire time."

"If she cries I'll deal with it." He then walked out of the kitchen.

SHEILA COULDN'T STOP her smile when Zeke walked out. She glanced down at Sunnie. "He's kind of bossy, isn't he?" She touched her lips. "And he's a darn good kisser."

She sighed deeply. "Not that you needed to know that. Not that you needed to see us lock lips, either."

She then moved around the kitchen as she cleared off the table. She was standing at the sink when Zeke returned with his briefcase. "How long do you plan to be here?" she asked him.

"For as long as you need to rest."

She nodded. "I'll be fine in a couple of hours. Will you wake me?"

Zeke stared at her, fully aware she had no idea of what she was asking of him. Seeing her in bed, under the covers or on top of the covers, would not be a good idea. At least she hadn't reminded him that she'd told him not to kiss her again. But what could she say, when she had kissed him back?

"I won't wake you, Sheila. You have to wake up on your own."

She frowned. "But Sunnie will need a bath later."

"And she'll get one, with or without you. For your information I do know a little about kids."

She looked surprised. "You do?"

"Yes. I was raised by my aunt and she has a daughter with twins. They consider me their uncle and I've kept them before."

"Both?"

"Yes, and at the same time. It was a piece of cake." Okay, he had exaggerated some. There was no need to tell her that they had almost totally wrecked his place by the time their parents had returned.

"How old are they?"

"Now they're four. The first time I kept them they were barely one."

She nodded. "They live in Austin?"

"No. New Orleans."

"So you're not a Texan by birth?"

He wondered why all the questions again. He had made a mistake when he mentioned Alicia and the twins. "According to my birth certificate, I am a Texan by birth. My aunt who raised me lives in New Orleans. I returned to Texas when I attended UT in Austin."

He had told her enough and, when she opened her mouth to say something more, he placed his hand over it. Better his hand than his mouth. "No more questions. Now, off to bed."

She glanced down at the baby when he removed his hand from her mouth. "Are you sure you want to handle her?"

"Positive. Now, go."

She hesitated for a minute and then drew in a deep breath before leaving the kitchen. He glanced down at Sunnie, whose eyes had followed Sheila from the room. Then those same hazel eyes latched onto him almost in an accusatory stare. Her lips began trembling and he had an idea what was coming next. When she let out a wail, he bent down and picked up the car seat and set it on the table.

"Shh, little one. Sheila needs her rest. Come on, I'm not that bad. She likes me. I kissed her. Get over it."

When her crying suddenly slowed to a low whimper, he wondered if perhaps this kid did understand.

CHAPTER FIVE

SOMETHING——SHEILA wasn't sure exactly what——woke her up, and her gaze immediately went to the clock on the nightstand: 7:00 p.m. She quickly slid out of bed and raced down the stairs then halted at the last step. There, stretched out on the sofa was Zeke with Sunnie on his chest. They were both asleep and, since the baby was wearing one of the cute pj sets they'd purchased yesterday, it was obvious he'd given her a bath. In fact, the air was filled with the fragrance of baby oil mixed with baby powder. She liked the smell.

She wished she had a camera to take a picture. This was definitely a Kodak moment. She slowly tiptoed to the chair across from the sofa and sat down. Even while sleeping, Zeke was handsome, and his long lashes almost fanned his upper cheeks. He didn't snore. Crawford snored something awful. Another comparison of the two men.

She wondered if he'd ever dumped a woman the way Crawford had dumped her. Good old Crawford, the traveling salesman, who spent a lot of time on the road…and as she later found out while he'd been on the road, in other women's beds. She remembered the time she would anxiously await his long-distance calls and how she would feel when she didn't get them. How lonely she would be when she didn't hear from him for days.

And she would never forget that day when he did show up, just to let her know he was marrying someone else. A woman he'd met while out peddling his medical supplies. He had wanted her to get on with her life because he had gotten on with his. She took his advice. Needing to leave Dallas, the next time an opportunity came for a transfer to another hospital, she had taken it.

She continued to stare at Zeke and wondered what his story was. He'd told her bits and pieces and she figured that was all she would get. So far he hadn't mentioned anything about a mother. His comment yesterday pretty much sealed the fact he hadn't known his father. And from what he'd told her today, his aunt in New Orleans had raised him. Had his mother died? She drew in a deep breath, thinking it really wasn't any of her business. Still, she couldn't help being curious about the hunk stretched out on her sofa. The man who had kissed her twice. The man who'd literally knocked sense right out of her brain.

And that wasn't good. That meant it was time for him to leave. Yesterday she had appreciated his help in shopping with her for baby items. Today she appreciated the pizza. There couldn't be a tomorrow.

Easing out of the chair, she crossed the room and gently shook him awake. She sucked in a deep breath when his eyes snapped open and his beautiful dark eyes stared up at her. Pinned her to the spot where she was standing. They didn't say anything but stared at each other for the longest time. She felt his stare as if his gaze was a physical caress.

And while he stared at her, she remembered things. She remembered how good his mouth felt on hers.

How delicious his tongue tasted in her mouth. How his tongue would slide from side to side while driving her to the brink of madness. It made her wonder just what else that tongue was capable of doing.

She blushed and she knew he'd noticed because his gaze darkened. "What were you thinking just now?"

Did he really expect her to tell him? Fat chance! Some things he was better off not knowing and that was definitely one of them. "I was thinking that it's time for me to put Sunnie to bed."

"I doubt that would have made you blush."

She doubted it, too, but she would never admit to it. Instead of responding to what he'd said, she reached for Sunnie. "I'm taking her upstairs and putting her to bed." Once she had the baby cradled in her arms, she walked off.

When she had gone up the stairs, Zeke eased into a sitting position and rubbed his hands down his face. Surprisingly, he'd gotten a lot of work done. Sunnie had sat in her car seat and stared at him the entire time, evidently fascinated by the shifting of the papers and the sight of him working on his laptop computer. He figured the bright colors that had occasionally flashed across the screen had fascinated her.

He stood and went back into the kitchen. There was no doubt in his mind that when Sheila returned she would expect him to be packed up and ready to go. He would not disappoint her. Although he would love to hang around, he needed to haul it. There was too much attraction between them. Way too much chemistry. When they had gazed into each other's eyes, the air had become charged. She had become breathless. So had he. That wasn't good.

All there was supposed to be between them was business. Where was his hard-and-fast rule never to mix business with pleasure? It had taken a hard nosedive the first time he'd kissed her. And if that hadn't been bad enough, he'd kissed her again. What had come over him? He knew the answer without thinking—lust of the most intense kind.

By the time he clicked his briefcase closed, he heard Sheila come back downstairs, and when she walked into the kitchen he had it in his hand. "Walk me to the door," he said softly, wondering why he'd asked her to do so when he knew the way out.

"Okay."

She silently walked beside him and when they got to the door, she reached out to open it, but he took her hand, brought it to his lips and kissed it. "I left my card on the table. Call me if you need anything. Otherwise, this was my last time coming by."

She nodded and didn't ask why. He knew she understood. They were deeply attracted to each other and if they hung around each other for long, that attraction would heat up and lead to something else. Something that he knew neither of them wanted to tangle with right now.

"Thanks for everything, Zeke. I feel rested."

He smiled. "But you can always use more. She'll probably sleep through the night, but she'll be active in the morning. That little girl has a lot of energy."

Sheila chuckled. "So you noticed."

"Oh, yeah, I noticed. But she's a good kid."

"Yes, and I still can't believe someone abandoned her."

"It happens, Sheila. Even to good kids."

He brushed a kiss across her lips. "Go back to bed."
Then he opened the door and walked out.

ZEKE FORCED HIMSELF to keep moving and not look back.
He opened the car door and sat there a moment, fighting
the temptation to get out of his car, walk right back up
to her door and knock on it. When she answered it, he
would kiss her senseless before she could say a single
word. He would then sweep her off her feet and take
her up to her bedroom and stretch her out on it, undress
her and then make love to her.

He leaned back against the headrest and closed his
eyes. How had it moved from kissing to thoughts of
making love to her? *Easily, Travers,* his mind screamed.
She's a beauty. She's hot. And you enjoy her mouth too
damn much.

He took a deep breath and then exhaled slowly. He
would be doing the right thing by staying away. Besides,
it wasn't as though he didn't have anything to do. He
had several people to interview tomorrow, including
several TCC members who wanted to talk to him. One
of them had called tonight requesting the meeting and
he wondered what it would be about.

He turned the key in the ignition and backed out the
driveway. He looked at the house one last time before
doing so. All the lights were off downstairs. His gaze
traveled to her bedroom window. The light was on there.
He wondered what she was doing. Probably getting
ready for bed.

A bed he wished he could join her in.

SHEILA CHECKED ON SUNNIE one more time before going
into her bathroom to take a shower. She felt heat rush to

her cheeks when she remembered waking Zeke earlier. The man had a way of looking at her that could turn her bones into mush.

A short while later after taking a shower and toweling dry her body, she slid into a pair of pajamas. She checked on Sunnie one last time and also made sure the monitor was set so she could hear her if she was to awaken. Zeke was convinced the baby would sleep through the night.

She drew in a deep breath knowing he'd told her he wouldn't be back. And she knew it was for the best. She would miss him. His appearance at her door tonight had been a surprise. But he had a way of making himself useful and she liked that. Crawford hadn't been handy with tools. He used to tell her he worked too hard to do anything other than what was required of him at his job. Not even taking out the trash.

And she had put up with it because she hadn't wanted to be alone.

Moving here was her first accomplishment. It had been a city where she hadn't known anybody. A city where she would be alone. Go figure. She had gotten used to it and now Zeke had invaded her space. So had Sunnie. The latter was a welcome invasion; the former wasn't.

As she slid into bed and drew the covers around her, she closed her eyes and ran her tongue around her mouth. Even after brushing her teeth she could still taste Zeke. It was as if his flavor was embedded in her mouth. She liked it. She would savor it because it wouldn't happen again.

THE NEXT DAY, Zeke leaned back on the table and studied the two men sitting before him and tried digesting their admissions.

"So the two of you are saying that you also received blackmail letters?"

Rali Tariq and Arthur Moran, well-known wealthy businessmen and longtime members of the TCC, nodded. Then Rali spoke up. "Although I was innocent of what the person was accusing me of, I was afraid to go to the authorities."

"Same here," Arthur said. "I was hoping the person would eventually go away when I didn't acknowledge the letters. It was only when I found out about the blackmailing scheme concerning Bradford that I figured I needed to come forward."

"That's the reason I'm here, as well," Rali added.

Zeke nodded. What the two men had just shared with him certainly brought a lot to light. It meant the blackmailer hadn't just targeted Brad, but had set his or her mark on other innocent, unsuspecting TCC members, as well. That made him wonder whether the individual was targeting TCC members because they were known to be wealthy or if there was a personal vendetta the authorities needed to be concerned with.

"Did you bring the letters with you?"

"Yes."

Both men handed him their letters. He placed them on the table and then pulled out one of the ones Brad had received. It was obvious they had been written by the same person.

"They looked the same," Rali said, looking over Zeke's shoulder at all three letters.

Arthur nodded in agreement.

"Yes, it appears that one person wrote them all," Zeke replied. "But the question is why did he carry out his threat against Brad but not on you two?"

He could tell by the men's expressions that they didn't have a clue. "Well, at least I'm finally getting pieces to the puzzle. I appreciate the two of you coming forward. It will help in clearing Brad's name. Now all we have to do is wait for the results of the paternity test."

An hour later he met Brad for lunch at Claire's Restaurant, an upscale establishment in downtown Royal that served delicious food. A smile curved Brad's lips after hearing about Zeke's meeting with Rali and Arthur.

"Then that should settle things," he said, cutting into the steak on his plate. "If Rali and Arthur received blackmail letters, that proves there's a conspiracy against members of the TCC. There probably are others who aren't coming forward like Rali and Arthur."

Zeke took a sip of his wine. "Possibly. But you are the only one who he or she carried out the threat with. Why you and not one of the others? Hell, Rali is the son of a sheikh. I would think they would have stuck it to him real good. So we still aren't out of the woods. There's something about the whole setup that bothers me."

He studied Brad for a moment. "Did you and Abigail Langley clear things up?"

Brad met his gaze. "If you're asking if I think she's still involved then the answer is no. Now I wished I hadn't approached her with my accusations."

A smile touched Zeke's lips. "I hate to say I told you so, but I did tell you so."

"I know. I know. But Abigail and I have been bad news for years."

"Yeah, but someone getting on your bad side is one thing, Brad. Accusing someone, especially a woman, of having anything to do with abandoning a child is another."

Brad held his gaze for the longest time. "And you of all people should know, right?"

Zeke nodded. "Yes, I should know."

Zeke took another sip of his wine. As his best friend, Brad was one of the few people who knew his history. Brad knew how Zeke's mother had abandoned him. Not on a doorstep, but in the care of his aunt. Although his aunt had been a godsend, he'd felt abandoned those early years. Alone. Discarded. Thrown away. No longer wanted.

It had taken years for him to get beyond those childhood feelings. But he would be the first to admit those childhood feelings had subsequently become adult hang-ups. That was one of the reasons he only engaged in casual affairs. He wouldn't let anyone walk out on him again. He would be the one doing the walking.

"Abigail certainly took my accusation hard," Brad said, breaking into Zeke's thoughts. "I've known her since we were kids and I've never known her to be anything but tough as nails. Seeing her break down like that really got to me."

"I could tell. You seemed to be holding her pretty tightly when I walked in."

He chuckled at the blush that appeared in Brad's features. "Well, what else was I supposed to do?" Brad asked. "Especially since I was the reason she'd gotten upset in the first place. I'm going to have to watch what I say around her."

Especially if it's about babies, Zeke thought, deciding not to say the words out loud. If Brad wasn't concerned with the reason the woman fell to pieces then he wouldn't be concerned with it, either. Besides, he had enough on his plate.

"So how's the baby?" Brad asked, breaking into his thoughts yet again.

"Sunnie?"

"Yes."

He leaned back in his chair as he thought about how she had wet him up pretty good when he'd given her a bath. He'd had to throw his shirt into Sheila's dryer. "She's fine. I checked on her yesterday."

"And the woman that's taking care of her. That nurse. She's doing a pretty good job?"

Zeke thought about Sheila. Hell, he'd thought about her a lot today, whether he had wanted to or not. "Yes, she's doing a pretty good job."

"Well, I hope the results from the paternity test come up quickly enough for her sake."

Zeke lifted a brow. "Why for her sake?"

"I would hate for your nurse to get too attached to the baby."

Zeke nodded. He would hate for "his" nurse to get too attached to Sunnie, as well.

"SHE IS SUCH a cutie," Summer Franklin said as she held Sunnie in her arms. Surprisingly, Sunnie hadn't cried when Summer had taken her out of Sheila's arms. She was too fascinated with Summer's dangling earrings to care.

Sheila liked Summer. She was one of the few people

she felt she could let her guard down around. Because Sheila had a tendency to work all the time, this was the first time she'd seen Summer in weeks.

"Yes, she is a cutie," Sheila said. "I can't imagine anyone abandoning her like that."

"Me, neither. But you better believe Zeke's going to get to the bottom of it. I'm glad Darius brought him on as a partner. My husband was working himself to death solving cases. Now he has help."

Sheila nodded, wondering how much Summer knew about Zeke, but didn't want to ask for fear her friend would wonder why.

Although Sunnie had slept through the night, she herself, on the other hand, had not. Every time she closed her eyes she had seen Zeke, looking tall, dark, handsome and fine as any man had a right to be. Then she also saw another image of him. The one sleeping peacefully on the sofa with the baby lying on his chest. She wondered if he would marry and have children one day. She had a feeling he would make a great dad just from his interaction with Sunnie.

"Oops, I think she's ready to return to you now," Summer said, breaking her thoughts. She smiled when she saw Sunnie lift her little hands to reach out for her, making her feel special. Wanted. Needed.

"You're good with her, Sheila."

She glanced over at Summer and smiled. "Thanks."

"I wonder who her real parents are."

"I wondered that, as well. But I'm sure Zeke is going to find out," Sheila said.

Summer chuckled. "I believe that, as well. Zeke comes across as a man who's good at what he does."

Sheila held the baby up to hide the blush on her face.

She knew for a fact that Zeke was good at what he did, especially when it came to kissing a woman.

ZEKE LET HIMSELF inside his home with a bunch of papers in his hand, closing the door behind him with the heel of his shoe. He'd been busy today.

He dropped the papers on his dining room table and headed straight to the kitchen to grab a beer out of the refrigerator. He took a huge gulp and then let out a deep breath. He'd needed that. That satisfied his thirst. Now if he could satisfy his hunger for Sheila Hopkins the same way....

Twice he had thought of dropping by her place and twice he had remembered why he could not do that. He had no reason to see her again until it was time to open the paternity test results. Considering what he'd discovered with those other two TCC members, he felt confident that the test would prove there was no biological link between Brad and Sunnie. But he was just as determined to discover whose baby she was. What person would abandon their child to make them a part of some extortion scheme? It was crazy. And sick. And he intended to determine who would do such a thing and make sure the authorities threw the book at them as hard as they could.

His thoughts shifted back to Sheila as he moved from the kitchen to the dining room. He had a lot of work to do and intended to get down to business. But he couldn't get out of his mind how he had opened his eyes while stretched out on her sofa only to find her staring down at him. If he hadn't had the baby sleeping on his chest, he would have been tempted to reach out and pull her down on the sofa with him. And he would have taken her mouth the way he wanted to do. Why was he torturing himself by thinking of something he was better off not having?

He drew in a deep breath, knowing he needed to put Sheila out of his mind. He had been going through various reports when the phone rang. He grinned when he saw it was Darius.

"Homesick, Darius?" he asked into the phone, and heard a resounding chuckle.

"Of course. I'm not missing you, though. It's my wife. I'm trying to talk Summer into catching a plane and joining me here—especially since there's a hurricane too close to you guys for comfort, but they're shorthanded at the shelter."

"So I heard."

"She also told me about the abandoned baby. How's that going?"

He took the next few minutes to bring Darius up to date. "I know Bradford Price and if he says the baby isn't his then it's not his," Darius said. "He has no reason to lie about it."

"I know, that's why I intend to expose the jerk who's out to ruin Brad's good name," Zeke said.

CHAPTER SIX

THREE DAYS LATER Sheila sat glued to her television listening to the weather report. It was the last month of hurricane season and wouldn't you know it...Hurricane Spencer was up to no good out in the gulf. Forecasters were advising everyone to take necessary precautions by stocking up on the essentials just in case the storm changed course. Now Sheila had Sunnie to worry about, and that meant making sure she had enough of everything— especially disposable diapers, formula and purified water in case the power went out.

Sunnie had pretty much settled down and was sleeping through the night. And they were both getting into a great routine. During the day Sheila had fun entertaining the baby by taking her to the park and other kid-friendly places. She enjoyed pushing Sunnie around in the stroller. Sunnie would still cry on occasion when others held her, but once she would glance around and lock her gaze on Sheila, she was fine.

Sheila had put the baby to bed a short while ago and was ready to go herself if only she was sleepy. Over the past couple of days she'd had several visitors. In addition to Summer and Jill, Dr. Greene had stopped by to check on the baby and Ms. Talbert from Social Services had visited, as well. Ms. Talbert had praised her for volunteering to care for Sunnie and indicated that considering the baby was both healthy and happy, she was doing a great job. The woman had further indicated there was a possibility the results of the paternity test might come in earlier than the two weeks anticipated. Instead of jumping for joy at the news, Sheila had found herself hoping that would not be the case. She had been looking forward to her two weeks with Sunnie.

She heard a branch hit the window and jumped. It had been windy all day and now it seemed it was getting windier. Forecasters predicted the hurricane would make landfall sometime after midnight. They predicted that Royal would be spared the worst of it.

She glanced around the room where she had already set out candles. The lights had been blinking all day; she hoped she didn't lose power, but had to be prepared if she did.

She was halfway up the stairs when the house suddenly went black.

THE WINDS HAVE increased and we have reports of power outages in certain sections of Royal, including the Meadowland and LeBaron areas. Officials are working hard to restore power to these homes and hope to do so within the next few hours….

Zeke was stretched out on the sofa with his eyes closed, but the announcement that had just blared from the television made him snap them open. He then slid into a sitting position. Sheila lived in the Meadowland area.

He knew he had no reason to be concerned. Hopefully, like everyone else, she had anticipated the possibility of a power failure and was prepared. But what if she wasn't? What if she was across town sitting on her sofa holding the baby in the dark?

Standing, he rubbed a hand down his face. It had been four days since he'd seen or talked to her. Four days, while working on clearing Brad's name, of trying hard to push thoughts of her to the back of his mind. He'd failed often, when no matter what he was working on, his thoughts drifted back to her.

What was there about a woman when a man couldn't get her out of his mind? When he would think of her during his every waking moment and wake up in the middle of the night with thoughts of her when he should be sleeping?

Zeke stretched his body before grabbing his keys off the table. Pushing aside the thought that he was making a mistake by rushing off to check on the very woman he'd sworn to stay away from, he quickly walked toward the door, grabbing a jacket and his Stetson on the way out.

SHEILA GLANCED AROUND the living room. Candles were lit and flashlights strategically placed where she might need them. It was just a little after ten but the wind was still howling outside. When she had looked out the window moments ago, all she could do was stare into darkness. Everything was total black.

She had checked on Sunnie earlier and the baby was sleeping peacefully, oblivious to what was happening, and that was good. Sunnie had somehow kicked the covers off her pudgy little legs and Sheila had recovered her, gazing down at her while thinking what the future held for such a beautiful little girl.

Sheila left the nursery and walked downstairs.

She had the radio on a station that played jazz while occasionally providing updates on the storm. It had stopped raining, but the sound of water dripping off the roof was stirring a feeling inside her that she was all too familiar with—loneliness.

Deciding what she needed was a glass of wine, she was headed to the kitchen when she heard the sound of her cell phone. She quickly picked it up and from caller ID saw it was Zeke.

She felt the thud in her chest at the same time she felt her pulse rate increase. "Yes?"

"I'm at the door."

Taking a deep breath and trying to keep her composure intact, she headed toward the door. The police had asked for cars not to be on the road unless it was absolutely necessary due to dangerous conditions, so why was he here? Did he think she couldn't handle things during a power failure? She was certain Sunnie was his main concern and not her.

She opened the door and her breath caught. He stood there looking both rugged and handsome, dressed in a tan rawhide jacket, Western shirt and jeans and a Stetson on his head. The reflections from the candles played across his features as he gazed at her. "I heard the reports on television. Are you and the baby okay?"

She nodded, at the moment unable to speak. Swallowing deeply, she finally said, "Yes, we're fine."

"That's good. May I come in?"

Their gazes stayed locked and she knew what her response should be. They had agreed there was no reason for him to visit her and Sunnie. But the only thing she could think about at that moment was the loneliness that had been seeping through her body for the past few hours, and that she hadn't seen him in four days. And whether she wanted to admit it or not, she had missed him.

"Please come in." She stepped aside.

Removing his hat, Zeke walked past Sheila and glanced around. Lit candles were practically everywhere, and the scent of jasmine welcomed his nostrils. A blaze was also roaring in the fireplace, which radiated a warm, cozy atmosphere.

"Do you want me to take your jacket?"

He glanced back at her. "Yes. Thanks."

He removed his jacket and handed it to her, along with his hat. He watched as she placed both on the coatrack. She was wearing a pair of gold satin pajamas that looked cute on her.

"I was about to have a glass of wine," she said. "Do you want to join me?"

He could say that he'd only come to check on her and the baby, and because they seem to be okay, he would be going. That might have worked if he hadn't asked to come in…or he hadn't taken off his jacket. "Yes, I'd love to have a glass. Thanks."

"I'll be back in a minute."

He watched her leave and slowly moved toward the fireplace. She seemed to be taking his being there well. A part of him was surprised, considering their agreement, that she hadn't asked him to leave. He was glad she hadn't. He watch the fire blazing in the fireplace while thinking that he hadn't realized just how much he had missed seeing her until she'd opened the door. She looked so damn good and it had taken everything within him not to pull her into his arms and kiss her, the way he'd done those other two times. Hell,

he was counting, mainly because there was no way he
could ever forget them.

And as he stood there and continued to gaze into
the fire, he thought of all the reasons he should grab
his jacket and hat and leave before she returned. For
starters, he wanted her, which was a good enough
reason in itself. And the degree to which he wanted
her would be alarming to most. But he had wanted her
from the beginning. He had walked into the hospital and
seen her standing there holding the baby, and looking
like the beautiful woman that she was. He had been
stunned at the intensity of the desire that had slammed
into him; it had almost toppled him. But he had been
able to control it by concentrating on the baby, making
Sunnie's care his top priority.

However, he hadn't been able to control himself that
day at his place when she had gotten in his face. Nor had
he been able to handle things the last time he was here
and he'd nearly mauled her mouth off. Being around
her was way too risky.

Then why was he here? And why was his heart
thumping deep in his chest anticipating her return? At
that moment he had little control of what he was feeling;
especially because they were emotions he hadn't ever
felt before for a woman. If it was just a sexual thing he
would be able to handle that. But the problem was that
he wasn't sure it was. He definitely wanted her, but there
was something about her he didn't understand. There
were reasons he couldn't fathom as to why he was so
attracted to her. And there was no way he could use
Sunnie as an excuse. Sunnie might be the reason they
had initially met, but the baby had nothing to do with

him being here now and going through the emotions he was feeling.

"Do you think this bad weather will last long?"

He turned around to face her and wished he hadn't. She had two glasses in her hand and a bottle of wine under her arm. But what really caught his attention was the way the firelight danced across her features, combined with the glow from the candles. She looked like a woman he wanted to make love to. Damn.

She was temptation.

Zeke moved to assist her with the glasses and wine bottle, and the moment their hands touched, he was a goner. Taking both glasses, as well as the wine bottle, from her hands, he placed both on the table. And then he turned back to her, drew her into his arms and lowered his mouth to hers.

SHEILA WENT INTO his arms willingly, their bodies fusing like metal to magnet. She intended to go with the flow. And boy was she rolling. All over the place.

She could feel his hand in the small of her back that gently pressed her body even closer to his. And she felt him. At the juncture of her thighs. His erection was definitely making its presence known by throbbing hard against her. It was kicking her desire into overdrive. And she could definitely say that was something that had never happened to her before. Since her breakup with Crawford she had kept to herself. Hadn't wanted to date anyone. Preferred not getting involved with any living male.

But being in Zeke's arms felt absolutely perfect. And the way he was mating his mouth with hers was stirring a yearning within her she hadn't been aware she was capable of feeling. And when he finally released her mouth, he let her know he wasn't through with her when his teeth grazed the skin right underneath her right ear, causing shivers to flow through her. And then his teeth moved lower to her collarbone and began sucking gently there.

She tilted her head back and groaned deeply in her throat. What he was doing felt so good and she didn't want him to stop. But he did. Taking her mouth once again.

HE LOVED HER TASTE.

And he couldn't get enough of it, which was why he was eating away at her mouth with a relentless hunger. He was driven by a need that was as primitive as time and as urgent as the desire to breathe. He could feel the rise and fall of her breasts pressed to his chest and could even feel the quivering of her thighs against his.

He hadn't had the time or inclination to get involved with a woman since moving to Royal. Brad's problems meant putting his social life on hold. He had been satisfied with that until Sheila had come along. She had kicked his hormones into gear, made him remember what it felt like to be hard up. But this was different. He'd never wanted a woman to this extreme.

And kissing her wasn't enough.

Keeping his mouth locked to hers, he walked her backward toward the sofa and when they reached it, he lowered her to it. Pulling his mouth away, he took a lick of her swollen lips before saying, "Tell me to stop now if you don't want what I'm about to give you."

She gazed up at him as if weighing his words and his eyes locked with hers. His gaze was practically drowning in the desire he saw in hers. And then he knew that she wanted him as much as he wanted her. But still, he was letting her call the shots. And if she decided in his favor, there was no turning back.

Instead of giving him an answer, she reached up and wrapped her arms around his neck and pulled his mouth back down to hers. He came willingly. Assuaging the hunger they both were feeling. At the same time, his hands were busy, unbuttoning her pajama top with deft fingers.

He pulled back from the kiss to look down at her and his breath caught in his throat. Her breasts were beautiful. Absolutely beautiful. He leaned down close to her ear and whispered, "I want to cherish you with my mouth, Sheila."

NO MAN HAD ever said such a thing to her, Sheila thought, and immediately closed her eyes and drew in a deep breath when he immediately went for a breast, sucked a hardened nipple between his lips. She could feel her breasts swelling in his mouth. Her stomach clenched and she couldn't help moaning his name. She felt every part of her body stir to life with his touch.

Her response to his actions was instinctive. And when he took the tip of his tongue and began swirling around her nipple, and then grazing that same nipple with the edge of his teeth, she nearly came off the sofa.

She began shivering from the desire rushing through her body and when he moved to the next nipple, she felt every nerve ending in her breast come alive beneath his mouth. This was torture, plain and simple. And with each flick of his tongue she felt a pull, a tingling sensation between her legs.

As if he sensed the ache there, he pulled back slightly and tugged her pj bottoms down her legs. Then he stared down at the juncture of her thighs when he saw she wasn't wearing panties. He uttered a sound that resembled a growl, and the next thing she knew he had shifted positions and lowered his mouth between her legs.

He went at her as if this had been his intent all along, using the tip of his tongue to stir a fervor within her, widening her thighs to delve deeper. What he was doing to her with his tongue should be outlawed. And he was taking his time, showing no signs that he was in a hurry. He was acting as if he had the entire night and intended to savor and get his fill. And she was helpless to do anything but rock her body against his mouth. The more she rocked, the deeper his tongue seemed to go.

And then she felt it, that first sign that her body was reaching a peak of tremendous pleasure that would seep through her pores, strip her of all conscious thought and swamp her with feelings she had never felt before. She held her breath, almost fighting what was to come, and when it happened she tried pushing his mouth away, but he only locked it onto her more. She threw her head back and moaned as sensation swept through her. She felt good. She felt alive. She felt as though her body no longer belonged to her.

And as the sensations continued to sprint through her, Zeke kept it up, pushing her more over the edge, causing a maelstrom of pleasure to engulf her; pleasure so keen it almost took her breath away. She began reveling in the feelings of contentment, although her body felt drained. It was then that he released her and slowly pulled back. With eyes laden with fulfillment, she watched as he quickly removed his own clothes and sheathed his erection in a condom. And then he returned to her. As if he wanted her body to get used to him, get to know him, he straddled her and gyrated his hips so that the tip of him made circles on her belly, before tracing an erotic path down to the area between her legs.

Sensuous pressure built once again inside her, starting at the base of her neck and escalating down. And when he eased between her womanly folds and slowly entered her, she called his name as his erection throbbed within her to the hilt. It was then that he began moving, thrusting in and out of her as if this would be the last chance he had to do so, that she could feel her body come apart in the most sensuous way.

He stroked her for everything she was worth and then some, making her realize just what a generous lover he was. She locked her legs around him and he rocked deeper inside her. And then he touched a spot she didn't know existed and just in the nick of time, he lowered his mouth to hers to quell her scream as another orgasm hit.

Then his body bucked inside her several times, and he moaned into her mouth and she knew at that moment that both of them had gone beyond what they'd intended. But they couldn't turn back now even if they wanted to. He kept thrusting inside her, prolonging the orgasm they were sharing, and she knew at that moment this was meant to be. This night. The two of them together this way. There would be no regrets on her part. Only memories of what they were sharing now. Immense pleasure.

ENTERING SHEILA'S BEDROOM, Zeke's gaze touched on every single candle she had lit, bathing her bedroom in a very romantic glow. He had gotten a glimpse of her bedroom before, when he'd been in the room across the hall putting the crib together. Evidently she liked flowers, because her curtains and bedspread had a floral pattern.

He turned back the covers before placing her in the center of the bed. He joined her there and hoped Sunnie slept through the night as Sheila predicted she would. They had made a pit stop by the nursery to check on the baby and found her sleeping in spite of all the winds howling outside.

"Thanks for coming and checking on us," Sheila said, cuddling closer to him. He wrapped her into his arms, liking the feel of having her there. Her back was resting against his chest and her naked bottom nestled close to his groin.

"You don't have to thank me."

She glanced over her shoulder at him. "I don't?"

"No."

She smiled and closed her eyes, shifting her body to settle even more into his. He stayed awake and, lifting up on his elbows, he stared down at her. She was just as beautiful with her eyes closed as she was with them open. He then recalled what Brad had said about Sheila getting attached to Sunnie and could definitely see how that could happen.

He couldn't help wondering how she was going to handle it when Sunnie was taken away. And she would be taken away. Although Sunnie didn't belong to Brad, she did belong to someone. And if no one claimed her, she would eventually become a part of the system.

That was the one thing that had kept him out of trouble as a kid growing up, the fear of that very thing happening to him. Although he now knew his aunt would never have done such a thing, he hadn't known it then and had lived in constant fear that one day, if he did something wrong, his aunt would desert him in the same way his mother had.

But Clarisse Daniels had proven to be a better woman than her younger sister could ever be. A divorcée, which made her a single mother, she had raised both him and Alicia on a teacher's salary. At least child support had kicked in from Alicia's father every month. But neither his mother nor his father had ever contributed a penny to his upbringing. In fact, he'd found out later that his aunt had on several occasions actually given in to his mother's demand for money just to keep her from taking him away.

His father. He hadn't been completely honest with Sheila that day when he'd said he hadn't known his father. Mr. Travers was his father. He might not have known the man while growing up as Ezekiel "Zeke" Daniels, but he certainly knew his identity now. Matthew Travers. One of the richest men in Texas.

It seemed his mother had gotten knocked up by the man who hadn't believed her claim. In a way, considering what Zeke had heard, his father could have been one of two men. His mother hadn't known for certain which one had sired her son. She had gone after the wealthiest. Travers's attorney had talked her out of such foolishness and pretty much told her what would happen if she made her claim public. Evidently she took his threat seriously and he had grown up as Ezekiel

Daniels, the son of Kristi Daniels. Father unknown. His birth certificate stated as much.

It was only while in college attending UT that there was a guy on campus who could have been his identical twin by the name of Colin Travers. When the two finally met, their resemblance was so uncanny it was unreal. Even Brad had approached the guy one day thinking it was him.

Zeke was willing to let the issue of their looks drop, but Colin wasn't. He went back to Houston, questioned his father and put together the pieces of what had happened between Matthew Travers and Kristi Daniels many years before, and a year or so before Travers had married Colin's mother.

When Zeke had been summoned to the Travers mansion, it was Brad who'd convinced him to go. It was there that he'd come face-to-face with the man who'd fathered him. The man, who after seeing him, was filled with remorse for not having believed Kristi Daniels's claim. The man who from that moment on intended to right a wrong, and make up to Zeke for all the years he hadn't been there for him. All the years he'd been denied. Abandoned.

He'd also found out that day that in addition to Colin, he had five other younger brothers and a sister. His siblings, along with their mother, Victoria, immediately accepted him as a Travers. But for some reason, Zeke had resisted becoming part of the Travers clan.

He'd always been a loner and preferred things staying that way. Although his siblings still kept in contact with him, especially Colin, who over the years had forged a close relationship with Zeke, he'd kept a distance between him and the old man. But his father was determined, regardless of Zeke's feelings on the matter, to build a relationship with him.

It was Brad and his aunt Clarisse who had been there for him during that difficult and confused time in his life. It was they who convinced him to take the last name his father wanted him to have and wear it proudly. That's the reason why on his twenty-first birthday, he officially became Ezekiel *Travers*.

That's why he and Brad had such a strong friendship. And that was one of the main reasons his aunt meant the world to him. The first thing he'd done after being successful in his own right through lucrative investments was to buy Aunt Clarisse a house not far from the French Quarter. Alicia and her husband, both attorneys, didn't live too far away. He tried to go visit whenever he could. But now, he couldn't even consider going anywhere until he'd solved this case.

He glanced down at Sheila. And not without Sheila.

He immediately felt a tightening in his stomach. How could he even think something like that? He'd never taken a woman home to meet his family before. There had never been one he'd gotten that attached to, and he didn't plan to start doing so now.

He would be the first to say that tonight he and Sheila had enjoyed each other, but that's as far as things went. It just wasn't in his makeup to go further. Suddenly feeling as though he was suffocating and needed space, he eased away from Sheila and slid out of bed.

Tiptoeing across the hall, he went to where Sunnie was sleeping. She was lying on her stomach and sleeping peacefully. He wasn't sure what kind of future was in store for her, but he hope for her sake things worked out to her benefit.

All he knew was that the woman who'd given birth to the beautiful baby didn't deserve her.

CHAPTER SEVEN

"YOU WANT US to go to your place?" Sheila asked to make sure she'd heard Zeke correctly.

They had awakened to the forecaster's grim news that Hurricane Spencer was still hovering in the gulf. And although Royal was not directly in its path, if the storm did hit land, there would be a lot of wind and rain for the next day or so. The local news media had further indicated that although the electrical company was working around the clock, certain areas of town would remain without power for a while. Meadowland was one of them.

"Yes, I think it would be for the best for now—especially since you don't know when your power will be restored. I have a generator in case the power goes out at my house."

Sheila nibbled on her bottom lip. What he was offering made sense, but she was so used to having her own place, her own stuff. She glanced over at Sunnie, who was sitting in the middle of the kitchen table in her car seat. She had just been fed and was happy. And she hadn't seemed bothered by seeing Zeke. In fact, it seemed as if she smiled when she saw him.

"Sheila?"

"I was just thinking of all the stuff I'd have to pack up and carry with us."

"We can manage. Besides, I have my truck."

How convenient, she thought. She knew his idea made perfect sense, but going over to his place meant leaving her comfort zone. "Sunnie has gotten used to being here," she said.

"I understand, but as long as you're within her sight, she'll be fine."

Sheila nibbled on her bottom lip as she gave her attention back to the baby. Yes, Sunnie would be fine, but she wasn't sure she would be. Waking up in Zeke's arms hadn't been exactly what she'd planned to happen. But it had been so natural. Just like the lovemaking that had followed before they'd heard Sunnie through the monitor that morning.

She had just finished feeding Sunnie when Zeke had dropped what she considered a bomb. She had been thinking how, in a nice way, to suggest they rethink what had happened between them last night and give each other space to do so, when his idea had been just the opposite. Moving her and Sunnie into his house until the storm passed was not giving them space.

Deciding to come out and say what she'd been thinking, she glanced back over at Zeke. He was sitting across the kitchen, straddling a chair. "What about last night?"

He held her gaze. "What about it?"

Sheila's heart thumped hard in her chest. "W-we slept together and we should not have," she stammered, wishing she hadn't been so blunt, but not knowing what else she could have said to broach the subject and let him know her feelings on the matter.

"It was inevitable."

Her eyes widened in surprise at his comeback. "I don't think it was. Why do you?"

"Because I wanted you from the first and I picked up on the vibes that you wanted me, too."

What vibes? "I was attracted to you from the first, I admit that," she said. "But I wasn't sending off vibes."

"Yes, you were."

Had she unconsciously emitted vibes as he claimed? She tried to recall such a time and—

"Remember that day you woke me up when I'd fallen asleep on your sofa?"

She nodded, remembering. They had stared at each other for the longest time. "Yes, I remember."

"You blushed but wouldn't tell me what you were thinking, what was going through your mind to make you do so?"

"So you assumed…"

"No, I knew. I think I can read you pretty well."

"You think so?"

"Yes. I can probably guess with certainty the times we've been together when your thoughts of me were sexual."

Could he really? She didn't like that and to hear him say it actually irritated her. "Look, Zeke, I'm not sure about the women you're used to getting involved with, but—"

"But you are different from them," he finished for her. "And I agree you're different in a positive way."

"We've known each other less than a week," she reminded him.

"Yes, but we've shared more in that time than a lot of people share in a lifetime. Especially last night. The connection between us was unreal."

Sheila immediately thought of her friend Emily Burroughs. If she could claim ever having a best friend it would have to be Emily. They had been roommates in college. And she believed they had a special friendship that would have gotten even stronger over the years... if Emily hadn't died. Her friend had died of ovarian cancer at the young age of twenty-three.

Sheila had been with Emily during her final days. Emily hadn't wanted to go to hospice, preferring to die at home in her own bed. And she had wanted Sheila there with her for what they'd known would be their last slumber party. It was then Emily had shared that although she wasn't a virgin, she'd never made out with a guy and felt one gigantic explosion; she'd never heard bells and whistles. Emily had never felt the need to scream. She had died not experiencing any of that. And last night Sheila had encountered everything that Emily hadn't in her lifetime.

"Do you regret last night, Sheila?"

His question intruded into her thoughts and she glanced back over at him, wondering how she could get him to understand that she was a loner. Always had been and probably always would be. She didn't take rejection well, and every time the people she loved the most rejected her, intentionally put distance between them, was a swift blow to her heart.

"No, Zeke, but I've learned over the years not to get attached to people. My mom has been married five times and my sister from my father's first marriage doesn't want to be my sister because my mother caused her father pain."

He frowned. "You didn't have anything to do with that."

She chuckled. "Try telling Lois that. She blames both me and my mother and I was only four when they split."

"Did you talk to your father about it?"

She shook her head. "When Dad left, he never wanted to see me or my mother again. I guess I would have been a reminder of what she did. She cheated on him."

"But it wasn't your fault."

"No, it wasn't," she said, wiping the baby's mouth. "And I grew up believing that one day one of them, hopefully both, would realize that. Neither did. Dad died five years ago. He was a very wealthy man and over the years he did do right by me financially—my mother saw to that. But when he died, he intended to let me know how much I didn't mean to him by leaving Lois everything. I wasn't even mentioned in his will."

She paused a moment, glanced away from him to look out the window as she relived the pain. And then back at him and said, "It's not that I wanted any of his worldly possessions, mind you. It was the principle of the thing. Just acknowledging me in some way as his daughter would have been nice."

Sheila glanced over at Sunnie, who was staring over at her, as if she understood the nature of what she'd said, of what she was sharing with Zeke. She then wondered why she had shared such a thing with him. Maybe telling him would help him to realize that she could get attached to him, and why she couldn't let that happen.

"So, no, I don't regret last night. It was too beautiful,

too earth-shattering and mind-blowing to regret. But I have to be realistic and accept that I don't do involvement very well. I get attached easily. You might want a casual affair, but a part of me would long for something more."

"Something I can't give you," he said gently. The sound of his husky voice floated across the room to her.

"Precisely," she said, nodding her head while thinking that he did understand.

"I could say I won't touch you again, even if we spend time together."

She would have taken his words to heart if at that moment a smile hadn't curved his lips. "Yes, you could say that," she agreed.

"But I'd be lying. Mainly because you are temptation."

"Temptation?" she asked, and couldn't help chuckling at that.

"Yes."

She shook her head. She had been called many things but never temptation. "You can see me in the garden with an apple?"

His eyes seemed to darken. "Yes, and very much naked."

Sensing the change in the tone of his voice—it had gone from a deep husky to a seductive timbre—she decided maybe they needed to change the subject. "How is the case coming?"

Zeke recognized her ploy to change the subject. She had reservations about sleeping with him again and he could understand that. But what she needed to understand was that there were some things a man and a woman could not ignore. Blatant sexual chemistry was one of them—it pretty much headed the list. And that was what existed between them, connecting more than just the dots.

Making love to her and waking up with her last night had affected him in a way he didn't quite comprehend, and because he didn't understand it, he wasn't ready, or willing, to walk away.

And when she'd tried explaining to him why she preferred not getting involved in a relationship for fear of getting attached, it was like hearing his own personal reservations. He had this apprehension of letting any woman get too close for fear she would do to him the very thing his mother had done. Walk away and leave him high and dry...and take his heart with her. He'd been there and done that and would never go that way again.

She was protecting her heart the way he was protecting his, so they were on the same page there. Maybe he should tell her that. Then again, maybe he shouldn't. Opening himself up to anyone wasn't one of his strong points. He was a private person. Few people got to know the real Ezekiel Travers. Brad and his other college friend and Royal resident, Christopher Richards, knew the real Zeke. And he felt comfortable being himself around Darius Franklin. Over the past year, while working through the terms of their partnership, he had gotten to know Darius, a man he highly respected. And he thought Summer was the perfect wife for Darius.

One night over dinner Darius and Summer had shared their story. How things had ended for them due to a friend's betrayal. They had gotten reunited seven years later and intended never to let anything or anyone come between them again. He was convinced that kind of love could only be found by a few people. He would never think about holding out for a love that sure and pure for himself.

He decided to go with Sheila's change of subject. "The case is coming along. I'm still following up possible leads."

He told her about his conversations with Rali Tariq and Arthur Moran and their admissions that they too had received blackmail letters.

"You mean they received blackmail letters claiming they fathered babies, as well?"

"Not exactly. Both are married men and they received letters threatening to expose them as having cheated on their wives, which they both deny doing. But both knew doctored pictures could have shown another story. It would have been embarrassing for their families while they tried to prove their innocence."

Sheila shook her head as she took Sunnie out of the car seat. "But knowing Bradford Price wasn't the only one who got a blackmail letter gives legitimacy to your his claim that he's not Sunnie's father, and it's all a hoax to extract money from TCC members, right?"

"In a way, yes. But you'll still have some who have their doubts. The paternity test would clear him for sure." He saw a thoughtful look in her eye. Clearing Brad also meant that Sheila would have to give Sunnie up.

Zeke stood and glanced out the window. "It's stopped raining. If we're going to my place we need to do so before it starts up again."

She frowned. "I never said I was going to your place with you."

He slowly crossed the room to her. "I know. But considering everything, even your apprehension about spending time with me, is there a reason you should subject Sunnie to another night in a house without power?"

Sheila swallowed, knowing there it was. The one person she couldn't deny. Sunnie. She looked down at the baby she held in her arms. In the end it would always be what was best for Sunnie. Right now she was all the little girl had. And she would always put her needs first. Last night hadn't been so bad, but it was November; even with fire in the fireplace, the house was beginning to feel drafty. And she couldn't risk the baby catching a cold all because she couldn't resist a tall, dark, handsome and well-built man name Zeke Travers.

She looked at Zeke, met his gaze. "Will you promise me something?"

"What?"

"That while we're at your place you won't…"

He took a step closer. "I won't what?"

She nibbled on her bottom lip. "Try seducing me into sleeping with you again."

He studied her features for a moment and then he reached out and caressed her cheek with the back of his hand while he continued to hold her gaze. "Sorry, sweetheart, that is one promise I won't make you," he said in a low, husky tone. He took a step back. "I'll start loading up Sunnie's stuff in my truck."

Sheila held her breath until he walked out of the room.

ZEKE PRETENDED NOT to notice how well Sheila interacted with Sunnie as he loaded the last of the baby items into his truck. They would probably be at his place only a day at the most. But with everything Sheila had indicated she needed to take, you would think they were moving in for a full year. He chuckled. He had no complaints. He had a huge house and lately he'd noticed how lonely it would seem at times.

He heard the baby chuckle and glanced back over at her. He couldn't tell who was giggling more, Sunnie or Sheila, and quickly decided it was a tie. He pushed his Stetson back off his head, thinking, as well as knowing, she would make a great mother. She always handled Sunnie with care, as if she was the most precious thing she'd ever touched.

She glanced over at him, caught him staring and gave him a small smile. The one he returned had a lot more depth than the one she'd given him and he understood why. She still had misgivings about spending time at his place. He didn't blame her too much. He had every intention of finishing what had gotten started between them last night. By not agreeing to her request not to get her into his bed, he'd pretty much stated what his intentions were and he wasn't backing down.

But as he'd told her, there was no way he could make her that promise. It would have died a quick death on his lips as soon as he'd made it. And the one thing his Aunt Clarisse had taught him not to do was lie. She'd always said lies could come back to haunt you. They would catch up with you at the worst possible time. And he had believed her.

He moved from around the back of the truck. "Ready to go?"

He could tell she wasn't ready. But she widened her smile a little and said, "Yes. Let me get Sunnie into her seat."

He watched as she strapped the baby in her car seat, again paying attention to every little detail of Sunnie's security and comfort. He stepped back as she closed the door, and then he opened the passenger door for her and watched how easily she slid in across the leather. Nice, he thought. Especially when he caught a glimpse of bare thigh. He'd never given a thought to how much he appreciated seeing a woman in a skirt until now.

He got into the truck, backed out of her yard and was halfway down the road when she glanced over at him. "I want to use one of your guest rooms, Zeke."

"All right."

Zeke kept looking straight ahead, knowing she had glanced over at him, trying to decipher the quickness of his answer. She would discover soon enough that physical attraction was a very powerful thing. And now that they'd experienced just how things could be between them, it wouldn't be that easy to give it up. And it just so happened that his bedroom was right across the hall from the guest room he intended to put her in.

"I can make a pit stop and grab something to eat. What would you like?" he asked her.

"Oh, anything. I'm not that hungry."

He looked over at her when he brought the car to a stop at a traffic light. "Maybe not now, but you'll probably be hungry later."

And he didn't add that she should eat something to keep her strength for the plans he had for her after she put the baby to bed for the night. He felt a deep stirring inside him. There was something about her scent that made him want to mate. And mate they would again.

His peace of mind and everything male within him was depending on it. He couldn't wait for night to come.

But for now he would pretend to go along with anything she thought she wanted, and making sure by the time it was over she'd be truly and thoroughly convinced what she wanted was him. Usually, when it came to women, he didn't like playing games. He liked to be honest, but he didn't consider what he was doing as playing a game. What he was doing was trying to keep his sanity. He honestly didn't think she knew just how luscious she was. Maybe he hadn't shown her enough last night. Evidently he needed to give her several more hints. And he would do so gladly. He shifted in his seat when he felt tightness in the crotch of his pants while thinking how such a thing would be accomplished.

"You don't mind if I pull into that chicken place, do you?" he asked, gesturing to a KFC.

"No, I guess you're a growing boy and have to eat sometime," she said, smiling over at him.

Growing boy was right, and there was no need to tell her what part of him seemed to be outgrowing all the others at the moment.

SHEILA GLANCED AROUND the bedroom she was given. Zeke had set up Sunnie's bed in a connecting room. She loved his home. It looked like the perfect place for a family.

She pulled a romance novel out of her bag before sliding into bed. When they arrived here, she had helped him get everything inside. After that was done they had both sat down to enjoy the fried-chicken lunch he'd purchased. After that was done he had gone outside to check on things. The fierce winds had knocked down several branches and Zeke and his men had taken the time to clean up the debris. While he was outside, Sheila and Sunnie had made themselves at home.

So far he had been the perfect gentleman and had even volunteered to watch the baby while she had taken a shower. Sunnie had gotten used to seeing him and didn't cry when he held her. In fact, it seemed that she was giving him as many smiles as she was giving to Sheila.

Now Sunnie was down for the night and it had started raining again. Sheila could hear the television downstairs and knew Zeke was still up. She thought it would be better for her to remain in her room and read. She would see him in the morning and that was soon enough to suit her.

She had been reading for about an hour or so when she decided to go to the connecting room to check on Sunnie. Although the baby now slept through the night, Sheila checked on her periodically. Sunnie had a tendency to kick off her bedcovers while she slept.

Sheila tiptoed into the room. Already the scent of baby powder drenched the air and she smiled. Sunnie's presence was definitely known. When Sheila had come downstairs after taking a shower, Zeke had been holding the baby in his arms and was standing at the window. From Sunnie's giggles she could tell the baby had enjoyed seeing the huge raindrops roll down the windowpane.

It had been a spine-tilting moment to see him standing there in his bare feet, shirtless with his jeans riding low on his hips. A tall, sexy hulk of a man with a tiny baby in his arms. A baby he was holding as gently as if she was his.

She had watched them and thought that he would make a wonderful father. She wondered if he wanted kids one day. He had talked about his cousin's twins and she knew he didn't have an aversion to kids like some men did. Crawford would freeze up whenever the mention of a baby entered their conversation. That had been one topic not open for discussion between them.

Pulling the covers back over Sunnie's chubby legs, Sheila was about to exit when she felt another presence in the room. She turned quickly and saw Zeke sitting in the wingback chair with his legs stretched out in front of him. He was sitting silently and watching her, saying nothing.

The glow of the moon flowing in through the curtains highlighted his features and the look she saw in his eyes said it all. She fought not to be moved by that look, but it was more powerful than anything she'd ever encountered. It was like a magnetic force, pulling her in, weakening her, filling her with a need she had been fighting since awakening that morning.

She wished she could stop her heart from beating a mile a minute, or stop her nipples from pressing hard against her nightgown. Then there was the heat she felt between her legs; the feeling was annoying as well as arousing.

Then he stood and she had to tilt her head back to look at him. In the moonlight she saw him crook his finger for her to follow him into the hall. Knowing it was best they not speak in the room to avoid awakening Sunnie, she followed.

"I didn't know you were in there with Sunnie," she said softly.

He leaned against the wall. "I went in there to check on her...and to wait for you."

A knot formed in Sheila's throat. "Wait for me?" He seemed to have inched closer. She inhaled his masculine scent into her nostrils and her nipples stiffened even more.

"Yes. I knew you would be coming to check on Sunnie sooner or later. And I decided to sit it out until you did."

She shifted her body when she felt a tingling sensation at the juncture of her thighs. "Why would you be waiting for me?"

She was warned by the smile that tilted his lips at the same time as he slipped an arm around her waist and said, "I was waiting to give you this."

He leaned his mouth down to hers. And instinctively, she went on tiptoe to meet him halfway.

THIS WAS WELL *worth the wait*, Zeke thought as he deepened the kiss. There was nothing like being inside her mouth. Nothing like holding her in his arms. Nothing like hearing the sound of her moaning deep in his ear.

And he had waited. From the moment she had gone upstairs to put the baby to bed, he had waited for her to come back downstairs. She hadn't done so. Instead, she had called down to him from the top of the stairs to tell him good-night.

He had smiled at her ploy to put distance between them, and he put a plan into action. He figured there was no way she would settle in for the night without checking on Sunnie. So he had closed up things downstairs and gone upstairs and waited.

The wait was over.

She was where he wanted her to be. Here in his arms where he needed her to be. But he needed her someplace else, as well. His bed. Lifting his mouth from hers, he gazed down into the darkness of her eyes and whispered against her moist lips, "I need to make love to you, sweetheart. I have to get inside you."

Sheila nearly moaned at the boldness of his statement. And the desire she saw in his dark gaze was so fierce, so ferocious, that she could feel an intensity stirring within her that she'd never felt before. His need was rousing hers.

She reached up and wrapped her arms around his neck, brought her mouth close to his and whispered thickly, "And I want you inside me, too." And she meant it. Had felt each and every word she had spoken. The throbbing between her legs had intensified from the hardness of him pressing against her and she was feeling him. Boy, was she feeling him.

Before she could release her next breath, he swept her off her feet and into his arms and headed across the hall to his bedroom.

NOTHING, ZEKE THOUGHT, had prepared him for meeting a woman like Sheila. She hadn't come on to him like others. Had even tried keeping her distance. But the chemistry had been too great and intensified each and every time they were within a foot of each other.

The last time they'd made love had been almost too much for his mind and body to handle. And now he could only imagine the outcome of this mating. But he needed it the way he needed to breathe.

He placed her on the bed and before she could get

settled, he had whipped the nightgown from her body. She looked up at him and smiled. "Hey, you're good at that."

"At what?" he asked, stepping back to remove his own clothes.

"Undressing a woman."

As he put on a condom, he glanced at her. She was the only woman he wanted to undress. The only woman he enjoyed undressing. The only woman he wanted to make love to. Suddenly, upon realizing what his mind had just proclaimed, he forced it free of such an assertion. He could and never would be permanently tied to any one woman. That was the last thing he wanted to think about now or ever.

He moved back toward the bed. The way she was gazing at every inch of his body made him aware of just what she was seeing, and just what he wanted to give her. What he wanted them to share. What he intended them to savor.

He stopped at the edge of the bed and returned her gaze with equal intensity. Moonlight pouring in through his window shone on her nakedness. There she was. Beautiful. Bare. His eyes roamed over her uplifted breasts, creamy brown skin, small waist, luscious thighs, gorgeous hips and then to the apex of her thighs.

"Zeke."

She said his name before he even touched her. She rose on the bed to meet him. The moment their lips fused, it was on. Desire burst like a piece of hot glass within him, cutting into his very core. Blazing heat rushed through his veins with every stroke of his tongue that she returned.

He lowered her to the mattress and pulled back from

the kiss, needed the taste of her and proceeded to kiss her all over. He gloried in the way she trembled beneath his mouth, but he especially liked the taste of her wet center, and proved just how much he enjoyed it.

She came in an explosion that shook the bed and he cupped her bottom, locked his mouth to her while those erotic sensations slashed through her. And when his tongue found a section of her G-spot and went after it as if it would be his last meal, she shuddered uncontrollably.

It was only then that he pulled back and placed his body over hers. "I like your taste," he whispered huskily. He eased inside her, stretching her as he went deep. Her womb was still aching and he could feel it. Already she wanted more and he intended to give her what she wanted.

He began thrusting inside her, thinking he would never tire of doing so. He was convinced there would never come a time when he wouldn't want to make love to her. He slid his hands beneath her hips to lift her off the bed, needing to go even deeper. And when he had reached the depth he wanted, he continued to work her flesh. Going in and out of her relentlessly.

He threw his head back when she moaned his name and he felt her inner muscles clench him, hold him tight, trying to pull every single thing out of him. And he gave in to her demand in one guttural moan, feeling the veins in his neck almost bursting in the process. Coming inside a woman had never felt this right before. This monumental. This urgent.

He rode her hard as his body continued to burst into one hell of an explosion, his shudders combined with hers, nearly shaking the bed from the frame. This was lovemaking at its best. The kind that would leave you mindless. Yet still wanting more. When had he become so greedy?

He would try to figure out the answer to that later. Right now the only things he wanted to dwell on were the feelings swamping him, ripping into every part of his body, taking him for all it was worth and then some. It had to be the most earth-shattering orgasm he'd ever experienced. More intense than the ones last night, and he'd thought those were off the charts.

And he knew moments later when his body finally withdrew from hers to slump beside her, weak as water, that it would always be that way with them. She would always be the one woman who would be his temptation. The one woman he would not be able to resist.

CHAPTER EIGHT

ZEKE AND SHEILA were aware that the power had returned to her section of town. Yet neither brought up the subject of her returning home. Four days later and she was still spending her days and nights in Zeke's home and loving every moment of it.

The rain had stopped days ago and sunshine was peeking out over the clouds. Those sunny days were her favorite. That's when she would take the baby outside and push her around in the stroller. Zeke's property was enormous and she and Sunnie enjoyed exploring as much of it as they could. Sunnie was fascinated by the horses and would stare at them as if she was trying to figure out what they were.

Then there were the nights when she would fall asleep in Zeke's arms after having made love. He was the most generous lover and made her feel special each and every time he touched her. She was always encouraged by his bold sexuality, where he would take their lovemaking to the hilt. When it came to passion, Crawford had always been low-key. Zeke was just the opposite. He liked making love in or out of bed. And he especially enjoyed quickies. She smiled, thinking she was enjoying them, too.

Usually Zeke worked in his office downstairs for a few hours while she played games with Sunnie, keeping her entertained. Then when he came out of his office, he would spend time with them. One day he had driven them to a nearby park, and on another day he took them to the zoo.

On this particular day Zeke had gone into his office in town to work on a few files when his house phone rang. Usually he received calls on his cell phone, and Sheila decided not to answer it. The message went to his voice mail, which she heard.

"Hi, Ezekiel. This is Aunt Clarisse. I'm just calling to see how you're doing. I had a doctor's appointment today and he says I'm doing fine. And how is that baby someone left on the doorstep and claiming it's Brad's? I know you said you were going to keep an eye on the baby real close, so how is that going? Knowing you, you're probably not letting that baby out of your sight until you find out the truth one way or another...."

A knot twisted in Sheila's stomach. Was that why she was still here? Is that why Zeke hadn't mentioned anything about taking her home? Why he was making love to her each night? Was his main purpose for showing interest in her to keep his eye on Sunnie?

She fought back the tears that threatened to fall from her eyes. What other reason could there be? Had she really thought—had she hoped—that there could be another reason? Hadn't she learned her lesson yet? Hadn't her father, mother and sister taught her that in this life she had no one? When all was said and done, she would be left high and dry. Alone.

Her only excuse for letting her guard down was that usually to achieve their goal of alienating her the ones she loved would try putting distance between them. That's why her father never came to visit, why Lois preferred keeping her from Atlanta and why her mother never invited her to visit her and her husbands.

But Zeke had been the exception. He had wanted to keep her close. Now she knew the reason why.

She drew in a deep breath. When Zeke returned she would tell him she wanted to go home. He would wonder why, but frankly she didn't care. Nor would she tell him. It was embarrassing and humiliating enough for her to know the reason.

One day she would learn her lesson.

ZEKE GLANCED OVER at Sheila, surprised. "You want to go home?"

She continued packing up the baby's items. "Yes. The only reason Sunnie and I are here is because of your generosity in letting us stay due to the power being out at my place. It's back on now and there's no reason for us to remain here any longer."

He bit back the retort that she'd known the power was back on days ago, yet she hadn't been in a hurry to leave…just as he hadn't been in a hurry for her to go. What happened to make her want to take off? He rubbed the back of his neck. "Is something going on that I need to know about, Sheila?"

She glanced up. "No. I just want to go home."

He continued to stare at her. He'd known she'd eventually want to return home. Hell, he had to be realistic here. "Fine, we can take some of Sunnie's things now and you can come back for the rest later on in the week."

"I prefer taking all Sunnie's items now. There's no reason for me to come back. "

That sounded much like a clean break to him. Why?

"Okay, then I'd better start loading stuff up." He walked out of the room.

Sheila glanced at the door Zeke had just walked out of, suddenly feeling alone. She might as well get used to it again. Sunnie's days were numbered with her either way. And now that she knew what Zeke was about, it would be best if she cut the cord now.

In the other room Zeke was taking down the baby bed he'd gotten used to seeing. Why was he beginning to feel as if he was losing his best friend? Why was the feeling of abandonment beginning to rear its ugly head again?

Waking up with her beside him each morning had meant more to him than it had to her evidently. Having both Sheila and Sunnie in his home had been the highlight of his life for the past four days. He had gotten used to them being around and had enjoyed the time they'd spent together. A part of him had assumed the feelings were mutual. Apparently he'd assumed wrong.

A short while later he had just finished taking the bed down, when his cell phone rang. He pulled it out of his back pocket. "Yes?"

"I just got a call from my attorney," Brad said. "There's a possibility I might get the results of the paternity test as early as tomorrow. Hell, I hope so. I need to get on with my life. Get on with the election."

"That's good to hear." At least it would be good for Brad, but not so good for Sheila. Either way, she would be turning the baby over to someone, whether it was Brad or the system. And the way he saw it, there was a one-hundred-percent chance it would be the system.

"Let me know when you get the results," he said to Brad.

His best friend chuckled. "Trust me. You'll be the first to know."

A FEW HOURS later, back at her place, Sheila stood at the window and watched Zeke pull off. He had stayed just long enough to put up the crib. No doubt he'd picked up on her rather cold attitude, but he hadn't questioned her about it. Nor had he indicated he would be returning.

However, since his sole purpose in seeing her was to spy on her, she figured he would return eventually. When he did, it would be on her terms and not his. She had no problem with him wanting to make sure Sunnie was well taken care of, but he would not be using her to do so.

She turned from the window, deciding it was time to take Sunnie upstairs for her bath, when she heard the phone ringing. She crossed the room to pick it up. "Hello?"

"Ms. Hopkins?"

"Yes?"

"This is Ms. Talbert from Social Services."

Sheila felt an immediate knot in her stomach. "Yes?"

"We received notification from the lab that the results of Bradford Price's paternity test might be available earlier than we expected. I thought we'd let you know that."

Sheila swallowed as she glanced across the room at Sunnie. She was sitting in her swing, laughing as she played with the toys attached to it.

"Does Mr. Price know?"

"I would think so. His attorney was contacted earlier today."

She drew in a deep breath. It would be safe to assume that if Bradford Price knew then Zeke knew. Why hadn't he mentioned this to her? Prepared her?

"Ms. Hopkins?"

The woman reclaimed her attention. "Yes?"

"Do you have any questions for us?"

"No."

"Okay, then. How is the baby doing?"

Sheila glanced over at Sunnie. "She's fine."

"That's good. I'll call you sometime this week to let you know when to bring the baby in."

"All right." Sheila hung up the phone and forced the tears back.

ZEKE ENTERED HIS house convinced something in Sheila's attitude toward him had changed. But what and why?

He went straight into the kitchen to grab a beer, immediately feeling how lonely his house was. It had taken Sheila and the baby being here for him to realize there was a difference between a house and a home. This place was a house.

He had drunk his beer and was about to go upstairs when he noticed a blinking light on his phone. He crossed the room to retrieve his messages and smiled upon hearing his aunt's voice. Moments later a frown touched his lips. When had his aunt called? He played back the message to extract the time. She had called around noon when Sheila had been here. Had she heard it?

He rubbed his hands down his face, knowing the assumptions that would probably come into her mind if she had. Sunnie was not the reason he'd been spending time with her. But after hearing his aunt's message, she might think that it was.

He moved to the sofa to recall everything between them since returning home that day. Even on the car ride back to her place she hadn't said more than a few words. Although the words had been polite, and he hadn't detected anger or irritation in them, he'd known something was bothering her. At first he'd figured since this was the beginning of the second week, she was getting antsy over Sunnie's fate. He had tried engaging her in conversation, but to no avail.

He drew in a deep breath. Did she know that she had come to mean something to him? He chuckled. *Hell, man, how could she know when you're just realizing such a thing yourself?* Zeke knew at that moment that he had done with Sheila the very thing he hadn't wanted to do with any woman. He had fallen in love with her.

He didn't have to wonder how such a thing happened. Spending time with her had made him see what he was missing in his life. He had enjoyed leaving and coming home knowing she was here waiting for him. And at night when they retired, it was as if his bed was where she belonged.

He had thought about bringing up the subject of them trying their luck dating seriously. But he had figured they would have the opportunity to do that after everything with Sunnie was over. He envisioned them taking things slow and building a solid relationship. But now it looked as if that wouldn't be happening.

He then thought about the call he'd gotten from Brad, indicating the test results might be arriving sooner than later. He probably should have mentioned it to her, but after seeing her melancholy mood, he'd decided to keep the information to himself. The last thing he wanted her to start doing was worry about having to give up the baby she'd gotten attached to.

A part of him wanted to get in his car and go over to her place and tell her she had made wrong assumptions about his reason for wanting to be with her. But he figured he would give her space tonight. At some point tomorrow he would be seeing her, and hopefully they would be able to sit down and do some serious talking.

He stood from the sofa, when his cell phone rang. He quickly pulled it off his belt hoping it was Sheila, and then grimaced when he saw the caller was his father. Matthew Travers was determined not to let his oldest son put distance between them as Zeke often tried to do.

The old man made a point of calling often, and if Zeke got the notion not to accept the call, Matthew Travers wasn't opposed to sending one of his offspring to check on their oldest sibling. Hell, the old man had shown up on his doorstep a time or two himself. Zeke had learned the hard way his father was a man who refused to be denied anything he wanted.

Zeke shook his head thinking that must be a Travers trait, because he felt the same way about certain things. He was definitely feeling that way about Sheila. "Hello?"

"How are you doing, son?"

Zeke drew in a deep relaxing breath. That was always the way the old man began the conversation with him, referring to him as his son. Letting Zeke know he considered him as such.

Zeke sat back down on the sofa and stretched his legs out in front of him. "I'm doing fine, Dad."

At times it still sounded strange referring to Matthew

Travers as "Dad," even after twelve years. They hadn't talked in a while and he had a feeling that today his father was in a talkative mood.

THE NEXT DAY Zeke got to the office early, intending to follow up a few leads. Regardless of whether Brad was cleared of being Sunnie's father, there was still someone out there who'd set up an extortion scheme and had made several members of the TCC his or her victims.

He hoped he would be able to call it a day at Global Securities by five and hightail it over to Sheila's place. He hadn't been able to sleep for thinking about her last night. And he hadn't liked sleeping in his bed alone. Those days she'd spent with him had definitely changed his life.

He sat down at his desk remembering the conversation he'd had with his father. His father still wasn't overjoyed that Zeke had turned down the position of chief of security of Travers Enterprises to come work here with Darius. As he'd tried explaining to the old man, he preferred living in a small town, and moving from Austin to Houston would not have given him that.

And had he not moved to Royal, he thought further, *he would not have met Sheila.*

A few hours later while sitting at his desk with his sleeves rolled up and mulling over a file, his intercom buzzed with a call from his secretary. "Yes, Mavis?"

"Mr. Price and his attorney are here and want to see you."

Zeke glanced at the clock on his desk, a sterling-silver exclusive from his cousin. He frowned, not believing it was almost four in the afternoon. He couldn't help wondering why Brad and his attorney would be dropping by. "Please send them in."

Seconds later the door flew open and an angry Brad walked in followed by Alan Nelson, Brad's attorney. Zeke took one look at a furious Brad and a flustered Alan and knew something was wrong. "What the hell is going on?" he asked.

"This!" Brad said, tossing a document in the middle of Zeke's desk. "Alan just got it. It's a copy of the results of the paternity test and it's claiming that I'm that baby's father."

SHEILA HUNG UP the phone. It was Ms. Talbert again. She had called to say the results of the paternity test were in. Although the woman couldn't share the results with her, she told her that she would call back later that day or early tomorrow with details about when and where Sheila was to drop off the baby.

Sheila felt her body trembling inside. She was a nurse, so she should have known not to get attached to a patient. Initially, she had treated Sunnie as someone who'd been placed in her care. But that theory had died the moment that precious little girl had gazed up at her with those beautiful hazel eyes.

The baby hadn't wanted much. She just wanted to be loved and belong to someone. Sheila had certainly understood that, since those were the very things she wanted for herself. She hoped that Sunnie had a better chance at it than she'd had.

But not if she ends up in the system. And that thought bothered Sheila most of all. A part of her wanted to call Zeke, but she knew she couldn't do that. He hadn't gotten attached to her the way she had to him. Oh, he had gotten attached to her all right, but for all the wrong reasons.

She moved over toward the baby. Their time was limited and she intended to spend as much quality time as she could with Sunnie. Although the baby was only five months old, she wanted her to feel loved and cherished. Because deep in Sheila's heart, she was.

"CALM DOWN, BRAD." Zeke then glanced over at Alan. "Will you please tell me what's going on?" he asked Brad's attorney.

Brad dropped down in the chair opposite Zeke's desk, and Zeke could tell the older man seemed relieved. There was no doubt in Zeke's mind that once Alan had delivered the news to Brad he'd wished he hadn't.

The man took out a handkerchief and wiped sweat off his brow before saying, "The paternity report shows a genetic link between Mr. Price and the baby."

Zeke lifted a brow. "Meaning?"

"It means that although there's a link, it's inconclusive as to whether he is Jane Doe's father."

Zeke cringed at Alan's use of the name Jane Doe for Sunnie. "Her name is Sunnie, Alan."

The man looked confused. "What?"

"The baby's name is Sunnie. And as far as what you're saying, we still don't know one way or the other?"

"No, but again, there is that genetic link," Alan reiterated.

Zeke released a frustrated sigh. He then turned his attention to Brad. "Brad, I know you recall not having been sexually involved with a woman during the time Sunnie would have been conceived, but did you at any time donate your sperm to a bank or anyplace like that?"

"Of course not!"

"Just asking. I knew a few guys who did so when we were in college," Zeke said.

"Well, I wasn't one of them." Brad stood up. "What am I going to do? If word of this gets out I might as well kiss the TCC presidency goodbye."

Zeke knew the word would probably get out. He'd found out soon enough that in Royal, like a number of small towns, people had a tendency to thrive on gossip, especially when it involved the upper crust of the city.

"Who contacted you about the results?" Zeke asked Alan.

"That woman at Social Services," Alan replied. "She's the one who called yesterday afternoon, as well, letting me know there was a chance the results would be arriving sooner than expected. I called Brad and informed him of such."

Zeke nodded. And Brad had called him. "Did she mention she would be telling anyone else?"

"No, other than the woman who has custody of Jane Doe." Upon seeing Zeke's frown, he quickly said, "I mean Sunnie."

Zeke was immediately out of his chair. "She called Sheila Hopkins?"

"Yes, if that's the name of the woman keeping the baby. I'm sure she's not going to tell her the results of the test, only that the results are in," Alan replied. "Is there a problem?"

Yes, Zeke saw a problem but didn't have time to explain anything to the two men. "I need to go," he said, grabbing his Stetson and jacket and heading for the door.

"What's wrong?" Brad asked, getting to his feet and watching him dash off in a mad rush.

"I'll call you," Zeke said over his shoulder, and then he was out the door.

SHEILA HEARD A COMMOTION outside her window and, shifting Sunnie to her hip, she moved in that direction. Pushing the curtain aside, she watched as Summer tried corralling a group of pink flamingos down the street.

She had heard about the Helping Hands Shelter's most recent fundraiser. Someone had come up with the idea of the pink flamingos. The plan was that the recipient of the flamingos had to pay money to the charity for the opportunity to pass them on to the next unsuspecting victim, and then the cycle would start all over again.

Sunnie was making all kinds of excited noises seeing the flamingos, and the sound almost brought more tears to Sheila's eyes, knowing the day would come when she wouldn't hear that sound again. She knew she had to get out of her state of funk. But it was hard doing so.

She moved from the window when Summer continued to herd the flamingos down the street. Sheila was glad her friend hadn't ditched the flamingos on her. She had enough to deal with and passing on pink flamingos was the last thing she had time for.

She glanced down at Sunnie. "Okay, precious, it's dinnertime for you."

A short while later, after Sunnie had eaten, Sheila had given her a bath and put her to bed. The baby was usually worn-out by six and now slept through the night, waking to be fed around seven in the morning. Sheila couldn't help wondering if the baby's next caretaker would keep her on that same schedule.

She heard the doorbell ring as she moved down the stairs. She figured it was Summer dropping by to say hello, now that she'd dumped the flamingos off on someone's lawn. Quickly moving to the door so the sound of the bell wouldn't wake Sunnie, she glanced out the peephole and her heart thumped hard in her chest. It wasn't Summer. It was Zeke.

She didn't have to wonder why he'd dropped by. To spy on her and to make sure she was taking care of Sunnie properly. Drawing in a deep breath, she slowly opened the door.

CHAPTER NINE

SHE'D BEEN CRYING. Zeke took note of that fact immediately. Her eyes were red and slightly puffy, and when he looked closer, he saw her chin was trembling as if she was fighting even now to keep tears at bay. He wasn't sure if the tears she was holding back were for Sunnie or what she assumed was his misuse of her.

He wanted more than anything to take her into his arms, pull her close and tell her how wrong she was and to explain how much she had come to mean to him. But he knew that he couldn't do that. Like him, her distrust of people's motives didn't start overnight. Therefore, he would have to back up anything he said. Prove it to her. Show her in deeds instead of just words. Eventually he'd have to prove every claim he would make here tonight.

He may have been the one abandoned as a child, but she, too, had been abandoned. Those who should have loved her, been there for her and supported her had not. In his book, that was the worse type of abandonment.

"Zeke, I know why you're here," she finally said, after they had stood there and stared at each other for a long moment.

"Do you?" he asked.

She lifted that trembling chin. "Yes. Sunnie's asleep. You're going to have to take my word for it, and we had a fun day. Now, goodbye."

She made an attempt to close the door, but he put his foot in the way. "Thanks for the information, but that's not why I'm here."

"Then why are you here?"

"To see the woman I made love to several times. The woman I had gotten used to waking up beside in the mornings. The woman I want even now."

She lifted her gaze from the booted foot blocking her door to him. "You shouldn't say things you don't mean."

"Sheila, we need to talk. I think I know what brought this on. I listened to the message my aunt left on my answering machine. You jumped to the wrong conclusion."

"Did I?"

"Yes, you did."

She crossed her arms over her chest. "I don't think so."

"But what if you did? Think of the huge mistake you're making. Invite me in and let's talk about it."

He watched as she began nibbling on her bottom lip, a lip he had sucked into his mouth, kissed and devoured many times since meeting her. Had it been less than two weeks? How had he fallen in love with her so quickly and know for sure it was the real thing?

He drew in a huge breath. Oh, it was definitely the real thing. Somehow, Sheila Hopkins had seeped into his bloodstream and was now making a huge statement within his heart.

"Okay, come in."

She stood back and he didn't waste any time entering in case she changed her mind. Once inside he glanced around the room and noticed how different things looked. All the baby stuff was gone. At least it had been collected and placed in a huge cardboard box that sat in the corner.

Not waiting for him to say anything when she saw the way his gaze had scanned the room, she said, "And please don't pretend that you don't know that I'll be turning Sunnie over to someone, as early as tomorrow."

He lifted a brow. "And someone told you that?"

She shrugged. "No, not really. But Ms. Talbert did call to say the results of the paternity test had come in. And since you were so certain Sunnie doesn't belong to your friend, then I can only assume that means she's going into the system."

He moved away from the door to walk over to stand in front of her. "You shouldn't assume anything. My investigation isn't over. And do you know what your problem is, Sheila?"

She stiffened her spine at his question. "What?"

"You assume too much and usually you assume wrong."

She glared at him before moving away to sit down on the sofa. "Okay, then you tell me, Zeke. How are my assumptions wrong?"

He dropped into the chair across from the sofa. "First of all, my aunt's phone call. She knew about the case I'm handling for Brad. And she knows Brad is my best friend and that I intend to clear his name or die trying. She was right. I intend to keep an eye on Sunnie and that might be the reason I hung around you at first. But that's not what brought me back here. If you recall, four days went by when I didn't see you or the baby."

"Then what brought you back?"

"You. I couldn't stay away from you."

He saw doubt in her eyes and knew he had his work cut out for him. But he would eventually make her believe him. He had to. Even now it was hard not to cross the room and touch her. Dressed in a pair of jeans and a pullover sweater and in bare feet, she looked good. Ravishing. Stunning. Even the puffiness beneath her eyes didn't take away her allure. And where she was sitting, the light from the fading sun made her skin glow, cast a radiant shine on her hair.

"Why didn't you tell me there was a chance the test results would come back early, to prepare me?"

"Because I know how attached you've gotten to Sunnie and I didn't want to deliver bad news any sooner than I had to. And what you assumed regarding that is wrong, as well. The test results were not conclusive that Brad isn't Sunnie's father."

She leaned forward and narrowed her gaze accusingly. "But you were so convinced Bradford Price is not Sunnie's father."

"And I'm still convinced. The test reveals there is a genetic link. Now I'm going to find out how. It's not Brad's sister's child, but he did have a brother who died last year. I'd only met Michael once and that was when Brad and I were in college and he showed up asking Brad for money."

Zeke drew in a deep breath as he remembered that time. "Michael was his younger brother and, according to Brad, he got mixed up with the wrong crowd in high school, dropped out and became addicted to hard drugs. That's when Mr. Price disinherited him."

She nodded. "What happened to him?"

"Michael died in a drunk driving accident last year but foul play was never ruled out. There were some suspicious factors involved, including the amount of drugs they found in his system."

"That's horrible. But it would mean there was no way he could have fathered Sunnie."

"I thought about that possibility on the way here. He would have died a couple of months after she was conceived. It might be a long shot, but I am going to check it out. And Brad also has a few male cousins living in Waco. Like Brad, they enjoy their bachelor lifestyles, so I'll be checking with them, as well."

She leaned back on the sofa. "So what will happen with Sunnie in the meantime?"

"That decision will be up to Social Services. However, I plan to have Brad recommend that she remain with you until this matter is resolved."

He saw the way her eyes brightened. "You think they'll go for it?"

"I don't know why they wouldn't. This is a delicate matter, and unfortunately it puts Brad in an awkward position. Even if Sunnie isn't directly his, there might be a family link. And knowing Brad the way I do, he will not turn his back on her, regardless. So either way, he might be filing for custody. She's doing fine right here with you, and the fewer changes we make with her the better."

He stood and crossed the room to sit beside her on the sofa. Surprised, she quickly scooted over. "Now that we got the issue of Sunnie taken care of, I think there is another matter we need to talk about," he said.

She nervously licked her lips. "And what issue is that?"

He stretched his arm across the back of the sofa. "Why you were so quick to assume the worst of me.

Why you don't think I can care for you and refuse to believe that I'd want to develop a serious relationship with you."

"Why should I think you care and would want to develop something serious with me? No one else has before."

"I can't speak for those others, Sheila. I can only speak for myself."

"So you want me to believe it was more than just sex between us?" she asked stiffly.

"Yes, that's what I want you to believe."

It's a good thing he understood her not wanting to believe. How many times had he wanted to believe that if he got involved with someone seriously, they wouldn't just eventually disappear? And he knew deep down that's why he couldn't fully wrap his arms around the Travers family. A part of him was so afraid he would wake up one day and they would no longer want to include him in their lives. Although they had shown him more than once that was not the case, he still had those fears.

He stood and walked to the window and looked out. It was getting dark outside. He scrunched up his brow wondering why all those pink flamingos were across the street in Sheila's neighbor's yard and then remembered the TCC's fundraiser.

Drawing in a deep breath, he turned around to glance over at Sheila. She was watching him, probably wondering what he was about. What he had on his mind. "You know you aren't the only one who has reasons to want to be cautious about getting involved with someone. The main reason I shy away from any type of serious relationship is thinking the person will be here one day and gone the next."

At her confused expression he returned to sit beside her on the sofa. "My mother left me, literally gave me up to my aunt when I was only five. In other words, I was abandoned just like Sunnie. I didn't see her again until I turned nineteen. And that was only because she thought with my skills as a football player in college that I'd make the pros and would be her meal ticket."

He saw the pity that shone in Sheila's eyes. He didn't want her pity, just her understanding. "Since Mom left me, for a long time I thought if I did anything wrong my aunt would desert me, as well."

"So you never did anything wrong."

"I tried not to. So you see, Sheila, I have my doubts about things just like you."

She didn't say anything for a moment and then asked, "What about your father?"

He leaned back on the sofa. "I never knew my father growing up. My aunt didn't have a clue as to his identity. My mother never told her. Then when I was in college, the craziest thing happened."

"What?" she asked, sitting up as if she was intrigued by what he was telling her.

"There was a guy on campus that everyone said looked just like me. I finally ran into him and I swear it was like looking in the mirror. He was younger than me by a year. And his name was Colin Travers."

"Your brother?"

"Yes, but we didn't know we were brothers because I was named Ezekiel Daniels at birth. Colin found our likeness so uncanny he immediately called his father. When he told his father my name, his old man remembered having a brief, meaningless affair with my mother years ago, before he married. He also remembered my mother's claim of getting pregnant when the affair ended. But she'd also made that claim to another man. So he assumed she was lying and had his attorney handle the situation. My mother wasn't absolutely sure Travers was my father, so she let it go."

"When your father finally discovered your existence, how did he treat you?" she asked.

"With open arms. All of his family welcomed me. His wife and my five brothers and one sister. At his request, on my twenty-first birthday, I changed my last name from Daniels to Travers and to this day that's all I've taken from him. And trust me he's offered plenty. But I don't take and I don't ask. Since acknowledging him as my father twelve years ago, I've never asked him for a single thing and I don't intend to."

"And who is your father, Zeke?"

"Matthew Travers."

Her mouth dropped open. "The self-made millionaire in Houston?"

He couldn't help chuckling at the shock he heard in her voice. "Yes. That's him."

"Do you blame him for not being a part of your life while growing up?"

"I did, but once I heard the whole story, and knowing my mother like I did, what he told me didn't surprise me. He felt badly about it and has tried making it up to me in various ways, although I've told him countless times that he doesn't owe me anything.

"So you see, Sheila, you aren't the only one with issues. I have them and I admit it. But I want to work on them with you. I want to take a chance and I want you to take a chance, too. What I feel with you feels right, and it has nothing to do with Sunnie."

He shook his head. "Hell, Sunnie's a whole other issue that I intend to solve. But I need to know that you're willing to step out on faith and give us a chance."

SHEILA COULD FEEL a stirring deep in her heart. He was asking for them to have a relationship, something more than a tumble between the sheets. It was something she thought she'd had with Crawford, only to get hurt. Could she take a chance again?

"My last boyfriend was a medical-supply salesman. He traveled a lot, left me alone most of the time. I thought I'd be satisfied with his calls and always looked forward to his return. Then one day he came back just to let me know I'd gotten replaced."

"You don't need to worry about that happening," Zeke said quietly.

She glanced over at him. "And why wouldn't I?"

He leaned closer to her and said in a low husky tone, "Because I am so into you that I can't think straight. I go to sleep dreaming of you and I wake up wanting you. When I make love to you, I feel like I'm grabbing a piece of heaven."

"Oh, Zeke." She drew in a deep breath, thinking that if this was a game he was playing with her then he was playing it well. Stringing her as high and as tight as it could go. She wanted to believe it wasn't a game and that he was sincere. She so much wanted to believe.

"I will always be there for you, Sheila. Whenever you need me. I won't let you down. You're going to have to trust me. Believe in me."

She fought back the tears. "Please don't tell me those

things if you don't mean them," she said softly. "Please don't."

"I mean them and I will prove it," he said, reaching out and gently pulling her toward him.

"Just trust me," he whispered close to her lips. And then he leaned in closer and captured her mouth with his.

SHEILA THOUGHT BEING in Zeke's arms felt right, so very right. And she wanted to believe everything he'd said, because as much as she had tried fighting it, she knew at that moment that she loved him. And his words had pretty much sealed her fate. Although he hadn't said he loved her, he wanted to be a part of her life and for them to take things one day at a time. That was more than anyone before had given her.

And she didn't have to worry about him being gone for long periods of time and not being there for her if she needed him.

But she didn't want to think about anything right now but the way he was kissing her. With a hunger she felt all the way to her bones.

And she was returning the kiss as heat was building inside her. Heat mixed with the love she felt for him. It was thrumming through her, stirring up emotions and feelings she'd tried to hold at bay for so long. But Zeke was pulling them out effortlessly, garnering her trust, making her believe and beckoning her to fall in love with him even more.

She felt herself being lifted into his arms and carried up the stairs. They didn't break mouth contact until he had lowered her onto the bed. "Mmm," she murmured in protest, missing the feel of his lips on hers, regretting the loss of tongue play in her mouth.

"I'm not going far, baby. We just need to remove our clothes," he whispered hotly against her moist lips.

Through desire-laden eyes she watched as he quickly removed his clothes and put on protection before returning to her. He reached out and took her hand and drew her closer to him. "Do you know how much I missed waking up beside you? Making love to you? Being inside you?"

She shook her head. "No."

"Then let me show you."

Zeke wanted to take things slow, refused to be rushed. He needed to make love to her the way he needed to breathe. After removing every stitch of her clothing, he breathed in her scent that he'd missed. "You smell good, baby."

"I smell like baby powder," she said, smiling. "One of the pitfalls of having a baby around."

His chuckle came out in a deep rumble. "You do smell like a baby. *My* baby." And then he kissed her again.

Moments later he released her mouth and began touching her all over as his hands became reacquainted with every part of her. He continued to stroke her and then his hands dipped to the area between her legs and found her wet and ready. Now another scent was replacing the baby powder fragrance and he was drawn into it. His erection thickened even more in response to it. He began stroking her there, fondling her, fingering the swollen bud of her womanhood.

"Zeke..."

"That's right, speak my name. Say it. I intend for it to be the only name you'll ever need to say when you feel this way."

And then he lowered himself to the bed, needing to be inside her now. His body straddled hers and he met her gaze, held it, while slowly entering her. He couldn't help shuddering at the feel of the head of his shaft slowly easing through her feminine core.

She wrapped her legs around him and he began moving to a beat that had been instilled inside his head from the first time he'd made love to her. And he knew he would enjoy connecting with her this way until the day he took his last breath. He'd never desired a woman the way he desired her.

And then he began moving in and out of her. Thrusting deep, stroking long and making each one count. Shivers of ecstasy began running up his spine and he could feel his hardness swell even more inside her. He reached down, lifted her hips to go deeper still and it was then that she screamed his name.

His name.

And something exploded inside him, made him tremble while wrapped in tremendous pleasure. Made him utter her name in a guttural breath. And he knew at that moment, whatever it took, he was determined that one day she would love him back. He would prove to her she had become more than just temptation to him. She had become his life.

SHEILA SNUGGLED DEEPER into Zeke's arms and glanced over at the clock on her nightstand. It was almost midnight. They had gotten up earlier to check on Sunnie and to grab a light dinner—a snack was more like it. He had scrambled eggs and she had made hash browns. While they ate he told her more about his relationship with the Travers family. And she shared with him how awful things had been for her with Crawford, and how strained her relationships were with her mother and sister.

He had listened and then got up from the table to come around and wipe tears from her eyes before picking her up in his arms and taking her back upstairs where they had made love again. Now he was sleeping and she was awake, still basking in the afterglow of more orgasms tonight than she cared to count, but would always remember.

She gently traced the curve of his face with the tip of her finger. It was hard to believe this ultrahandsome man wanted her. He had a way of making her feel so special and so needed. Earlier tonight in this very bed she had felt so cold. But now she wasn't cold. Far from it. Zeke was certainly keeping her warm. She couldn't help smiling.

"Hmm, I hate to interrupt whatever it is you're thinking about that's making you smile, but…"

And then he reached up, hooked a hand behind her neck to bring her mouth down to his. And then he took possession of it in that leisurely but thorough way of his. And it was a way that had her toes tingling. Oh, Lord, the man could kiss. Boy, could he kiss. And to think she was the recipient of such a drugging connection.

He finally released her mouth and pulled her up to straddle him. He then gazed up at her as he planted his hands firmly on her hips. "Let's make love this way."

They had never made love using this position before, and she hesitated and just stared at him, not sure what he wanted her to do. He smiled and asked, "You can ride a horse, right?"

She nodded slowly. "Yes, of course."

"Then ride me."

She smiled as she lifted the lower part of her body and then came down on him. He entered her with accurate precision. She stifled a groan as he lifted his hips off the bed to go deeper inside her. She in turned pressed down as hard as she could, grinding her body against his.

And then she did what he told her to do. She rode him.

BRAD GLANCED ACROSS the desk at Zeke. "Is there a reason you ran off yesterday like something was on fire?"

Zeke leaned back in his chair. He had left Sheila's house this morning later than he'd planned, knowing he had to go home first to change before heading into the office. He wasn't surprised to find Brad waiting on him. He'd seen the newspaper that morning. Brad's genetic connection to Sunnie made headline news, front page and center, for all to read.

When Zeke had stopped by the Royal Diner to grab a cup of coffee, the place where all the town gossips hung out, it seemed the place was all abuzz. There must have been a leak of information either at the lab where the test was processed or at the hospital. In any case, news of the results of the paternity test was all over town.

Everyone was shocked at the outcome of the test. Those who thought the baby wasn't Brad's due to the blackmailers hitting on other TCC members—even that news had somehow leaked—were going around scratching their heads, trying to figure out how the baby could be connected to Brad.

"It had to do with Sheila," he finally said.

Brad lifted a brow. "The woman taking care of the baby?"

"Yes."

Brad didn't say anything as he studied him, and Zeke knew exactly what he was doing. He was reading him like a book, and Zeke knew his best friend had the ability to do that. "And why do I get the feeling this Sheila Hopkins means something more to you than just a case you're working on?" Brad finally asked.

"Probably because you know me too well, and you're right. I met her less than two weeks ago and she has gotten to me, Brad. I think...I've fallen in love with her."

Zeke was certain Brad would have toppled over in his chair if it had not been firmly planted on the floor. "Love?"

"Yes, and I know what you're thinking. And it's not that. I care for her deeply." He leaned forward. "And she is even more cautious than I am about taking a chance. I'm the one who has to prove how much she means to me. Hell, I can't tell her how I feel yet. I'm going to have to show her."

A smile touched Brad's lips. "Well, this is certainly a surprise. I wish you the best."

"Thanks, man. And you might as well know one of her concerns right now is what's going to happen to Sunnie. She's gotten attached to her."

He paused a moment and then said, "Since you're here I have a video I want you to watch."

"A video?"

"Yes. I want you to look at that video I pulled that shows a woman placing the car seat containing the baby on the TCC doorstep. All we got is a good shot of her hands."

"And you think I might be able to recognize some woman's hands?" Brad asked.

Zeke shrugged. "Hey, it's worth a try." He picked up the remote to start rolling the videotape on the wide screen in his office.

Moments later they looked up when there was a tap on the door. He then remembered his secretary had taken part of the morning off. "Come in."

Summer entered. "Hi, guys, sorry to interrupt. But you know it's fundraiser time for the shelter and I—"

She stopped talking when she glanced at the wide screen where Zeke had pressed Pause and the image had frozen on a pair of hands. "Why are you watching a video of Diane Worth's hands?"

Both men stared at her. Zeke asked in astonishment, "You recognize those hands?"

Summer smiled. "Yes, but only because of that tiny scar across the back of her right hand, which would have been a bigger scar if Dr. Harris hadn't sutured it the way he did. And then there's that little mole between the third and fourth finger that resembles a star."

Her smile widened when she added, "And before you ask, the reason I noticed so much about her hand is because I'm the one who bandaged the wound after Dr. Harris examined her."

Zeke got out of his chair to sit on the edge of his desk. "This woman came through the shelter recently?"

Summer shook her head. "Yes, around seven months ago. She was eight months pregnant and her boyfriend had gotten violent and cut her on her hand with a bowie knife. She wouldn't give the authorities his name, and stayed at the shelter one week before leaving without a trace in the middle of the night."

Zeke nodded slowly, not believing he might finally have a break in the case. "Do you have any information you can give us on her?"

"No, and by law our records are sealed to protect the women who come to the shelter for our protection. I can tell you, however, that the information she gave us wasn't correct. When she disappeared I tried to find her to make sure she was okay and ran into a dead end. I'm not even sure Diane Worth is her real name."

Zeke rubbed his chin. "And you said she was pregnant and vanished without a trace?"

"Yes, but Abigail might be able to help you further."

Brad lifted a brow. "Abigail Langley?"

Summer nodded. "Yes. It just so happened the night Diane disappeared, we thought she might have met with foul play. But Abigail had volunteered to man our suicide phone line that night, and according to Abigail, when she went out to put something in her car, she saw Diane getting into a car with some man of her own free will."

"That was a while back. I wonder if Abigail would be able to identify the guy she saw?" Brad mused.

"We can pay Abigail a visit and find out," Zeke said. He looked over at Summer. "We need a description of Diane Worth for the authorities. Can we get it from you?"

Summer smiled. "With a judge's order I can do better than that. I can pull our security camera's tape of the inside of the building. There were several in the lounge area where Diane used to hang out. I bet we got some pretty clear shots of her."

Adrenaline was flowing fast and furious through Zeke's veins. "Where's Judge Meadows?" he asked Brad.

Brad smiled. "About to go hunting somewhere with Dad. Getting that court order from him shouldn't be a problem."

"Good," Zeke said, glancing down at his watch. "First I want to pay Abigail Langley a visit. And then I want to check out those videotapes from the shelter's security camera."

"I'm coming with you when you question Abigail," Brad said, getting to his feet.

Zeke raised a brow. "Why?"

Brad shrugged. "Because I want to."

Zeke rolled his eyes as he moved toward the door. "Fine, but don't you dare make her cry again."

"You made Abigail cry?" Summer asked, frowning over at him.

"It wasn't intentional and I apologized," a remorseful-sounding Brad said, and he quickly followed Zeke out the door.

CHAPTER TEN

"You NEED A husband."

Sheila groaned inwardly. Her mother was definitely on a roll today. "No, I don't."

"Yes, you do, and with that kind of attitude you'll never get one. You need to return to Dallas and meet one of Charles's nephews."

Sheila shook her head. Her mother had called to brag about a new man she'd met. Some wealthy oilman and his two nephews. Cassie had warned her that they were short for Texans, less than six feet tall, but what they lacked in height, they made up for in greenbacks.

"So, will you fly up this weekend and—"

"No, Mom. I don't want to return to Dallas."

Her mother paused a moment and then said, "I wasn't going to mention it, but I ran into Crawford today."

Sheila drew in a deep breath. Hearing his name no longer caused her pain. "That's nice."

"He asked about you."

"I don't know why," she said, glancing across the room to where Sunnie was reaching for one of her toys.

"He's no longer with that woman and I think he wants you back," her mother said.

"I wouldn't take him back if he was the last man on earth."

"And you think you can be choosy?"

Sheila smiled, remembering that morning with Zeke. "Yes, I think I can."

"Well, I don't know who would put such foolishness into your head. I know men. They are what they are. Liars, cheaters, manipulators, all of them. The only way to stay ahead of them is to beat them at their own game. But don't waste your time on a poor one. Go after the ones with money. Make it worth your while."

A short time later as she gave Sunnie her bath, Sheila couldn't help thinking of what her mother said. That had always been her mother's problem. She thought life was a game. Get them before they get me first. There was no excuse for her cheating on her first husband. But then she had cheated on her second and fourth husbands, as well.

Her phone rang and she crossed the room to pick it up, hoping it wasn't her mother calling back with any more maternal advice. "Yes?"

"Hi, beautiful."

She smiled upon recognizing Zeke's voice. "Howdy, handsome."

She and Zeke had made love before he'd left that morning and she had felt tingly sensations running through her body all day. They had been a reminder of what the two of them had shared through the night. And to think she had ridden him. Boy, had she ridden him. She blushed all over just thinking about it.

"I think we have a new lead," he said excitedly.

"You do? How?"

He told her how Summer had dropped by when he was showing the videotape in his office to Brad, and that she had identified the hands of the woman who had left Sunnie on the TCC's doorstep. He and Brad were now on their way to talk to Abigail Langley. There was a chance she could identify the man who the pregnant woman had left with that night. Then they would drop by the shelter to pull tapes for the authorities. There was a possibility Sunnie's mother was about to be identified.

By the time she'd hung up the phone from talking to Zeke, she knew he was closer to exposing the truth once and for all. Was Diane Worth Sunnie's biological mother? If she was, why did she leave her baby on the TCC's doorstep claiming she was Bradford Price's child?

ABIGAIL LED ZEKE and Brad into the study of her home. "Yes, I can give you a description of the guy," she said, sitting down on a love seat. "I didn't know who he was then, but I do now from seeing a picture of him flash on television one night on CNN when they did an episode on drug rings in this country. His name is Miguel Rivera and he's reputed to be a drug lord with an organization in Denver."

"Denver?" Zeke asked, looking at Brad. "Why would a drug lord from Denver be in Royal seven months ago?"

Brad shrugged. "I wouldn't know unless he's connected to Paulo Rodriguez." Brad then brought Zeke up to date on what had gone on in Royal a few years ago when the local drug trafficker had entangled prominent TCC members in an embezzlement and arson scandal.

"I think I need to fly to Denver to see what I can find out," Zeke said. He glanced over at Abigail. "I appreciate you making time to see us today."

"I don't mind. No baby should have been abandoned like that."

Knowing that the subject of the baby was a teary subject with her for some reason, Zeke said, "Well, we'll be going. We need to stop by the shelter to see what we can find out there."

They were about to walk out the study, when Brad noticed something on the table and stopped. "You still have this?" he asked Abigail.

Zeke saw the trophy sitting on the table that had caught Brad's eye.

"Yes. I was cleaning out the attic at my parents' house and came across it," she said.

Intrigued, Zeke asked. "What is it for?"

"This," Brad said, chuckling as he picked up the trophy and held it up for Zeke to see, "should have been mine. Abigail and I were in a spelling bee. It was a contest that I should have won."

"But you didn't," she said, laughing. "I can't believe you haven't gotten over that. You didn't even know how to spell the word *occupation*."

"Hell, I tried," Brad said, joining her in laughter.

"Trying wasn't good enough that day, Brad. Get over it."

Zeke watched the two. It was evident they shared history. It was also evident they had always been rivals. He wondered if they could continue to take their boxing gloves off and share a laugh or two the way they were doing now more often.

After a few moments, the pair remembered he was there. Brad cleared his throat. "I guess we better get going to make it to the shelter. Goodbye, Abby."

"Bye, Brad, and I'll see you around, Zeke."

"Sure thing," Zeke responded, not missing the fact this was the second occasion that he'd heard Brad refer to her as Abby. The first time occurred when he'd been holding her in his arms, comforting her. Um, interesting.

"So what do you think?" Brad asked moments later while snapping on their seat belts in Zeke's car.

Zeke chuckled. "I think it's a damn shame you couldn't spell the word *occupation* and lost the spelling bee to a girl."

Brad threw his head back and laughed. "Hey, you didn't know Abigail back then. She was quite a pistol. She could do just about anything better than anyone."

Zeke wondered if Brad realized he'd just given the woman a compliment. "Evidently. Now to answer your question about Miguel Rivera, I think I'm going to have to fly to Denver. If Diane Worth is Sunnie's mother, I want to know what part Miguel Rivera is playing in her disappearance. I think all the answers lie in Denver."

Brad nodded. "And you think there's a possible connection to my brother, Michael?"

"I'm not sure. But I know that baby isn't yours and she has to belong to someone. And you and I know Michael was heavy into alcohol and drugs."

"Yes, but as a user, not a pusher," Brad said.

"As far as we know," Zeke countered. "When you went to collect his belongings, was there anything in them to suggest he might have been involved with a woman?"

"I wasn't checking for that. Besides, there wasn't much of anything in that rat hole he called an apartment. I boxed up what he had, if you want to go through it. I put it in storage on my parents' property."

"I do. We can check that out after we leave the shelter." Zeke backed out of Abigail's driveway.

"YOU'RE LEAVING FOR Denver tomorrow?" Sheila asked hours later, glancing across the kitchen table at Zeke. He was holding Sunnie, making funny faces to get her to laugh. Sheila tried to downplay the feeling escalating inside her that he was leaving her.

This is work, you ninny, a voice inside her said. *This is not personal. He is not Crawford.* But then she couldn't help remembering Crawford's reasons for leaving were all work-related, too.

"Yes, I need to check out this guy named Miguel Rivera. He might be the guy who picked Diane Worth up from the shelter that night. Thanks to security cameras inside the shelter, we were able to get such good shots of the woman that we've passed them on to law enforcement."

The woman who might be Sunnie's mother, she thought. "How long do you think you'll be gone?" she asked.

"Not sure. I don't intend to come back until I find out a few things. I have a lot of questions that need to be answered."

Sheila nodded. She knew his purpose in going to Denver would help close the case on Sunnie and bring closure. It was time, she knew that. But still… "Well, I hope you find out something conclusive. For Sunnie's sake," she said.

And for yours, Zeke thought, studying her features. He knew that with each day that passed, she was getting attached to Sunnie even more. The first thing he'd noticed when he arrived at her place was Sunnie's things were once again all over the place.

"So what are you going to be doing while I'm gone?" he asked her, standing to place the baby back in her seat.

"You can ask me that with Sunnie here? Trust me, there's never a dull moment." She paused and then asked quietly, "You won't forget I'm here, will you?"

He glanced up after snapping Sunnie into the seat. Although Sheila had tried making light of the question, he could tell from the look on her face she was dead serious. Did she honestly think when he left for Denver that he wouldn't think of her often, probably every single day? And although he would need to stay focused on solving the case, there was no doubt in his mind that she would still manage to creep into his thoughts. Mainly because she had his heart. Maybe it was time for him to tell her that.

He crossed the room to where she sat at the table and took her hands into his and eased her up. He then wrapped his arms around her waist. "There's no way I can forget about the woman I've fallen in love with."

He saw immediate disbelief flash across her features and said, "I know it's crazy considering we've only known each other for just two weeks but it's true. I do love you, Sheila, and no matter what you think, I won't forget you, and I am coming back. I will be here whenever you need me, just say the word."

He saw the tears that formed in her eyes and heard her broken words when she said, "And I love you, too. But I'm scared."

"And you think I'm not scared, too, baby? I've never given a woman my heart before. But you have it—lock, stock and barrel. And I don't make promises I don't keep, sweetheart. I will always be here for you. I will be a man you can count on."

And then he lowered his mouth and sealed his promise with a kiss, communicating with her this way and letting her know what he'd just said was true. He wanted her, but he loved her, too.

She returned his kiss with just as much fervor as he was putting into it. He knew if they didn't stop he would be tempted to haul her upstairs, which couldn't happen since Sunnie was wide awake. But there would be later and he was going to start counting the minutes.

SHEILA WOKE WHEN the sunlight streaming through the window hit her in the face. She jerked up in bed and saw the side next to her was empty. Had Zeke left for Denver already without telling her goodbye?

Trying to ignore the pain settling around her heart, she wrapped the top sheet around her naked body and eased out of bed to stare out the window. Was he somewhere in the skies on a plane? He hadn't said when he was returning, but he said he would and that he loved her. He *loved* her. She wanted so much to believe him and—

"Is there any reason you're standing there staring out the window?"

She whipped around with surprise all over her face. "You're here."

He chuckled. "Yes, I'm here. Where did you think I'd be?"

She shrugged. "I assumed you had left for Denver already."

"Without telling you goodbye?"

She fought back telling him that's how Crawford would do things, and that he had a habit of not returning when he'd told her he would. Something would always come up. There was always that one last sale he just had to make. Instead, she said, "What you have to do in Denver is important."

He leaned in the doorway with a cup of coffee in his hand. "And so are you."

He entered the room and placed the cup on the nightstand. "Come here, sweetheart."

She moved around the bed, tugging the sheet with her. When she came to a stop in front of him, he said, "Last night I told you that I had fallen in love with you, didn't I?"

"Yes."

"Then I need for you to believe in me. Trust me. I know, given your history with the people you care about, trusting might not be easy, but you're going to have to give me a chance."

She drew in a deep breath. "I know, but—"

"No buts, Sheila. We're in this thing together, you and me. We're going to leave all our garbage at the back door and not bring it inside. All right?"

She smiled and nodded. "All right."

He was about to pull her into his arms, when they heard the sound of Sunnie waking up on the monitor in the room. "I guess we'll have to postpone this for later. And later sometime, I need to look through some boxes Brad put in storage that belonged to his brother. His cousins in Waco swear they are not Sunnie's daddy, and since Michael is not here to speak for himself, I need to do some digging. But I am flying out for Denver tomorrow sometime."

He took a step back. "You go get dressed. Take your time. I'll handle the baby. And please don't ask if I know how to dress and feed her. If you recall, I've done it before."

She chuckled. "I know you have. And you will make a great father."

His smile widened. "You think so?"

"Yes."

"I take that as a compliment," he said. "And like I said, take your time coming downstairs. Sunnie and I will be in the kitchen waiting whenever you come down."

ZEKE DECIDED TO do more than just dress and feed Sunnie. By the time Sheila walked into the kitchen, looking as beautiful as ever in black slacks and a pretty pink blouse, he had a suggestion for her. "The weather is nice outside. How about if we do something?"

She raised a brow. "Do something like what?"

"Um, like taking Sunnie to that carnival over in Somerset."

"But I thought you had to go through Brad's brother's boxes," she said.

"I do, but I thought we could go to the carnival first and I can look through the boxes later. I just called the airlines. I'll be flying out first thing in the morning, and I want to spend as much time as I can today with my two favorite ladies."

"Really?"

He could tell by her expression that she was excited by his suggestion. "Yes, really. What do you say?"

She practically beamed. "Sunnie and I would love to go to the carnival with you."

Considering how many items they had to get together for Sunnie, it didn't take long for them to be on their way. He had passed the carnival a few days ago and had known he wanted to take Sheila and Sunnie there. It had been only a couple of weeks, but Sunnie had become just as much a part of his life as Sheila's.

Although he'd told her how he felt about her, he could see Sheila was still handling him with caution, as if she was afraid to give her heart to him no matter how much she wanted to. He would be patient and continue to show her how much she meant to him. As he'd told her, considering her mother, sister and ex-boyfriend's treatment of her, he could definitely understand her lack of trust.

"And you're sure Brad is okay with you putting the investigation on hold to spend time with me and Sunnie?"

He glanced over at her as he turned toward the interstate. "Positive. A few hours won't hurt anything. Besides, I'll probably be gone most of next week and I'm missing you already."

It didn't take them long to reach the carnival grounds. After putting Sunnie in her stroller, they began walking around. It was Saturday and a number of people were out and about. He recognized a number of them he knew and Sheila ran into people she knew, as well. They ran into Brad's sister, Sadie, her husband, Ron, and the couple's twin daughters.

"She is a beautiful baby," Sadie said, hunching down to be eye level with Sunnie.

And as usual when strangers got close, Sunnie glanced around to make sure Sheila was near. "Yes, she is," Sheila said, smiling. She waited to see if the woman would make a comment about Sunnie favoring her brother or anyone in the Price family, but Sadie Price Pruitt didn't do so. But it was plain to see she was just as taken with Sunnie as Sheila was with Sadie's twins.

They also ran into Mitch Hayward and the former Jenny Watson. Mitch was the interim president of the TCC, and Jenny, one of his employees, when the two had fallen in love. And they had a baby on the way.

But the person Zeke was really surprised to see was Darius. He hadn't known his partner had returned to town. "Darius, when did you get back?" he asked, shaking his business partner's hand.

"Last night. We finished up a few days early and I caught the first plane coming this way."

Zeke didn't have to ask why when Darius drew Summer closer to him and smiled down at her.

"I would have called when I got in, but it was late and…"

Zeke chuckled. "Hey, man, you don't have to explain. I understand." He was about to introduce Darius and Sheila, but realized when Darius reached out and gave Sheila a hug that they already knew each other.

"And this is the little lady I've heard so much about," Darius said, smiling at Sunnie. "She's a beautiful baby."

They all chatted for few minutes longer before parting ways, but not before agreeing to get together when Zeke returned from Denver.

"I like Darius and Summer," Sheila said. "That time when Summer and I worked together on that abuse case, Darius was so supportive and it's evident that he loves her very much."

Zeke nodded and thought that one day he and Sheila might share the kind of bond that Darius and Summer enjoyed.

CHAPTER ELEVEN

ZEKE WAS GRATEFUL for the friendships he'd made while at UT on the football team. The man he needed to talk to who headed Denver's Drug Enforcement Unit, Harold Mathis, just so happened to be the brother of one of Zeke's former teammates.

Mathis wasted no time in telling Zeke about Miguel Rivera. Although the notorious drug lord had been keeping a low profile lately, in no way did the authorities believe he had turned over a new leaf. And when they were shown photographs of Diane Worth, they identified her as a woman who'd been seen with Rivera once or twice.

Zeke knew he had his work cut out in trying to make a connection between Diane Worth and Michael Price. Michael's last place of residence was in New Orleans. At least that's where Brad had gone to claim his brother's body.

His belongings hadn't given a clue as to who he might have associated with, especially a woman by the name of Diane Worth. But Zeke was determined to find out if Diane Worth was Sunnie's mother.

The Denver Drug Enforcement Unit was ready to lend their services to do anything they could to get the likes of Miguel Rivera off the streets. So far he had been wily where the authorities were concerned and had been able to elude all undercover operations to nab him.

Since Zeke knew he would probably be in Denver awhile, he had decided to take residence in one of those short-term executive apartments. It wasn't home, but it had all the amenities. He had stopped by a grocery store to buy a few things and was reminded of the time when he had gone grocery shopping with Sheila and the baby when they'd stayed over at his place. He had been comfortable walking beside her and hadn't minded when a few people saw them and probably thought they were an item. As far as he was concerned, they were.

He glanced out a window that had a beautiful view of downtown Denver. He was missing his *ladies* already. Sunnie had started to grow on him as well, which was easy for her because she was such a sweet baby. She no longer screamed around strangers, although you could tell she was most comfortable when he or Sheila was around.

Sheila.

God, he loved her something awful and was determined that distance didn't put any foolishness in her mind, like her thinking he was falling out of love with her just because he didn't see her every day. Already he'd patronized the florist shop next door. They would make sure a bouquet of flowers was delivered to Sheila every few days. And he intended to ply her with "thinking of you" gifts often.

He chuckled. Hell, that could get expensive because he thought of her all the time. The only time he would force thoughts of her from his mind was when he was trying to concentrate on the case. And even then it was hard.

He picked up the documents he had tossed on the table that included photographs of both Rivera and Worth. A contact was working with hospitals in both New Orleans and Denver to determine if a child was born to Diane Worth five months ago. And if so, where was the baby now?

He was about to go take a shower, when his phone rang. "Hello."

"I got another blackmail letter today, Zeke."

He nodded. Zeke figured another one would be coming sooner or later. The extortionist had made good his threat. But that didn't mean he was letting Brad off the hook. It was done mainly to let him know he meant business. "He still wants money, right?"

"Yes, and unless I pay up, Sunnie's birth records will be made public to show I had a relationship with a prostitute."

Of course, that was a lie, but the blackmailer's aim was to get money out of Brad to keep a scandal from erupting. It would have a far-reaching effect not only for Brad's reputation but that of his family.

"I know it's going to be hard for you to do, but just ignore it for now. Whoever is behind the extortion attempt evidently thinks he has you where he wants you to be, and we're going to prove him wrong."

By the time Zeke ended his call with Brad, he was more determined than ever to find a link between Rivera and Worth.

"YOU'RE THINKING ABOUT getting married?" *Again?* Sheila really should not be surprised. Her mother hated being single and had a knack for getting a husband whenever she wanted one....

"Um, I'm thinking about it. I really like Charles."

You only met him last week. And wasn't it just a couple of weeks ago she'd asked her about Dr. Morgan? Sheila decided not to remind her mother of all those other men she'd liked, as well. "I wish you the best, Mom." And she did. She wanted her mother to be happy. Married or not.

"Thanks. And what's that I hear in the background? Sounds like a kid."

Sheila had no intention of telling her mother the entire story about Sunnie. "It is a baby. I'm taking care of her for a little while." That wasn't totally untrue since she was considered Sunnie's caretaker for the time being.

"That's nice, dear, since chances are you won't have any of your own. Your biological clock is ticking and you have no prospects."

Sheila smiled, deciding to let her mother think whatever she wanted. "You don't have to have a man to get pregnant, Mom. Just sperm."

"Please don't do anything foolish. I hope you aren't thinking of going that route. Besides, being pregnant can mess up a woman's figure for life."

Sheila rolled her eyes. Her mother thought nothing of blaming her for the one stretch mark she still had on her tummy. She was about to open her mouth and say something—to change the subject—when her doorbell sounded.

"Mom, I have to go. There's someone at the door."

"Be careful. There are lunatics living in small towns."

"Okay, Mom, I'll be careful." At times it was best not to argue.

After hanging up the phone, she glanced over at

Sunnie, who was busy laughing while reaching for a toy that let out a squeal each time Sunnie touched it. She was such a happy baby.

Sheila glanced through the peephole. There was a woman standing there holding an arrangement of beautiful flowers. Sheila immediately figured the delivery was for her neighbor, who probably wasn't at home. She opened the door. "Yes, may I help you?"

The woman smiled. "Yes, I have a delivery for Sheila Hopkins."

Sheila stared at the woman, shocked. "I'm Sheila Hopkins. Those are for me?"

"Yes." The woman handed her a huge arrangement in a beautiful vase. "Enjoy them."

The woman then left, leaving Sheila standing there, holding the flowers with the shocked look still in place. It took the woman driving off before Sheila pulled herself together to take a step back into the house and close the door behind her as she gazed at the flowers. It was a beautiful bouquet. She quickly placed the vase in what she considered the perfect spot before pulling off the card.

I am thinking of you. Zeke.

Sheila's heart began to swell. He was away but still had her in his thoughts. A feeling of happiness spread through her. Zeke, who claimed he loved her, was too real to be true. She wanted to believe he was real...but...

She turned to Sunnie. "Look what Zeke sent. I feel special...and loved."

Sunnie didn't pay her any attention as she continued to play with the toy Zeke had won for her at the carnival. Sheila was satisfied that even if Sunnie wasn't listening, her heart was. Now, if she could just shrug off her inner fear that regardless of what he did or said, for her Zeke was a heartbreak waiting to happen.

A FEW DAYS later, during a telephone conversation with a Denver detective, Zeke's hand tightened on the phone. "Are you sure?" he asked.

"Yes," the man replied. "I verified with a hospital in New Orleans that Diane Worth gave birth to a baby girl there five months ago. We could pick her up for questioning since abandoning a baby is a punishable crime."

Zeke inhaled a deep breath. "She could say the baby is living somewhere with relatives or friends, literally having us going around in circles. We need proof she's Sunnie's mother and have that proof when she's brought in. Otherwise, she'll give Miguel Rivera time to cover his tracks."

Zeke paused a moment and then added, "We need a DNA sample from Worth. How can we get it without her knowing about it?"

"I might have an idea." The agent then shared his idea with Zeke.

Zeke smiled. "That might work. We need to run it by Mathis."

"It's worth a try if it will link her to Rivera. We want him off the streets and behind bars as soon as possible. He's bad news."

Later that night, as he did every night, Zeke called Sheila. Another bouquet of flowers as well as a basket of candy had been delivered that day. He had been plying her with "thinking of you" gifts since he'd been gone, trying to keep her thoughts on him and to let her know how much he was missing her.

After thanking him for her gifts, she mentioned that Brad had stopped by to see how Sunnie was doing. Sheila had been surprised to see him, but was glad he had cared enough about the baby's welfare to make an unexpected visit. She even told Zeke how Sunnie had gone straight to the man without even a sniffle. And that she seemed as fascinated with him as he had been with her.

Zeke then brought her up to date on what they'd found out about Diane Worth. "It seems she has this weekly appointment at a hair salon. One of the detectives will get hair samples for DNA testing. Once they have a positive link to Sunnie, they will bring her in for questioning."

"What do you think her connection is to Michael Price?" Sheila asked.

"Don't know for sure, but I have a feeling things will begin to unravel in a few more days."

They talked a little while longer. He enjoyed her sharing Sunnie's activities for that day, especially how attached she had gotten to that toy he'd won for her at the carnival.

"I miss you," he said, meaning it. He hadn't seen her in over a week.

"And I miss you, too, Zeke."

He smiled. That's what he wanted to hear. And since they were on a roll… "And I love you," he added.

"And I love you back. Hurry home."

Home. His chest swelled with even more love for her at that moment. "I will, just as soon as I get this case solved." And he meant it.

A FEW DAYS later things began falling into place. As usual, Worth had her hair appointment. It took a couple of days for the DNA to be matched with the sample taken from Sunnie. The results showed Diane was definitely Sunnie's biological mother.

Although Zeke wasn't in the interrogation room when Worth was brought in, she did what they assumed she would do—denying the abandoned child could be hers. She claimed her baby was on a long trip with her father. However, once proof was presented showing Sunnie was her child and had been used in a blackmail scheme, and that her hand had been caught on tape, which could be proven, the woman broke down and blurted out what she knew of the sordid scheme.

She admitted that Rivera had planned for her to meet Michael Price for the sole purpose of having him get her pregnant. Once Rivera found out Michael was from a wealthy family, he set up his plan of extortion. She was given a huge sum of money to seduce Michael, and once her pregnancy was confirmed, Rivera had shown up one night and joined the party. Throughout the evening at Diane's, he'd spiked Michael's drinks with a near-lethal dose of narcotics and made sure he got behind the wheel to drive home. What had been made to look like a drunk-driving accident was anything but—Michael had been murdered. She also said that up until that night, Michael had been drug-free for almost six months and had intended to reunite with his family and try to live a decent life. With Worth's confession linking Rivera to Michael's death, a warrant was issued and Rivera was arrested.

Zeke had kept Brad informed of what was going on. The Price family was devastated to learn the truth behind Michael's death and looked forward to making Sunnie part of their family. Brad, who had never given up hope that Michael would have eventually gotten his life together if he'd survived, had decided to be Sunnie's legal guardian. He felt Michael would have wanted things that way.

That night when he called Sheila and heard the excitement in her voice about receiving candy and more flowers he'd sent, he hated to be the deliverer of what he had to tell her. Although it was good news for Sunnie, because she would he raised by Brad and kept out of the system, it would be a sad time for Sheila.

"The flowers are beautiful, Zeke, and the candy was delicious. If I gain any weight it will be your fault."

He smiled briefly and then he said in a serious tone, "We wrapped things up today, Sheila. Diane Worth confessed and implicated Miguel Rivera in the process. He then told her how things went down and how in the end the authorities had booked both Worth and Rivera. Since Worth worked with the authorities, she would get a lighter sentence, and Rivera was booked for the murder of Michael Price."

"That is so sad, but at least we know what happened and why Brad had a genetic link to Sunnie," she said softly.

"Yes, and Brad is stepping up to the plate to become Sunnie's legal guardian. He's going to do right by her. Already his attorneys have filed custody papers and there is no doubt in my mind he will get it. That's another thing Worth agreed to do to get a lighter sentence. She will give up full rights to Sunnie. She didn't deserve her anyway. She deliberately got pregnant to use her baby to get money."

Zeke paused and then added, "She claims she didn't know of Rivera's plans to kill Michael until it was too late."

"I guess that means I need to begin packing up Sunnie's stuff. He'll come and get her any day," Sheila said somberly.

"According to Brad, Social Services told him the exchange needs to take place at the end of the week. I'll be back by then. I won't let you be alone."

He thought he heard her sniffing before she said, "Thanks, Zeke. It would mean a lot to me if you were here."

They talked for a little while longer before saying good-night and hanging up the phone. Zeke could tell Sheila was sad at the thought of having to give up Sunnie and wished he was there right now to hold her in his arms, make love to her and assure her everything would be all right. They would have babies of their own one day. All the babies she could ever want, and that was a promise he intended to make to her when he saw her again.

A COUPLE OF days later, after putting Sunnie down after her breakfast feeding, Sheila's phone rang. "Hello?"

"Sheila, this is Lois. Are you okay?"

Sheila almost dropped the phone. The last time her sister called her was to cancel her visit to see her and her family. "Yes, why wouldn't I be?"

"You were mentioned on the national news again. The Denver police and some hotshot private investigator solved this murder case about a drug lord. According to the news, he'd been using women to seduce rich men, get pregnant by them and then using the resulting babies as leverage for extortion. I understand such a thing happened in Royal and you are the one taking care of the abandoned baby while the case was being solved."

Sheila released a disappointed sigh. Ever since the story had broken, several members of the media had contacted her for a story and she'd refused to give them one. Why did her sister only want to connect with her when she appeared in the news or something? "Yes, that's true."

"That's wonderful. Well, Ted was wondering if perhaps you could get in touch with the private investigator who helped to solve the case."

"Why?"

"To have him on his television talk show, of course. Ted's ratings have been down recently and he thinks the man's appearance will boost them back up."

Sheila shook her head. Not surprising that Lois wanted something of her. Why couldn't she call just because?

"So, do you have a way to help Ted get in touch with his guy?" Lois asked, interrupting Sheila's thoughts.

"Yes, in fact, I know him very well. But if you or Ted want to contact him you need to do it without my help," she said. "I'm your sister and the only time you seem to remember that is when you need a favor. That's not the kind of relationship I want with you, Lois, and if that's the only kind you're willing to give then I'm going to pass. Goodbye."

She hung up the phone and wasn't surprised when Lois didn't call back. And she wasn't surprised when she received a call an hour later from her mother.

"Really, Sheila, why do you continue to get yourself in these kinds of predicaments? You know nothing about caring for a baby. How did you let yourself be talked into being any child's foster parent?"

Sheila rolled her eyes. "I'm a nurse, Mom. I'm used to taking care of people."

"But a kid? Better you than me."

"How well I know that," she almost snapped

Her mother's comments reminded her that in two days she would hand Sunnie over to Bradford Price. He had called last night and they had agreed the exchange would take place at the TCC. It seemed fitting since that was the place Diane Worth had left her daughter—although for all the wrong reasons—that she would begin her new life there again.

Sheila wasn't looking forward to giving up Sunnie. The only good thing was that Zeke would be flying in tonight and she wouldn't be alone. He would give her his support. No one had ever done that for her before. And she couldn't wait to see him again after almost two weeks.

ZEKE PAUSED IN the middle of packing for his return home and met DEA Agent Mathis's intense gaze. "What do you mean Rivera's attorney is trying to get him off on a technicality? We have a confession from Diane Worth."

"I know," Mathis said in a frustrated tone, "but Rivera has one of the slickest lawyers around. They are trying to paint Worth as a crackhead and an unfit mother who'd desert her child for more drugs, and that she thought up the entire thing—the murder scheme—on her own. The attorney is claiming his client is a model citizen who is being set up."

"That's bull and you and I know it."

"Yes, and since he drove from Denver to New Orleans instead of taking a flight, we can't trace the car he used." Mathis let out a frustrated sigh and added, "This is what we've been dealing with when it comes to Rivera. He has unscrupulous people on his payroll. He claims he was nowhere near New Orleans during the time Michael Price was killed. We have less than twenty-four hours to prove otherwise or he walks."

"Damn." Zeke rubbed his hand down his face. "I refuse to let him get away with this. I want to talk to Worth again. There might be something we missed that can prove that now she's the one being set up."

A few hours later Zeke and Mathis were sitting at a table across from Diane Worth. "I don't care what Miguel is saying," she said, almost in tears. "He is the one who came up with the plan, not me."

"Is there any way you can prove that?" Zeke asked her. He glanced at his watch. He should be on a plane right this minute heading for Royal. Now he would have to call Sheila to let her know he wouldn't be arriving in Royal tonight as planned. He refused to leave Denver knowing there was a chance Miguel Rivera would get away with murder.

She shook her head. "No, there's no way I can prove it." And then she blinked as if she remembered something. "Wait a minute. When we got to New Orleans we stopped for gas and Miguel went inside to purchase a pack of cigarettes. The store clerk was out of his brand and he pitched a fit. Several people were inside the store and I bet one of them remembers him. He got pretty ugly."

Zeke looked over at Mathis. "And even if they don't

remember him, chances are, the store had a security camera."

Both men quickly stood. They had less than twenty-four hours to prove Miguel was in New Orleans when he claimed that he wasn't.

SHEILA SHIFTED IN BED and glanced over at the clock as excitement flowed down her spine. Zeke's plane should have landed by now. He would likely come straight to her place from the airport. At least he had given her the impression that he would when she'd talked to him that morning. And she couldn't wait to see him.

She had talked to Brad and she would deliver Sunnie to him at the TCC at three the day after tomorrow. It was as if Sunnie had detected something was bothering her and had been clingy today. Sheila hadn't minded. She had wanted to cling to the baby as much as Sunnie had wanted to cling to her.

She smiled when her cell phone rang. She picked it up and checked caller ID. It was Zeke. She sat up in bed as she answered it. "Are you calling to tell me you're outside?" she asked, unable to downplay the anticipation as well as the excitement in her voice.

"No, baby. I'm still in Denver. Something came up with the case and I won't be returning for possibly three days."

Three days? That meant he wouldn't be there when she handed Sunnie over to Bradford Price. "But I thought you were going to return tonight so you could be here on Thursday. For me."

"I want to and will try to make it, but—"

"Yes, I know. Something came up. I understand," she

said, trying to keep the disappointment out of her voice. Why had she thought he was going to be different?

"I've got to go, Zeke."

"No, you don't. You're shutting me out, Sheila. You act as if I'd rather be here than there, and that's not true and you know it."

"Do I?"

"You should. I need to be here or else Miguel Rivera gets to walk away scot-free."

A part of her knew she was being unreasonable. He had a job to do. But still, another part just couldn't accept he wasn't doing a snow job on her. "And, of course, you can't let him do that," she said snippily.

He didn't say anything for a minute and then, "You know what your problem is, Sheila? You can't take hold of the future because you refuse to let go of the past. Think about that and I'll see you soon. Goodbye."

Instead of saying goodbye, she hung up the phone. How dare he insinuate she was the one with the problem? What made him think that he didn't have issues? She didn't know a single person who didn't.

She shifted back down in bed, refusing to let Zeke's comments get to her. But she knew it was too late. They already had.

CHAPTER TWELVE

TWO DAYS LATER, it was a tired Zeke who made it to
the Denver airport to return to Royal. He and Mathis
had caught a flight from Denver to New Orleans and
interviewed the owner of the convenience store. The
man's eyewitness testimony, as well as the store's security
camera, had pinned Rivera in New Orleans when he said
he hadn't been there. With evidence in hand, they had left
New Orleans to return to Denver late last night.

After reviewing the evidence this morning, a judge
had ruled in their favor and had denied bail to Rivera and
had refused to drop the charges. And if that wasn't bad
enough, the lab had delivered the results of their findings.
DNA of hair found on Michael's jacket belonged to
Rivera. Zeke was satisfied that Rivera would be getting
just what he deserved.

He glanced at his watch. The good thing was that he
was returning to Royal in two days instead of three. It
wasn't noon yet and if his flight left on time, he would
arrive back in Royal around two, just in time to be
with Sheila when she handed Sunnie over to Brad. He
had called her that morning from the courthouse in
Denver and wasn't sure if she had missed his call or
deliberately not answered it. He figured she was upset,
but at some point she had to begin believing in him. If
for one minute she thought she was getting rid of him

she had another thought coming. She was his life and he intended to be hers.

A few moments later he checked his watch again thinking they should be boarding his plane any minute. He couldn't wait to get to Royal and see Sheila to hold her in his arms, make love to her all night. He hadn't meant to fall in love with her.

An announcement was made on the nearby intercom system, interrupting his thoughts. *"For those waiting on Flight 2221, we regret to inform you there are mechanical problems. Our take-off time has been pushed back three hours."*

"Damn." Zeke said, drawing in a frustrated breath. He didn't have three hours. He had told Sheila he was going to try to be there, and he intended to do just that. She needed him today and he wanted to be there for her. He could not and would not let her down.

He knew the only way he could make that happen. He pulled his phone out of his pocket and punched in a few numbers.

"Hello?"

He swallowed deeply before saying, "Dad, this is Zeke."

There was a pause and then, "Yes, son?"

Zeke drew in another deep breath. He'd never asked his father for anything, but he was doing so now. "I have a favor to ask of you."

"THANK YOU FOR TAKING care of her, Ms. Hopkins," Bradford Price said as Sheila handed Sunnie over to him at the TCC headquarters.

"You don't have to thank me, Mr. Price. It's been a joy taking care of Sunnie these past few weeks,"

Sheila said, fighting back her tears. "And I have all her belongings packed and ready to be picked up. You paid for all of it and you'll need every last item." Sunnie was looking at her, and Sheila refused to make eye contact with the baby for fear she would lose it.

"All right. I'm make arrangements to drop by your place sometime later, if that's all right," Brad said.

"Yes, that will be fine." She then went down a list of dos and don'ts for the baby, almost choking on every word. "She'll be fussy if she doesn't eat breakfast by eight, and she sleeps all through the night after being given a nice bath. Seven o'clock is her usual bedtime. She takes a short nap during the day right after her lunch. She has a favorite toy. It's the one Zeke won for her at the carnival. She likes playing with it and will do so for hours."

"Thanks for telling me all that, and if it makes you feel better to know although I'm a bachelor, I plan to take very good care of my niece. And I know a little about babies myself. My sister has twin girls and I was around them a lot when they were babies."

"Sorry, Mr. Price, I wasn't trying to insinuate you wouldn't take good care of her."

Bradford Price smiled. "I know. You love her. I could see it in your eyes when you look at her. And please call me Brad. Mr. Price is my father."

A pain settled around Sheila's heart when she remembered Zeke's similar comment. Then later, he had explained why he'd said it. She was missing him so much and knew she hadn't been fair to him when he'd called two days ago to explain his delay in returning to Royal.

"Yes, I love her, Brad. She's an easy baby to love. You'll see." She studied him a minute. He was Zeke's best friend. She wondered how much he knew about their relationship. At the moment it didn't matter what he knew or didn't know. He was going to be Sunnie's guardian and she believed in her heart he would do right by his niece.

"I'm looking forward to making her an integral part of my family. Michael would have wanted it that way. I loved my brother and all of us tried reaching out to help him. It was good to hear he was trying to turn his life around, and a part of me believes that eventually he would have. It wasn't fair the way Miguel Rivera ended his life that way."

"No, it wasn't," she agreed.

"That's why Zeke remained in Denver a couple more days," Brad said. "Rivera's shifty attorney tried to have the charges dropped, claiming Rivera wasn't in New Orleans when Michael died. Zeke and the DEA agent had to fly to New Orleans yesterday to get evidence to the contrary. Now Rivera will pay for what he did. And I got a call from Zeke an hour ago. His flight home has been delayed due to mechanical problems."

Sheila nodded. Now she knew why Zeke wasn't there. She understood. She should have understood two nights ago, but she hadn't given him the chance to explain. Now, not only was she losing Sunnie, she had lost Zeke, as well.

She'd pushed him away because she couldn't let go of the past. She was so afraid of being abandoned; she couldn't truly open her heart to him. And now she feared she was truly alone.

She continued to fight back her tears. "I call her Sunnie," she said, fighting to keep her voice from breaking. "But I'm sure you're going to name her something else."

Brad smiled as he looked at the baby he held. "No, Sunnie is her name and it won't get changed. I think Sunnie Price fits her." He then glanced over at her. "What's your middle name?"

She was surprised by his question. "Nicole."

"Nice name. How does Sunnie Nicole Price sound?"

Sheila could barely find her voice to ask. "You'll name her after me?"

Brad chuckled. "Yes, you took very good care of her and I appreciate it. Besides, you're her godmother."

That came as another surprise. "I am?"

"I'd like you to be. I want you to always be a part of my niece's life, Sheila."

Joy beamed up inside Sheila. "Yes, yes, I'd love to. I would be honored."

"Good. I'll let you know when the ceremony at the church will be held."

"All right."

"Now I better get her home."

Sheila leaned up and kissed Sunnie on the cheek. The baby had taken to Brad as easily as she had taken to her and that was a good sign. "You better behave, my sunshine." And before she could break down then and there, she turned and quickly walked away.

Sheila made it to the nearest ladies' room and it was there that the tears she couldn't hold back any longer came flooding through and she began crying in earnest. She cried for the baby she'd just given up and for the man she had lost. She was alone, but being alone was the story of her life, and it shouldn't have to be this way. She wanted her own baby one day, just like Sunnie, but she knew that would never happen. She would never find a man to love her again. A man who'd want to give her his babies. She'd had such a man and now he probably didn't want to see her again. He was right. She couldn't take hold of the future because she refused to let go of the past.

She saw that now. Zeke was right. It was her problem. But he wasn't here for her to tell that to. He had no reason to want to come back to her. She was a woman with issues and problems.

"Excuse me. I don't want to intrude, but are you all right?"

Sheila turned at the sound of the feminine voice and looked at the woman with the long, wavy red hair and kind blue eyes. She was a stranger, but for some reason the woman's question opened the floodgates even more and Sheila found herself crying out her pain, telling the woman about Sunnie, about the man she loved and had lost, and how she'd also lost the chance to ever have a child of her own.

The stranger gave her a shoulder to cry on and provided her with comfort when she needed it. "I understand how you feel. More than anything I'd love to have a child, but I can't have one of my own," the woman said, fighting back her own tears.

"My problem is physical," she continued as a slow trickle of tears flowed down her cheeks. "Every time I think I've accepted the doctor's prognosis, I discover I truly haven't, so I know just how you feel. I want a child so badly and knowing I can't ever have one is something I've yet to accept, although I know I must."

Sheila began comforting the woman who just a moment ago had comforted her.

"By the way, I don't think I've introduced myself. I'm Abigail Langley," the woman said once she'd calmed down.

"I'm Sheila Hopkins." She felt an affinity for the woman, a special bond. Although they had just met, she had a feeling this would be the start of an extraordinary friendship. She was convinced she and Abigail would be friends for life.

A short while later they managed to pull themselves together and with red eyes and swollen noses they walked out of the ladies' room, making plans to get together for lunch one day soon.

The sun was shining bright when Sheila and Abigail stepped outside. Sheila glanced up into the sky. Although it was a little on the chilly side, it was a beautiful day in November. The sun was shining and it made her think of Sunnie. Thanksgiving would be next week and she had a feeling Brad would have a big feast to introduce the baby to his entire family.

Abigail nudged her in the side. "I think someone is waiting for you."

Sheila glanced across the parking lot. It was Zeke. He was standing beside her car and holding a bouquet of flowers in his hand. At that moment she was so glad to see him. Her heart filled with so much love. He had come back to her, with her problems and all. He had come back.

As fast as her legs could carry her, she raced across the parking lot to him and he caught her in his arms and kissed her hard. And she knew at that moment he was also her sunshine and that her heart would always shine bright for him.

GOD, HE'D MISSED her, Zeke thought as he continued to deepen the kiss. Two weeks had been too long. And the more she flattened her body to his, the more he wanted to take her then and there. But he knew some things came first. He pulled back to tell her how much he loved her. But before he could, she began talking, nearly nonstop.

"I'm sorry, Zeke. I should have been more supportive of you like I wanted you to be supportive of me. And you were right, I do have a problem, but I promise to work on it and—"

He leaned down and kissed her again to shut her up. When he pulled his mouth away, this time he handed her the flowers. "These are for you."

She looked at them when he placed them in her hands and for a moment he thought she was going to start crying. When she glanced up at him, he saw tears sparkling in her eyes. "You brought me more flowers after how mean I was to you on the phone?"

"I know you were upset, but your being upset was not going to keep me away, Sheila."

She swiped at a tear. "I'm glad you think that way. I thought your plane had gotten delayed. How did you get here so fast?"

"I called my dad and asked a favor. I needed to get here for you, so I swallowed my pride and asked my father if I could borrow his jet and its crew to get me here ASAP."

He knew the moment the magnitude of what he'd said registered within Sheila's brain. The man who had never asked his father for anything had asked him for a favor because of her.

"Oh, Zeke. I love you so much," she said as fresh tears appeared in her eyes.

He held her gaze. "Do you love me enough to wear my last name, have my babies and spend the rest of your life with me?"

She nodded as she swiped at her tears. "Yes."

It was then and there, in the parking lot of the TCC, he dropped down on his knee and proposed. "In that case, Sheila Hopkins, will you marry me?"

"Yes. Yes!"

"Good." He then slid a beautiful ring on her finger.

Sheila's mouth almost dropped. It was such a gorgeous ring. She stared at it and then at him. "But... how?"

He chuckled. "Another favor of my dad. He had his personal jeweler bring samples on the plane he sent for me."

Sheila blinked. "You father did all that?"

"Yep. The plane, the jeweler and a travel agent on board."

She lifted a brow. "A travel agent?"

Zeke smiled as he stood and reached into his pocket and pulled out an envelope. "Yes, I have plane tickets inside. We'll marry within a week and then take off for a two-week honeymoon in Aspen over the Thanksgiving holidays. I refuse to spend another holiday single. Since neither of us knows how to ski, Aspen will be great— we'll want to spend more time inside our cabin instead of out of it. I think it's time we start working on that baby we both want."

Sheila's heart began to swell with even more love.

He'd said she was his temptation, but for her, he would always be her hero. Her joy.

"Come on," he said, tucking her hand firmly in his. "Let's go home and plan our wedding...among other things. And before you ask, we're taking my car. We'll come back for yours later."

Clutching her flowers in her other hand, she walked beside him as she smiled at him. "You think of everything."

He chuckled as he tightened her hand in his. "For you I will always try, sweetheart."

And as he led her toward his car, she knew within her heart that he would. He was living proof that dreams did come true.

Epilogue

JUST AS ZEKE had wanted, they had gotten married in a
week. With Summer's help she was able to pull it off and
had used the TCC's clubhouse. It was a small wedding
with just family and friends. Brad had been Zeke's best
man and Summer had been her maid of honor. And her
new friend, Abigail Langley, had helped her pick out
her dress. It was a beautiful above-the-knee eggshell-
colored lace dress. And from the way Zeke had looked
at her when she'd walked down the aisle, she could tell
he had liked how she looked in it.

As nothing in Royal could ever be kept quiet, there
had been mention of the wedding and small reception
to be held at the TCC in the local papers. The story had
been picked up by the national news wires as a follow-up
to the stories about Zeke's heroics in the Miguel Rivera
arrest.

Apparently, news of the wedding had reached as far as Houston and Atlanta.

Cassie had arrived with her short Texan in tow, and Sheila could tell she was trying real hard to hook him in as husband number six. Even Lois had surprised her by showing up with her family. It seemed Ted intended to take advantage of the fact Zeke was now his brother-in-law.

Then there were the Traverses. Lois's mouth dropped when she found out Zeke was one of "those" Travers. But she was smart enough not to ask Sheila for any favors. Sunnie was there dressed in a pretty, pink ruffled dress and it was quite obvious that Brad was quite taken with his niece. Sheila was Sunnie's godmother and Zeke was her godfather.

"I can't get over how much you and your siblings look alike," she whispered to Zeke, glancing around. "And your father is a handsome man, as well."

Zeke threw his head back and laughed. "I'll make sure to tell him you think so."

He glanced across the room and saw Brad talking to Abigail. They sure seem a lot friendlier these days, and he wondered if the truce would last when the election for president of the TCC started back up again. But for now they seemed seen to have forgotten they were opponents.

He glanced back at his wife, knowing he was a very lucky man. And they had decided to start working on a family right away. And he was looking forward to making it happen. "We'll be leaving in a little while. You ready?"

"Yes." Sheila smiled as she glanced over at Sunnie,

who was getting a lot of attention from everyone. She appreciated the time she had spent with the baby.

"What are you smiling about?" Zeke leaned down to ask her.

Sheila glanced back at her husband. "You, this whole day, our honeymoon, the rest of our lives together...the list is endless, need I go on?"

Zeke shook his head. "No need. I know how you feel because I feel the same way."

And he meant it. She was everything he'd ever wanted in a woman. She would be his lover, his best friend and his confidante. The woman who was and always would be his temptation was now his wife. And he would love and cherish her forever.

* * * * *

SPONTANEOUS

To my husband, the love of my life and my best friend,
Gerald Jackson, Sr.

To everyone who enjoys reading a Brenda Jackson novel,
this one is for you!

Happy is the man that findeth wisdom,
and the man that getteth understanding.
—*Proverbs* 3:13

CHAPTER ONE

MY BROTHER HAS hit gold.

That thought ran through Duan Jeffries's mind while he stood on the sidelines and watched Terrence "Holy Terror" Jeffries escort his bride, Sherri Griffin Jeffries, around the huge ballroom as they thanked the numerous guests for attending their wedding.

From the moment Duan had met Sherri, he'd known she was the one woman who could make his younger brother happy. Just being in their presence was to feel the love radiating between them. And even though he was a downright cynical bastard when it came to the notion of true love, the two of them had made him somewhat of a believer.

The same held true for his sister, Olivia, and the man she'd married last year, Senator Reggie Westmoreland. That was definitely another love match. So okay, two cases weren't bad. He shifted his glance across the room to his father and the woman by his side and chuckled inwardly. All right, he would make that three cases. His father had finally married his devoted administrative assistant a few months back. Duan didn't know any man who deserved the love of a good woman more than Orin Jeffries, especially after all the hell the mother of his three offspring put him through.

Not wanting to think about the woman who'd given birth to him, the same one who'd deserted her husband and three children when Duan was twelve, Terrence ten and Libby three, he glanced at his watch, feeling tired and edgy. He had arrived in Chicago yesterday and come straight from the airport to the church, just in time to make the rehearsal dinner.

A private investigator, for the past three months he'd been working practically around the clock trying to gather enough evidence to hand over to an attorney friend who was convinced a man he was representing had been wrongfully accused of murder. It had been a hard case to crack and even harder to deliver the news that it was the man's wife who'd set him up. With the evidence needed to clear the man of all charges, Duan had taken off from Atlanta on a direct flight to Chicago.

He glanced at his watch. He had another hour or so before the wedded couple headed for O'Hare and a two-week honeymoon in Paris. After they departed he would go up to his hotel room, get out of his tux and change into something more comfortable and...

Do what?

He didn't have any immediate plans. Word had gotten around that some of Reggie's brothers and cousins were hosting a card game later tonight in one of their rooms. He wasn't surprised. He had known most of the Westmorelands from his high-school years in Atlanta and had rekindled friendships with them since Reggie had married Libby. The one thing he knew about them was that they liked to gamble, and their game of choice was poker.

Duan decided to pass after remembering what happened the last time he'd played with them. When the game ended he'd been three hundred dollars poorer.

If not poker, then what else was there to do?

He shifted his gaze to the woman standing across the room talking to the bride's parents. Immediately, he felt a primitive thrumming heat run through him. Kimani Cannon. He would definitely love to *do* her.

She was the best friend of the bride and he had been attracted to her from the first moment they'd been introduced a few months ago at Terrence and Sherri's engagement party in the Keys. He had immediately picked up on the strong sexual chemistry flowing between them, and the look Kimani had given him promised that they would hook up later to wear out somebody's sheets. But before they could make that happen, he'd received an important tip on a case he was working and had to leave.

She was definitely nice to look at with her dark, sultry eyes, a cute pixie nose and full and shapely lips. He particularly liked the mass of dark brown spiral curls that crowned her creamy cocoa-colored face.

She was downright sexy from the top of her head past those shapely curves and gorgeous legs to the soles of her feet. And speaking of feet, he had a weakness when it came to women in high heels, especially if they had the legs for them, which she did. And the strapless satin baby-blue maid-of-honor dress that hit below the knees looked damn good on her, but he'd much prefer seeing her naked. He wanted to find out if his dreams came close to the real thing.

He took a sip of his drink and continued to watch her. Lust after her was more like it. And it wasn't helping matters when all kind of wicked fantasies danced around in his head. He could envision doing something hot, naughty and X-rated with her—like locking himself between her legs and staying there until there wasn't anything left to give or take.

His fingers tightened on the stem of the wineglass, not sure what part of her he enjoyed staring at the most, and quickly decided he liked everything about her. Even from across the room she stirred his blood, fired his senses and made him think about hot sex under silken sheets.

He dragged in a deep breath and reached up to loosen his tie, which suddenly felt tight. Hell, even his briefs were restricting. And the rumble deep in his gut, trickling down toward his groin, could only mean one thing. After a six-month abstinence, he needed to get laid. And he wondered if the woman across the room would in any way be accommodating.

No sooner had that thought worked its way into his mind then she glanced over in his direction. Their gazes locked and the chemistry flowing between them thickened, stirred and escalated. Heat shimmered in the air and then she broke eye contact with him. Placing her wineglass on the tray of a passing waiter, she headed out of the ballroom. He watched, mesmerized by the sway of her hips and those gorgeous legs in high heels.

Suddenly, he felt his feet moving to follow her.

KIM RELEASED A DEEP breath as she walked down the hall that led to the room the bridesmaids had used earlier to dress in. She heard footsteps behind her and didn't have to turn around to know the identity of the person following her.

Duan Jeffries.

There was something about him that made her immediately think of sex, sex and plenty more sex. In that brief moment they'd made eye contact in the ballroom, she had detected the raw hunger within him, a need that was both possessive and magnetic, and it had drawn her to him, filled her with a desire to take him on right now.

Due to budget cuts at the hospital where she worked as an E.R. nurse, she hadn't had much of a social life lately. Seeing Duan made her realize just how much she longed for some skin-to-skin contact. Licking him from head to toe would be a good start, but she figured they wouldn't have enough time for that. A quickie would have to do.

She'd known the instant she met him four months ago that they would eventually get together. The vibes had been strong and she was disappointed when he'd left the Keys unexpectedly. The only reason she hadn't initiated jumping his bones after the rehearsal dinner last night was because she and Sherri had planned to hang out with her cousins one last time in Sherri's hotel room.

A shiver of anticipation flowed through her body when she came to a stop in front of the room. Without looking over her shoulder, she turned the knob, pushed opened the door and stepped inside.

It was only when she heard the sound of the door closing and the lock clicking in place behind her that she turned to stare up into what had to be the most gorgeous dark eyes any man could possess. And then there were the perfect angles, seamless planes and sensuous lines that made up an impressive and sinfully handsome face.

He took a step closer and she sucked in a quick breath when she felt his erection poke into her belly. She wasn't sure who made the first move after that. It wasn't really important. All that mattered was the mouth that swooped down, taking hers with a hunger that she reciprocated.

When she met his tongue with her own, he deepened the kiss and then it was on. Something frantic broke within her, within them, and a need as raw as it could get took over.

She felt his hand lifting her dress. The sound of silk rustling against silk inflamed her mind, and when those same hands made contact with the apex of her thighs, not even her panties were a barrier against the busy fingers that sought and found an easy opening.

And then those fingers were moving through the curls, beyond the folds, stirring her wetness and massaging her clit. She moaned at the invasion as well as the pleasure, and instinctively reached for his fly and eased down the zipper. Quickly inserting her hand beneath the elastic waistband of his briefs, she gripped the engorged hardness of his sex. He pulled his mouth from hers and released a guttural groan, and the primitive sound was something she understood and identified with.

"Condom." He said that one word in a ragged breath and she relinquished her hold on him so he could fish into the pockets of his pants for his wallet. He pulled out a square packet.

She shifted her gaze from the condom to his erection, jutting proudly from a dark thatch of curls. The head of his shaft was big and smooth, and the veins running along the sides were thick.

Heat burning in every part of her body, she watched as he sheathed himself with such ease and accuracy that she figured he'd done this numerous times. When that task was completed, he glanced up and the eyes that stared at her nearly scorched her skin and made her regret they only had time for a quickie. Leisurely savoring every inch of him was something she would just love doing. But for now she would take what she could get. Leaning up on tiptoe, she pressed her moist lips against his.

His mouth immediately captured hers, kissing her hungrily, and she felt him tug her dress up. She had a feeling this mating would be a quickie like nothing she'd ever experienced.

He lifted her, cupping her hips in his hands, and she instinctively wrapped her legs around him. Like radar his engorged sex found its mark and he pushed forward, sliding between her wet folds. The size of him stretched her, filled her to capacity. And it seemed his erection got larger as he delved deeper and deeper…pressing her back against the wall.

He paused, as if he wanted to experience the feeling of being embedded within her, and in protest her inner muscles clamped down hard on him, then let go, repeating the process a few times. He snatched his mouth from hers, threw his head back and released a massive growl.

To her satisfaction he began moving, pounding in and out of her in a rhythm that matched the beat of her heart. She hoped and prayed the room on the other side of the wall was empty. She would hate for anyone to want to investigate what all the noise was about.

She felt his every thrust all the way to her toes—toes that were curled around his waist at that very moment. His erection was throbbing inside her with the intensity of a volcano about to erupt.

He leaned down and imprisoned her mouth again, kissing her hungrily. Was there anything this man couldn't do perfectly? She moaned and worked her body against his, meeting him stroke for stroke, thrust for thrust.

She pulled back from the kiss, needing to see him, to look into his face, to know he was feeling the same things she was. Pure feminine satisfaction poured through her at the intense look on his features that told her he was. And if that didn't convince her, then his thrusts did. They were powerful, each one an accurate hit, centering on her G-spot with clear-cut precision and a mastery that had her panting. And still he thrust deeper, pounded harder.

And then she felt it, the first signs of the explosive tension building inside her and inside him, as well. His muscular thighs began quivering with an intensity that she felt through his tuxedo pants. And then he let out a deep moan followed by a release that triggered her own eruption, and he clamped his mouth on hers to quell her scream.

Their tongues tangled once again and she was devoured by his greedy mouth. Giving in to pent-up passion and bridled lust, she wrapped her arms around him as he continued to rock into her, as if taking her this way was his due. His every right.

And at that moment, it was.

Duan SHOVED HIS SHIRT into his pants as he glanced over at Kimani. She was smoothing her dress over those luscious curves. The woman was something else, and even now, while aftershocks of his orgasm were still flitting through his system, his body was aching for more. What was it about her that made him into one greedy ass where her body was concerned?

He breathed in deeply. The scent of sex mingled with the perfume she was wearing had to be filling her nostrils the way it was his. He liked the aroma. When she reached up and ran fingers through her curls to bring order back to her hair, he thought she looked simply beautiful.

He shook his head. He'd just made out with the maid of honor at his brother's wedding. Hell, they were right down the hall from the reception.

"We need to move quickly if we want to be there when Terrence and Sherri leave," she said, slipping into the shoes she had discarded earlier. Those high heels he liked so much.

He knew it was a stupid thought, but the only place he could imagine being at the moment was right here with her. "And just what will happen if we're not there?" he asked.

She glanced up at him with that *duh* look. "Everyone will wonder where we are. Have you forgotten that you're the best man and I'm the maid of honor?"

He wished he could forget if it meant another round with her. This was not a good time to tell her they'd probably already been missed. There might not be anyone keeping tabs on her, but he was certain Libby would have noticed his disappearing act by now. When it came to him and Terrence, his sister didn't miss a thing. Getting married hadn't changed that about her.

"You look nice in your tux, by the way."

He met her gaze and couldn't help but smile. He thought she had a pair of gorgeous eyes. "And you look good in your dress. But can I be honest with you about something?"

"Yes."

"I really wanted to see you naked."

He waited, fully expecting her to say something like this had been one of those done deals and there wouldn't be a next time so he could chalk it up as a missed opportunity. Instead, she strolled over to him, reached up to straighten his tie, then stood on tiptoe and leaned closer to whisper, "That can be arranged. I'm in Room 822."

She then slipped out of his reach, and after tossing a saucy smile over her shoulder, she unlocked the door and walked out.

KIM HEARD HER NAME being called the moment she re-entered the ballroom. She glanced over and saw Sherri heading toward her. She was so excited for her best friend and truly believed she and Terrence would be happy together.

"And just where did you slip off to?" Sherri was asking. "I've been looking for you."

Kim threw her head back and laughed. "You mean your husband finally let you out of his sight? Unbelievable."

She and Sherri shared a smile and then Sherri said, "Yes, but only for a minute." Her expression turned serious. "Promise me that you're going to celebrate your good news."

Kim thought about the official letter she had received a couple of days ago. The one informing her she'd been accepted into medical school. "I promise that I will celebrate."

She'd always wanted to become a doctor, but her parents had split in her senior year of high school, which made money tight. Out of spite, her poor excuse for a father had emptied the savings account her mom had set up to defray the cost of college. As a result Kim had to resort to student loans and eventually had to settle on a master's degree in nursing.

She found being a nurse rewarding and was dedicated to the profession, but now it was time to move on and pursue her dream to become a doctor.

Her gaze shifted from Sherri as she caught sight of Duan across the room. Just like she'd told him earlier, he looked good in his tux. On some men a tuxedo looked only so-so, but on Duan it was spine-tingling sexy. Definitely eye candy of the sweetest kind. As if he felt her watching him, he glanced over at her and she tilted her head and smiled.

Sherri noticed the exchange and lifted a brow. "Now, isn't that strange?"

Kim broke eye contact with Duan and turned back to Sherri. "What is?"

"Terrence was searching for Duan at the same time I was looking for you. Imagine that."

Kim shrugged, trying to keep a straight face. "Yes, imagine that."

"You know what I think?" Sherri was grinning.

"Haven't a clue."

Her friend gave her an assessing glance. "I think you've started celebrating already."

DUAN STOOD OFF to the side and watched the newlyweds leave amidst a shower of rice and well-wishes. He took a long drink of his champagne and kept his gaze on Kim, while at the same time pretending interest in the conversations going on around him.

He had already turned down an invitation from Lucas McCoy and Stephen Morales, Terrence's close friends from his college days, to join them and their wives for a night out on the town. And as predicted, the Westmorelands were hosting a poker game in one of their suites.

"You sure you don't want to join us later, Duan?" Stone Westmoreland asked. Duan and Stone had been in the same softball league while growing up and had played football together in high school.

"I'm positive," he said, noting the exact moment Kim began walking toward an exit door. "I had a rough week and need to get to bed early."

Most of what he said was true. No one needed to know that the bed he would be getting into wasn't his.

He exchanged conversation with Stone and the other

Westmorelands for a few minutes and then bid everyone a farewell and a safe return home. Like him, most
of them would be checking out of the hotel sometime
tomorrow. Placing his empty champagne glass on a
table, he picked up his pace as he headed toward the
elevators.

KIM GLANCED AROUND her hotel room and saw the bottle
of champagne Sherri had ordered earlier sitting in a
bucket of ice. She hadn't told anyone but Sherri about
her acceptance into medical school at the University of
California, San Francisco.

She had a couple months to accept their offer. She
had applied to three other universities and would wait
to hear from them before making a decision.

She smiled as she kicked off her shoes. She was very
much aware that Duan had been watching her when
she'd left the reception, which meant he was probably
on his way up. The quickie earlier had relieved some
of the sexual tension between them but not all of it.
She had issued the invitation to complete what they'd
started, so she had no problem with him taking her up
on it.

She liked him, and after what happened earlier, she
liked him even more. Even with a limited amount of
time he hadn't been a selfish lover. She couldn't say
the same for the last guy she'd dated, a surgeon at the
hospital. He'd left a lot to be desired.

Kim walked over to the window to take in the view
of Lake Michigan. Several small fishing vessels were
out on the lake, as well as a number of other boats in
various sizes. It was so beautiful she could just stand

there a while and watch. Her mother had planned to come to the wedding with her, but had called two days ago and said something had come up and she wouldn't be able to make it. She would have enjoyed being here.

At the thought of her mother, Kim shook her head. She'd been forced to tell a lie to her mom and Aunt Gertrude. She loved the two women to death and they meant well, but recently Aunt Gert had submitted Kim's name to the producers of the reality show *How to Find a Good Man*. That was a bit too much. And when Aunt Gert's essay had won and Kim had been selected as a contestant, she'd come up with the only plausible reason to turn down what her mother and aunt thought was a golden opportunity. Kim had convinced them she'd found a good man on her own.

She turned at the sound of the knock on the door. In a way she had found one, at least for this weekend. A sense of heated anticipation gripped her and she inhaled deeply, more than ready to enjoy another round of hot, heavy and mind-blowing sex.

And this time there wouldn't be any time restraints.

KIM OPENED THE DOOR and immediately heat began stirring through every part of her body. She took a step back when he entered the room.

"Would you like a drink, Duan?"

The smooth smile that formed on his lips made Kim's nipples harden.

"No, thank you," he said, stepping closer.

"In that case..."

She reached up and placed her arms around his neck, going straight for his mouth. In response, turbulent emotions consumed her and made her deepen the kiss at the same time he did.

She felt him moving, walking her backward, and when the bed hit her legs she pulled away to break from the kiss. Kim glanced up at him and saw the taut lines of his jaw and the moist sheen of his lips. And then she felt his hand working its way to her back to ease down her zipper. He tugged her dress down her body, right along with her bra. The man knew what he was after. He'd said he wanted to see her naked and wasn't wasting any time getting her that way.

He then proceeded to use both hands to cop a feel of her bare breasts. The moment the pad of his thumbs came in contact with the budded nipples, she felt the crotch of her panties get wet.

His gaze caught hers just moments before he leaned forward and captured a nipple between his lips, savoring it as if it were the best thing he'd ever tasted. He sucked aggressively. Licked profusely. Hard. Hungrily. Moments later he switched to the other breast.

When Kim thought she couldn't handle any more, she felt herself being lowered to the bed, felt the mattress and thick bedcovers beneath her back. He threw his leg over her middle and she moaned at the feel of the material of his pants rubbing against her inner thigh. When she was totally convinced his mouth was about to push her over the edge he released her nipple, lifted his head and met her gaze.

"You have nice breasts," he said in a deep, husky voice.

"Glad to know you like them," she responded, reaching up and brushing her fingers against the length of his jaw.

Someone once said you could tell the strength of a man by his jawbone. If that was the case then Duan Jeffries was the equivalent of Samson. He certainly had a lot of sex appeal.

"We need to get you out of the rest of your clothes," he said, slowly sliding his hands down her body and then back up again, letting his fingertips gently caress her skin, sending heated bliss wherever he stroked.

Kim's pulse rate increased and she dragged air into her lungs as the feel of his touch tormented her flesh. She eased herself up in the bed and he moved to give her room while she removed her stockings, tossing the items aside. She was completely naked except for her panties. And when she leaned back on her elbows and lifted her hips off the bed with a bold unmistaken invitation in her eyes, he reached out and slid her panties down her thighs and legs.

Duan pulled in a deep heated breath as he let his gaze roam over Kim's naked form. Something within him had driven his desire to see her this way and he was not disappointed.

Before he realized what she was doing, she had eased off the bed to kneel in front of him and was sliding down his zipper. She then tugged down his pants and briefs and he stepped out of them. Tossing the pieces of clothing out of the way, she leaned back on her haunches and tilted her head to look up him and smile. "I wanted to do this earlier but time wouldn't allow it."

He pulled in a deep breath when her tongue began licking him from top to bottom and front to back. She then opened her mouth and greedily slid him inside, letting her tongue wrap around his head and then the length of his entire manhood.

His breath caught and he wondered if he would ever be able to breathe again. The sensations were so powerful he could have died right then and there. He'd been given head before, but never with such bold deliberation. And there was a sweetness to her lips that even extended to this.

He threw his head back and growled as she worked her mouth and tongue over his rod. The sight of her on her knees with him fully planted inside her mouth, bobbing her head up and down while her hands played gently with his balls, had his erection throbbing to an almost explosive state. He reached down and grabbed hold of a fistful of her hair to hold her mouth still when the unbearable pleasure intensified. Every cell in his body seemed electrified.

His nerve endings were stretched to the limit and the sensations firing through him shuddered deep in his gut.

When he felt himself almost pushed over the edge, he grabbed her chin and pulled his rod out of her mouth. Ignoring her whimper of disappointment, he lifted her into his arms and quickly crossed back to the bed and placed her on it. He came down with her, and before she could straighten her body, he was there pushing her backward. His hands grabbed hold of her hips and his head went between her legs. Now it was time for his tongue to pleasure her.

His fingers parted her folds, and the moment his tongue slid inside her and he was introduced to her taste, a rush of new sensations surged through him, made him clasp her hips tighter to bring her closer to his mouth. His tongue moved frantically inside her and he knew the exact moment he found what he was seeking.

"Duan!"

He withdrew his tongue and let the tip play with her clit. His lips then came together and greedily devoured it. He had to hold her down with his hands when she began moving frantically beneath his mouth as he savored her unique taste of honey.

She shuddered just seconds before she screamed. It was only after the last spasm passed through her body that he loosened his hold on her and pulled back to retrieve a condom from his wallet.

He sheathed himself and moved back toward the bed to find her still stretched out in that same position, as inviting as any woman could be.

That pose made him ease onto the mattress on all fours, like a lion capturing his prey, and when he had straddled her, effectively pinning her beneath him, he met her gaze. He leaned in and captured her mouth at the same moment that he slid inside her, not stopping until he was buried deep.

And then he began making love to her, deciding there would be nothing quick in their mating this time around.

CHAPTER TWO

DUAN OPENED HIS EYES and squinted against the bright sunlight flowing in through the hotel-room window. It was at that moment he felt the soft feminine naked body resting against him, his front spooning her backside.

A shiver of pleasure flowed through him when he remembered everything that had happened—all he'd done over the past fourteen-plus hours. And he wasn't feeling one moment of regret. In fact, he felt electrified in a way he'd never felt before. Kim had satisfied a fierce need inside him. Making love to her had been everything he'd wanted, and more.

She had met him on every level and together they had shared climax after magnificent climax. But for some reason what they'd shared was a lot more than sex. She had managed to tap into a Duan Jeffries few people saw. The one who longed not to be so disciplined. The one who didn't necessarily want to be a good guy *all* the time.

Growing up he'd had no choice. He was the oldest and was expected to set a good example for Terrence and Olivia. His mother had caused his father enough scandal, and Orin Jeffries hadn't needed his oldest son to follow in his wife's footsteps. So he had done everything right. He had gotten the best grades in school and had gone into law enforcement after college to keep the bad guys off the street. In a way his occupation as a private investigator was still doing that. He enjoyed his work. He loved preserving the peace and making sure those who broke the law were put behind bars.

But still...

It had been fun slipping off in the middle of his brother's wedding reception for a quickie. And if that hadn't been shameful enough, before Terrence and Sherri could make it to the airport for their honeymoon, he had come up to Kim's room, driven with a desire to see her naked and to engage in more sex. Shameful to some but total pleasure for him.

He was simply enthralled and could only wonder what there was about Kim that made him respond to her with a spontaneity that he found disconcerting as well as fascinating. What was there about her that dared him to become a risk taker?

His thoughts were interrupted when she shifted in sleep, snuggling her luscious backside even closer to him. Already his rod was awake, and the damn greedy bastard was stretching. It obviously liked the feel of Kim's bare bottom pressed against it.

He suppressed the urge. For some reason he didn't want to do anything more than just lie there and hold her, share the essence of her heat.

When he draped his arms across her middle she snuggled closer into him. He liked the feel of having her there, and with that thought firmly planted in his mind, he closed his eyes and joined her in sleep.

"WHAT TIME DO YOU plan to check out today, Kim?"

Kim looked up from her breakfast plate. They had

awakened a short while ago, and after taking a shower they'd ordered room service for breakfast. Now, wearing the complimentary bath robes provided by the hotel, they were eating in bed.

"I asked for a late checkout," she replied. "That means I won't be leaving before two. What about you?"

"I asked for a late checkout, as well. My plane doesn't fly out until five and that will give me plenty of time to get to O'Hare."

"I don't fly out until six. Want to share a taxi to the airport?" she asked, taking a sip of coffee.

His smile sent a warm feeling all through her in a way even the coffee hadn't done. "Yes, that will work."

She resumed eating. She would be returning to the Keys and he to his home in Atlanta. Although they both lived in the southeastern part of the country, a long-distance affair was out of the question. She'd tried it once, only to discover the man had been living a double life with girlfriends on both the east and the west coast.

"I appreciated yesterday and last night, Kim."

She glanced over at him and the corners of her lips eased up. Duan could definitely make her smile, among other things. She considered what he'd just said and wondered how many men actually thanked a woman for sex.

She chuckled. "You're a man who probably appreciates a willing woman. And I was definitely willing." She pushed her plate aside and propped herself against a pillow. "You didn't even have to hit me with any good lines. I saved you the trouble, but it was well worth it."

Over the rim of her coffee cup, she studied him lounging in bed with his robe on. Like her he was naked underneath. He had to be the most sexually compelling man she'd ever met. During their shower they had done a number of scandalous things and she could feel her pulse speed up just thinking about it.

"So tell me something about Duan Jeffries that I may not know," she prompted.

A grin touched his lips. "Is that a prerequisite to sharing a cab ride with you?"

"I could make it one." She smiled. "You never know who you can trust these days."

He laughed. "And you can say that after the past fourteen-plus hours we've shared together?"

"Sure, why not? So tell me."

He took another sip of his coffee. "You tell me what you think you already know."

She scrunched up her face as if she were thinking real hard and Duan couldn't help but chuckle. "Hey, I'm not that complicated."

"Didn't say you were, so let's not get testy," she replied.

She tapped her chin a couple of times. "I know you're thirty-six—used to be a cop and then got promoted to detective. Now you own a P.I. firm with four other guys. You've never been married and as far as anyone knows, you don't have any children. And you date on those rare occasions you're not swarming the country doing investigative work."

"I see my sister's been talking."

Kim shrugged. "What makes you think it was Olivia?"

"Because Terrence knows better. A brother's creed. He won't tell my secrets and I won't tell his."

Kim leaned forward, her brow arched. "Terrence has secrets?"

Amusement flitted in Duan's eyes. "None that Sherri needs to be concerned about, if that's why you're asking. They're all in the past. The Holy Terror is now a changed man."

"So tell me your secrets, Duan. The good, the bad and the ugly."

He smiled. "Um, the good is that I volunteer my time with the boys' club whenever I can." He paused a moment. "The bad is that I have a low tolerance for those who break the law and then, because of some damn loophole in the legal system, get away with it."

Kim heard the anger in his voice. "Is there a particular case that rubbed you the wrong way?"

There was no amusement in his eyes now. "There have been several, but the one that sticks out in my mind is a case I worked involving a woman who was kidnapped, raped and left for dead. We had all the evidence we needed. It should have been open and shut."

"But it wasn't?"

"No. One of our officers obtained evidence without a search warrant."

Kim pulled back, afraid to ask. "They dropped the charges?"

"No, but he was sentenced on a lesser charge."

Kim could understand his frustration. As a nurse she had no tolerance for red tape. She'd seen people who needed to receive treatment denied the care because of administrative issues. That was one of the reasons she transferred to the emergency room. Less red tape.

"More coffee?"

His question pulled her out of her thoughts and she smiled. "No, thanks, I'm good." She stared at him for a moment. "You've told me the good and the bad, so what's the ugly?"

Duan studied his nearly empty cup. Now that was an area he didn't want to cover with her or anyone else. The ugliness in his life was his inability to forgive the person who'd given birth to him. God knew, he'd tried. And he'd gone so far as to search for her as a grown man of thirty, to let her know he'd forgiven her for what she'd done and to find closure for himself.

What he'd found instead was a woman who didn't deserve his forgiveness. Or Terrence's or Libby's. And definitely not the forgiveness of the man who'd loved her.

"That's a discussion for another day," he said, getting off the bed and reaching for the coffeepot. He refilled his cup and glanced over at Kim. "So what about you? What's the good, the bad and the ugly?"

She smiled. "That's easy to answer and I prefer going from last to first."

He tipped his cup at her. "Go ahead."

"The ugly is my father, the wife beater and drunk. I always wanted to become a doctor and he knew it, especially since I was the one who had to heal the bruises Mom got at his hands. For years she worked extra hours to save money to make my dream come true, only for my father to take it out of their bank account when it was time for me to go to college."

She paused a minute. "The bad is that I'll probably never marry because most men see me as too strong-willed. I intimidate the doctors at the hospital, and when it comes to guys outside the hospital, they claim I'm too outspoken. People, mostly men, don't understand me."

Duan figured he must like strong-willed women because he definitely liked her. He would even say he liked outspoken women. And he certainly felt he understood her. She was a woman who didn't mind going after what she wanted. Yesterday, last night and this morning, she had wanted him. He had no complaints.

"What's the good?" he asked.

Her face brightened when she glanced over at the bottle of unopened champagne. "That," she said, pointing to the ice bucket. "I have my own celebrating to do. That's the good."

"What are you celebrating?"

He could swear he saw her chest stick out with pride when she said, "My admission into med school. It took me long enough but I'm going to finally do it."

"Congratulations. What school?" he asked, truly interested.

"University of California, San Francisco." Excitement tinged her voice. "I applied to three others so there's no telling where I might end up if I'm accepted by them, as well. But it doesn't matter really. My dream's finally coming true and I've waited a long time for it."

She was thoughtful a moment. "I'm going to miss being a nurse. I've enjoyed it tremendously, but I feel I have so much more to offer as a doctor."

A huge smile lit his face and he set his cup aside and went back to the bed. Reaching out, he took her hands in his. "I'm happy for you and this does call for a celebration," he said, placing a kiss on her knuckles.

He released her hand and headed for the bucket of champagne. "I usually don't indulge in a drink this early, but it's for a very special occasion." A few moments later he popped the cork and poured some of the bubbly into two flutes.

Kim realized he was genuinely happy for her and it wasn't just a put-on. A conversation she'd once had with Olivia came back to her. His sister told her it had always been Duan's dream to one day own his own P.I. company, but that after college he'd joined the Atlanta police force. However, he'd never lost sight of his dream and a few years ago had started his own P.I. firm.

As Kim watched him cross the room with their champagne, she figured he knew all about following one's dreams. "Thanks," she said, taking the glass he offered.

He smiled down at her and held up his own glass. "I propose a toast to the future Dr. Kimani Cannon."

Kim couldn't help but beam with both pride and excitement as she touched her glass to his and took a sip, enjoying the sparkling taste as it flowed down her throat.

Duan eased onto the bed beside her and relieved her of her glass, setting it on the nightstand. "Now for some real celebrating," he said, still holding his glass with one hand while untying the belt at her waist with the other. She wet her lips as she watched him open her robe, revealing her nakedness.

And then with his fingertips he reached up and slowly traced a trail from the base of her throat to her breasts, downward to her navel and lower still to the curls between her thighs.

"So what do you say about us really getting down-right festive?" he suggested. And before she figured out what he was about to do, he tilted his glass until champagne splashed on her.

She drew in a sharp breath as the cool liquid contacted her skin. A shiver went through her when it followed the same trail from her breasts downward.

"Oops, sorry, I'm rather clumsy," he said, placing his glass beside hers on the nightstand. "I guess I'm going to have to lick it off you."

And he proceeded to do just that.

KIM'S CELL PHONE RANG the moment she was settled in the backseat of the taxi. She flipped open her phone and smiled after seeing the caller. "Yes, Mom, how are you? You missed a great wedding."

She glanced over at Duan. He was sitting beside her, leaning back against the seat. He had his hand on her thigh and was staring at her with a look that said it wouldn't take much for him to push her down and have his way with her.

She understood. From the moment they'd sneaked out of the wedding reception to make out in that room, something crazy had happened between them. It was like an addiction. One that would hit them with the urge to have sex whenever, wherever and however. The only reason they were controlling themselves now was because they didn't want to scandalize the cab driver. And there was also the risk of getting arrested.

Kim shook her head. This was crazy. Nothing like

this had ever happened to her before. It was as if their bodies were acting on impulse without any logical thought. That would explain why two adults had made out in an elevator on the way down to catch their cab.

Sex between them was off the charts, the best she'd ever had. Every orgasm—and there had been plenty— had proven better than the one before. And she appreciated the fact that Duan was such a skillful lover. The past twenty-four hours had been the most pleasure-producing—and memorable—she'd ever had.

"I'm fine, baby, and I hate that I missed the wedding," her mother was saying, pulling Kim's attention back to the conversation but not fully away from Duan. She could feel sensations stirring in her belly at his nearness, at the way he was looking at her with all that heat.

"I'll give Sherri a call once she returns from her honeymoon," her mother added. "But now I'm ready to tell you why I wasn't able to join you in Chicago."

"All right." Kim tried to focus completely on the conversation with her mother…at least as much as she could.

Each time she glanced over at Duan she would get aroused. With him she'd gained a boldness that was new to her. To make out with a man in an empty room during her best friend's wedding reception was certainly over the top.

She forced her attention back to her mother. When she had called a few days ago she had been pretty secretive about the reason she could not make the wedding. After convincing Kim that she was fine, Wynona Cannon-Longleaf-Higgins-Gunter had assured her daughter she would tell her everything later.

The last time her mother had behaved in such a manner there had been a man involved. Kim didn't begrudge her mother meeting someone and being happy. At fifty-five Wynona was still attractive, although it had taken Kim a long time to make her mother believe that. Her abusive father had convinced his wife that if she left him, no other man would want her, and where would she be without a man taking care of her.

Unfortunately, Wynona had remained with her husband, taking his abuse, both physically and mentally. Kim would never forget how in her senior year of high school her mother had landed in the emergency room from one of those beatings, and it was then that Wynona had made up her mind it would be the last whipping any man would give her. She had tearfully told Kim she didn't want her daughter to assume that physical abuse was something any woman should tolerate.

While Kim was grateful her mother had finally gotten the strength to leave her dad, the only other thing Wynona needed to rid herself of was the notion that a woman needed a man to survive. That belief was the reason Kim had eventually ended up with three stepfathers. Although none were abusive like her father, the men had lacked substance, and none of the marriages had lasted more than a year or two.

When her mother didn't say anything, Kim prompted, "So, why weren't you able to make it to the wedding, Mom?"

"I've met someone," her mother said.

Kim could hear the excitement in her mother's voice and imagined the giddy smile that must be on her face. *Oh, brother,* she thought, as she leaned back against her seat. The movement brought her closer to Duan and he automatically placed his arm around her shoulder. Heat swept through her as if he'd pressed some button.

"And who did you meet?" Kim heard herself asking her mother.

"His name is Edward Villarosas and he's nice."

They all are in the beginning, Kim thought, remembering the other men her mother had married. First there was Boris Longleaf, whom Wynona had met during her prison ministries. At least he hadn't been a prisoner but one of the guards. He seemed nice enough until her mother had discovered a year into the marriage that Boris preferred men.

Then there was Albert Higgins, a maintenance man in the apartment complex her mother had moved into after her divorce from Boris. There was something about Albert that Kim hadn't trusted and her suspicions were confirmed when he'd been arrested for his part in a car-theft ring.

And last but not least was Phillip Gunter, the one who'd tried coming on to her. During all her mother's marriages Kim had been away at college and was only around the men whenever she came home for spring break or the holidays.

She'd known from the first moment she'd seen Phillip that he would be trouble, and when he tried cornering her in the laundry room, she had used the knee-jab-in-the-groin move that she'd seen on television. When her mother had rushed downstairs after hearing the man howling in pain, he'd had the audacity to tell her that Kim had been the one trying to come on to him. Of course her mother hadn't believed it and had sent him packing.

So after four failed marriages, Kim hoped her mother would eventually find someone to make her happy. But with Wynona's track record, she wasn't so sure of that happening.

"Tell me all about nice Edward," Kim said, trying to keep the sarcasm out of her voice.

"Edward and I met at the grocery store and things between us began getting serious pretty fast."

Kim rolled her eyes. "I bet."

"You're going to like him."

I doubt it. That's what you said about the others. "When can I meet him?"

"Um, when you come to the wedding in three weeks."

"What!" Kim nearly jumped out of her seat.

"Are you all right, Kim?" Duan asked, leaning close to her in concern. His heated breath against her cheek had sensations stirring within her.

She nodded quickly and whispered, "Yes, I'm fine."

"Kim, who are you with? The man you're engaged to?"

Kim rolled her eyes and shook her head. It had been nearly two months since she'd told that lie and now everyone was still waiting to meet her fiancé.

"Kim?"

Instead of addressing the issue of her fabricated fiancé, she said, "Mom, you can't get married in three weeks. What do you know about this guy?"

"I know enough to believe Edward is a good man. He's a divorcé like me and we enjoy each other's company. He asked me to marry him and I accepted. Be happy for me. I'm happy for you. You don't know how happy I was when you told me and Aunt Gert about your guy. For so long I've blamed myself for you not wanting to get married because I stayed with your father when he was so abusive to me. I know that's what turned you off marriage. I should have left him sooner."

Yes, you should have left him sooner, Kim thought. *Not for my sake but for your own.* Although she would be the first to admit she'd never wanted to marry because of the abuse she'd witnessed by her father, she didn't want her mother to feel guilty about that.

Kim pushed frustrated air out of her lungs. "Mom, please promise you won't do anything until I get there."

"And when do you plan to come? The family wants me to have another wedding, but Edward and I are tickled with the idea of just taking off and flying to Vegas and—"

"No, Mom, please not Vegas again. Haven't you learned anything?"

"Kimani Cannon, I won't allow you to take that tone with me. I didn't call to get your permission to marry Edward. I'm just letting you know about him. But if you really want to meet him, then I suggest you make time to do so."

"I think that I will, Mom."

"Fine. And don't you dare come without bringing your young man with you," Wynona said in a stern voice. "I can't wait to meet him, and like I said, the fact that you're in love has lifted a load off my heart that I've been carrying around for a long time."

"Mom, I—"

"No, sweetie, please let me finish. I know you don't understand why I keep going from man to man. Maybe I'm trying to find something I missed out on all those years I was with your daddy, letting him hit me around. I'm fine now. I like Edward. He'll be good for me. But to know that you've gotten beyond the abuse you saw in our household has been my prayer. I've been praying for a good man to come into your life and now he has. I can't wait to meet him, so don't you dare think of coming home to Shreveport without him. Goodbye, sweetie."

Her mother hung up and Kim realized she hadn't told her the good news about being accepted into med school. She sighed deeply, knowing she'd gotten herself into a sticky situation with the lie about a fiancé. Sherri had warned her it was bound to catch up with her eventually.

"Is everything all right, Kim?"

Kim glanced over at Duan. For a moment she'd forgotten he was in the taxi with her as they cruised through the streets of Chicago on their way to the airport.

She sighed deeply, and when he opened his arms she cuddled up closer to him. "Is your mother okay?" he asked, concern in his voice.

Kim chewed on her bottom lip and then said, "If you call planning wedding number five okay, then yes, she's doing just fine."

CHAPTER THREE

DUAN WASN'T SURE he'd heard her correctly. "Your mother has been married four times?"

"Yes."

He found that simply incredible since his own mother had been married that many times, as well. He shifted in his seat and Kim's body automatically moved with his. He'd done one-night stands before but none had stretched into breakfast the next morning or a cab ride to the airport the next day. When it was over, it was over. There hadn't been any exchange of business cards or promises to follow up. But he knew that he and Kim would see each other again. This weekend hadn't been enough.

"I told you a little about my father being the ugly in my life this morning and how he abused my mother. What I didn't tell you was that they split while I was in high school. I counted it as one of the happiest days of my life. He was a bully of the worse kind."

"And your mom stayed with him all those years?"

"Yes. She was always convinced he would get better. He was smart enough to move us to New Orleans, away from her family during that time. She moved back to Shreveport a few years ago to be close to her family and to take care of my grandmother, who's since died.

Now Mom wants to get her life together and believes there is a good man out there destined to be hers. So far she's had four misfits and I'm afraid this fifth might be the same."

He shook his head. It was ironic that her mother was looking for a good man when his mother had had one and hadn't been satisfied. Go figure.

"My mother's been married four times, as well," he heard himself saying.

"She has?"

"Yes." He wondered why he'd told her that. He never discussed his mother with anyone. And it was only on rare occasions that her name came up with Terrence and Olivia.

Kim was sitting close to him, practically in his lap. He felt his desire for her on the rise again and hoped the cab arrived at the airport before he was tempted to do something that could make headlines in the *Chicago Sun-Times*.

"The last I saw her," he said, "she was contemplating husband number five. But that was six years ago. She might have made it to number ten by now."

Kim gave him an odd look. "You're joking, aren't you?"

His expression was unreadable when he said, "I never joke when it comes to the woman who birthed me."

There was an edge of steel in his voice and Kim figured the subject of his mother's desertion was a sore one with him, just like her mother's obsession with finding the perfect man was with her.

The perfect man.

Such a man didn't exist. But that was her mother's dream and Kim knew all about chasing dreams. Just like she understood her mother's desire to see her only child married. Wynona thought she'd failed in both the mother and wife departments. Neither was true, but until mother and daughter were happily married, she would always believe that.

The backseat of the cab got quiet, as if Duan was allowing her time to think, and then he asked, "When is the wedding?"

She rubbed a hand down her face. "They want to marry in three weeks, which will put me in more hot water because of a lie I've told."

"What lie?"

"That I'm engaged."

At his surprised look, she said, "Okay, I'll admit that was a big one, but I had a reason for lying in this case. Mom and her sister, my aunt Gertrude, believe my exposure to my parents' relationship for all those years is the reason I'm not in what they call a *healthy relationship* with a man."

He shrugged. "That's probably true. At least I know it is for me. I'm not sure I can fully trust a woman after what my mother did to my dad. I know all women aren't the same, like I'm sure you know all men aren't the same. But still, it's understandable for anyone who's witnessed all that to want to protect their heart."

Kim nodded. What he said made sense. Her parents' marriage had influenced her way of thinking.

"But I don't want Mom to beat herself up about it and worry unnecessarily. I'm happy with my marital status, and I think Mom would ease off if it wasn't for Aunt

Gert. She's a bona fide romantic. She's also a reality TV junkie. A couple of months ago, without me knowing, she submitted my name and bio to *How to Find a Good Man*. Believe it or not, I was the one selected to go on a televised scavenger hunt to find a good man."

Duan chuckled. "You're kidding, right?"

"Trust me, I kid you not. Anyway, they wanted to surprise me, and they sure did when the film crew showed up at the hospital. The only way I could get out of it was to lie and say I'd gotten engaged after Aunt Gert had submitted my personal info."

She shook her head. "That made everyone happy and I was left alone. And to this day, no one has asked me the name of my fiancé. But just like Sherri warned, the lie has caught up with me. Now Mom wants to meet him. I can't put it off any longer."

"Just tell them the truth."

She rolled her eyes. "You don't know my family, especially Aunt Gert. I would go so far as to tell her to butt out of my business, but I know she means well, so I can't. When I go home next week I not only have to meet what could be my fourth stepfather, but also take a man with me to Shreveport as my fiancé. A fake one at least."

Duan thought it might be wise for her to just fess up and tell her family the truth. But if she didn't do that and took a man home…a part of him didn't like the thought of that for some reason. He knew what she did was her business. But still…

"You have any prospects?" he asked, looking down at her. Not for the first time he thought how gorgeous her brown eyes were. He could recall staring into them while climaxing. Several times.

She lifted an arched brow. "Prospects?"

"You know. Guys willing to play the part of your fiancé."

Kim shrugged. She immediately thought of Winslow Breaker. He was a surgeon at the hospital who'd been after her for months. The only problem was that she could just imagine what good old Winslow would expect in return. And she just wasn't feeling it with Winslow. Never had.

"Possibly," she heard herself say.

Duan cursed under his breath, wondering why he even gave a damn. Like he'd thought earlier, what she did was her business.

He noticed the huge marker that indicated the airport was less than ten miles away and knew what he wanted to do before they parted ways.

Shifting in the seat, he reached out and ran the tip of his finger down the side of her face, his gaze fastened on her lips. "Sounds like you have a plan and I'm sure things are going to work out in your favor. In the meantime—" his voice dipped a little lower, became throatier "—I appreciate being with you this weekend."

And then he lowered his mouth to hers.

DUAN HAD THOUGHT her taste was sweet before, but after thrusting his tongue between her parted lips and greedily drinking in her flavor, he realized she was the most alluring woman he'd ever had the pleasure of knowing. Definitely the tastiest.

Their tongues met, melded, mated and were stirring waves of pleasure inside him. And then there was the passion she returned wantonly and flagrantly each and every time they kissed. He would take charge of the kiss, she would follow, and then she would turn the tables and stake her control.

It was while savoring the wet heat and hunger of her sizzling passion that he yielded to full awareness of what being with her entailed. With Kim there was no sensual limit, no restricted areas and no borders to guard. There was just this—absolute surrender and a yearning for more.

"You did say you were flying out on Delta, right, mister?"

Duan released Kim's mouth and inclined his head to look at the taxi driver, who had turned around to stare at them with a silly grin on his face. Understandably so, since he and Kim had been caught in a heated kiss. And he had managed to pull her onto his lap and drape her body across his.

"Yes, I'm flying out on Delta." Then ignoring the man, he leaned up and brushed his lips across hers once more to whisper, "Have a safe trip back to Key West, Kim."

Reluctantly he eased her off his lap. Something pulled inside Duan at the thought that this was where he went his way and she went hers. When the driver brought the taxi to a stop, Duan opened the door and made a move to get out. He then looked back at Kim.

At that moment, something pushed him to say, "I have some free time coming up, so how about adding me to your list of prospects?"

He smiled at the stunned look on her face. "You're serious? You would consider doing that for me?"

"Yes, I would." He reached for her hand, lifted it to his lips and placed a kiss on her knuckles. Immediately he felt the sizzling between them.

Releasing her hand, he shifted and turned to get out of the taxi.

"Don't be surprised if I decide to take you up on your offer, Duan," she warned. "Then all I'll have to concentrate on is making sure Mom knows what she's doing with Edward Villarosas."

Duan turned back, gave her his full attention. Fighting to keep the frown off his face, he repeated, "Edward Villarosas?"

She nodded. "Yes. He's the man my mother plans to marry."

DUAN PULLED OUT his cell phone the moment he cleared security. He wasted no time dialing the number to his office. Landon Chestnut, one of the private investigators who worked with him at the Peachtree Private Investigative Firm, usually came into the office on Sunday afternoons. There were three other guys in the firm—Antron Blair, Brett Newman and Chevis Fleming.

"Hey, man, how was the wedding?" Landon asked, answering on the third ring.

"Real nice. The newlyweds should have reached Paris by now." Duan paused and then asked, "Ready for a blast from the past?"

"About what?"

"It's not what, Landon, but who. Edward Villarosas."

Duan heard his friend's expletives and understood why. Landon had always felt Villarosas was the one he'd let get away when he was still a detective with the force. Duan had already left the department and was working to start his own P.I. business when the Villarosas case had fallen into Landon's lap.

The guy's two wives had come up missing, five years apart, but nothing could be found to connect him with their disappearance. To this day, Duan could recall the frustration and grief Landon had gone through every time he hit a dead end during his investigation. There had been plenty of dead ends but no dead bodies. If Villarosas was guilty, he had covered his tracks well. Landon's failure with the case was one of the reasons he'd left the force to join Duan's P.I. firm.

"I don't think I'll ever forget him," Landon finally said.

"Well, if it's the same Edward Villarosas, and I have a hunch that it is, he's about to remarry," Duan told him, taking a seat near his designated gate.

"Is it to anyone you know?" Landon asked.

"Not directly. The intended bride is the mother of Terrence's wife's best friend. She mentioned it a few moments ago in a cab ride we shared to the airport. Seems he's living in Louisiana now."

"I heard he'd moved from Atlanta. Do you think he told his future bride that on two occasions he was suspected of bumping off his previous wives?"

"I doubt it," Duan said.

"I would have to agree. I'd love to reopen those cases to see if there's anything I missed the first time. The man did have ironclad alibis, but there was something about him that didn't sit well with me. In the end, there was nothing solid that we could use to move the case from missing persons to homicide. He claimed they left him for other men."

"I might have the opportunity to gather more information if I'm invited to the wedding in three weeks. Kimani Cannon needs a date, and I'm figuring since she'll be meeting Villarosas for the first time, she might want to go to Shreveport a little early."

"The opportunity to spend even a week with Villarosas might trip him up to reveal something that he didn't five years ago," Landon said. "During the investigation he had his stories together. Another plus is that he wouldn't recognize you since you had already left the force."

Duan knew Landon was right; he did have an advantage. But he wasn't absolutely certain Kim would ask him to go with her.

"When will you know if you'll be Ms. Cannon's escort?"

"Possibly early next week. I'll give her a call to remind her that I'm available."

"Will you tell her what's going on?"

He considered Landon's question for a moment. If he were to tell Kim, she definitely wouldn't let her mother go through with the wedding. Besides, as much as he might think otherwise, the former cop in him had to remember the man was innocent until proven guilty. And although Villarosas had been a prime suspect in Landon's book, he was never charged with any crime.

"No, I won't tell her yet," he said.

He ended his connection with Landon, and a short

while later when the announcer called his flight, he knew that he couldn't waste any time putting a plan into place to make sure he was the man Kim took home to Shreveport with her.

CHAPTER FOUR

KIM WOKE UP MONDAY morning in her own bed with her hormones overacting. And all because of last night's dream, which basically reenacted those moments she'd spent in bed with Duan over the weekend.

There had been something about his touch that was different from any other man's. She chuckled when she recalled Dr. Allen Perry, one of the hospital's prized surgeons, who thought his hands, both in and out of the operating room, were extraordinary. But those hands had nothing on Duan's. The way his fingers had glided across her skin, stroking her in certain areas, especially between her legs, stirring longings in her that she'd never felt before.

She squeezed her eyes shut. Since she was off work today, she could grab another hour or so of sleep, to relive those naughty moments in Duan's arms. She wasn't due back at the hospital until tomorrow, and then she needed to clear her calendar for next week to go home to Shreveport.

She smiled as she remembered growing up in Shreveport among family before her father had convinced her mother to move to New Orleans in search of better job opportunities. That was when the beatings began, and no matter how much Kim had tried, she could not convince her mother to leave him and return home to her family.

The sound of the phone ringing ended any hope of further sleep. Opening her eyes, she leaned up and reached for her cell phone, not recognizing the caller and hoping it was a wrong number. "Hello."

"I'm sitting here at my desk and remembering an incredible weekend."

She smiled, recognizing the deep, husky voice immediately. There was no need to ask how he got her number since she had given it to him before they'd departed the hotel. She'd figured he would look her up the next time he was in the Keys visiting Terrence. She didn't have a problem with him doing that. She had enjoyed his company and his bedroom manners had been perfect.

Kim was also smart enough to know that when a man called to compliment you on how much he enjoyed his time with you, he was probably about to hit you up again for a repeat.

"Can you believe I'm doing the same thing," she said, not feeling the least awkward in admitting it.

"Glad to hear it. And I was wondering…"

A smile of anticipation touched her lips. "Wondering what, Duan?"

"I promised Terrence I'd check on things at his place while he was gone this week. Seems he and Sherri ordered a new bedroom suite and it's to arrive on Friday. I told him I'd be glad to fly to the Keys to make sure it's delivered okay."

A soft chuckle escaped Kim's lips. The new bedroom

suite had been Sherri's idea. Her best friend preferred not seeing all those notches on Terrence's bedpost.

"And I was wondering if I could see you again while I'm in town," Duan was saying.

Kim pulled herself up in bed, propped her back against the pillow. There was nothing wrong with enjoying herself as long as she knew what side of the bread was getting buttered. And the one thing she *did* know was that any affair with Duan would be a safe one since he wasn't any more interested in a serious relationship than she was.

Personally, she didn't have the time or inclination for anything serious. Like she'd told Duan, she couldn't fully trust a man because of her dad. And now she had been given the opportunity to pursue the dream that had gotten waylaid for a number of years. She was back on track and there was no man alive who would get her off. Besides, she'd made a decision not to get involved in a long-distance relationship ever again.

And she knew he wasn't interested in anything serious because he'd pretty much made that clear during the cab ride to the airport. He'd stated that he could never fully trust a woman because of his mother.

"I'd love to see you again." And because she knew exactly what this call was about, she added, "To spend time between the sheets with you."

There was no need to be coy, and when it came to sex she had no qualms about taking the driver's seat if she had to, especially if it meant getting where she wanted to go.

There was a slight pause on the line and then he asked, "I love the way you think, Kimani Cannon. How does your schedule look this weekend? Terrence left me the use of his boat and I was thinking about taking it out on Saturday to get in some fishing. Would you like to come along?"

She knew Terrence owned a real forty-foot luxury miniyacht. "Sounds great and I'd love to," she said, thinking of all the possibilities. According to Sherri, Terrence's yacht had a cabin with a comfy bed. Kim doubted they would be doing much fishing, which was fine since she'd never made love on a boat before.

"Wonderful. I'll pick you up at your place Saturday morning around eight. What's the address?"

She rattled it off to him and then they ended the call.

There was no denying it. She was definitely looking forward to this weekend.

DUAN CLICKED OFF the phone and eased back in his chair. He was helpless against the rapid thumping in his chest at the prospect of spending the weekend with Kim again. And deep down he knew that even without the issue of accompanying her to Louisiana, he would still want to spend time with her. The woman had that kind of effect on him, something he still didn't quite understand.

He'd had sexual encounters of the most intense kind before, but what he'd shared this past weekend with Kim had been so incredible that even now he could barely breathe just thinking about it.

There was nothing like waking up to a hot feminine body next to his, an early morning hard-on poking between a pair of curvaceous buttocks.

His mouth had traveled every inch of her and he re-

membered how she would shiver with awareness all the
way to her toes when he licked certain parts of her. He
didn't know of a more responsive woman.

But a part of him knew it had been more than just
the sex. He'd enjoyed talking to her, and because she'd
had issues with one of her parents while growing up,
she'd known exactly how he felt regarding his mother.

He glanced up at the knock on his door and wasn't
surprised when the four men walked in. Landon Chestnut. Chevis Fleming. Brett Newman. Antron Blair. Due
to the number of cases they handled and the traveling
involved, it was unusual for all five of them to be in the
same place at the same time.

Duan had met the four while working as a cop in
Atlanta. They had started the academy together and
had eventually gotten promoted to detectives. He had
been the first to venture out on his own and Landon
followed. Within another year, Brett and Chevis had
joined them as partners.

Antron had eventually followed in his father's footsteps and become an FBI agent until an undercover
sting operation had nearly ended his life. After that,
he'd decided to join the others at the firm.

What Duan liked about their setup was that, although they worked individual cases, each had a spe-
cialty. He had an analytical mind and was good at
deciphering leads from an investigative report. Landon
had a knack for finding missing persons. Chevis had
a gift when it came to interrogations. Brett was computer savvy and was considered their technical expert,
and Antron had exemplary undercover skills, and his
contacts within the FBI were invaluable.

Over the past five years they had handled a number of cases, working closely with their allies in the Atlanta police department and the attorney friends they'd met over the years.

"Landon told us you might be working on a case and you could use our help," Brett said.

"Yes." Duan nodded. "It would definitely make things a lot easier. I know you have your own cases, but I'd appreciate your assistance in checking into a few things."

It didn't take long for him to provide the details. First they would contact a detective they knew with the Atlanta police department to reopen the two cases. Then they would gather information to see what Villarosas had been up to since he'd moved from Atlanta a few years ago. They also needed to contact the family and any friends of the missing women to see if either woman had been sighted or heard from since her disappearance. There was still the chance the women *had* run off with other men like Villarosas claimed. However, for two wives to do the same thing was a bit of a stretch.

After the guys had left his office, Duan settled back in his chair once again. He was determined that before Kim's mother married Edward Villarosas, they would know whether he was guilty of killing his former wives.

CHAPTER FIVE

LIKE CLOCKWORK KIM'S doorbell rang at eight o'clock on Saturday morning. She glanced down at herself as she headed for the door. The weather forecast indicated it would be a beautiful day for boating and she was wearing a new outfit for the occasion.

She opened the door and a blade of sunlight came through, nearly blinding her, but not before she took stock of the man standing on her doorstep. She angled her head and squinted to look up at him. He flashed a sexy smile and immediately she felt weak in the knees. It was going to be one of those days when she would find it almost impossible to keep her hands off him. He had just that kind of an effect on women. Her in particular. Standing there in a pair of jeans that tapered down muscular thighs, a T-shirt covering his broad shoulders, he looked every bit of sexy and that wasn't helping matters any. For a split second, all she could do was stand there and drool.

"Good morning, Kim."

It took her a moment to find her voice and respond. But watching the movement of his mouth had made her remember all the things that same mouth had done to her. Naughty, naughty. "Good morning, Duan."

"Are you ready?"

A memory of being ready for him—naked and waiting—flickered through her mind and she forced it away. "Yes, I just need to grab my jacket and bag."

"All right. Take your time."

Kim quickly headed back into her living room to collect the jacket and duffel bag. She knew the moment Duan stepped over the threshold to enter her home and closed the door. The air between them began to thicken and it seemed as if the air-conditioning had stopped working. Heat was coming through the vents instead.

He gave her living room an appreciative glance before turning his dark eyes to her. Every nerve in her body felt stretched tight when his gaze roamed over her, as if he could see through her outfit. He'd seen her naked before, had tasted practically every inch of her skin, and he knew all her hot spots and exactly what he needed to do to make them hotter.

She swallowed, wondering if he was thinking about any of those things. Was he remembering last weekend like she was doing? Was he as aware of her as she was of him? From the way his eyes were darkening, she figured he was.

"I guess it's not going to happen, Kim," he said, breaking the silence, his husky voice making her nipples harden.

She pulled in a deep breath. "What's not going to happen?"

"That we can wait to get to the boat before we do anything."

She could really play dumb and ask what he meant, but figured why waste her time or his. Goose bumps formed on her skin and she couldn't help skimming her gaze over him like he'd done with her earlier. She had already checked him out pretty good at the front door. But now, thanks to the huge bulge behind his zipper, there was more of him, and the woman in her appreciated that fact.

"So what do you think we need to do about it?" he asked.

"Why think?" In addition to the thrumming sensations in the pit of her stomach, she could also feel the steam floating between them.

He was right. They couldn't wait. Their desire for each other was urgent. It was spontaneous. And like before, they needed to deal with it right now. She didn't have a problem with that and proceeded to yank her T-shirt over her head, glad she wasn't wearing a bra.

Duan didn't waste any time crossing the room and pulling Kim into his arms. And when she parted her lips, he thrust his tongue between them until it was firmly planted inside her mouth. His hands were on the move and the moment his fingers found her breasts, his erection strained against his zipper. Touching her nipples wasn't enough. He needed to taste them. He remembered her flavor well and intended to become reacquainted with it this weekend.

His mouth replaced his fingers as he ended the kiss, drawing her nipples between his lips and sucking hard. He heard her moan deep in her throat, and when she clutched his head to hold it to her breasts, his hands automatically lowered and slid between the waistband of her shorts.

Shit. She's not wearing panties, either.

His erection became even more engorged when he

touched bare skin, then delved into the thickness of the curls covering her sex. The moment his hand touched her intimately, her thighs automatically parted and he eased his fingers into her soft flesh, the essence of her dewy core. He pushed apart her legs even more with his knee, and still latching onto her breasts with his mouth, he inserted his fingers deeper inside her. The moment he found her clit, she exploded in a climax of gigantic proportions and he clamped his mouth on hers to smother her scream.

The scent of her orgasm filled the air and he pulled the aroma deep into his nostrils. Before she could recover, he swept her into his arms and carried her over to the kitchen table and placed her on top of it.

His hands grasped the waistband of her shorts and pulled them down her legs. Before she could open her eyes, he lowered his head between her thighs, hungry enough to eat her alive.

His teeth scraped across her clit then he eased the torture with the tip of his tongue as he tasted her deeply.

He couldn't remember the last time he'd taken a woman on her kitchen table and quickly realized he'd never done such a thing. It seemed everything with Kim was wild, spontaneous and crazy. And when he felt her on the brink of yet another orgasm, he didn't intend to let her have it without him.

He pulled away and, still feasting his gaze on her body stretched out before him, kicked off his shoes and proceeded to remove his clothes. Standing in her kitchen completely naked, he put on a condom and turned his full attention back to her.

Duan reached out and wrapped her legs around his

neck. Then he parted her thighs and entered her, going all the way to the hilt. He tried to maintain control of his senses but her body seemed to be summoning him on a primal level and he was too weak to deny the call. Not that he intended to.

Mercy. The feel of being back inside her was sending all kinds of sensations rippling through him. Grabbing firmly on to her thighs, he began thrusting inside her while her body rocked with every movement he made. He knew the exact moment he'd touched her G-spot and the stroking took on a whole new meaning.

He watched her expression each time he entered and withdrew, keeping up the rhythmic pace while her inner muscles clenched him tight, trying to milk him for all they could get. He'd never made love before with this intensity, this need. This hunger. He couldn't explain it. Wouldn't know how to explain it. Right now he could only accept it. This fiery mating. One that touched every fiber of his being. Every part of his soul.

And then he felt her shudder, felt the way she arched her back, the way her legs tightened around his neck, and knew he had to push both of them over the edge.

He thrust harder and the sound of her scream made something inside him snap. He needed this mating like he needed his next breath and he lifted her hips in his hands for a deeper penetration. Head flung back, his body bucked into yet another explosion without fully recovering from the first.

He kept going until there was nothing left inside him. After giving it all, he slumped down on her and took a quick lick of her breasts before his face settled blissfully between them.

IT WAS A BEAUTIFUL DAY to be out on the ocean and to Duan's surprise the fish were biting. He enjoyed fishing and recalled it was one of the few things he and Terrence did with their father that didn't include Olivia. It wasn't that she hadn't been invited to go with them, but after he'd shown her how to bait her hook that first time, she had refused to come back.

He glanced over at Kim. She looked beautiful sitting on the bench seat next to him in one hot-looking bikini, the sunlight dancing off her features. She claimed this was her first time fishing, and she hadn't been at all squeamish when he'd shown her how to bait the hook. She reminded him that she was a nurse and nurses didn't get woozy at the sight of blood and guts.

She had been thrilled at her first catch and a part of him was excited about having her there. He'd gotten used to fishing alone, preferring the solitude. But not today. He wasn't ready to figure out why.

Another thing he had to get his mind around was the intense chemistry between them. The sexual chemistry was so strong, so overwhelming, that the need to have each other took precedence over anything else. Sounded crazy, but it was true.

Prime example was the incident back at her place. He had taken her on her kitchen table, of all places. His only excuse was that he'd arrived this morning filled with one hell of a lustful need after thinking about her, dreaming of her, all week.

The moment she'd opened the door, every primitive male instinct within him had erupted. He figured no woman had a right to look so damn good that early. He wasn't even sure whether she was wearing makeup.

Didn't matter. And she had a baseball cap on her head. That didn't matter, either. What mattered was that she was a woman his body seemed to desire whenever he saw her. Any time and any place.

She was becoming an addiction.

She must have felt his gaze and looked up from working her fishing pole. "I like doing this, Duan."

He chuckled as he leaned back in his seat and tilted his cap back. It was on the tip of his tongue to say he liked doing her. "It's hard to believe you've lived in the Keys for over a year now and have never gone fishing. What a waste of water." He noticed the hands holding the fishing rod. Most women he dated did up their nails but not Kim. He figured in her line of work it was best she didn't. He liked her fingers. He remembered sucking on them the last time. The memory made something pull deep within his groin.

"Well, to be honest, I'm not much for being out on or in the water," she said, interrupting his thoughts. "Makes me nervous."

He lifted his brow. "Then how did you learn to swim?"

"I didn't."

He stared at her, not believing what she'd said. "You don't know how to swim?"

"No. I always planned to take lessons but ended up chickening out."

He glanced around and then back at her. "So, you're out here with me in the middle of the ocean, wearing a very sexy bathing suit and don't know how to swim."

She smiled. "The key words are that I'm out here

with you. You won't let anything happen to me. Sherri will never forgive you if you do."

He returned her smile. He could believe that. "I've never asked how the two of you met."

She leaned back and propped her feet up on the side of the boat. He liked the way her bathing suit fit. She had used the facilities below to change out of the shorts set into the bikini as soon as they'd gotten on the boat. He had changed into swimming trunks, as well. It was a beautiful day in April and there were other boaters taking advantage of the perfect weather.

"Sherri and I met in college and were roommates for all four years. After college we decided to pursue opportunities in the same cities. If it wasn't for Sherri, I would probably still be living in D.C. She talked me into moving to the Keys. My life hasn't been the same since."

He nodded. "Is that good or bad?"

"At the time it was good because I needed a change. The guy I was involved with wanted more out of the relationship than I was willing to give. He knew going in that I wasn't looking for anything long-term and claimed he wasn't, either. Somewhere along the way he changed his mind."

"But he didn't change yours."

It was presented as a statement and not a question, but she answered anyway. "I doubt there is anything or anyone that will change my mind about that."

She paused for a moment. "I told you about my father and all his ugliness. Well, then there was that one time one of my stepfathers tried to come on to me. If I hadn't known a little about defending myself, there's no telling what might have happened. His actions only added to my distrust of men in general."

The thought of someone trying to take advantage of her filled him with anger. "So there's never been anyone you'd want to marry?"

A bright smile touched her lips. "Sure," she joked. "Denzel Washington. But I don't see Pauletta giving him up anytime soon. But on a serious note, I've told you my reasons for not wanting to indulge in a long-term affair. Short-term serves me just fine. I watch my mother live her life believing she can't survive without a man and I refuse to let that happen to me, so marriage is not in my future."

He knew the feeling.

"But I do like kids and want to have a child some-day," she added.

Her statement didn't surprise him. Although he'd never seen her around children, for some reason he believed she would be a good mother and nothing like the woman who'd birthed him. As far as kids went for him, he liked them but wasn't sure he could ever be the father his dad had been. Orin Jeffries had been a rock for his kids. He had always been there for them, and when his poor excuse of a wife had walked out, he had taken on the role of single father without much sweat.

Duan pulled in a deep breath, wondering who he was fooling. He shifted his gaze from Kim and stared out over the water, thinking that for his father, there had been *both* sweat and tears. He would never forget the day he'd walked in on his father standing in the middle of his bedroom, staring at his wife's picture and crying. Actually crying over the woman who'd humiliated him by running off with another man. Duan had backed out of the room without his father knowing he'd been there. That day stuck out in his mind because it was then that he'd decided he didn't want any woman to ever cause him the pain he'd seen on his father's face.

"What about you?" Kim asked.

He glanced back over at her. "What about me?"

"How do you feel about marriage and children?"

It had been a long time since any woman asked him that. "I don't ever plan to marry. And as long as there are such things as condoms, I don't ever intend to produce a baby, either, although I like them. I just don't want to parent one. Don't know how good I'd be, so I'd rather not take any chances." He turned from Kim and stared out over the ocean again.

"I guess we'll have to wait on Sherri and Terrence."

He glanced back at her. "Wait on them for what?"

She smiled. "Babies. I'll be godmother to any baby they have. That's a given."

He couldn't help but chuckle at that. "Is it?"

"Yes."

And any baby his brother and sister-in-law produced would make him an uncle. *Uncle Duan.* He liked the sound of that, but he wasn't so sure it would be Terrence and Sherri who would be bestowing the honor upon him first. For some reason, he had a feeling it would be Reggie and Libby.

Deciding to change the subject to the one they needed to discuss, he asked, "How are things with your mother?"

The face she made told him the answer before she opened her mouth to say anything. "Basically the same.

I've talked to her twice this week and at least she's agreed not to do anything rash about her marital status until after I get there."

"When are you leaving?"

"Friday, and I plan to be there for a week. That will give me a few days to spend with her and to get to know the man she wants to marry."

He nodded. "And are you still contemplating taking a fake fiancé with you?"

She tilted her head back and met his gaze. "It depends."

He lifted a brow. "On what?"

"On whether or not you were serious about going with me."

THERE, SHE'D SAID IT and now she was trying to decipher his response, Kim thought, studying Duan. She had been tempted to bring up the subject all morning but hadn't known how to.

Although he'd made the offer last weekend, it had been post-sex, when they'd still been caught up in the hot time they'd shared in her hotel room. When she'd played the offer over and over in her mind this week, she'd tried to convince herself that he had been serious, but she wasn't so sure. This was one way to find out for certain.

He placed his fishing pole aside and leaned over her. "Then I guess I just became your pretend fiancé since I was dead serious, Kim."

She swallowed. He was giving her *that* look. "You do know what that will mean when it comes to my mother and aunt, don't you? They will be asking you questions, trying to pin us down to a wedding date and all that stuff. It won't be easy."

He shrugged. "And it won't be hard. You tell me what to say and I'll say it."

She tilted her head and continued to hold his gaze. "And just what will you get out of this?"

A smile touched his lips and that smile made sensations flutter all through her. "I'm surprised that you would ask me that, especially after last weekend and this morning," he said in a throaty voice. "But just in case you don't have a clue, let me break it down to you." He leaned closer. "I'll be getting you, Kimani. I like kissing you. I enjoy having sex with you."

His smile widened as he added, "Um, I *especially* like having sex with you."

She couldn't help noticing he'd specifically pointed out they'd had sex and not made love. Why did his description of what they'd done bother her, when the same terminology from any other man would not have? She pushed the thought from her mind and wriggled up to wrap her arms around his neck. Looking up at him, she smiled. "Then I guess we are officially pretend engaged."

"DUAN ACTUALLY VOLUNTEERED to go to Shreveport and pretend to be your fiancé?" Sherri asked Kim a few days later. Terrence had left their hotel room to grab them breakfast and she'd taken the time to give Kim a call.

"Yes, can you believe my luck? Seeing me with him will satisfy Aunt Gert I've got a man."

"Is there something you aren't telling me about you and Duan, Kim? Sounds serious."

Kim chuckled. She knew just what Sherri was hinting at. "Not serious, just sexual. I don't do serious, Sherri. You of all people know that. And Duan isn't looking for anything serious, either. It's the perfect arrangement."

Before her best friend could ask her any more questions, Kim quickly said, "Now hang up the phone before your husband returns. You *are* on your honeymoon, you know."

"I know, and I am so happy I have to pinch myself to make sure it's real."

Kim could hear the sheer contentment in Sherri's voice. She laughed. "Why pinch yourself? Just look at the size of that rock on your hand if you have any doubt."

Moments later, she hung up the phone and glanced across the room at her packed luggage. She would be flying out of the Keys in a few hours and would catch a connecting flight in Atlanta, where Duan would be joining her to continue on to Shreveport.

Strolling from the living room to the kitchen, she couldn't help but smile when she glanced over at her table. She was consumed with memories every time she walked past it. Even now her mind was filled with memories of their lovemaking on Terrence's boat. To be totally honest, there wasn't a single night since the wedding that she hadn't thought about all the lovemaking she and Duan had done.

He was definitely a man who knew how to have a good time and she remembered how quickly she had slid her bikini bottoms down her legs and untied her top. It hadn't taken Duan any time at all to remove his swimming trunks, and using the rocking motion of the boat on the water, they had taken each other hard, fast and often.

And they would be back together again for a third weekend. She shouldn't, but she was beginning to consider him as her weekend lover, and his ability to turn any fantasy she'd ever had into reality was simply amazing.

Kim glanced at her watch. It was time to begin loading her luggage into the car. As she headed up the stairs she couldn't squash her anticipation at the thought that in a few hours she would be seeing Duan again.

CHAPTER SIX

DUAN PULLED INTO the airport parking lot and then into the space his car would occupy for the next ten days. He patted the pocket of his shirt to make sure the ring he'd slid inside was still there. He had volunteered to come up with an engagement ring and thought the one he already had in his possession was perfect. It was the ring his grandmother had left him to present to the woman he would one day marry. When he'd mentioned it to Kim, she'd thought using that ring was a good idea, as well.

He had to remind himself that the ring's purpose was twofold. First, it was personal since he was helping out a woman he'd come to consider a friend. It was also business, in that he hoped to determine if Edward Villarosas was guilty of murder.

The Atlanta police department had agreed to reopen the two cases and was putting together a list of family and friends that would be interviewed again. According to the cold case file, wife number one hadn't returned home from what should have been a weekend trip to Orlando with her two girlfriends ten years ago.

The other women acknowledged that Mandy Villarosas had been acting strange and had left their hotel room right after breakfast, saying she was meeting someone. When she hadn't returned for lunch, they'd begun to worry and had called Edward, who'd encouraged them to notify the police.

The other women claimed they had no idea who Mandy was supposed to meet, but indicated there had been a man in a club the night before who Mandy had been flirting with. Two years later, Villarosas had divorced his wife on grounds of desertion, and a year after that, he remarried.

He and Sandra Villarosas had been married two years when he'd reported her missing. She hadn't shown up for work and one of her coworkers had gotten concerned. Edward was out of town on a fishing trip in Florida with friends and had left two days before. In fact, Sandra was the one who had taken him to the airport. Several witnesses verified that, and also the fact she had been seen around town afterward.

Neither woman had been heard from since, and Edward's alibis were verified by family and friends.

Duan walked inside the airport terminal, which was busy as usual. Any other day he might have wished he were someplace else, even in his office totally absorbed in another case. But not today.

If Kim's flight left on time she would be here in less than an hour. It had been five days since they'd been together and he was anxious to see her again. With that admission, he felt a punch to his stomach and something close to panic. He was reminded that the last thing he needed to do was get wrapped up with any woman. Women, he knew for a fact, had the ability to wrap a man around their finger, then walk away and not look back.

Instead he switched his thoughts from Kim to the real purpose of this trip. Edward Villarosas. Going to Shreveport to meet Kim's family would afford him the opportunity of being in the man's company for almost a week, and with a bit of luck he'd notice or discover something that the other detectives who'd worked the case hadn't. For the time being, the less Kim knew about what was going on, the better.

If Villarosas was guilty, then he was a man who'd successfully gotten away with two crimes. It was going to be up to Duan to figure out how Kim's mother played into any of this. Was the man looking to knock off wife number three? He had read the two case files over and over, and there was nothing in them to indicate Villarosas was a man who married women and then got some sort of sick kick getting rid of them.

But Duan did not intend on taking any chances. He would be on full alert until he figured out just what type of man they were dealing with. At no time did he plan on putting Kim or her mother in danger. A deep frown settled on his face at the thought of anything happening to Kim. He would protect her with his life if he had to, and wouldn't let Villarosas or anyone else harm a single strand of hair on her head or her mother's.

Right now he didn't want to question why he'd become so protective of Kimani; he just accepted that was the way it was. While his partners were out in the field gathering information, Duan's job in Shreveport over the next few days was to get close to Villarosas and develop a rapport with him in hopes the man would let his guard down.

Even without meeting the guy he had a gut feeling the man was bad news, and the quicker that could be proven, the better.

KIM GLANCED AROUND when she approached her gate. Duan's head could be seen above everyone else's, making him easily recognizable. In addition to that, he was the man most women were giving a second look.

She glared at one such woman when she passed, then frowned, wondering why it annoyed her that other women found him as desirable as she did. It wasn't like he was her man. Everything between them was strictly casual. They enjoyed having sex with each other. No big deal.

Kim breathed in deeply, wondering who she was fooling. It was beginning to become a big deal. There was something about this affair with Duan that was different. Emotions were starting to come into play, at least on her end, and she never let emotions creep into any of her relationships. There was no place for them.

And as she got closer to where he stood, she didn't want to analyze what those strange feelings were about. The only thing she wanted to do was concentrate on him. He was wearing a polo shirt and a pair of khaki pants and he looked good. Instinctively, she walked into his open arms and a part of her wished all those drooling women took notice.

"Good seeing you again, Kim," he murmured, brushing a kiss across her temple.

The moment his lips touched her skin, Kim felt the muscles in her belly tighten. He pulled her closer and she melted into him easily. Already he was hard and erect. She tilted her head and looked up at him. There was never any other way with them. Their desire for each other was spontaneous. They saw; they wanted.

"That was just a public kiss," he whispered. "I'm going to give you a very private one later when we're alone."

She smiled. "I can't wait. And speaking of waiting, have you been here long?"

He shrugged as he released her and took her hand. "This is a busy airport so I figured it was best to arrive early. There are a couple of eating places around here if you're hungry. We have a couple of hours before our flight leaves."

"No, I'm fine. What about you?"

That elicited a laugh. "I could use something else but will settle for a cup of coffee."

She had an idea what he meant. "Okay."

He took her hand and led her toward the food court. He glanced over at her. "You look cute."

"Thanks."

She had deliberately worn this outfit, a short denim skirt and a green tank top with spaghetti straps. She hadn't missed the way he'd scanned her appreciatively from head to toe.

She followed him to an empty table and a waitress came to take Duan's coffee order. Before the woman left he glanced over at her. "You sure you don't want anything?"

"Um, I would like some vanilla ice cream."

He lifted a brow after the waitress walked off. "Ice cream? This early?"

She laughed. "It's not *that* early, Duan." She checked

her watch. "In fact, it's a few minutes past ten. I love ice cream and I'm known to eat it for breakfast. It used to drive Sherri crazy."

He smiled. "I bet. And before I forget, give me your left hand."

Instinctively she did as he asked and watched him pull a small jewelry box out of his shirt pocket. He placed it on the table beside her and opened it up.

"Wow! It's beautiful, Duan." And she meant it. The ring was dazzling. "And this was your grandmother's?"

"Yes," he said, taking it out of the box and sliding it onto her ring finger. It was a perfect fit and she watched in surprise as he lifted her hands and kissed her knuckles.

"When she died she left it for me since I was her oldest grandson," he said, releasing her. "However, since I have no plan to ever marry I thought about giving it to Terrence, but Dad figured I should keep it anyway since it was left to me. I think she felt bad for the way her daughter turned out."

Kim fluttered her fingers, admiring the ring Duan had just placed on it. "Well, regardless, I think it's beautiful and—"

"Oh, my goodness! Did the two of you just get engaged?"

Both Kim and Duan glanced up at their waitress. She was standing there holding a coffee in one hand and a cup of vanilla ice cream in the other, a delighted look on her face.

Kim opened her mouth to answer but Duan beat her to the punch. "Yes, we did."

"Congratulations!" the woman exclaimed. "That's wonderful and it's a beautiful ring."

A huge smile spread over Duan's face. "Thanks."

He glanced expectantly at Kim. She then caught on to what he was doing and smiled up at the woman. "Yes. Thanks."

The waitress placed the coffee in front of Duan and gave Kim her ice cream. She gave both of them another huge smile before leaving. Kim leaned over the table. "Why did you let her think we've just gotten engaged?"

He shrugged. "For all intents and purposes, we have."

She rolled her eyes. "We're role-playing for Mom and Aunt Gert, not necessarily for strangers."

He chuckled. "Who's to say she doesn't know some-one who might know you? You'd be surprised how small this world is sometimes. Besides, telling her we're engaged gave me some practice time."

"Practice for what?"

"Smiling whenever anyone congratulates us. I'm sure we'll be hearing a lot of that over the next few days. Did I seem genuinely pleased?"

She momentarily clamped her mouth shut, not sure what to say or to question why she felt irked by what he'd said. Of course they were role-playing, but for some reason she was bothered by the thought.

When he continued to stare at her, waiting for her response, she pasted a smile on her face and said in a syrupy tone, "You were simply marvelous, darling."

He wiggled his eyebrows. "Ready for an Oscar?"

She rolled her eyes. "Um, I wouldn't go that far."

He laughed as he reached out and took her hand in

his, caressing the finger that wore his ring. "But you would say I was good, wouldn't you?"

The smile that touched her lips that moment was genuine. "Yes, Duan, you were good."

And then she gently pulled her hand away from his to eat her ice cream.

CHAPTER SEVEN

"DUAN, I'D LIKE YOU to meet my mother, Wynona Cannon-Longleaf-Higgins-Gunter. Mom, this is Duan Jeffries, my fiancé."

Duan kept his mouth from dropping completely open. Kim's mother was a very attractive woman. Kim had said she was fifty-five, but to his way of thinking, she looked a lot younger. He offered the older woman his hand. "How do you do, Mrs...." Already he'd forgotten her names.

She beamed happily. "Just call me Wynona. I don't know why Kim insisted on saying all those names."

Kim smiled. "Because they're yours. All four of them." She glanced around. "And where is the man who might be number five?"

Wynona gave her daughter a frown. "Edward will be here any minute. He's probably stuck in traffic since he lives on the other side of town."

She returned her attention to Duan. "Your last name is Jeffries?"

"Yes, ma'am."

"And before you ask, Mom, the answer is yes," Kim said. "He's Terrence's older brother."

"Best friends marrying brothers. How nice."

She studied his features for a moment and then

asked, "And you're willing to wait for Kim to finish med school before the two of you marry?"

Duan gave Kim a loving smile and slipped his arm around her waist to bring her closer. That was number one on the list of questions Kim had known her mother would ask. Wynona had asked her that same thing when she'd told her mother about her acceptance into medical school. Evidently she was hoping for a different answer.

"Whatever Kim wants, that's what we'll do," he said, leaning over and placing a kiss on Kim's lips. He could tell from the expression that appeared on Wynona's face that she wasn't pleased with his comment.

"But we're talking about four, maybe five years," the older woman pointed out. "Don't you think that's way too long to wait?"

He opened his mouth to respond but Kim beat him to it. "Maybe you ought to try it, Mom. You, of all people, should know that rushing into marriage serves no purpose other than a quick divorce. Which is why I think you and Mr. Villarosas should take more time to get to know each other before the two of you contemplate marriage."

Instead of agreeing or disagreeing with Kim's comment, Wynona smiled at him and said, "And what do you do for a living, Duan?"

"I used to be a cop but now I'm a private investigator. I own my own business." Now he knew how it felt to be interrogated.

"And I take it that you love my daughter."

Duan looked at Kim again, and something about being asked that question bothered him. Nonetheless, he plastered a smile on his face before saying, "Very much so. I wouldn't be marrying her if I didn't."

Wynona opened her mouth, but at that moment there was a knock at the door. She smiled. "Excuse me. That's probably Edward."

As soon as Wynona exited the room Kim turned to Duan. "So far so good. You're handling Mom's interrogation well."

Before Kim could say anything else, Wynona returned with a tall, slender man by her side. He was smiling as he approached them.

"Well, now, Wynona, this has to be your daughter. She favors you." He came to stand before Kim and Duan, but only gave Duan a cursory glance. Kim had his full attention.

"Yes, Edward, this is my daughter," Wynona said, beaming proudly. "Kim, this is the man I plan to marry in a few weeks."

Kim extended her hand to him. "Nice meeting you, Edward. And this is the man I plan to marry, Duan Jeffries. Duan, this is Edward Villarosas."

It was only then that Edward met Duan's gaze, and Duan felt the smile he bestowed upon him wasn't genuine. That feeling in his gut intensified. "Duan, nice meeting you." Edward offered him his hand.

"Likewise," Duan said, taking it.

Wynona leaned close to Edward. "Don't they make a lovely couple, Edward?"

Edward smiled up at her. "Just as lovely as we do." He then turned his attention back to Kim. "I understand you have doubts about me making your mother happy."

Kim lifted a brow. "And you plan to rid me of those doubts, right?"

He chuckled. "I certainly do. Your mother is the only woman for me."

"So this is your first marriage?" Duan asked, pinning the man with a direct gaze.

Villarosas seemed surprised by the question, and the look he gave Duan indicated he didn't appreciate being asked. "No. In fact, I've been married twice and both ended in divorce."

Duan nodded. At least Villarosas was up front about that.

"But I'm determined to make sure this time is the last time," he added, taking Wynona's hand to his lips and kissing her knuckles.

A part of Duan wished everything the man said was true. That he was innocent in the disappearances of his two wives. Not for Villarosas's sake but for Kim's mother's sake. She was a nice lady who deserved better.

"Mom, Duan and I are going to check in to the hotel now and—"

"But Gert will want to come by later to see you," Wynona said.

Kim shrugged. "I'll see Aunt Gert tomorrow. We'll come join you and her for breakfast since I know you're making a big deal out of it in the morning. I can just imagine who all you've invited."

Wynona smiled. "Just family and friends. They're looking forward to seeing you and meeting Duan."

Kim chuckled. "I just bet they are, but I had a rough week at work and the flight was a long one and I want to rest up a bit. So, we'll see you in the morning." Turning to Edward, she said, "It was nice meeting you, Edward."

"Same here, Kim." He glanced over at Duan. "And you, too."

Duan almost laughed at that. "Likewise, Edward," he said with a serious expression.

Duan and Kim were about to walk out the door when Edward called out, "Sorry, Duan, but you didn't say what you did for a living."

Duan wondered what business it was of Villarosas's, but answered, "Yes, I did, but you weren't here at the time. I'm an ex-cop turned private investigator."

Villarosas's brows lifted. "In Key West?"

Duan smiled. "No, in Atlanta."

Villarosas wasn't quick enough to hide the startled look in his eyes. And Duan could just imagine the questions rolling around in the man's mind right about now.

"And you didn't say what you did for a living, Edward," Duan ventured.

Again Villarosas seemed taken aback that Duan would question him about anything. He hesitated a moment before saying, "I'm retired."

"Oh, I see." Duan placed his hand in the center of Kim's back and they continued out the door.

KIM WALKED INTO THE hotel room and tossed her purse on the sofa. She wished she could read Duan's thoughts. He had been quiet during most of the car ride from her mother's and she wanted to know what he was thinking.

She doubted it was obvious to her mother, whose inability to read people was legendary, but it hadn't gone unnoticed by her that Duan had taken an immediate dislike to Edward and she wondered why.

She glanced over at Duan and noticed him looking around the room. After they had picked up a rental car, they had come here directly from the airport but only long enough to drop off their luggage before heading over to her mother's place. Now they were back and he was checking things out.

The suite had a separate sitting room with a sofa that pulled out to a bed. There was a spacious bath with a hot tub and the bedroom area had a king-size bed. There was no doubt in her mind that she and Duan would be sharing that bed.

"I have an idea what you're thinking, Duan," she said.

It was then that he glanced over at her. "I doubt very seriously that you do. But if you want to take a stab at it, then go ahead and tell me."

"You're probably wondering what the hell you're doing here, and wishing you were someplace else."

He looked down at the carpeted floor and then lifted his gaze back to hers. "I'm alone in this hotel room with you, with a king-size bed, and you think I'd rather be someplace else?"

She released an exasperated laugh. "Be serious, Duan."

He stared at her for a moment. "I am serious when it comes to you, me and the bed."

She nodded. "And how serious are you about Edward? I could tell you don't like him. Why?"

Duan moved across the room to stand in front of Kim. She had asked a good question, and maybe it would be best for all concerned if he answered it. To be fair to the man, he hadn't planned to tell her what he suspected until he had something concrete, not speculation. But Kim was very observant, and it would be best for the investigation if he leveled with her now and hoped she would understand and not blow his cover.

"Duan?"

"We need to talk." He reached out and took her hand in his and gently led her toward the couch. She sat beside him and he saw the curiosity in her eyes.

Her hand tightened on his. "What is it, Duan?"

He muttered a silent curse. He would tell her, but he would also make sure she understood that although Villarosas might think Duan was on to him, it was important to keep him guessing. Duan had long ago discovered that a man with something to hide would begin messing up if he thought he had a reason to look over his shoulder.

He pulled in a deep breath and began talking. "The moment you mentioned Edward Villarosas's name to me that day we were leaving Chicago, it sounded familiar. All it took was a phone call to one of my partners for confirmation."

Kim's eyes widened. "Your partner? Are you saying Edward is in some kind of trouble?"

"I'm not sure yet."

Kim shook her head and released Duan's hand to stand. She stared down at him with numerous questions in her eyes. "Not sure? Duan, we're talking about a man my mother is planning to marry. Just what *are* you sure about?"

Duan stood also. He knew she was not going to

like what he was about to tell her, and would probably wonder why he hadn't told her sooner. "A few years ago, on two occasions, Edward came under suspicion for a crime, but nothing was proven."

Kim placed her hands on her hips and met his gaze. Duan could clearly see the worried look in her eyes. "What was he suspected of doing?"

A part of Duan wished they weren't having this conversation, but another part of him was glad they were. He hadn't like withholding information from her. "He was married twice."

Kim nodded. "Yes, he admitted as much, but according to him he got a divorce in both situations. Are you saying that he didn't?"

"No, there were divorces."

Duan paused a moment. "Both women turned up missing during the marriage, and to this day have not been heard from."

Kim bit down on her lip and fought to keep her composure. "Are you saying what I think you are?"

He nodded. "Yes. On two occasions Edward was a suspect in his wives' disappearances. No one was able to prove foul play on his part because he had real good alibis."

Kim's eyes widened. "But if he *was* in some way responsible, that means…"

He knew what she was thinking, although it was apparently hard for her to say it out loud. "Yes," he said softly, gazing deep into her eyes. "That's what it means."

CHAPTER EIGHT

"OH, MY GOD." Kim closed her eyes and drew in a deep breath. She felt her body trembling at the same time she felt Duan's strong hands gently stroking her back.

"It's okay, Kim. Nothing is going to happen to your mother," he whispered in a deep, husky voice close to her ear. "I give you my word on that."

She shook her head. She heard his words but didn't fully understand how he could say them. In fact, a part of her brain refused to comprehend any of what he'd said. She was imagining things—yes, that had to be it. There was no way Duan had insinuated that the man her mother planned to marry could be responsible for the deaths of his previous two wives.

She opened her eyes and stared up into Duan's face, and knew from his expression that she hadn't imagined anything. It was true.

She wrenched away from him as anger consumed her. "And you've known this since that Sunday in Chicago when we shared a cab ride to the airport?" she asked in an accusing tone. "You knew what Edward Villarosas was capable of doing, yet you didn't tell me when you were aware my mother was spending time with him? Planning to marry him?" Cold, hard fear struck Kim in the chest at the very thought of Edward Villarosas and her mother together.

Duan knew Kim was upset. Highly pissed was more like it. He'd guessed what her reaction would be, which was why he hadn't told her sooner. Now that she knew, it was imperative that he convince her Wynona wasn't at risk and exactly what was at stake and why they needed to do things his way.

"The reason I didn't tell you as soon as you mentioned the name was because I had to verify we were talking about the same person."

"And when you discovered it was the same person?" she asked hotly, pressing the issue.

"Then it was a matter of acknowledging the first rule of law." He leaned against the wall and crossed his arms over his chest. "No matter how things might look, a person is innocent until proven guilty, and after two investigations, some of Atlanta's finest detectives couldn't come up with anything to nail Villarosas. He had ironclad alibis. He and his wives weren't even in the same cities when they disappeared."

"Then why on earth do you think he's guilty of anything?"

Duan knew it would be a waste of time to explain about a cop's intuition. Landon had only worked on the second case, but when he'd learned about the first, which happened a good five years before he'd become a cop, he'd tried making a connection but hadn't been able to do so. That didn't necessarily mean there wasn't one, but time and city budget cuts had prevented the force from following up on every plausible lead.

"A few things didn't add up," he heard himself

saying. "But they weren't enough to get a conviction if we had wanted to take things that far."

He remembered the evidence wasn't even enough to get the man locked up for the night as a suspect. People had verified his whereabouts and the two incidents had been five years apart.

"But you just said he wasn't in the same cities as his wives when they disappeared." She was thoughtful a moment. "So what did Edward think happened to them? It is odd both wives disappeared."

"He said they were having affairs and left him for other men."

She lifted a brow. "I wonder if he realizes that doesn't make him look very good—as if he was lacking in certain areas."

"Yes, you could think that. But there were others who knew the women and claimed they definitely liked to flirt. The witnesses believed they were involved in affairs, though no one knew the names of the men."

Kim pushed a curl behind her ear. She still had a lot of questions but at least she had an answer to one of them, the one she'd asked herself just last week. Why would Duan want to come to Shreveport with her? She now saw that it had nothing to do with him enjoying her company, at least not to the extent she'd assumed. Men liked sex and she would be the first to admit that what was between them was off the charts. However, now that she was aware of his real motivation, she wouldn't be surprised to find out that he'd had his bags packed, ready to come here and nail Edward Villarosas, the moment she'd mentioned his name.

She glanced up to find Duan staring at her. "And you

think you'll be able to crack a case—two cases—in one week? Do you honestly believe that Edward will give something away to make that happen?"

She watched as he dragged in a deep breath. "If cracking the cases was just dependent on me, then I would say no. But I'm not the only one working them. I have four other men in the firm who're just as determined to solve this, and I consider them the best there are. One is even a former FBI agent. The first thing we had to do was get the Atlanta police to agree to reopen the files. And now that that's been done, we have technical equipment at our disposal that wasn't on the market a few years ago. I feel certain if there was foul play in either case, we're going to find out this time. We have the time, manpower and the resources to do it."

Kim began pacing as she tried to make sense of everything Duan had said. Moments later, she stopped and glanced over at him.

He was leaning against the wall, arms crossed. His expression was unreadable, but she was certain hers showed that she was still upset.

Thinking she had paced long enough, she moved over to the sofa and sat down. "I gather there wasn't sufficient motive in either case. He couldn't collect on insurance policies since the women—according to him—weren't dead, just missing."

"True."

"So the only thing you and your friends have to go on is gut instincts?" When he lifted his brow, she said, "Yes, I know all about gut instincts. I dated a detective while living in D.C. It was a short-term affair but long enough to get an idea of how a cop thinks. That's one of the things he and I didn't agree on, because people in the medical field, we base our decisions on scientific data."

"And so do we, to a certain extent," he said. "The use of DNA proves that. But still, there are times when you know something doesn't add up, but you just can't prove it. And unfortunately, there're not always unlimited funds available to prove your theories. The city of Atlanta was undergoing budget cuts, so without evidence to support a lengthy investigation the cases stayed in missing persons and never made it over to homicide."

He paused to allow what he'd said to sink in before adding, "Landon Chestnut, the detective who originally worked the second case, felt something was missed in the first, which hindered him from doing a good job. Now he can pursue both with a full team behind him."

Duan finally moved away from the wall to take the chair across from Kim. He was fully aware that over the past twenty minutes or so, in the midst of their conversations, something was taking place between them that had nothing to do with sex but everything to do with trust. She was upset, understandably so, yet she'd been willing to listen while he explained things.

"I wish I could say that after meeting Villarosas I think Landon is wrong," he spoke up and said. "But before I flew out here I was able to read documentation on both cases, and I think there's more to it than two women deciding they no longer wanted to be married and hauling ass, never to be heard from again."

His opinion did nothing to relieve her anxiety. It only

worsened it. "If what you say is true, then how can you think my mother's life is not in danger, Duan?"

He leaned forward and rested his elbows on his thighs. "First of all, if Villarosas has gotten rid of two wives, he wouldn't risk there being a third without raising a lot of suspicions. And he and your mother aren't married yet and he has no reason to think she's being unfaithful like the other two were. Besides that, he asked about my profession before we left your mother's house, so he knows I'm an ex-cop. He even knows I'm an ex-cop from Atlanta and he's probably wondering if I'm familiar with the investigation."

Kim sighed and leaned back in her chair. "But solving a case can take weeks, months, possibly years. You met my mother, Duan. You saw how her face lit up when Edward got there. She's fallen for him, and if he's not what he's pretending to be then she should know it and I'm the one who should tell her."

"If you were to tell her now, would she believe you? How do you know he hasn't already told her that he's had two wives run off and made it seem it was their choice? And would knowing that about him make your mother leery of him? In Wynona's mind, he's a good man, so unless you can present concrete evidence to the contrary, she'll take anything you say as an attempt to keep them apart."

Kim was silent for a while because what Duan had said was the truth. Her mother could very well know about Edward's two wives. She certainly hadn't reacted when he'd answered Duan's question earlier about whether he'd ever been married. He hadn't hesitated to admit to two divorces, so chances were he'd told her mother about his wives' disappearances, as well. Kim knew her mother wouldn't suspect Edward of any foul play.

"I can't let her marry him until I know for sure he's innocent, Duan," she said, glancing over at him.

He nodded. "And like I said earlier, with all five of us working the case, not to mention the detective with the Atlanta police department, I feel we should come up with something—even if nothing more than a motive."

"And then what?"

"And then we present what we have to the police, and to your mother. Until then, she won't believe mere speculation on our part." He leaned back in his chair. "There is no doubt in my mind that Villarosas is a manipulator. I watched your mother while he was talking. He's convinced her that he's the best thing since sliced bread."

Kim felt that was a pretty good assessment, one she'd made herself. "So what can we do?"

"Right now, nothing. My partners know how important it is that we determine once and for all what happened to those women, and if that means starting back at square one, then that's what we'll do."

His words didn't give Kim much comfort. What he was anticipating doing could take time, and time was something they didn't have, not when her mother intended to marry Edward in a few weeks.

"There has to be something we can do now," she said in a frustrated tone.

"There is. I need you to act as if he's winning you over. That's going to be important to him. I'm sure he's already figured out that he's rubbed me the wrong way, and he either doesn't give a damn or he's going to do his best to get on my good side, if for no other reason than to try to figure out what I know."

"Won't he become suspicious if he finds out the cases have been reopened?"

"Possibly. But he won't connect me to anything. In fact, I'm going to make him believe I know nothing about it. I was up front with him about being a former police officer, and he's probably thinking I wouldn't have done so had I recognized his name."

He stood up and crossed over to her, reaching out his hand. She stared at it for a moment before placing her own hand in his. He tugged her to her feet, and when he wrapped his arms around her waist she made a feeble attempt to pull away. He tightened his hold, not letting her go.

"You should have told me," she said, narrowing her eyes at him.

He lifted her chin to connect their gazes. He couldn't help but see the hurt in the depths of her dark brown eyes and it was like a kick in the gut. He'd never meant to hurt her.

"Things had to be done this way, Kim. Any false move could blow up in our face—cause potential evidence to be thrown out. I can't risk him wiggling through any loopholes. Would you want that, especially if he's guilty?"

"No."

"Had I told you any sooner you would have caught the first plane here to confront both Villarosas and your mother, without any proof. That would only have pushed them closer together. They would have eloped before you could have stopped them. This way we both know what we have to do and we'll work together to nail him." He paused to let his words sink in.

"So, are we a team or not?" he asked after a few moments.

A part of Kim wanted to go somewhere and cry her eyes out. Finding out that the one man her mother believed could make her happy was a fake and possible murderer was bad enough. And then to be reminded that sex was the only thing between her and Duan, and that the only reason he was there was to work undercover—

"Kim?"

She tilted up her chin, scowling fiercely. "What?"

"Are we or are we not a team? Do we not want the same thing here?"

She sighed and looked up at him. "Yes, but I want to know everything I can about Villarosas and those two cases. Did you bring those reports with you?"

"Yes."

"Good, because I intend to read them. If Edward is innocent I'll be the first to apologize to him and Mom for doubting him, but if he's guilty of any crimes then I want to make sure he pays for what he's done."

CHAPTER NINE

KIM PUT DOWN the documents she'd been reading for the past hour and rubbed her eyes. As a nurse she was used to reports, some even thicker than the three-hundred-page document Duan had given her. However, most of them were medical in nature and reached a conclusion at the end, a diagnosis. Although a lot of information was documented from various sources in this investigative report, there was no definite finding.

"Here, looks like you can use this."

She smiled when Duan placed a cup of coffee in front of her. "Thanks."

He eased into the chair beside her. After she'd started to read the report he had pulled out a laptop. For the past hour they had worked in amiable silence, the only sounds in the room those of her turning pages and him clicking on the keyboard.

But the one thing she was constantly aware of was his presence. Just knowing he was there within arm's reach was a comforting thought. All she had to do was sniff the air to breathe in the manly scent of his aftershave. Occasionally she would glance over at him, see how intense he was, and she realized how seriously he took his job as a private investigator.

She'd never been a woman who needed or even desired to have a man underfoot, but having Duan here with her felt good. And knowing they were, as he called it, a team made it even better. After giving her the report, he had reminded her that he had asked her to consider him as a pretend fiancé *before* she'd mentioned Villarosas's name. That was the only comforting thought in this entire thing.

She took a sip of her coffee. It was good. Not for the first time, she wondered if there was anything Duan Jeffries wasn't good at. She glanced back down at the report, thinking he'd certainly made it easy for her to follow along. The highlighted sections might as well have been her own, and all the questions he'd jotted on sticky notes were the same ones she would have asked.

"Is the report boring you with all that investigative jargon?"

She glanced over at him. Earlier he had been sitting on the sofa with the computer in his lap. Now he had placed the laptop on the table to take a break and enjoy a cup of coffee with her. And he had changed clothes. He was wearing a pair of jeans and a T-shirt and he was in his bare feet. He looked at home. Sexy.

"No, I find all that stuff interesting and I'm amazed at how police officers and detectives can tie it all together and bring the case to a conclusion."

"Trust me, it's not always easy," he said, smiling over at her. "And in a lot of cases there are loose ends, things that don't add up."

She nodded. "Yes, I saw those."

"And the sad thing is that without time, resources and money, those loose ends are never thoroughly checked out. There are a number of them listed in the report, but without proof it all boils down to speculation."

"And a lot of legal loopholes to slip through."

He held her gaze for a moment, then nodded.

She gave a frustrated sigh, beginning to understand more about him and his work. A couple of weeks ago she'd asked him to tell her about himself, the good, the bad and the ugly. This had been his bad. The inability to right a wrong because of legal loopholes.

"I refuse to let this be one of them, Duan. I will never be satisfied until I know the truth about what really happened to those women, and we don't have months or years to find it out. There has to be something else we can do. Every day Mom is falling deeper and deeper in love with him, and I can't live my life with her here in Shreveport. Whether in the Keys or wherever I'll be living while in medical school, I'll be constantly wondering if she's safe or if Villarosas has decided to make her his next victim. If something has pushed him over the edge to make him want to harm her."

She stood and began pacing. "There is so much we don't know about him. So much that Mom doesn't know. Maybe we should go back there tonight and tell her that we've decided to stay at her place instead of at the hotel so we can keep an eye on things."

"And how do you suggest we explain our decision to do that without her getting suspicious of anything?" he asked.

She slid her hands into the back pockets of her jeans and threw her head back. "Do you have any better ideas?" she snapped.

This woman knew how to pump up his adrenaline, Duan thought, for the good and for the bad. He felt her anger, he understood her frustration and knew her mother was her main concern. And knowing that, he would deal with anyone who dared to hurt her or someone she cared about. Mainly because he was beginning to feel this connection to her that he didn't want to feel.

He stood and moved toward her and she gave him a look that all but said, *Don't mess with me.* He shrugged. She was a spitfire and was having one of her moments. He would help her through it.

He came to a stop in front of her. "Yes, I have a few ideas that we can discuss in detail later. Most of them involve those blue sticky notes I've placed throughout the report. But right now I think you need to chill and work off some anger. I'm going to help you do that."

She rolled her eyes. "I bet. And how do you plan to accomplish that?" she asked with a look that said quite simply that whatever he had in mind, now was not the time to try it.

Duan smiled, reading her thoughts and knowing her assumptions were wrong. "Give me a couple of minutes and I'll have things ready for you," he said, moving away and heading toward the bedroom.

Kim looked confused. "Have what ready for me? Where are you going?"

He turned and a smile touched the corners of his lips. "You need to be pampered so I'm going into the bathroom to prepare your bubble bath."

KIM SANK DOWN DEEPER in the tub beneath all the bubbles and closed her eyes. No man had ever prepared a bath for her. Duan had done more than just run the bathwater; he had made her feel special. And what she found so amazing was that he probably wasn't even aware he'd done so. Certain kinds of deeds seemed to be an ingrained part of his nature. She figured it had to have come from being the oldest and looking out for his younger siblings. Although she couldn't imagine him ever being Terrence's keeper, Olivia was a different matter.

When she'd come to the Keys to be fitted for their bridesmaid dresses, Olivia had told her and Sherri that both of her brothers had been overprotective while she was growing up, Duan more so than Terrence. There were some things she could pull over on Terrence that she wouldn't dare try with Duan. Kim could believe that.

Kim breathed in the scented bubbles as she thought about her mother. More than anything she wished there weren't so many unanswered questions in the hundred or so pages she'd already read on that first case involving Edward. With all the evidence and eyewitnesses interviewed, no one would have reason to suspect foul play of any kind.

It seemed that Mandy Villarosas had been a bona fide flirt. Even the girlfriends with whom she'd gone away for the weekend had verified she had met some man in the club the night before she disappeared.

That was close to ten years ago, before video cameras were used in most businesses. After reading that report one could almost sympathize with Edward for having a wife with loose morals.

But what she wanted to gather from the reports—

and she still had the second case to read—was whether there were similarities between the two women, physical or emotional. And more important, whether there were similarities between her mother and the two women. People became serial killers for any number of reasons.

She shuddered at the thought that Villarosas was a serial killer, but until he was cleared of all suspicions, she would do everything within her power to make sure her mother didn't marry the man.

"Time's up."

Kim opened her eyes and glanced over at Duan. He was standing in the doorway with a huge bath towel in his hand. "But, it's only been—"

"Almost an hour. Look at the bubbles."

She did. Most were gone. Talk about not having any staying power. "I'm disappointed. I thought you would be joining me," she said, easing her body to sit up straight. "The tub's big enough."

"Yes, but you needed this time to yourself."

She agreed that she had needed the time. He was thoughtful not only knowing it but making it happen. "I'm still worried about Mom, Duan."

He nodded as he slowly walked toward her and the hot tub. "Sure you are. You wouldn't be the daughter that you are if you weren't. Your mother has always meant a lot to you."

And yours meant a lot to you until you learned to stop caring, to shield the pain, Kim wanted to say. But she didn't. Instead, when he reached the edge of the tub and opened the huge velour towel, she unashamedly stood up and he wrapped the towel around her before effortlessly lifting her out.

He placed her on her feet and began toweling her dry, patting her wet skin. Never had she felt so taken care of. She could get used to this kind of attention.

A part of her wanted to tell him that she could do it herself, but she didn't. She liked the feel of his touch. And she especially liked his tender ministrations as he gently stroked every inch of her flesh. So she stood there while he took his time drying her wet shoulders, all around her breasts and down to her stomach.

He bent down in front of her to dry her hips and thighs before gently patting dry the curls between them. She watched him and saw how long his lashes were, then noted that his breathing had changed. Without warning he grabbed one of his T-shirts and pulled it over her head, working her arms through the sleeves. It was then that he swept her off her feet and into his arms.

"Where are you taking me?" she asked, looking up at him, studying the jaw that she found so fascinating.

He looked down at her from beneath those long lashes. "The living room. I want to hold you for a while."

A part of her wanted to protest and say she didn't need to be held. And that she didn't want any man to assume she was a weakling that needed his attention. When he lowered his body on the sofa and cuddled her into his arms, for a moment she stared up at him, and he stared back. Then she snuggled closer to him, her head coming to rest against the warmth of his broad chest, and she could actually feel the beating of his heart beneath her cheek.

She closed her eyes thinking that yes, she liked being held by him.

DUAN THOUGHT THERE was something just plain sensual about a woman who was comfortable within her own skin. A woman who knew what she wanted and didn't mind going after it, no matter what it was.

He stood by the bed glancing down at Kim. She was a woman who embraced her sexuality like she had every right to do so, a woman so damn beautiful that his eyes were feeling sore just looking at her.

She had fallen asleep in his arms and he figured she would rest better in the bed. But for a while he had simply enjoyed holding her, listening to her even breathing. It was a peaceful slumber, one he had helped make possible, and he was pleased with that.

Over the years he'd had affairs with many women, but he could now say, quite truthfully, he'd never been involved with one as bold, brazen and gorgeous as this one. But then tonight, she had surrendered to his care and he had enjoyed pampering her, trying to ease her stress and tension. In a way, he wanted her to know that with him she could lighten whatever load she was carrying.

She was worried about her mother and he knew that. And he was well aware that if she could do so, she would pack up and go stay at Wynona's home for the rest of the trip. But he knew that wouldn't be a smart move since they needed to convey as much normalcy in their relationship as possible so Villarosas wouldn't

suspect anything. Like he'd told Kim, they were now
a team.

A team.

For some reason he liked the sound of that. While on
the police force he'd had a female partner once. A very
competent woman who was good at what she did, and
he'd always felt secure that she was covering his back.
But he and Kim were a different kind of team. He felt
a bond with her that he couldn't explain but knew existed.

She shifted position in bed and the ring she wore
drew his attention. The ring he'd placed there earlier
that day. He felt a sudden tightness in his chest. Seeing
that ring—his ring—on her hand did something to him.

He never wanted to see it on anyone else's hand.

Sweet mercy. He rubbed his hands down his face,
knowing what that admission meant. For all his ban-
tering about how he never wanted to share his life with
any woman, he knew if the circumstances were different, if she didn't have dreams to pursue, he would
make her a permanent part of his life. He could honestly
say that he had never wanted a woman as badly as he
wanted her. And that intense desire had originated the
first time he'd set eyes on her.

He had been drawn to her because deep down, in
spite of all the sexual chemistry they generated, there
had been another pull just as strong.

They were alike in a number of ways. Both had pa-
rental issues they couldn't let go of. Her father and his
mother had turned them off ever having a fulfilling
marriage of their own. But he could now say that the
thought of settling down and committing his life to a

woman didn't scare the hell out of him like it once had,
and he credited that to Kim. She was nothing like Susan
Jeffries, and he believed she would never desert the
man she loved or the children she'd given birth to. She
was loyal and dedicated to a fault. Definitely the kind
of woman any man would want to claim as his own.

And the thought of any man doing that was something he didn't want to think about.

CHAPTER TEN

KIM TRIED TO FEIGN SLEEP at the feel of a hard erection poking her in the back, dead center where her butt cheeks came together, and a hot wet tongue gliding across the skin at her nape.

She closed her eyes and decided she wasn't ready to let Duan know she was awake yet. She curled her hands into fists when he shifted and his tongue began moving down her spine.

"Since you're awake, how about flipping on your back so we can play," a deep husky voice said, his heated breath sending sensuous sensations uncoiling in her belly.

She smiled and glanced over her shoulder before turning onto her back. "How did you know I was awake?"

He looked up into her face. "By the way you were breathing. I didn't touch you until I knew I had your attention. You didn't fool me."

And before she could make a comment to that, he shifted his body and leaned down to kiss her. The first thing that came to her mind was that his tongue was full of energy this morning, and the second was that she didn't have one single complaint about it, especially after the way he'd pampered her last night.

She so loved the feel of his mouth on hers, the way he seemed to put everything into every kiss they shared. And how he seemed to greedily lap her up, feast hungrily on her as he drove his tongue deeper and deeper inside her mouth.

The ringing of her cell phone had them breaking apart, sucking in hard breaths. "That's probably Mom making sure we don't forget breakfast," she said, shifting to reach for the ringing phone.

Before she got too far away, Duan reached out, grabbed a thigh and leaned down to place a kiss right in the center of her stomach before sliding off the bed and grabbing his own cell phone off the nightstand. He had heard the humming sound as it vibrated before daybreak, but had decided to miss the call since he didn't want to wake Kim.

He saw the missed call had come from Landon. While Kim chatted with her mother he moved toward the balcony to return Landon's call. "Hey, man, what's up?"

"Just wanted to check in to see if you've met Villarosas yet."

"Yes, I met him and you were right. He seems like an arrogant ass. How is Chevis doing with the first case?"

"He's trying to find out the identity of the man Mandy Villarosas was supposed to have flirted with that night at the club. Chev is convinced someone might remember something."

"Even after ten years?"

"Yes. According to the report taken from one of the women, a class reunion party was also going on at the club that night, which means there was probably a lot of picture-taking. Chev is going to track down some of the partygoers to see if he can gather photos. I'll let you know what we find out."

Duan ended the call and flipped off the phone as he reentered the hotel room. He glanced over at Kim. She returned his gaze with troubled eyes. It was obvious something was wrong.

"Are you okay?" he asked.

She shrugged her shoulders. "Yes, I guess. I just finished talking to Mom and she sounded so happy and excited." She laughed bitterly and a fiery look appeared in her eyes. "It pisses me off that the man that has brought so much joy to her life could end up being a damn murderer."

Duan knew how she felt, but he also knew they needed to play the game well with Villarosas, which meant perfecting their acting abilities. "Forget the personal now, Kim. Put a lid on the anger. We need to concentrate on nailing this guy if he's guilty, and the only way we can do that is to find out everything there is to know. We've come this far and the last thing we need is to have my cover blown. Villarosas has to believe he has us snowed, especially you. You can't in any way let him know you suspect something. The questions you ask him should be the same ones you would ask any man about to marry your mother. And you want to make him feel comfortable in telling you anything you want to know."

He reached out and traced the line of her jaw with his fingertips. "Can you do that, Kim? If you can't, I'll understand. No questions asked. No explanation required. But a lot is at stake and—"

"I can do it, Duan," she said with clear certainty and unwavering confidence. "And I *will* do it. If he isn't what Mom thinks he is, then I need to help expose him. We're not doing this just for my mother. I have to remember the families of those other two women who don't know if they're alive somewhere or really dead. I have to do it for them, too."

He smiled and cupped her jaw before lowering his mouth down to hers. The moment their lips touched, a fiery heat exploded within his gut and he slid his tongue inside her mouth, tangled with hers, and laved the insides from corner to corner. And when she wrapped her arms around his neck he dropped his hand from her jaw and slid it around her waist.

Her body melted into his and he could only continue to kiss this woman who affected him like no other. The woman responsible for making him want things he never wanted before. The woman who made it possible for him to consider all the possibilities, but only with her.

She was one and done. If he could not have her, then he would not have anyone, because he was convinced she was his other half, the one that made him whole. He was letting his emotions come into play and get the best of him, but he couldn't do anything to stop it.

Reluctantly, he pulled his mouth away and pressed his forehead against hers. There was so much passion between them. How could that be possible?

He took a step back. "I was just talking to Landon and he indicated that Chevis is in Orlando following up a possible lead. The report you read indicated that the night before Mandy Villarosas, wife number one, disappeared there was a party at the club—a high-school reunion."

Kim nodded. "Yes, I recall reading that in the report."

"As with most reunions, there're always people taking a lot of pictures at random. We're contacting a few of the attendees to see if someone got a shot of this man—the person Mandy supposedly flirted with that night. The women she went out of town with that weekend think he's the same man that she was to meet the day she disappeared."

Kim frowned. "But if that's true and there is a possibility there was another man involved, then…"

She stopped talking, hoping Duan was following her train of thoughts. He was.

"That means if there was another man involved, then that man could very well be the person behind her disappearance," Duan replied. "Remember, we've never said Villarosas is guilty of any crime, but he is under suspicion."

"With the scenario you just presented, I don't know how he can be a suspect, Duan. What if the man at the club is the same man she went to meet? He would be the main suspect, wouldn't he?"

Duan nodded. "Yes and no. There're still a lot of gray areas. That's why we're looking into all the possibilities. Just remember, it wasn't the first case that roused Landon's suspicions because he never worked that one. It was the second case and now we have access to both. And we're going to proceed as if Edward is innocent until proven guilty, or at least until we can establish a motive."

"And if Mom insists on marrying him before then?"

"Then we'll level with her and tell her our suspicions. But as I told you, chances are she might not want to believe that he's capable of harming anyone. And you need to apprise me of everyone your mother might be inviting to the breakfast this morning so there won't be any surprises. I don't want to be caught off guard about anything. You can school me on the drive over."

"Okay."

"And remember, no matter what, we're a team."

She smiled. "I'll remember."

Duan glanced at the clock on the wall. "Ready to take a shower?" he asked, heading in the direction of the bathroom.

"You go ahead, I need to call the hospital and check on someone who came through E.R. Thursday, a little boy who'd gotten bitten by a poisonous snake. They were flying in the anti-venom and I want to see how he's doing."

"Okay." He turned to enter the bathroom and then stopped to look back at her. As if he needed to taste her again, he walked over and pulled her into his arms, covering her mouth with his.

Unlike the one earlier, this kiss was unexpected, spontaneous, and sensations immediately flooded Kim's body. The breath she'd been about to take was reduced to a shudder. His tongue was making a quick but thorough study of her mouth and the tip of his finger was making erotic circles on her back. She needed this. She wanted this. And he was giving it to her in perfect measure, using his tongue to stroke her into tranquility, to give her the peace and calm she needed at that moment.

Reluctantly, he pulled back and released her. He held her gaze for a moment, and then without saying a single word he crossed the room to the bathroom and closed the door behind him.

CHAPTER ELEVEN

"So, how did you and Kim meet?"

Duan smiled down at Aunt Gert, who appeared to be in her early sixties. Kim had warned him that her aunt would ask a lot of questions. And she was right.

Breakfast had become a Saturday-morning brunch outside on the terrace. Wynona and Aunt Gert had done most of the cooking, and Duan had to agree the women were great cooks. He couldn't help noticing that Edward had avoided him most of the morning, but was in Kim's face every chance he got.

"Kim and I met when her best friend, Sherri, whom I'm sure you know, became engaged to my brother Terrence," he answered truthfully.

"So, was it love at first sight?" Aunt Gert asked with a hopeful look on her face.

He was inclined to agree with her on that. "Let's just say there were a lot of things about Kim that drew me to her. Things I definitely liked and admired." He took a sip of iced tea. Kim had said her Aunt Gert was a die-hard romantic and she was right. The woman was really taking this all in.

He glanced across the room at Kim. She was talking to a man she had introduced earlier as her mother's neighbor, Benjamin Sanders, whom she fondly called Mr. Bennie.

Duan suddenly realized just how true the statement was that he'd made to Aunt Gert. There had been a number of things he'd liked about Kim right off the bat. Her looks headed the list, of course. But it didn't take long to discover that she was a very intelligent woman who had a profound sense of caring for others, and he hadn't been surprised to learn she was a nurse. Another thing he liked about her was her spunk.

"Well, I'm just glad she finally got serious about a man. For a while, I was concerned about her."

"Concerned?" he asked.

"Yes, concerned."

Duan chuckled at the elderly woman's words. "You were concerned that she hadn't gotten serious about a man?"

"Yes, after all, she's twenty-seven."

"Yes, ma'am."

"In today's society, if a woman her age doesn't have a man, people start to think things," Aunt Gert said.

"Is that why you sent her résumé to that television show—because you were concerned whether she even *liked* men?" he asked incredulously, having caught on to what Aunt Gert was insinuating.

She met his gaze. "Yes."

At that moment he would have thought unkindly of the woman if he hadn't seen all the love she felt for Kim radiating in her face. "Trust me, no one has to wonder about Kim. She's all the woman any man would ever want or need." And he knew all the way to the base of his groin that statement was true.

The woman's face lit up in a smile. "I'm glad to hear it. And I like that ring you've put on her finger. It looks just like it belongs there."

Duan couldn't help but smile himself. "Yes, I think so, as well. So rest assured, Aunt Gert. My woman is doing just fine."

He took a slow sip of his lemonade. *My woman.* His thoughts floated back to that morning. She had indeed been *his* woman. He hadn't expected her to join him in the shower, but once she'd found out the little boy was recovering from the snake bite, she had. Together they had given the word *steam* a whole new meaning. One that made sensations stir from his chest to his groin just thinking about it.

His gaze sought Kim out across the room. Someone had placed a baby in her arms, one of her cousins' babies, he assumed. She looked like a natural holding it, and then he recalled that she'd told him she wanted children one day, but didn't intend to marry. He continued to look at her and doubted if his own mother had ever had such a look on her face while holding him, Terrence or Olivia.

"Well, I've consumed enough of your time, Duan. Wynona is hoping that everyone will hang around for dinner because she's fixing a feast. I'll go see if she needs help with anything in the kitchen."

When she walked off, he felt someone looking at him and met Edward Villarosas's gaze. He was standing with a group of men but his attention was on Duan. Deciding the man had avoided him long enough that day, Duan crossed the room when the men Edward had been talking to walked off.

"So, Edward, how are things going?" Duan asked.

Edward smoothed his hand over his bald head. "Fine. I see that you're fitting in rather nicely."

Duan chuckled. "I'm trying to. Tell me," he said, meeting Edward's gaze, "was it easy for you?"

"To do what?"

"Fit in."

"Oh, sure. Wynona has nice relatives." Edward hesitated a moment then said, "So, you were a cop in Atlanta. I lived in Atlanta for a while. For ten years."

Duan widened his eyes as if he were surprised by the statement. "That's a long time. Why did you leave?"

Edward shrugged. "After my divorces there was nothing there for me anymore. I wanted a fresh start so I moved here." After taking a sip of his lemonade he asked, "How long were you a cop?"

"Seven years," Duan said.

"Were you always on the beat?" Edward asked.

Duan shook his head. "No, I made detective after my second year. After doing detective work for a number of years, I decided to get my own private investigative firm. I'm proud to say I'm doing well with it."

"That's good to hear."

"What about you? What did you do for a living while in Atlanta?"

"I was a mechanic for a long time and had my own shop, mostly working on antique cars."

"Really?" Duan said, as if he hadn't known that fact. "What was the name of it?"

"Villarosas Auto Shop. It was located in College Park."

The man glanced around the room. "Excuse me,

Duan, but I need to go see Wynona for a second." Duan watched him head outside to the patio.

"How are things going?"

He glanced up and saw that Kim had approached. "Okay. What about with you?"

"Edward is asking a lot of questions."

"About what?"

"You. And I hope I gave him all the right answers."

Duan frowned. "What sort of questions?"

"Questions I'd assume a father would ask when his daughter brought a guy to the house for their first date. How long were you a cop? Are you a detective, and if so, how long? Where did you live in Atlanta and for how long? Those sorts of questions."

Duan nodded. "And what did you tell him?"

"What we agreed that I would."

"Good. I might add you to my P.I. firm yet," he teased, leaning toward her and placing a kiss on her lips. Anyone looking at them would assume they were sharing a loving moment.

She chuckled. "No, thank you. I'll stick to the medical field. Anyway, I think I surprised him when I finally told him that considering he was going to marry my mom, the two of you should get to know each other. And that if he wanted to know anything else about you, he needed to ask you himself."

Duan smiled. "He did, but I'm sure more questions are coming later."

He placed his arm around her shoulder and tried to downplay the tingle he felt in his gut from touching her. No matter where she'd been in the room all morning, he'd been aware of her.

"How did things go with you and Aunt Gert?" she asked.

"I think she likes me."

"How was the rest of your day with Edward?" Duan asked. "I couldn't help noticing a few times he had you stuck in a corner all to himself." It was later that evening and they were heading back toward the hotel, momentarily stuck in traffic as a train passed.

Kim glanced over and gave him a faint smile. Everyone had hung around for dinner and afterward several people played a game of cards. Duan was right. Edward had participated in one or two games, but most of the time he'd cornered her. She wasn't surprised Duan had noticed. In fact, she had picked up on him watching her a lot that day. And knowing his gaze was on her had given her sensuous shivers. The thought that he had that effect on her no longer came as a surprise.

"Yes, I did everything you'd suggested and kept him talking. He didn't say a lot about his marriages, but he did tell me he didn't have any kids and that was his one regret in life. So, he's looking forward to becoming my stepfather." She sighed. "That's basically it. And he did talk about how happy he plans on making Mom. So, what did you find out?"

"Not a whole lot. He likes playing golf and going fishing. He suggested we do both while I'm here. Of course, I didn't turn down the opportunity to spend more time with him. I also got him to talk about his past life in Atlanta. But other than telling me about the auto mechanic shop he used to own in College Park, he was rather tight-lipped."

"That doesn't tell us a lot, does it?" Kim asked.

"No. However, as days go on—"

"But that's just it, Duan. Instead of spending time getting to know the man my mother is marrying for the right reasons, I'm questioning him for all the wrong ones, only because—"

"I know what you're about to say, Kim, and I understand. But—"

"Does there have to be a *but,* Duan?"

"In this case, yes. Now tell me about your mom's neighbor."

She glanced over at him in surprise. "Who? Mr. Bennie?"

"Yes."

"Why would you want to know anything about him?"

"He seems to like your mom."

Kim rolled her eyes. "Of course he likes Mom. They've lived next door to each other for years and have known each other even longer. They attended school together. The house Mom is living in now used to be my grandparents' house and the house Mr. Bennie lives in used to be his parents' house, so he and Mom were neighbors growing up. He's a few years older than she is."

She shifted a little in her seat to look at Duan. "When his mother died, Mr. Bennie and his wife and only daughter moved back to Shreveport to take care of his father. But his dad only lived a year after that. And around eight years ago, Mr. Bennie's wife, Ms. Diana, died of breast cancer."

Duan nodded, thinking the house Mr. Bennie was

living in had experienced a lot of sadness. "Where's his daughter?"

"Valerie, who is a year older than I am, left for college in New Jersey and met a guy there. Now they're married with a little girl. I get to see them when I come home for Christmas. She usually comes and spends the holidays with Mr. Bennie like I do with Mom every year."

"He's never remarried?"

"No, he never remarried. I like Mr. Bennie. He's a really nice man who helps Mom out a lot with the yard and by doing odds and ends around the house."

Kim didn't say anything for a moment, then asked, "Why do you think he likes Mom *that* way?"

Duan smiled. "There are little things I notice, things I can now recognize as signs. Trust me when I say they went past me with my own father. And they went past Terrence, as well. Olivia pointed them out to us and made us aware that Cathy, our dad's secretary, had been in love with him for years. We thought Libby was crazy until she told us to pay more attention, so we did. At first we didn't pick up on anything, but then we noticed the looks Cathy would give Dad when he wasn't looking and how she would do anything for him."

"And you saw Mr. Bennie looking at Mom when he thought she wasn't looking?"

"Yes. And then there's the way his face lights up whenever she walks into a room. Trust me. I'd say he's definitely smitten. And sometimes people have a tendency not to notice someone who's always there, even if that person's the best thing for them."

At that moment, Duan's cell phone went off. Luckily they were still stalled in traffic, so he lifted his hip to pull the phone from his belt clip.

"Yes, Landon. What's up?"

"We may have found the guy in question. One of the women recognized him from some of the photos as the same guy Mandy Villarosas flirted with that night."

Duan nodded. "Did anyone recognize him as a former classmate?"

"No. So now we have a face, but we need a name. Brett is going to provide that."

Duan chuckled. Brett could do just about anything with a computer. "Let me know when he finds out something."

He clicked off the phone and glanced over at Kim. "We have a make on the guy that Mandy Villarosas was supposed to have met."

"So you know who he is?" she asked, not hiding her excitement.

"No, but he was captured in several pictures, so at least that's a start. We're not sure if he went there with someone, or if he knew anyone at the club. Remember, this was ten years ago."

Her hope deflated, Kim sank back into her seat. "So it will be like pulling a needle out of a haystack."

Duan laughed. "Not really. Especially since Brett is working that end of things."

"Brett? One of the guys in your firm?"

"Yes."

"Why?"

"Brett is our computer and technical expert and he's developed this high-tech network. All he has to do is scan in this guy's picture and it'll be distributed to all his databases. It goes to probably every law enforcement agency in the country, as well as the FBI's database. I'll give him less than forty-eight hours to find out the identity of the man."

"But like you said, it's been ten years," she reminded him.

"Yes, and the beauty of the equipment Brett has developed is that it can do an age enhancement. If we know what he looked like then, you can be certain we'll know what he looks like now. Brett has had quite a few successes."

"Wow."

Duan chuckled. "Yes, now we're getting somewhere."

He shifted his head to look out the windshield. It was dark and they were on a two-lane road with cars in front and back of them, all at a standstill. "Hell, how long is that train? It seems like we've been stopped for a while."

"Not sure. I told you to go this way because it's a short cut back to the hotel. I forgot about the train crossing."

He glanced back over at her and grinned. "Are you anxious to get back to the hotel?"

"Aren't you?"

Duan leaned back in his seat. "Yes."

"Why? You can't be hungry since my mother fed you plenty. What's the rush?"

The smile on his lips widened. "I'm surprised you have to ask, and it's probably the same reason as yours," he said throatily.

"You think?"

"I know. This is our third weekend together, Kim."

She was surprised he remembered. She thought only women recalled things like that. "And you want to celebrate?"

"Yeah, something like that."

She released her seat belt and edged closer to him on the bench seat. "Why wait until we get back to the hotel? We can start things right here."

"There is the matter of all these cars," he pointed out.

"Yes, but no one is beside us and it's dark. It will be like this for a while. So to my way of thinking we don't have to wait until we get back to the hotel to do certain things."

He swallowed deeply as she reached across his lap to push the button that slid their seats back.

He raised a brow. "Just what do you think you're doing?"

"You'll see."

He watched as her fingers pulled his zipper down. He had started getting hard the moment she mentioned them getting back to the hotel room.

"Kim, don't you think—"

"Shh. I don't think, Duan, and I don't want you to think, either. I just want you to relax and enjoy. And be a little daring."

And while she had been saying those words, she had slowly worked his shaft from his jeans. It was standing straight up and almost hitting the steering wheel.

"Gosh, you're an impressive man," she said, licking her lips while working her hands over his erection. And then before he could stop her, she dipped her head to his lap and took him into the warmth of her mouth.

"Kim!"

He called out her name but by now stopping her was a lost cause. He watched her head bob up and down and his entire groin ached at the feel of her mouth on him.

He felt hot, ready to explode, from the head of his penis all the way to his balls. Every lick of her tongue was pushing him slowly and deliciously over the edge. And every long, slow suck was almost causing him to come. He was tempted...boy, was he tempted, to fill her mouth with his release. If only she knew what she did to him. All the pleasure she was lavishing on him. Not just with her mouth, but with every part of her.

He let out a deep groan, thinking if he had to get stuck in traffic, then this was the best way to pass the time. The woman was definitely something else. He almost cursed when he saw the train's flashing last car, which meant they would be moving again soon.

"Kim?"

She didn't answer but continued feasting on him as if it were her last meal. She kept licking and went right on sucking and then he couldn't hold back.

"Kim!"

He came hard. Busting a nut had never been so spectacular, so damn fantastic. He tried to get a grip but it was too late. His body exploded and every nerve erupted. He tightened his hand on the steering wheel as electricity rushed through every part of him, and through it all her mouth did not let go of him. She kept it locked down on him as white fire spread through him, touching every cell in his body.

He moved a hand from the steering wheel to rub through the curls on her head, gently tugging, trying to pull her away from him. But she wouldn't let up, so he let her have her way as intoxicating sensations continued to rush through him. She had a way of satisfying every needy bone in his body and her sense of giving overwhelmed him.

When he had nothing left to give and she kept her mouth on him anyway, he whispered in a hoarse voice, "Kim, sweetheart, the train's gone by. You have to stop. The cars will start moving in a minute."

She lifted her head and looked up at him, holding his rod just mere inches from her wet lips. "You sure that's it?"

She was amazing. "For now. But when I get you back to the hotel…"

"What are you going to do?"

"You'll see." The blasting of a horn behind them signaled it was time to put the car in gear and move forward.

After tucking his shaft back inside and zipping his jeans, she returned to her seat, all the while licking her lips. "That was good."

"Mercy," he said, putting the car in gear and easing on the gas pedal. He was grateful to hit a traffic light. He needed to get his senses back in control. His shaft was still throbbing, but he knew that had to have been the most marvelous thing he'd ever experienced.

He glanced over at her. "I'm going to get you for that, Kim," he warned in a husky voice that rumbled deep from his gut.

She smiled at him sweetly. "You were going to *get* me anyway, weren't you, Duan?"

What she'd said was true, and the mere thought of it increased the throbbing in his groin. This was crazy. You would think after what she'd just done to him, his shaft would be satisfied for days.

The traffic light changed and the car moved forward. He couldn't wait to get her back to the hotel.

CHAPTER TWELVE

"YOU DO KNOW this is the third weekend straight that we've shared Sunday-morning breakfast in bed," Duan said, glancing over at Kim as he took a sip of his coffee.

Wearing a bathrobe, Kim sat cross-legged in the middle of the bed. She smiled over at him. "If we keep this up it might become one of those hard habits to break."

Duan placed his cup aside and leaned over to kiss her with a passion that Kim felt all the way to her toes.

After he pulled away she stared at him for long moments before saying, "Mom is going to call us when she and Edward are ready to head over to the county fair. In the meantime, what do you think we should do while we're waiting?"

He shook his head and chuckled. "Get the hell out of this room before we kill ourselves. I've had more sex with you in the past twenty-four hours than I've had all year."

She glanced away, nervously fiddling with the belt around her bathrobe. There was that word again. *Sex.* Was that all they'd been sharing for the past three weeks? When did a man stop thinking of it as nothing more than sex?

Evidently for Duan, it wouldn't be any time soon.

But then, why should it? Just because she had started dealing with a bunch of crazy emotions was no reason to think he was doing the same.

Of their own accord her eyes skimmed down the muscular plane of his chest, reminding her how much she liked rubbing her fingers over it.

Kim forced herself to look at his face. "Is that what you want to do? Get out of the room?" she asked nervously, her tongue licking her top lip.

He stared at her. "No. Especially not when you do something like that with your tongue," he said in a voice so deep and sexy it made her shiver.

And then, as if he intended to make her do more than shiver, he raked his gaze from her lips down the rest of her body, taking in everything in his path, making her feel naked even while wearing her robe. The look in his eyes hinted at more than lust; it showed a hunger so hot that parts of her felt as if she were on fire.

Duan was about to lean forward to cop another kiss when his cell phone went off. He reached over toward the nightstand. "Whatever thoughts you were thinking, hold them until after I take this call."

He answered the phone. "This is Duan."

"Hey. Brett's been busy."

Duan smiled. That could only mean one thing. "What did he find?"

"Our man."

"Who is he?"

"His name is Stein Green and at the moment he's serving time in a Florida prison for armed robbery that involved the death of a police officer. It's pretty safe to say that Green will be behind bars for a while—he's serving a life sentence with no chance of parole. Chevis is on his way to Florida as we speak."

Duan nodded. "Let me know when Chevis finds out anything."

Moments later, he hung up the phone and glanced over at Kim. She looked gorgeous, even when she was sitting there staring at him expectantly.

"That was Landon," he said. "Brett has ID'd that guy—the one in the photos."

She nodded. "And?"

"And he's serving time for armed robbery in a jail in Florida. Chevis is on his way to pay him a visit."

Kim propped herself against one of the pillows. That was his favorite position. Well...one of his favorites. He much preferred seeing her on her back.

"That's good news," she said. "Do you think he'll tell him anything?"

"It depends. But I do know if there's one man who can get information out of someone, it's Chevis."

He eased off the bed. "Now is a good time for us to go over those case files since you've read both reports."

Kim watched him move across the room to get the reports from the table. He was only wearing a pair of briefs and she couldn't help thinking, not for the first time, that the man was built. Her gaze traveled up his sturdy long legs, flat tummy and broad chest. And his tush could make a woman drool, especially when he was wearing tight jeans.

She glanced at the digital clock on the nightstand. Her mother had gone to church and they would be getting together with her and Edward to go to the county fair around two.

Kim sighed. They had spent the entire day with her mother and the family yesterday, and intended to do the same for the remaining days she would be in Shreveport.

The thought of Wynona spending any time alone with Edward still bothered her, but she couldn't make a flap about it or it might push her mother even deeper into the man's arms. Edward Villarosas was certainly a charmer, or at least he tried to be.

She was supposed to leave next Sunday. She hoped, if nothing else, she could convince her mother to postpone her wedding plans for a while. She certainly intended to try.

KIM STEPPED AWAY from the car and glanced around. She recalled how each year when a county fair came to New Orleans, she'd looked forward to going. That was the only time her father actually acted like a normal human being.

He had enjoyed taking her and her mother, and before their eyes he would transform into another person. It was as if he'd needed—if only for a little while—the chance to act like a kid again. He would head for the roller coasters first, which was probably the reason she'd inherited a fondness for the daring rides.

Her mother, who'd come to stand beside her, smiled and then leaned down and kissed her cheek. As if she knew what she'd been thinking, Wynona said, "I know you don't want to hear this, Kimani, but your father wasn't all bad."

Kim rolled her eyes. Her mother was right; she really

didn't want to hear it. She glanced over and saw Duan and Edward standing by the car talking. The conversation appeared to be going well. She turned back to her mom. It wasn't the first time Wynona had tried convincing her of her father's goodness, so it wouldn't be the first time she'd had a problem believing it.

"Your father had a rough childhood," her mother went on to say.

"Please, Mom, give me a break. The man used to beat the crap out of you all the time."

"Yes, but only after he'd been drinking," her mother said defensively.

"Then that was almost every Friday night," Kim said. She really wasn't in the mood to rehash this bit of family history.

"Please remember those other days when he would be the fun, caring husband that I married."

Kim didn't say anything but a tightness in her stomach pushed her to ask, "Do you know where he is and do you ever hear from him?"

From the look on her mother's face Kim knew the answer. "You *do* know where he is and you *do* hear from him, don't you?" she asked in what she knew was an accusing voice.

Her mother didn't back down. "Yes to both, and the only reason he hasn't contacted you is because he's afraid you wouldn't accept him, and that would truly break his heart."

Kim frowned. "And I'm supposed to care about breaking his heart?"

Instead of answering, her mother rushed on, "He's your father and he has gotten help over the years."

"Good for him."

"Kim, listen, we—"

"No, Mom," she whispered so her voice wouldn't carry to the men. "When it comes to my father, there is no *we*. I don't hate him. I won't waste that much energy. He has to come to terms with how he treated you. Treated us."

"He never hit you."

"No, Mom, he didn't have to. He had you for his punching bag."

"But he's gotten better over the years. He's even in the church now."

Kim twirled her finger in the air and simultaneously rolled her eyes. "Whoop-de-do."

"Kim."

"Just what do you want from me, Mom?"

"I want you to find it in your heart to forgive your father. You've made the first step by finding a man to love, but before you can really move on you're going to have to forgive him. I had to do so and that's why I can get on with my life. He's a part of my past that I won't repeat. I've found someone who wants to make me happy."

"You sure of that?"

"Yes. Edward is a good man."

Kim bit down on her lower lip so she would not respond. A part of her hoped and prayed Duan and his partners were wrong about Edward and that he was a good man like her mother assumed. But she wasn't holding out for that. Duan had gone over the cases with her earlier, and she had a good idea how an investigator's mind worked. No stone would be left uncovered this time around.

She and her mother ended the conversation when they saw Edward and Duan approaching. "Looks like we're going to have a lot of fun today," Edward said, excitement in his voice. For a split second he reminded Kim of her father and that wasn't a good thing.

"I can't wait," Wynona responded, a huge smile on her face.

Kim glanced over at Duan. He reached out and took her hand in his, then leaned over and brushed a kiss across her lips. It was as if he'd read her emotions and knew she was bothered by something.

"Well, you guys," Edward announced, grabbing Wynona's hand, "I'm going to take my lady and we're heading for the Scorpion and from there to the Ferris wheel."

"See you guys later," Wynona called over her shoulder, increasing her pace to keep up with Edward.

Duan glanced over at her and tightened his hand on hers. "You okay?"

She saw concern in the depths of his eyes. "Yes, I'm fine. I just had one of those 'daddy' moments."

"Come on, let's walk," he said, keeping her hand in his. "Want to tell me about it?"

For some reason she didn't mind airing the family's dirty laundry to Duan. She'd done it before. "Fairs used to be one of my daddy's favorite places. When he took us it would be one of the few times he was normal. He would actually stay sober for a few weeks after visiting a fair. After that, it was every Friday night as usual. He would get off work and head for the nearest bar with his homies. Luckily there was always someone in the group who would bring him home later and not let him drive."

She grimaced. "It would have been better if they'd checked him in to a hotel to let him sleep it off instead of bringing him home. That would have spared Mom the beatings once he got there."

A bitter smile formed on her lips. "He would sleep late on Saturdays while I was bandaging up Mom's wounds. Then he would wake up around noon and see her bruises and become all apologetic, asking her forgiveness and telling her it wouldn't happen again. He'd become the loving husband and father, and Mom was eager to believe the best so she'd eventually forgive him. I lived to regret Fridays, Duan. Most kids in school looked forward to the weekends, but I wasn't one of them since I knew what would happen at my house."

"I'm sorry, Kim." Duan's voice was gentle. "That kind of life must have been hell to endure each week."

"It was. Because of my father I've endured a lot of hell. Forgiving doesn't come easy for me, and Mom can't seem to understand that."

"And all this time I've been the one hosting a pity party thinking the Jeffrieses were the family with all the garbage." Duane shook his head. "When my mom left, I was angry, madder than hell. I was the oldest and I had Terrence to deal with. He was a holy terror even back in the day. And then there was Olivia, who tried to take Mom's place. It's still hard to believe how a woman could leave her husband and family without looking back."

He stopped walking and so did she. He met her gaze.

"I have one hell of a father, and I can't tell him enough how much I appreciate him. He had to step in and do both roles as a parent and he did it. I'm sure it wasn't easy, yet he never complained. I admire him for what he did, and I'm not sure that I could have done the same if I'd been in his place."

They began walking again and a few moments later they stopped at a vendor to buy a bag of popcorn to share. When they started walking again she asked, "Have you seen your mom since she left?"

"I didn't for a long time, almost eighteen years, in fact. She left when I was twelve. A few days before my thirtieth birthday, after I'd celebrated the opening of my investigative firm, I decided to put my skills to the test and find her. I actually wanted to see her. I *needed* to see her for closure—at least I told myself it was closure. But I was hoping that when I tracked her down and she saw me, she would be remorseful, ashamed for not having the decency to pick up a phone to see how her kids were doing."

He shook his head. "But when I found her, there was no remorse or shame on her part, just annoyance at being bothered. She told me, in a not-too-nice way, that she'd gotten out of our life for a reason. She never wanted kids, wasn't the motherly type and that she didn't want to renew a relationship with any of us."

"Wow, that's deep," Kim said.

"Yes, it was. I caught a plane back to Atlanta to hear Terrence's taunting that he'd told me so. Somehow he'd known. He hadn't seen her, he hadn't wanted to see her and had been determined to move on with his life. He'd accepted her walking out on us at face value. Her betrayal, her abandonment had left its mark on the three of us, but especially on Dad."

Kim heard the bitterness in his voice. She knew it well. It was the same whenever she discussed her father with anyone. A father she hadn't seen in at least five years now. The last time had been at her paternal grandmother's funeral. He hadn't looked in the best of health and even then she guessed he was still hitting the bottle and she'd even smelled alcohol on his breath.

She glanced ahead and saw her mother and Edward. They were standing in line to get on another ride. She didn't want to think how her mother would handle it if what they suspected about Edward was true. That would definitely be a heartbreaker and her mother didn't deserve that.

Duan glanced down at her. "I know you're still worried about your mom, but you're going to have to believe that I'll do everything I can to find out the truth about Villarosas, good or bad. You're going to have to trust me."

She nodded. "I do trust you, Duan."

Kim looked away, fearful she might also admit that she had fallen in love with him.

CHAPTER THIRTEEN

DUAN EASED OUT OF BED when he heard his cell phone vibrating on the nightstand. He picked it up and quickly moved toward the bathroom. Kim was still asleep, lying naked on top of the covers. He felt his shaft get hard as he entered the bathroom. Closing the door behind him, he leaned against it as he flipped on his phone.

"Kind of late for you, isn't it, Landon?" he asked, wiping a hand down his face. It was just past midnight.

"Sorry about that. I'm still at the office."

Duan wasn't surprised. It had been that way for Landon ever since he'd lost Simone, just two days before their wedding day. She and two of her brides-maids had shared a ride from the bachelorette party. A drunk driver had run a traffic light and the impact had been so great both vehicles had burst into flames, killing everyone involved. That had been close to four years ago and Duan knew Landon was still grieving. "I'm wondering about you not having a life, Lan."

Landon's chuckle came across the line. "Don't wonder too much, otherwise you'll sound like my mom. Anyway, I surfed the internet and found something interesting."

"What?"

"Several old police reports, dated twenty or so years

ago. They're on Villarosas. He went under the name Eduardo Villarosas then. Probably calls himself Edward for short these days."

Duan nodded. "What are the police reports about?"

"Domestic calls. Most were from neighbors complaining that he and his girlfriend were disturbing the peace with their frequent arguments. There is one where the girlfriend placed a 911 call when Villarosas threatened her because he thought she was being unfaithful."

"So there were a lot of lovers' spats."

"Seems that way. On one particular call, the girlfriend said he threatened her with bodily harm if she moved her things out of the apartment they were sharing. According to the report, she claimed Villarosas has a mean jealous streak. Police suggested she get a restraining order, which she did."

"Anything else?"

"I spoke to Chev. He's meeting with prison officials today to request time with Stein Green. Hopefully, the man will be cooperative. In the meantime, I've located a current address for Edward's old girlfriend. She still lives in the area, so I think I'll pay her a visit. I'll let you know what I find out."

From the first, Landon had assumed the disappearance of Villarosas's second wife was a hit job, a good old-fashioned murder for hire. And if that was the case, it was probably the same for Edward's first wife, as well. But without a concrete motive or a dead body, the police hadn't been able to come up with anything that would stick.

Duan couldn't wait to hear whatever Chevis could

get from that guy in prison. Was he the man Mandy had met up with that day? Had he been a lover or an assassin?

"Villarosas and I are going fishing tomorrow," Duan said. "I'm going to engage him in a lot of conversation, but I don't expect him to say much. He's been pretty tight-lipped around me."

"Yeah, but there's that one chance he might lower his guard and say something meaningful."

"If I can be so lucky," Duan said.

"Well, with all of us working on this, something has to give sooner or later," Landon replied.

Duan certainly hoped it was sooner. He and Kim were supposed to leave next Sunday and he knew she had no intention of doing that without letting her mother know about their suspicions of Villarosas, proof or not.

"Let's hope so," he said.

Moments later, he ended the call and softly opened the door to walk out of the bathroom. But he paused when he immediately picked up the scent of a woman. *His woman.*

His heartbeat thundered in his chest. This was the second time he'd thought of her as his woman. But then, he would be the first to say his relationship with Kim was rather unique. What was supposed to have been a one-night stand had evolved into something a lot more. The thought of them parting ways on Sunday sent something plummeting deep in his gut. He couldn't imagine a day of not seeing her, not being with her.

He glanced across the room and saw her standing at the window. She had put on his T-shirt and had her back to him, unaware he had come out of the bathroom. That gave him a chance to just stand there and stare at her, feeling his body getting aroused in the process.

Like most men, he'd always had a pretty healthy sexual appetite, but with Kim his craving for sex was downright voracious, as insatiable as it could get. She would tempt him to no end, and the more she did, the more ravenous he became. But with her there were other things that turned him on, as well. Like the way she would lean into a kiss whenever his mouth descended on hers, and the way she would smile at him for no reason at all.

Then there was the way she would open up to him whenever she told him about her past. She had allowed him to feel the pain of her childhood, and miraculously, he had allowed her to feel the pain of his, which was something he hadn't ever done with any woman. His relationship with his mother—or his lack of one—was something he'd kept bottled up inside him. But with Kim the conversation had come easily and without any anger or feelings of guilt.

And with Kim he could have fun, like the time they'd gone fishing in the Keys on Terrence's boat, and earlier today at the fair. With a host of other folks around them, they had strolled from ride to ride, vendor to vendor, and for a few hours he had forgotten that their attachment to each other had been nothing but a show. For that period of time their relationship had seemed real.

Then there was the time when they had sat together on a bench waiting for her mother and Villarosas to get off one of the rides. He and Kim had shared a bag of cotton candy, and he'd gotten turned on watching her tongue dart out of her mouth to lick away the sticky and sweet confection from her lips. Unable to resist, he had leaned over and used his own tongue and mouth to help, and had even gone so far as to lick a bit of the sugar off her fingers. He had to stop himself from kissing her so many times today, kisses he wanted to give her for no reason at all.

Just because.

Just because he thought she was simply adorable. Just because she had to be the most sensuous woman he'd ever met. And just because everything they did was spontaneous. Especially when they made love.

"I hope there's a reason for that smile, Duan."

He hadn't noticed she'd turned around. "There is a reason, but it has nothing to do with that call I just got from Landon," he said, crossing the room to place his cell phone back on the nightstand. "The smile has everything to do with you and your behavior at the fair today."

She looked at him, surprised. "My behavior? And just what was wrong with my behavior?"

He forced his conversation with Landon to the back of his mind and crossed his arms over his chest, not bothered by the fact that he was standing in front of her totally naked and fully aroused. She was used to seeing him hard, as well as nude, since that was the way he slept every night. That was the way she slept, too, although she admitted it was something she'd only begun doing since being with him.

"I couldn't believe how many of those wild and crazy rides we went on," he said, grinning. "Most women would have backed off, claimed they were too scary. But not you. Makes me wonder just what else you like doing for kicks." Not that he didn't have a good idea. In the time they'd spent together, he had come to know her pretty well.

"I like to cook, but I wouldn't say I do it for kicks," she said, chuckling. "Mainly for survival."

Yes, he knew she liked to cook. She had awakened him that Sunday morning after their fishing trip to breakfast in bed—pan-seared pieces of the fish they'd caught, grits and the best buttermilk biscuits he'd ever eaten.

"Tell me something about you that I don't know," he suggested, moving closer to place a kiss on her nose and then her lips.

"We've already covered the good, the bad and the ugly. Besides, I can't think when you kiss me," she protested as his mouth slid to her neck.

"Do you want me to stop?" he asked, sliding his arms around her waist and proceeding to run his hands down her hips, the portion not covered by the T-shirt. He then cupped her naked backside to bring her smack against him.

"If you stop, I might have to hurt you," she threatened in a voice that sounded close to a moan. And when he returned his lips to hers, she opened her mouth to take his tongue and wrap her arms around his neck.

The scent of her aroused him even more, and he deepened the kiss while pulling her closer to him. There was this chemistry between them that had him wanting to lay his hands on her every chance he got. Even when they were just sitting together—alone or with others—

he had a tendency to place his hand on her thigh, as if he liked having that connection.

From the first he'd never questioned why he liked touching her so much. He'd just accepted it, like he was doing now. He no longer had to analyze why things were the way they were between them. Why he enjoyed getting naked with her, sinking deep into her body and reaching a climax where his release seemed endless, especially when it mingled with hers.

And why, despite the lust and desire he felt for her, he still enjoy doing simple things with her, such as sharing breakfast in bed, listening to her talk about her job at the hospital, hearing her excitement about going to med school.

He looked forward to breathing in the same air that she did, looking into her face while they ate, waking up with her scent all over him and her limbs entwined with his. Before being with her, he'd much preferred sleeping alone. Now he wondered how he would ever sleep alone again.

In an unexpected move, she withdrew her mouth from his. "Hey, Jeffries, you're slow. You're already naked, so what's the holdup with me?" She took a step back and whipped the T-shirt over her head, tossing it aside. "Don't you like to see me without clothes anymore?"

If only she knew. "I always enjoy seeing you without clothes, Kim," he said, reaching out and bringing her naked body back to him. And that was no lie. There wasn't a part of her body that he didn't like looking at, touching or tasting.

"Then I can't have you losing your touch," she said,

rubbing against him. His erection got harder when it came into contact with her wet heat.

"I'll never lose my touch when it comes to you, beautiful," he said, sweeping her off her feet and into his arms. He headed toward the bed. The primitive male in him wanted her with a need that was consuming every part of his body, sending heat rumbling in his belly.

She kissed his nose and lips. "I love a confident man."

When she slid out of his arms onto the bed, he ran his hands all over her, needing to touch her everywhere. A degree of hot energy surged in his groin, and when she propped herself on a pillow in that position he loved so much, he leaned down and with the tip of his finger traced a path down her throat and chest, pausing when he got to her stomach.

He drew circles around her navel while thinking about the child she'd said she wanted one day, and wondered about the man who would eventually plant his seed inside her to make it happen. He inhaled sharply when the mere thought of such a thing—Kim having another man's baby—snatched his breath away.

Fighting back a crazy impulse that was running through his mind, he removed his hand from her to retrieve a condom from the nightstand. How many of these had they gone through already? Hell, he wasn't counting and he figured neither was she. The main thing was that they were acting as responsible adults and using them.

He sheathed his penis in the condom, and when he glanced over at Kim, the eyes watching him were filled with hot desire. He had come to recognize that look—

an urgent and silent message that told him how desperate she was for him to get inside her. That thought sent what felt like liquid fire rushing through his veins.

"You like torturing me, don't you, Duan?"

"No more than you like torturing me—the way you're doing now, lying there with your legs spread open. Whenever I see you that way all I can think about is getting inside you." But it was more than that. He craved her like a man who craved a woman who was in his blood. His head reeled at the very thought.

He watched as she took her hand and slid it down to her thigh, then back up to splay it across her stomach, the same stomach he'd gazed at moments ago. Then she shifted her body to spread her legs even wider, giving him a pure, unadulterated visual of what lay between them. His erection stirred at the same time his heart did.

Unable to resist any longer, he moved toward the bed. "I want you, Kim."

"Prove it."

She tossed the words out the moment he placed one knee on the bed and reached for her. "Come here," he said, lifting her off the bed into his arms and toward his waiting and hungry mouth. And then he tumbled on his back with her on top of him, their mouths still locked.

Kim gripped Duan's shoulders and concentrated on kissing him with the same intensity that he was kissing her, with a hunger that was sending hot blood racing through her veins. Their mouths fitted together perfectly, like those Lego blocks she had as a kid, and they mated with a fervor that was unrelenting.

He raked his fingers through the curls on her head and she gripped his shoulders tightly as their tongues dueled and tangled, sucked and licked while something fierce and potent tugged deep inside her.

She tried to focus on his mouth and not on what she was feeling in her heart. This wasn't just sex for her. This was love in a way she'd never thought possible.

She pulled her mouth away and released a moan from deep within her throat, staring down at him. The look in his eyes was as hot and as predatory as anything she'd ever seen. And behind those dark pupils she sensed a need, the magnitude of which had her inner muscles gripping and tensing something awful.

She moved her hands from his shoulders and took hold of his wrists, placing them on both sides of his head to make him her prisoner, not of war but of love. She could feel her love in every inch of him, in everything about him.

Holding his hands in her tight grip, she widened her legs and lowered her body toward his erection, angling herself in such a way that allowed for deeper penetration. She began easing down slowly and watched in heated fascination as his erection slid between the folds of her sex until she had taken in his entire length.

She heard the hitch in his breath and saw his jaw tighten. The hands she was gripping felt hot and his solid thickness stretched her, bathing her in sensations until she was shuddering almost uncontrollably.

He stared up at her and she lost herself in the depths of his gaze. He was so powerfully male and she quivered at the thought of him being embedded so deep inside her. It was as if she could feel him touching her womb, and the realization stroked her heart.

The moment she released his hands, he automatically reached out and gripped her hips, lifting his own off the bed to thrust even deeper into her. Then he pulled back and plunged into her again.

"Ride me, Kim."

The plea, spoken in a guttural groan, unraveled her senses, fragmented her control, and she—who'd never ridden a horse in her life—began imitating what she'd seen on television. Clutching his sides with her knees as if she was riding bareback, she established a steady rhythm, moving up and down his shaft as he penetrated her more deeply.

She continued to ride him, building her confidence, flexing her inner muscles to squeeze everything out of him. When he lifted his head off the pillow to suck on her shoulder and then capture a nipple with his mouth, it seemed that every single thing inside her exploded.

She threw her head back as she continued to ride him, needing to possess him that way, needing him to surrender everything to her and knowing the moment he did. And the thought that he did set her on fire.

His hips rose off the bed as he let out a guttural groan and thrust into her. His hands locked around her hips and she felt him come inside her and knew at that moment that the condom had broken. The heat of his semen was filling her core and plunging her into one earth-shattering orgasm. She opened her eyes and met his gaze and knew he was aware of what had happened but had no intention of stopping now.

He clenched his jaw and thrust deep inside her once

more as he came yet again. The air surrounding them was filled with the thick aroma of sex, but the only thing Kim could focus on was all the pleasure he was giving her. She gripped his shoulders more firmly as sensation upon sensation washed over her, through her.

Moments later, she slumped down on him, unable to move after what had to be the most intense mating session any one woman could endure.

"Kim?"

She heard him whisper her name and was fully aware of his concern. She lifted her head slightly and met his gaze. She knew what he was about to say. "It's okay. I'm on the Pill."

"Oh."

Was that disappointment she heard in his voice? Part of her knew it couldn't be, but another part wished that it were. They held each other's gaze for a long moment, and then his arms closed around her. Without disengaging their bodies, he snuggled her closer into his arms, kissed her so tenderly it almost brought tears to her eyes. Then she rested her head in the cradle of his shoulder.

She closed her eyes and knew if she never made love to another man again, this would be enough.

CHAPTER FOURTEEN

"DID LANDON HAVE any updates?"

The bedcovers rustled as Kim shifted position to ease off him. Duan lay on his side to face her, missing the feel of her warm body on top of his. He'd hoped she had forgotten about Landon's midnight call.

He glanced down and saw the damage done to the condom. They weren't cheap, which presented proof of the intensity of their lovemaking. He needed to go into the bathroom, but first he would answer her, not sure how much he would tell her. Already the thought of her mother spending any time with Villarosas bothered her. If he were to level with Kim that he had reason to believe the man had a jealous streak, there was no telling what she might say or do.

But still, he knew he had to tell her. She deserved to know. She had every right to know. "Landon spent most of the day surfing the Net and got some information on Villarosas that he figured we should know."

She lifted a brow. "What kind of information?"

"About twenty years ago, Villarosas and his girlfriend at the time had had a number of disorderly peace citations when their arguments got out of hand."

"And?"

Of course she'd know there was more, Duan thought.

"And according to the woman, he has a tendency to display a jealous streak on occasion."

Concern flashed in her eyes and she made a move to get off the bed, but he quickly reached out and grabbed her wrist. "Hey, that's the woman's side of things. Her accusations. No charges were ever filed against Villarosas and he never physically touched the woman. They just caused a lot of ruckus that got on their neighbors' nerves. Who knows, the girlfriend might have given him a reason to be jealous. Some women do that sort of thing to get their man's attention."

It took a while for what he'd said to sink in and then she asked, "And you're sure there were no charges of any type of abuse?"

He nodded. "Positive."

She seemed to relax somewhat and he released her wrist. "My mother is probably the last person I should worry about when it comes to physical abuse. She swore my father was the last man who would ever touch her that way. While I was in college she and some of the ladies in the apartment complex where she was living got together and arranged for one of the police officers who patrolled the area to teach a self-defense class. She enjoyed it so much that when the class was over she took additional lessons at the junior college."

He nodded, impressed. "How good is she?"

Kim shrugged. "She's not a black belt, but she has a yellow belt."

"Some women don't have that."

She smiled faintly. "I know, including me. While Mom was taking those classes, I was motivated to do the same, but I was away at college and studying all the time. Then later, my excuse was the long hours I was working at the hospital."

Duan glanced over at the clock as he eased out of bed. It was past two in the morning. "I need to go into the bathroom to take care of this," he said. "I'm sorry this happened, Kim. It's a first for me, but I assure you I'm in good health. I take that seriously."

She waved off his words. "No sweat, and rest assured that I'm in good health, as well. It was an accident. I don't want you to lose sleep over it because I won't. Like I told you, I'm on the Pill so I'm good."

Duan nodded. He figured hearing that again should make him feel a whole lot better, but it didn't. He turned and headed toward the bathroom thinking it would not have bothered him in the least if she hadn't been on the Pill.

He pulled in a shaky breath, knowing why he felt that way. He had fallen in love with her.

KIM SAT AT THE TABLE in her mother's kitchen and sipped her hot chocolate. Duan and Edward had left hours ago to go fishing and her mother was busy baking a cake for a sick member of the church. She was glad her mother was back to baking again. Spending time in the kitchen had always been one of Wynona's favorite pastimes.

Three consecutive knocks sounded at the back door. "Come on in, Bennie—it's open," her mother called out.

When Mr. Bennie walked in, Kim immediately remembered what Duan had said a few days ago about the man having a thing for her mom. "Good morning, Mr. Bennie," she greeted him.

He looked over in her direction and returned her smile. "Hey there, Sunshine," he said, calling her by the name he'd given her years ago when she was a toddler. She was Sunshine and his daughter Valerie had been Sweet Pea. "Are you doing okay this morning?"

"Yes, sir, I'm fine. What do you have there?" she asked as he placed a huge basket on the kitchen counter.

"Vegetables for your mom from my garden," he said proudly. "Sweet potatoes, squash, tomatoes and okra. I always share with Nona."

"That's nice," Kim said, closely watching the interaction between the two.

Her mother had crossed the room to check out the basket, and Mr. Bennie said something to make her laugh. But he'd always made her mother laugh. They were old friends and enjoyed each other's company, which was why Kim had never paid them any attention before.

And she had never paid any attention to the fact that Mr. Bennie was rather nice-looking. Tall, with dark hair, gray eyes and a roasted-almond skin tone. It was quite obvious that he had kept himself in good physical shape for a fifty-seven-year-old man. For years he'd owned a hardware supply store in town but had sold it not long after Valerie graduated from college.

Wynona crossed the room to open the refrigerator and Kim watched as Mr. Bennie's gaze followed her mother's every step. And then, as if he remembered she was in the kitchen, he glanced over at Kim and gave her a nervous smile, knowing he'd been caught ogling her mother.

He cleared his throat. "So, Sunshine, how long will you be in town?"

"Just until the weekend. I'm flying back out on Sunday," she said, hoping that was true. She was thinking about contacting the hospital for extended time if she needed to do so.

Her mother returned to the counter with the eggs for the cake. "Kim came home to meet Edward," Wynona said, smiling. "She was afraid we would marry before she had a chance to do that. Now she's talked to me about putting off the wedding until next month, when she could get more time off work. Of course, Edward will have to agree to it."

Mr. Bennie nodded, and Kim could tell that Wynona's wedding to Edward was not something he wanted to talk about. "I called Sweet Pea last night and told her all about you making medical school," he said, as if he needed to change the subject. "She told me to tell you congratulations and that she knows one day you'll make a fine doctor."

Kim smiled. "Thanks."

"And just so you know, Sunshine, I like your young man. He's nice."

Flutters kicked in Kim's stomach. If only Duan was really hers. "Thanks again."

Mr. Bennie rubbed his hands down his jeans. "Well, I'd better be getting back next door. I need to check in on my computer to see if any orders came in this morning." Kim knew he had an online business that specialized in selling figurines. Customers placed orders through the internet and he sent them to the factory where the merchandise was kept. That way he didn't have to worry about inventory. "I hope to see you again before you leave, Sunshine," he said.

Kim nodded. "And I hope to see you, as well. In fact, I'm going to make a point of stopping by and saying goodbye. You have a nice day, Mr. Bennie."

"You do the same, Sunshine." He smiled at her mother. "I'll talk to you later, Nona."

When the door closed behind him, Kim knew Duan was right. Although her mother was clueless, Mr. Bennie was sweet on her.

"HEY, YOU'RE NOT a bad fisherman," Edward said, smiling over at Duan.

Duan forced a smile back. "Thanks. I try to get out on the water as often as I can. It relaxes me."

"Same here. Do you own a boat?"

Duan shook his head. "No, but my brother has a beauty of one in the Keys. He lets me use it whenever I want, and I fly down there every chance I get."

Edward nodded. "And that's how you met Kim?"

Duan remembered Kim had told the story of how they met to both Edward and Wynona and wondered if perhaps the man was trying to compare their versions. "Yes. Her best friend, Sherri, is married to my brother, Terrence."

Edward grinned. "That's right, the *Holy Terror*. I used to keep up with him when he was playing pro with the Miami Dolphins. I hated when he called it quits."

"A number of people did, but it was his decision to make. Terrence had played football since he was in grade school and always said he only wanted to play until he was thirty. He didn't want an injury to take him out. I agreed with and respected his decision."

"So are you and Kim thinking of having kids?"

Duan nearly dropped his fishing rod, wondering where that question had come from. "Probably one day. Kim has plans to go to medical school." Again he was aware that Edward knew that. Was this another verification question?

"Wynona is hoping Kim can squeeze in marriage and a baby before she becomes a doctor," Edward said, casting out his rod.

Duan shrugged. "It's whatever Kim wants," he said. "The beauty of our relationship is that we're in agreement on just about everything."

"And I guess you trust her completely."

The statement sounded sarcastic. "Yes, I trust her completely. Just like I'm sure you trust Wynona completely."

Edward nodded. "Oh, yeah. Sure. I trust Wynona. I wouldn't be marrying her if I didn't."

Duan studied the man for a second. "I guess you wouldn't since this will be your *third* marriage, right?"

The beer bottle Edward had been holding nearly slipped from his grasp and he quickly glanced over at Duan. "Yes, it will be my third marriage."

"Hey, you know what they say. Three's a charm."

Duan wasn't sure whether Edward's smile was genuine. "Yes, you're right," Edward said. "Three's a charm."

LATER THAT NIGHT, Duan got a call from Chevis. "I was able to convince the warden of my need to talk to Green and he agreed. Our meeting is set for Wednesday at noon. Has anyone heard from Tron?"

"Landon spoke with him a few days ago," Duan said of the former FBI agent turned private investigator, Antron Blair. "He's checking out Edward's cell phone records from five years ago and his land phone records from ten years ago, as well as his bank statements for the same period. I hope to hear something from him soon."

He shoved off the bed when Kim walked out of the bathroom. Wynona had gone to Bible study at church, and instead of accepting her invitation to join her, he and Kim had decided to go to a movie at the multiplex around the corner from the hotel. He usually would not have wasted his time or money on the flick, but he would suffer through it for her.

"All right, Chevis, keep me informed on how things turn out with your meeting with Stein Green on Wednesday."

After flipping off the phone, he gave Kim his total attention. There was no hope for it. She was wearing a hot-pink tank top and a short black skirt that showed what good-looking legs she had. He'd much prefer staying in the hotel room tonight and messing around with her, but he knew she had her heart set on seeing this movie. Still…

He crossed the room when he saw the trouble she was having putting her necklace on. He came to stand behind her. "Need help?"

She glanced over her shoulder at him. "Yes, thanks."

He pushed her curls aside to have access to her neck. She smelled so good. But then, she always did.

"You were right, Duan."

"About what?"

"Mr. Bennie having a thing for Mom. I can't believe I've never noticed it before."

He finished with the necklace and leaned down to place a kiss on her neck at the same time she brushed her backside against his crotch. He sucked in a deep breath at the contact. Damn, it felt good. "I hate to say that I told you so," he said, wrapping his arms around her middle to bring her even closer to him.

"You know what I wish?" she said, shifting to look over her shoulder at him.

He leaned in and brushed a kiss across her lips. "No, what do you wish?"

"That Mom would notice, too. But they've been friends for so long she probably doesn't see him as anything other than a friend."

"I can believe that." Duan went back to her neck, sucking in his favorite spot, not caring that a passion mark would probably be visible tomorrow. "Dad didn't start noticing Cathy until she turned up the heat."

"How did she do that?"

Duan chuckled. "Hell if I know, but I'm sure Olivia does. Terrence and I figured the less we knew, the better. All we do know is that they went to New York on a business trip together and things changed for them after that."

He sucked in another deep breath when Kim intentionally wiggled her backside against his crotch again. "Hey, I wouldn't do that too many times if I were you," he warned.

She laughed when he took a step back. "Whatever," she said, turning around to him. "Ready to go?"

"I guess."

She lifted a brow. "You don't sound too anxious."

He smiled. "Well, I'd rather see a lot of blood and guts instead of a lot of kissy, kissy, bed, bed."

She threw her head back and laughed, and the way the curls on her head went flying around her face sent sensations all through his gut. He thought at that moment she was simply beautiful.

Taking his hand, she pulled him toward the door. "We'll see a blood-and-guts movie the next time. I promise."

Duan allowed himself to be dragged out of the room. He hoped she remembered the promise she'd just made because he intended for her to keep it.

CHAPTER FIFTEEN

KIM TRIED TO KEEP BUSY while Duan talked on the phone.
The call had come early Thursday morning, waking
them up at seven. At first she'd thought he was talking
to Landon, but after a while it became obvious a conference call was taking place and he was conversing with
several people. She had showered and had taken care
of her hair but he was still on the phone.

The expression on his face looked serious. She tried
to remain calm and not jump to any conclusions. To kill
time, she walked around the room, tidying up a little
bit. Although the hotel had someone to come in and
clean their room every day, there was no need for the
person to think they were slobs. Although she would
have to admit the only untidy spot was the bed.

Bedcovers were strewn all over the floor, the sheets
were all twisted and a couple of pillows were at the foot
of the bed. She didn't have to figure out how that happened. Last night she and Duan had tried several new
positions, and one required her at one end of the bed
with him at the other, their heads buried between each
other's thighs. Talk about a fantasy come true. Pleasure
stirred her insides just remembering it.

She turned toward him when she heard his phone
flip shut and met his gaze. Immediately, she knew—

for better or for worse—that he'd found out something. She inhaled deeply to prepare herself for whatever he had to say.

"Come here, Kim," he said in that deep, throaty voice she loved so much.

She crossed the room to the wingback chair where he sat and he reached out and pulled her down into his lap. She turned to him. "Yes?"

"That was everyone," he said, draping his hands across her thighs.

"Everyone?" she asked. "All four of them?"

"Yes, Landon, Antron, Brett and Chevis. We had a conference call since there were several updates."

She nodded. "So what did they find out?"

When Duan hesitated she knew he was looking for the right words. "Go ahead, Duan. Tell me. Is my mother in any danger?"

Instead of answering her, he said, "Landon went to talk to Villarosas's old girlfriend and she backed up her claim of over twenty years ago. She said Villarosas has a nasty jealous streak and that he'd threatened to get rid of her several times when he thought she was unfaithful to him. She claims she wasn't, but had gotten sick and tired of him making false allegations and threats that she believed he would carry out, so she split."

Kim nodded. "But that was over twenty-some years ago. Right?"

"Right. Now, Chevis went to a prison in Florida yesterday to visit Stein Green. After some intense questioning—relentless interrogation Chevis-style—Green admitted that Edward Villarosas hired him to get rid of both of his wives because they were unfaithful."

Kim leaped out of Duan's lap. "And that bastard thinks he's going to marry my mother?" she said in a raised voice.

"Kim, calm down."

"Have the police been notified? When will he be arrested? When is—"

"Kim, please let me finish," he interrupted, standing up as well. "What we have is an allegation from a convicted killer, a man already serving a life sentence with no chance of parole for armed robbery where a police officer was gunned down. All he's done is verify what we suspected all along, especially with Villarosas's ironclad alibis. But we need more than just the word of a criminal. We need concrete proof and we're working with Green to get that. No court of law will bring charges against Villarosas based on Green's word."

"What kind of proof is needed?"

"Finding their bodies would be nice."

Kim's hands flew to her mouth and Duan knew she was remembering the two women. "Oh, my God, Duan, something has to be done. My heart goes out to their families."

"And something will be done to the fullest extent of the law. But we don't have enough to uphold a conviction. Right now, all we have is a criminal's word. Until we have evidence to substantiate his claim, there's nothing we can do. But rest assured, we're getting that evidence."

"How?"

"From Villarosas's old bank accounts, we can show that large amounts of money were withdrawn during the times Green claims he was paid."

"That's not enough proof?"

"No. We've also obtained old phone call records between Green and Villarosas, but again, that doesn't prove anything since there are no recorded conversations. It will be Green's word against Villarosas's, and who do you think a jury would believe? A man already in jail for life or a man who appears to be a model citizen? Those incidents with Villarosas's girlfriend over twenty years ago would not be admissible."

"So what's going to be done?"

"As we speak, a team of both local and federal officers are searching a wooded area near Orlando and another in Atlanta where Green said the remains are. Regardless, Villarosas will be picked up and brought in for questioning today. Detectives from the Atlanta police department are already on their way here for that. If those remains are located, Villarosas will be charged immediately and extradited back to Georgia."

Duan sighed deeply and rubbed a hand over the top of his head. "What we need to do now is talk to your mother. Villarosas is going to be questioned and it's best she finds out from us. I will also need to come clean with her and tell her my role in all of this."

Kim nodded. "I agree, and we should tell her in person. She isn't expecting Edward to come over until later since this is the day he plays golf. So hopefully we can talk to her alone. Mom is going to be crushed."

"Yes, but when the evidence is laid out before her, I'm sure she'll agree that these are serious charges and those allegations being made are—"

Duan's cell phone went off. "Excuse me." He flipped

it on. "Yes, Landon?" He nodded a few times. "Yes, okay, and thanks for letting us know."

He flipped off the phone and met Kim's gaze. "That was Landon. He wanted to let me know remains were found exactly where Green said they would be, and the authorities are working to obtain positive IDs. If they are Villarosas's missing wives, then it's safe to say he'll be booked and extradited back to Atlanta to face murder charges."

Kim was already grabbing her purse off the bed. "I need to get to Mom and tell her."

Duan was already moving toward the door. "Come on, let's go."

"I STILL CAN'T REACH Mom," Kim said, putting her cell phone back in her purse. She glanced over at Duan as he drove the rental car out of the hotel parking lot. "I want to at least let her know we're on our way over there so she won't go anywhere. She visits Aunt Gert on occasion."

"It's a nice day so she might be out in the yard."

"Yes," Kim said, smiling. "She loves her flower garden."

She was trying to think of positive things, but it was hard to do so knowing how close her mother had come to marrying Edward. The thought that the man had arranged for his two wives to be killed sent chills down her body. She dreaded telling her mother, but at least all this was coming to an end before her mom could become his next victim.

"Thanks for all the hard work you and your friends did. Just think of how long Villarosas has gotten away with this. With Green already in jail for an unrelated crime, he probably thought he was home free."

"That's a good assumption to make. The man evidently has mental issues, and I won't be satisfied until he's behind bars where he belongs."

Kim nodded. "I'm surprised Stein Green decided to talk."

"He had nothing to lose since he's already doing life with no chance of parole. He probably feels good about squealing on Villarosas since he's in prison and Villarosas is still out enjoying freedom." Duan pulled to a stop at the red light.

"In that case, why didn't he speak up sooner?"

"Green probably figured no one was going to take him seriously, but since Chevis came around asking, he was more than ready to spill his guts. According to Chevis, the man was full of information and didn't hesitate in telling them where the women's bodies were."

"And he admitted to killing them?"

"Yes, after beating them up first. He claimed those were Villarosas's instructions to teach his cheating wives a lesson."

Kim shuddered at the thought and was glad when Duan pulled into her mother's driveway. She had unsnapped her seat belt and was out of the car as soon as it came to a complete stop. She began racing toward the front door.

"She's not at home, Sunshine."

Kim stopped walking so fast that she almost missed the step to the door. Duan's arm reached out to steady her.

She glanced across the yard at Mr. Bennie, who was

working in his flower garden. "She's not here? Do you know if she went to visit Aunt Gert?"

He shook his head as he took off his work gloves. "No, she left early this morning with Edward Villarosas. She had an overnight bag so I assume they've gone out of town."

"What! Oh, my God, I hope you're wrong about that, Mr. Bennie." Kim frantically fished through her purse for her mother's door key, spilling most of the contents on the ground.

"I'll get the door," Duan said, bending down to retrieve the items that had fallen from her purse, including the keys. With his arms planted firmly around Kim's waist, he slid the key in the door and pushed it open. She rushed past him and was inside before he could draw his next breath.

A piece of paper was sitting on the dining-room table and she quickly raced over to pick it up. When she finished reading it, she turned to Duan, her eyes filled with anger. "The bastard talked Mom into eloping to Vegas," she said heatedly, letting the paper fall from her hand onto the floor. "She can't marry him! She can't!"

Duan crossed the room and pulled her into his arms. "No, she can't, and if we have to contact every wedding chapel in Vegas to make sure that she doesn't then—"

"Excuse me, I don't mean to intrude, but is everything all right?"

Duan and Kim glanced over to see Mr. Bennie standing in the doorway. Kim pulled out of Duan's arms and rushed over to him. "Mr. Bennie, when you saw Mom this morning, did she look okay? Did it appear as if she was being forced to leave or anything like that?"

The man's eyebrows shot up, as if surprised by Kim's line of questioning. "No, she seemed to be leaving of her own free will and was in a good mood, as always. She smiled and waved when she saw me. I was putting out the garbage. That was around seven this morning."

Kim nodded. She found some comfort in knowing Edward hadn't killed the other two women himself, which meant her mother was probably not in any immediate danger. But still, the thought of Wynona traveling alone with the man was unsettling.

"What is it, Sunshine? What's wrong?"

Duan walked over to them. "If you don't mind coming inside, Mr. Bennie, we can explain things."

"All right."

Duan closed the door behind the man and pulled Kim close to his side. She was shivering in both fear and anger.

"Mr. Jeffries, I know you might think it's none of my business, but if there's something wrong, please tell me. Nona and I are very good friends. I care about her deeply."

"I know you do, Mr. Bennie," he said truthfully. "And she's going to need you a lot when this is all over."

The man glanced over at Kim in concern. "I'll always be there for her. Now please tell me what's going on."

Duan inhaled deeply. "Edward Villarosas is wanted for questioning by the police."

Mr. Bennie looked surprised. "The police? What for?"

Duan's arms tightened around Kim's waist. "For arranging the deaths of his two wives."

CHAPTER SIXTEEN

KIM WAS PACING the floor and so was Mr. Bennie. They both had worried looks on their faces. Kim had tried a number of times to reach her mother by phone but was unsuccessful.

Duan had contacted the Shreveport police and then placed a call to the airlines to check flights for Vegas. He'd been able to find out Wynona and Edward's flight number, and according to the airline, the flight had landed in Vegas over an hour ago. So why wasn't Wynona answering her phone?

The Vegas police had been contacted and a warrant had been issued for Villarosas's arrest. The one good thing was that Wynona wasn't taken by force, which meant she still didn't know the type of man Villarosas really was. Duan was of the opinion that Villarosas had no reason to harm Wynona since he probably felt secure in their relationship. At least for now.

He looked over at Kim and she gave him a faint smile. A part of him realized why he loved her so much. She cared about her family. She was loyal. And she was nothing like the woman his father had married, who had deserted her husband and children. Kim was all goodness. All caring. And she wanted children.

He understood why he enjoyed sleeping so close to

her at night, their bodies touching, and then awakening beside her every morning for playtime. He enjoyed seeing her eat, swallow, lick cotton candy from her lips. He had enjoyed their late-night talks where he would sit with her in his lap for hours. He even enjoyed sitting next to her at the movies, sharing buttered popcorn with her. And although the movie wasn't anything he'd wanted to see, it hadn't mattered as long as she was there beside him. Just hearing her chuckle through a couple of scenes had been music to his ears.

He had fallen in love with a woman who didn't have room for him in her future.

He knew all about her plans. Four years in medical school. What right did he have to ask her to do anything differently now that he knew he loved her? And why would she even consider such a thing? Although he had fallen in love with her, that didn't mean she had fallen in love with him. As far as he knew, and as she'd reminded him several times, she had no intentions of having a serious relationship with a man, and what he was considering was a serious as it could get.

She deserved to have her dream and he wouldn't rob her of it like her father had done when he'd taken that money. This was her chance to do the one thing she'd always wanted to do, and he loved her too much to stand in her way. So he would stick to his original plan.

When all this was over, he would leave for Atlanta. But he intended to keep up with what she was doing through Sherri, because no matter where Kim went or what she did, she would always unknowingly have his heart.

Duan was pulled from the depths of his thoughts as a car door slammed. He glanced out the window and saw an unmarked patrol car pull into the yard, then watched as three men got out. He recognized one of them as Landon. He assumed one man was a detective from the Atlanta police department who'd come to question Villarosas, and the other was a detective from Shreveport.

Kim heard the car, as well, and she quickly moved toward the front door, holding her breath with every step she took. And she didn't have to glance over her shoulder to know Duan was right behind her.

She looked into the faces of the three men. "Yes, may I help you?"

"Ms. Cannon?"

"Yes."

One of the men flashed a badge in front of her. "I'm Detective Mark Hogan of the Shreveport police department, this is Detective Arnold Reddick with the Atlanta police department and Landon Chestnut from the Peachtree Private Investigative Firm."

Kim's gaze swept by the two men and went straight to Landon. Duan had mentioned he would be accompanying the detective coming from Atlanta.

After shaking hands with the men, she said, "Yes, please come in."

Introductions were made to Duan and Mr. Bennie. She watched the easy comraderie between Duan and Landon, indicating the long friendship between the two. Landon, who seemed to be a couple of years younger than Duan, was a very handsome man. But in her opinion no man was more handsome than Duan.

"Have you heard anything?" Kim asked anxiously.

Detective Hogan glanced over at her. "The police department in Vegas has been notified and they're checking the registry of all the hotels. There's quite a number of them. A current photograph of your mother and Villarosas was wired to Vegas and everyone is on the lookout for them. We've also alerted several popular chapels."

At that moment Kim's cell phone rang and she raced across the room to pick it up from the table, not recognizing the phone number. "Yes?"

"Kim?"

"Mom!" she nearly screamed with both relief and excitement. Everyone raced across the room to her.

"Mom! Where are you? I've been trying to reach you and—"

"Kim, sweetheart, please listen. I had to call you. Edward is acting weird and accusing me of all sorts of stuff. I'm in Las Vegas, and on the way from the airport to our hotel I convinced him that I needed to use the bathroom and couldn't wait. So we stopped at one of those fast-food restaurants. I'm using this woman's phone that I met here in the ladies' room. The battery in my phone died so I couldn't call you, and when I asked Edward about using his phone he accused me of wanting to call Bennie."

"Mr. Bennie?" Kim asked, glancing over at the neighbor, who stared back at her with a curious look on his face.

"Yes. Edward dropped by unexpectedly last night while Bennie was there. I don't know what's got into him. He was fine until we got to Vegas and then he began yelling and accusing me of all sorts of things, especially having an affair with Bennie."

Kim struggled to stay calm. "Mom, listen, don't go back out to Edward's car. Use the lady's phone and call 911 and tell them exactly where you are."

"Kim, it's not that serious. Edward just needs time to think about what he's saying and—"

"Mom, please do what I ask. Edward is wanted by the police." Kim hadn't wanted to break the news to her mother this way, but she didn't have a choice.

"Wanted by the police? Kim, that is utter nonsense."

"No, it's not, Mom. The police detective is here and needs to talk to you. Please listen to what he says and tell them where you are."

Kim handed Detective Hogan her cell phone and then moved aside to inform Duan, Mr. Bennie and Landon of what her mother had said. Detective Reddick was talking on his cell, contacting the police in Vegas, letting them know of her mother's phone call.

"Edward began acting strange," Kim said. "And he accused Mom of having an affair with you, Mr. Bennie. Mom said Edward got that idea when he dropped by last night and you and Mom were together."

Mr. Bennie nodded. "Yes, I was here last night. Nona and I were shelling peas."

"Well, evidently Edward got upset, which is probably what prompted him to convince her to fly off to Vegas with him."

"Why didn't she contact you on her cell phone?" Duan asked.

"Her battery died. And according to her, Edward wouldn't let her use his phone, so she pretended she had to go to the ladies' room, which got him to make a stop. She called from the ladies' room of a fast-food restaurant using another woman's phone. That's where she is now."

Kim glanced over at the two detectives. Hogan was still talking to her mother and she eased closer to hear what was being said.

"Yes, Ms. Cannon. He needs to be brought in for the murder of his two wives." He paused and then said, "Yes, ma'am, murder. I know this comes as a shock, but it's true. His hired killer told us where to find the bodies. We've contacted the Vegas law enforcement as to where you are and they're on their way."

Hogan nodded. "Yes, I would advise you to keep the bathroom door locked until they get there." He nodded again. "Good thinking. Yes, please hold for a minute."

Hogan then relayed to the others what was happening. "The lady whose phone she's using has agreed to stay with her and they've locked themselves in the restroom. Edward has knocked on the door twice, but Ms. Cannon has kept him at bay by saying she had a little emergency and needed more time."

"The Vegas police are a couple of blocks away," Reddick said, before returning to his own call.

Hogan conveyed that information to Wynona. He nodded at whatever she was saying and then replied, "Yes, ma'am, you're right. People are not always what they seem to be."

Kim swallowed, wondering how her mother was going to feel when she found out that Duan had been an imposter, as well.

"The police are there now?" Hogan glanced over at

Reddick, who nodded to confirm. "Yes, then it's safe to unlock the bathroom door and yes, everything is going to be all right, Ms. Cannon. You did a smart thing getting away from Villarosas." He nodded again. "Yes, she's right here."

Hogan glanced over at Kim. "Your mother would like to speak with you."

Kim quickly moved forward to take the phone. "Yes, Mom, I'm glad it's over and that you're all right." She actually felt her heart ache for her mother, especially when she heard the sobs in her mother's voice.

Her eyes began getting teary, and Duan came forward and pulled her closer to his side when she said, "Yes, Mom, we want you to come home, too."

FOUR HOURS LATER, Wynona was back home. Kim had hoped the family would not get wind of what had happened for a while, but when Edward's arrest made the evening news everyone began calling.

Kim thought her mother a real trouper after enduring questioning by the Vegas, Shreveport and Atlanta police departments. Edward had been transported from Vegas straight to Atlanta. Wynona said he'd asked to see her and she had agreed, although it had been hard. He hadn't denied the charges and instead had tried to get her to see why his wives deserved to die. Basically, he'd ended up confessing his crimes to her and the Vegas detectives.

Wynona returned to Shreveport on a law enforcement plane, had been given a sedative and was now resting comfortably. Kim had managed to keep the family members away and for once appreciated that they understood her mother's need to rest.

She sat in the chair beside the bed watching her mother sleep. She had contacted the hospital to ask for an additional week off, knowing she would need to stay with her mother to help her through this traumatic episode.

She sighed. Wynona deserved a man to love, respect and cherish her. After Edward's actions, she wondered if her mother would finally realize that you couldn't seek your happiness in others—it had to first come from within.

That lesson was something that she herself would have to accept in the coming days. No matter what, she couldn't let despair take hold of her at the thought that pretty soon she and Duan would be parting ways.

Once her mother woke up and they had a chance to talk, she would tell Wynona everything, including the fact that Duan was not her fiancé and that his sole purpose in being in Shreveport was to prove or disprove Edward's guilt.

Duan and his associates had worked hard to do just that. And now with the two cases finally closed, there was nothing to keep him in Shreveport. She wondered if he planned to fly out with Landon first thing in the morning.

Kim fought back her tears, thinking no one had asked her to fall in love with Duan. Their relationship was never meant to be long-term. She had known that, yet she had allowed her heart to get involved in what should have been nothing more than red-hot sex. She could only blame herself for the outcome.

A warm pair of lips touched the side of her face and she didn't have to look up to know that Duan was there. And then she felt strong arms lift her up and carry her out of the room.

She knew she had to pull herself together and not think of the man she was losing, since he'd never been hers anyway.

"I know you wanted to watch over your mother, but you don't need to sleep in that chair, Kim," Duan whispered against her forehead.

"And just where are you taking me?" she asked, cuddling deeper into his arms, knowing this would probably be the last time she would have a chance to do so.

"To one of the guest bedrooms. Then I'm leaving to go pack up our things at the hotel. I figure you'll want to be close to your mom for a while, especially tonight. I'll be flying out with Landon to Atlanta first thing in the morning to provide what information I have for the women's families."

Kim tried to keep her heart from breaking but it shattered into little pieces anyway. He wasn't wasting any time putting distance between them. "I can go back to the hotel with you to help you pack things up and—"

"No, you need to stay here with your mom. She needs you."

And I need you, she wanted to scream, but fought the urge to do so. More than anything she wanted to make love with him one final time, to release him from her heart and soul.

"Where is Landon?" she asked when she felt him gently place her on the bed.

"He left to go over to police headquarters and file

our reports." He stretched out beside her on the bed, pulling her into his arms.

"Are you hungry, Kim? I prepared a pot of soup for you and your mom."

She shook her head as she settled her body against his. "Thanks, but I'm not hungry. Is Mr. Bennie still here?"

"No, he left, but I have a feeling he'll be back. It wouldn't surprise me if he makes his feelings for your mother known to her. He admitted to me that he's been in love with her for a long time. At least three years now, but he was afraid to make his move, afraid she would turn him down as a suitor and then he would lose her as a friend."

Kim hoped Mr. Bennie did let her mother know of his feelings. Wynona would need time to heal from Edward's betrayal, but Kim was sure Mr. Bennie would give her all the time she needed.

"Kim?"

She looked up at Duan. "Yes?"

"Everything worked out, didn't it?"

She nodded. "Yes, and I have you and your friends to thank for that. I don't want to think about what could have happened if you hadn't remembered Edward's name. What if Mom had married him? He was a time bomb just waiting to go off. The man truly has a mental problem and I hope he gets the treatment he needs."

"At least he's out of your mother's life, and with the love of you, her family and Mr. Bennie, I believe she'll get over it."

Kim nodded. She believed that, as well. She felt herself being pulled closer into Duan's arms and then he leaned down and kissed her in a long, deep and devouring kiss. A part of her wished it could last forever, and that what was between them could last forever, as well, but she knew it wasn't meant to be. He had his life and she had hers. She would pursue her dream of becoming a doctor.

He finally broke off the kiss and tucked her body against his, but not before his lips skimmed hers once more. When she yawned, he smiled. "You're tired. Go on to sleep. I'll call you tomorrow from Atlanta."

Kim heard Duan say a few more words before the warmth of his body, the calmness of his voice and the tender kisses he was placing on her face compelled her to close her eyes and drift off to sleep. It was a good sleep. A restful sleep in the arms of the man she loved.

DUAN CONTINUED TO LIE there and hold Kim long after she had drifted off to sleep. More than anything he wanted to spend the rest of his life with her. Loving her and giving her every single thing she needed. But he knew that wasn't possible. Her life was already mapped out the way she wanted it. The dream she'd given up before was within her reach. So it was just as well that they ended things now, on a good note.

The tightening around his heart couldn't be helped. All he had to do was close his eyes and remember all the good times they'd shared. A part of him wanted to wake her up so they could make love one last time, but he knew that wouldn't happen.

He eased from the bed and headed toward the door. But before he could get there he turned around. That same tightening had moved to his throat. He wondered if she would remember the words of love that he'd spoken as she'd drifted off to sleep. Probably not. It was for the best.

He forced himself to turn and walk out of the room. And with every step he told himself that ending things this way was the right thing to do.

WHEN KIM AWAKENED hours later she glanced out the window to see it was dark outside and the house was quiet. The ceiling light in the hallway illuminated her luggage letting her know Duan had brought it from the hotel.

She eased off the bed and left the room to go check on her mother. Wynona seemed to be in a peaceful sleep. Kim hoped that it was.

She left her mother's room and went into the kitchen. Duan had used some of her mother's fresh vegetables to make a soup and it smelled delicious. It was then that she saw the note he had scribbled and left on the counter.

Take care of yourself and Ms. Wynona.
Duan.

Kim swallowed the lump in her throat. This was his way of saying goodbye. He wasn't coming back. She had dreamed that he'd held her and told her he loved her, but she knew it had only been a dream.

She glanced around the kitchen and was almost overwhelmed in misery, but fought it back. She needed all her strength and energy to get her mother through this.

It wasn't about her own heartbreak and pain; it was about her mother's.

Kim knew she was a fighter. She had a great future looming ahead of her. Medical school was within her reach. She would continue her life just the way she had before Duan entered into it.

She would survive and she would pursue and achieve her dreams. A part of her hoped and prayed that doing so would be enough.

CHAPTER SEVENTEEN

"Duan? Why aren't you going to Sherri's birthday party in the Keys next weekend?"

For a long time Duan didn't say anything. He just stared across his office at his sister, wishing he could ignore the question. But he knew Olivia well enough to know she would hound him until he came up with what she considered a good answer. Married life had definitely made her bossier.

"I'm working on a case that requires my full concentration, Libby," he said, knowing that wasn't true. The case he was working on wasn't going to be that difficult to solve. What was difficult was giving it his full concentration.

"And before you ask, the answer is no," he said. "I haven't told Terrence I won't be coming, but I will. In fact, I plan to call him later today."

He knew Libby's concern. As kids growing up they'd always shared their birthdays together and had made them special. Even when Libby lived in Paris, it was easy to do since she came home for the holidays and her birthday was two days before Christmas. And since Sherri, Reggie and Cathy were now official members of the Jeffries family, it was expected that everyone be present for their birthday celebrations, as well.

His sister crossed the room and placed her hands on his desk, looking directly into his eyes. "A difficult case has never stopped you before, Duan, so what's going on?"

He forced himself to maintain a pleasant expression. Otherwise, his sister, who didn't miss much when it came to her brothers, would see the pain lurking deep in his eyes. "Nothing's going on," he said, picking up a folder and making a pretense of browsing through it.

"You sure?"

He met her gaze again. "Yes, I'm sure." He glanced at his watch. "I thought you said you were on your lunch break."

She smiled as she leaned back. "When you're the boss, you can take a few liberties."

Duan knew he couldn't very well disagree with that. For a wedding gift, Reggie had purchased his wife an art gallery and a building to house it in a perfect location in Atlanta. Reggie had had the building remodeled to her specifications and *Libby's*—Olivia had chosen the name—was doing extremely well.

"Besides, I had a doctor's appointment."

He raised a concerned brow. "You're doing okay?"

She smiled. "Nothing eight months won't cure. Reggie and I are having a baby."

Duan blinked a few times to let her words fully sink in. A huge smile spread across his face and he pushed his chair back to stand. "Come here, sport."

When she came around his desk he pulled her into his arms. His little sister was going to be a mother, and he knew without a doubt that she would do a better job at it than their own mother had done.

"I'm sure Reggie knows already," he said, releasing her with a big grin. "Those damn Westmorelands believe in being fruitful and replenishing the Earth."

Olivia threw her head back and laughed. "Reggie actually knew before I did. We did the at-home pregnancy test a week ago, but the visit to the doctor today made it official. He was there with me when the doctor confirmed everything. Senator Reginald Westmoreland is definitely a happy man."

Duan nodded as he sat on the edge of his desk. "What about Dad and Terrence?"

"Dad knows and, of course, he and Cathy are delighted to become grandparents. I haven't told Terrence yet. I plan to call him and Sherri tonight."

She glanced down at her watch. "I better go since I do have an appointment at three with an artist whose work we want to display."

After his sister left, Duan wasn't able to get back to work. He leaned back in his chair and stared out the window. It had rained earlier but now the sun was out. Everywhere flowers were blooming, typical for May.

It had been three weeks since he had left Shreveport, and although he had spoken to Kim twice since then, that hadn't been enough. He knew her mother's outlook on life was improving, and that Mr. Bennie had stated his intentions to Wynona. The two adults were taking things one day at a time as they moved from friends to a more serious relationship. Duan had sent a bouquet of flowers to Wynona last week for Mother's Day, and she had called and left a message on his cell phone thanking him.

He knew Kim had told her mother and family the

truth about their fake engagement. She had returned the ring to him a couple of weeks ago with a note thanking him for all he'd done. She'd also written that the family was so concerned about her mother's well-being that they hadn't dwelled on the fact that she'd lied to them.

The last time they talked he had told her that Villarosas had been charged in connection to his wives' deaths and was waiting trial. Villarosas still wasn't remorseful for what he'd done to his two wives and was trying to convince anyone who would listen that he had valid reasons for his actions.

When Duan had gotten the ring back he had stared at it remembering the exact moment he had placed it on Kim's finger. He'd been tempted to send it back to her and tell her to keep it since it looked as if it belonged on her hand. He still might do so, but knowing Kim, she would only return it.

Thanks to information he pulled from Terrence, he knew Kim had returned to the Keys and was back at work. He also knew the main reason he wouldn't be going to Sherri's birthday party: he wasn't ready to see her again. He wasn't sure if he could look at her and pretend not to want her and love her. So he had made the decision not to make the trip to Key West next weekend, and as he had told Libby, he would call Terrence and explain things.

Deciding that now was as good a time as any, he reached over and picked up the phone.

KIM GLANCED AROUND when she walked into Club Hurricane. Terrence was expecting her. Sherri's birthday party was coming up and he'd enlisted her help to make it special. The huge celebration would be held here at the club and Terrence had put her in charge of decorations.

"Hello, Ms. Cannon." Debbie, one of the club's hostesses, greeted her with a friendly smile on her face.

"Hi, Debbie. Is Terrence in? I believe he's expecting me, although I never told him what time I could make it. Working E.R. makes that impossible."

"Yes, I understand, and he said to send you right on up to his office whenever you arrived."

"Thanks." Kim headed into an elevator and leaned against the back panel. She checked her watch and saw it was a little past three in the afternoon. Since she had come straight from work she still wearing her nurse's scrubs.

She allowed her thoughts to drift to a subject she'd been trying to avoid thinking about and failing miserably. Duan. It had been three weeks since she'd seen him, three weeks since he had held her in his arms and kissed her with a passion that only he could deliver. And there was not a single day that went by that she didn't think of him and remember the time they'd spent together.

She had talked to him a few times when he'd called to see how she was doing and to check on her mother. But their conversations seemed rushed. He was afraid she would say something related to their time together and he hadn't wanted that. She had accepted that what they'd shared had meant more to her than it had to him and she'd moved on. At least she was trying to. The only thing she still had to do was decide which medi-

cal school she wanted to attend in the fall since several
more offers had come in.

And she had finally been able to move beyond the
issues she'd had with her father, although she was
taking things one step at a time. After hearing about
what had happened to her mother after Edward's arrest
made national news, he had shown up in Shreveport
while she was there.

Louis Cannon's appearance had drastically improved
since she'd last seen him, and she could tell he was
trying to take control of his life. He'd shared with both
her and her mother that he hadn't taken a drink in over
three years and was active in his church and had remarried. She was happy for him.

And she was also happy for her mother, who now
had Mr. Bennie in her life. They, too, were taking
things one step at a time. But Kim was convinced Mr.
Bennie was the person her mother needed.

The elevator came to a stop and the door opened.
Immediately, she could hear Terrence talking in a loud
voice to someone on the speakerphone. She had taken
a few steps toward his door when she recognized the
voice of the person Terrence was conversing with. And
when Terrence said her name, Kim stopped walking
and listened.

"Hey, man, I hear what you're saying but I think
you're wrong for not letting Kim know how you feel."

"I couldn't do that," Duan said in a voice filled with
anguish. "I couldn't tell her that I love her so much I
ache inside just thinking about her. She wants to go to
med school. She's always wanted to go and someone

took that dream away from her once. I won't be the one to take it away from her again."

"She can still go to med school, Duan. That's all I'm saying. When two people love each other, they can work through anything. The two of you can even have a long-distance relationship."

"She tried that before with a guy and it didn't work out so that's not an option. Besides, I'm not even sure she feels the same way about me. Our time together may not have meant as much to her as it meant to me. She never gave me any indication that she loved me."

Duan paused for a moment before continuing, "Look, Terrence, I didn't call to lay all this on you. It's my problem. I just wanted you to know the reason why I won't be coming to Sherri's birthday party next weekend. There is no way I can see Kim and not give away how much I want her. How much I love her. And I hope you understand."

Tears clouded Kim's eyes as she began backing away from Terrence's office door. She returned to the elevator and pressed the button that would take her back down. Her heart began filling with happiness at the thought that Duan loved her. All those times they *had* been making love and not just having sex. He actually loved her and wasn't telling her for fear of coming between her and her dream of attending medical school.

Didn't he know he was now part of her dream and that she had a chance to have it all with him? Apparently not. So she intended to be the one to tell him and she wouldn't waste any time doing so.

"You're through with your meeting with Terrence already?"

Kim blinked, realizing the elevator door had opened and Debbie was standing in front of it, staring at her.

"Oh, no. I've just got an emergency that I need to take care of. Let Terrence know I'll call him later to reschedule our meeting."

"All right."

Kim quickly headed for the exit door, pulling her car keys out of her purse. She would drive herself to the airport. Destination? Atlanta, Georgia.

CHAPTER EIGHTEEN

DUAN RECALLED the conversation he'd had with Terrence before leaving the office. Maybe his brother was right and he should let Kim know how he felt.

To anyone who didn't know Duan, he probably appeared to be a calm, cool and collected guy. A man defined by his achievements, someone who knew what he wanted and was proud of what he had. A man not willing to show his emotions to too many people. A private person. Definitely not a man who would bare his soul to anyone. And Duan could admit that before he'd met Kim, that image was probably right on the money.

But now he was also a man who knew how it felt to love a woman, truly love a woman. Now he understood his father's tears that day. He understood the pain of loving someone and not having that love returned. Although he was certain the depth of his father's misery was deeper than his because of his wife's betrayal, the bottom line was that love was love no matter how you looked at it. And he could admit that he was a man in love. And the sad thing was that the woman who had his heart didn't have a clue.

He headed toward the kitchen to prepare one of those microwave dinners when his doorbell rang. He pivoted,

SPONTANEOUS

wondering who the hell it could be. He wasn't in a good mood and the last thing he wanted was company.

Without bothering to glance out the peephole, he flung open the door, ready to give the person hell for having the nerve to bother him on a Thursday night.

His breath caught in his throat and he felt himself stagger back a foot. He blinked, thinking he was seeing things, and when he realized he wasn't, he asked in a shocked voice, "Kim, what are you doing here?"

She smiled and that smile did something to him that he couldn't explain, and all the frustration and anger he'd felt earlier seemed to melt away. "I was wondering, Duan, if you wanted to play."

DUAN BLINKED AGAIN, but when he fully realized what she'd asked, he reached out and pulled her into his arms, covering his mouth with hers. He then swept her off her feet and slammed the door shut with his foot.

He had a vague memory of Kim tossing her purse on his sofa. But what stood out in his mind more than anything was when he carried her into his bedroom and proceeded to strip her naked before tearing off his own clothes, popping buttons in his haste.

Oh, yeah, they would play. Then afterward they would talk.

He glanced over at her and almost had an orgasm right then and there. She was propped back on his pillows in that sexy, mouth-watering pose he liked. Her legs were open, showing him everything, and her scent was driving him insane. It was definitely an aphrodisiac moment.

He moved toward her but thought he needed to make one thing clear right now. "We're not having sex, Kim."

She smiled. "We're not?"

"No."

"Then what is it that we're about to do?"

"Make love," he quickly replied.

His knee touched the mattress of the bed and he reached out for her. Pulling her closer to him, he whispered against her lips, "I could never just have sex with the woman I love."

There, he'd said it, and he hoped and prayed Terrence was right, that maybe, quite possibly, things could work out between them and that she cared for him, too.

She rose up on her knees and wrapped her arms around his neck. He dragged in a deep breath at the feel of her hard nipples pressed into his chest. She held his gaze, flicking out her tongue a few times to trace the outline of his lips before saying, "That's good to hear, Duan, because you're the man I love."

At that moment everything within Duan snapped and he grabbed the back of her neck and lowered his mouth to hers, devouring her in a kiss that only the two of them could share. It was a kiss that let them know beyond a shadow of a doubt that no matter what, they belonged together and they *would* be together.

He took his time to cherish every part of her body, loving her, tasting her and transforming her into sexual energy in his arms. And when he lowered his head between her thighs and gently parted her folds with his fingers, he eased his tongue inside and began stroking her all the way to the tip of her clit, darting in and out of her, lapping her with a hunger that was consuming him. She screamed out his name and reached down to grab hold of his head to push his tongue even deeper inside her. Giving him more of her taste. More of her as an orgasm ripped through her body.

Before her climax could ease away, he slid between those same open thighs and entered her, throwing his head back in a guttural groan at how good it felt being back inside her. And when he felt himself all the way to the hilt, he began moving in long, deep strokes, delving in and out, back and forth, mating with her, making love to her, making both their bodies tremble in what had to be the most precious pleasure any two individuals could share.

And when she screamed his name again, he knew he was about to follow her lead, and as everything erupted inside him, exploded to the nth degree, he shot his semen all the way to her womb.

"Kim!"

He screamed out the name of the woman he loved. The woman who had made him whole. The only woman he ever wanted to belong to. This woman. His woman. And then he busted another nut when an orgasm slammed into him again. He felt her inner muscles clench him, taking everything he had.

And when he had nothing left to give, he slumped down on her in mindless ecstatic pleasure and contentment.

"TELL ME, KIM. You knew, didn't you?"

A very drained Kim glanced up at the eyes staring down at her, the eyes of the man she loved. "Yes, but only recently," she responded in a strained whisper.

She saw the confusion enter his eyes. "But how...?"

"I had an appointment with Terrence after work today to go over his plans for Sherri's party, and when I stepped off the elevator I heard him talking to you. He had placed you on the speakerphone and I overheard what you said."

More confusion flashed in the dark depths of his eyes. "But that was just a couple of hours ago."

She smiled. "I know. Once I heard you say you loved me, but that you weren't sure I loved you, I knew I had to come here and tell you in person. So, without Terrence even knowing I'd been there, I left and drove directly to the airport."

A look of incredulity shone on Duan's face. "Without a ticket?"

Kim managed a chuckle. "A ticket was the least of my problems. I had to call to let the hospital know I wouldn't be in tomorrow. Luckily I was scheduled to be off this weekend anyway. But the biggest goof of all was when I discovered I didn't have a house address for you until I got in the cab and the driver asked where I was going. I had to call Sherri to get it."

Duan threw his head back and laughed.

She couldn't help but join in when she thought about it, although it hadn't been funny at the time. "So, I guess you can say that my visit here was rather spontaneous."

Duan grinned from ear to ear. "Yes, I think it would be safe to say that. *Spontaneous* is definitely the word of the day, and it seems the norm for us."

"And if you noticed, I was wearing my nurse's uniform, which means unless you plan to have me walking around nude all weekend, I'll need more clothes. And a few toiletries."

"You walking around naked won't be a problem for me," Duan informed her. "In fact, I rather like the idea. And as for the toiletries, just make a list of everything you need and I'll go out and get them."

He reached out and rubbed the tip of his finger across her chin. "I meant what I said to Terrence, Kim. I won't stand in the way of your dream. You *are* going to med school."

The corners of her lips tilted into a smile. "Yes, I am going to medical school. But Terrence was right, Duan. You and I can work out anything because we love each other. I will go to med school, and on the flight here I decided which one, since I've received several offers. I'm going to accept the offer from Emory University here in Atlanta. That means you're going to have a roommate for a while, Duan Jeffries."

Kim scrutinized his face to see how the thought of her moving in with him would go over, especially when she would be unemployed and going to school full-time. From the smile on his face, she knew he was fine with the idea.

"I would love for you to share this place with me, Kim," he said, leaning closer to her. "But only as a short-term roommate."

He reached in the drawer to the nightstand behind him and pulled out a small box. Kim recognized it immediately. It was his grandmother's ring. The ring she had returned to him a few weeks ago. The ring she had grown used to wearing. The one she'd fallen in love with. The ring that looked perfect on her hand.

Tears filled her eyes as he took her hand in his. "I'd rather have you as my wife instead of a roommate. Kim, will you marry me? Be the mother of our babies? Trust me to make you happy? And know that on the day you become Dr. Kimani Cannon Jeffries, I will be just as happy as you, and that I will cherish you, honor you and forever love you."

Kim smiled and raised her eyebrows. "And will you play with me anytime I want?"

He chuckled. "Yes, sweetheart, I will play with you anytime you want."

"In that case, yes, I will marry you."

Duan slid the ring on her finger and leaned down and kissed her with all the longing and hunger of a man in love. When he finally pulled back she smiled up at him, placed her arms around his neck and said, "I'm ready to play some more."

And they did.

* * * * *

PASSION

For a spicier, decidedly hotter read—
this is your destination for romance!

COMING NEXT MONTH
AVAILABLE DECEMBER 6, 2011

#2125 THE TEMPORARY MRS. KING
Kings of California
Maureen Child

#2126 IN BED WITH THE OPPOSITION
Texas Cattleman's Club: The Showdown
Kathie DeNosky

#2127 THE COWBOY'S PRIDE
Billionaires and Babies
Charlene Sands

#2128 LESSONS IN SEDUCTION
Sandra Hyatt

#2129 AN INNOCENT IN PARADISE
Kate Carlisle

#2130 A MAN OF HIS WORD
Sarah M. Anderson

REQUEST YOUR FREE BOOKS!
2 FREE NOVELS PLUS 2 FREE GIFTS!

♦ Harlequin®

Desire

ALWAYS POWERFUL, PASSIONATE AND PROVOCATIVE

HDES11B

*Lucy Flemming and Ross Mitchell shared a magical,
sexy Christmas weekend together six years ago.
This Christmas, history may repeat itself when they find
themselves stranded in a major snowstorm...
and alone at last.*

**Read on for a sneak peek from
IT HAPPENED ONE CHRISTMAS
by Leslie Kelly.**

Available December 2011, only from Harlequin® Blaze™.

EYEING THE GRAY, THICK SKY through the expansive wall of
windows, Lucy began to pack up her photography gear.
The Christmas party was winding down, only a dozen or so
people remaining on this floor, which had been transformed
from cubicles and meeting rooms to a holiday funland. She
smiled at those nearest to her, then, seeing the glances at her
silly elf hat, she reached up to tug it off her head.

Before she could do it, however, she heard a voice. A
deep, male voice—smooth and sexy, and so not Santa's.

"I appreciate you filling in on such short notice. I've
heard you do a terrific job."

Lucy didn't turn around, letting her brain process what
she was hearing. Her whole body had stiffened, the hairs on
the back of her neck standing up, her skin tightening into
tiny goose bumps. Because that voice sounded so familiar.
Impossibly familiar.

It can't be.

"It sounds like the kids had a great time."

Unable to stop herself, Lucy began to turn around,
wondering if her ears—and all her other senses—were
deceiving her. After all, six years was a long time, the mind

could play tricks. What were the odds that she'd bump into *him*, here? And today of all days. December 23.

Six years exactly. Was that really possible?

One look—and the accompanying frantic thudding of her heart—and she knew her ears and brain were working just fine. Because it was *him*.

"Oh, my God," he whispered, shocked, frozen, staring as thoroughly as she was. "Lucy?"

She nodded slowly, not taking her eyes off him, wondering why the years had made him even more attractive than ever. It didn't seem fair. Not when she'd spent the past six years thinking he must have started losing that thick, golden-brown hair, or added a spare tire to that trim, muscular form.

No.

The man was gorgeous. Truly, without-a-doubt, mouthwateringly handsome, every bit as hot as he'd been the first time she'd laid eyes on him. She'd been twenty-two, he one year older.

They'd shared an amazing holiday season.

And had never seen one another again.

Until now.

Find out what happens in
IT HAPPENED ONE CHRISTMAS
by Leslie Kelly.
Available December 2011, only from Harlequin® Blaze™

Every woman wants him. But he wants only her…

New York Times and *USA TODAY* bestselling author

BRENDA JACKSON

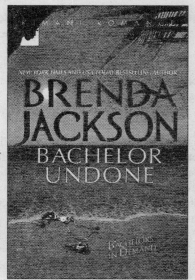

BACHELOR UNDONE

When Darcy Owens leaves snowy weather for some Jamaican sun, the city planner isn't expecting to meet the hero of her fantasies. But sexy security expert York Ellis comes pretty close….

Pick up your copy on November 22, 2011, wherever books are sold.